SCIONS OF CHANGE

CADICLE: VOLUME 7

A K DUBOFF

SCIONS OF CHANGE

www.cadicle.com

Published by Epic Realms Press

ISBN: 1-95434404X
ISBN-13: 978-1954344044
Copyright Registration Number: TXu002058268

0 9 8 7 6 5 4 3

Produced in the United States of America

CONTENTS

PART 1: DESTINY

CHAPTER 1

THE APPARENT VOID of space was alive, if one knew how to see. As Wil Sietinen gazed into space from the surface port on Earth's moon, his consciousness roamed in the distance.

It was one of the luxuries he allowed himself now that so much of his life was spent confined in the TSS Headquarters facility. With his children training as Agents, he rarely left, lest he leave them unprotected. Too much was at stake to take any chances with their safety.

He left his physical form and roamed the depths of space, projecting his consciousness farther than many ships had traveled. Over the years, he'd continued pushing himself to see how far he'd be able to go, and with practice, he no longer had the need for Seconds to serve as a tether. He'd surprised himself with the results, particularly when he reached the outer boundaries of the galaxy's Orion Arm. At first, he had considered trying to span the unfathomable distance to the Andromeda Galaxy, but he ultimately decided that anything he might find there would be irrelevant.

His next venture took him deeper into the Milky Way Galaxy, toward the core. He passed by the network of Taran worlds and through the ruined corner of space previously occupied by their Bakzen enemies—so twisted from their Taran roots that they may as well have been the aliens his people had come to see them to be.

Though Tarans often talked about themselves as populating the entire Milky Way Galaxy, that was a considerable exaggeration. At best, their territory occupied a quarter of the galaxy, with the occasional rogue world beyond. Since the advent of advanced terraforming techniques millennia prior, new planets could be colonized as long as the conditions and the star were sufficient. Moving planets into orbits more ideally located in habitable zones had even been possible in past ages of the Taran civilization, and he marveled at some of those efforts as he passed by.

Where Wil was going, though, was beyond the Taran realm. Somewhere out there were the Aesir. They had left Tararia before the last revolution that brought the sinister Priesthood into power, and he suspected they still possessed all that technology that had been suppressed in recent years.

He'd made an agreement for the Aesir to wait to test his children, as they'd once tested him—but the agreement was struck before the Priesthood had captured his daughter, Raena, and her boyfriend, Ryan, for their perverse genetic experimentation. Only after their escape had Wil realized that Raena didn't need those five years to prepare for the Aesir's test. She was ready from the moment of her Awakening, and he wanted her insights. The problem was, he was afraid if she discovered the true extent of her abilities, she might take a path that would lead her away from Tararia, where she was needed in their generations-long plan to unseat the Priesthood.

But the Priesthood had relayed information that Wil needed verified, and the Aesir were the only group capable of offering informed commentary. He wished to meet with them outside the circumstances of a test, to see if a partnership of any sort was possible.

However, he had no idea where they called home. The galaxy was simply too vast for him to search. He'd been calling out to them for months, hoping for a reply, but none had come.

Wil halted the movement of his consciousness in his journey beyond the edge of his civilization. He wasn't sure exactly where he was, but something told him to wait.

"*Are you there?*" he questioned in the void.

No reply came, only the eternal background hum of the energy that formed the basis of reality.

He was about to return to his physical self when a whisper broke through the darkness. "*Why have you come here?*"

At last, the Aesir had answered his call. A tingle of excitement rippled through his mind. "*I wish to know what future path to take.*"

"*That is something that she must see. You have already seen your truth.*"

Wil had been prepared for that answer. "*May we meet with you?*"

"*You told us to give you time,*" the Aesir replied.

"*That was before what I know now.*"

The Aesir didn't reply for a minute. "*The Priesthood fears you won't do what needs to be done for the future of all Tarans.*"

"*The Priesthood reached out to you?*" That was a possibility Wil hadn't seen coming. When the two organizations diverged more than a thousand years prior, his assumption had been that they'd severed all contact. After all, the Aesir hadn't communicated with anyone—as far as Wil knew—in hundreds of years before they came to test him as a young Agent. However, perhaps that was not the case. The notion of the Priesthood and Aesir working together on any matter was unnerving.

"*You already know your line holds the genetic key. The Priesthood's analysis has raised concerns.*"

"*You've messed with us enough,*" Wil replied. "*The genetic legacy of our people won't mean anything if our entire civilization collapses. The Priesthood will enslave everyone if we let them.*"

The Aesir waited again before replying. "*We agree. Eliminating the Priesthood must be the top priority. But our future is still at stake. The Bakzen were not our only threat.*"

A chill gripped Wil's core. "*What do you mean?*"

"*Travel to the Rift and you will see. Only then can we meet with you.*" As quickly as they'd appeared, the Aesir's presence vanished.

Wil's consciousness traced back to his physical self, and he returned to his surroundings with a gasp.

He found that the spaceport was still deserted, as it had been when he'd begun his projection. When he checked his handheld, he discovered that only half an hour had passed—it seemed impossible to have covered such a vast distance in so little time.

Shaking off the aftereffects of being disconnected from his physical self, he began processing the Aesir's cryptic words. *There's something for me to see in the Rift, and Raena needs to go with me.*

Raena and Jason already got enough attention within the TSS as the children of the High Commander and Lead Agent, so he was hesitant to plan a trip to the Rift just for them. Furthermore, he'd tried to avoid the Rift as much as possible, finding the intensity of energy within it to be too strong a reminder of how his own abilities had been used for destruction during the war. He was reluctant to go back, but everything the Aesir had stated in the past had come true. If they were going to venture into the final standoff with the Priesthood completely informed and prepared, then they'd need the Aesir on their side.

What, Wil pondered, *is a good excuse to go to the Rift?*

— — —

The twenty members of the Primus Elite Trainees floated in the simulated starscape within the spatial awareness chamber deep inside TSS Headquarters. Raena Sietinen glanced at the other side of the circle of Trainees and caught Ryan's eye, telepathically flashing him a smile in his mind.

He returned her smile with a mental caress, careful not to have his external gaze linger on her for too long.

"*Looking forward to our upcoming field trip?*" Raena asked him.

"*Absolutely,*" Ryan replied. "*Ever since we learned about the Rift, I've wanted to see it in person.*"

"*It'll be wild.*" Raena's parents had told her about the enhanced energy within the Rift, and she was quite curious to see how that would feel.

"Attention!" Michael, the Primus Elite's primary trainer, shouted out loud and in their minds.

Raena's arms straightened at her sides. *"Back to work."*

Ryan smirked, and she realized her tone had been more sarcastic than she'd intended. However, even after several months in the TSS, it was still difficult for her to see Michael in any way other than the close family friend he'd been to her while growing up on Earth. She respected him as a mentor, but she didn't share the same awe of Agents as some of her fellow Trainees—after all, her own parents were the High Commander and Lead Agent of the Tararian Selective Service.

Michael pushed off the wall near the entry door and took up position in the center of the circle with a set of six metal spheres, each the size of his fist.

"I'd like to spend some more time today honing your electromagnetic sensitivity," he said as he fanned the spheres around him in the center of the circle.

"Those are new," Liam commented.

"New tools for new exercises." Michael waved his hand over the spheres, causing blue lights to illuminate around the equator of each. He then telekinetically drew himself toward the facet of the icosahedron functioning as the ceiling relative to the group's current orientation. Adopting a position in space perpendicular to the students, he requested a volunteer.

"I'll go," Raena's brother, Jason, offered.

Raena playfully rolled her teal eyes at him. He grinned back.

Michael sighed. "This is getting boring. I need some fresh guinea pigs!"

Next to Raena, Tiff tightened her short, dark brown ponytail. "Isn't New Guinea a country on Earth? What does a pig from there have to do with anything?"

Raena laughed. "I'm so happy we ended up with a trainer who grew up on Earth, too. For once, I'm not the one left out of the loop with idioms."

Tiff wrinkled her nose and narrowed her copper-brown eyes. "Idiom or not, it doesn't make sense. What's so special about New Guinea's pigs?"

"Geography and pigs have nothing to do with the phrase," Raena sighed. "Just… never mind."

While they were talking, Michael had telekinetically drawn

Jason into the center of the circle and arranged the metal spheres around him, from head to foot, his sides, and front and back.

"Now, Jason," Michael explained, "I'm going to activate the spheres in sequence and I want you to point to the one that's emitting an electromagnetic pulse."

"All right," he acknowledged.

"For the rest of you, try to test your own perception of the pulses. It will be more difficult without having the pulses around you, but hopefully you can get some indication," their instructor stated. "Everyone, close your eyes."

Raena complied with the request. She visualized the spheres surrounding her brother and the energy signatures of the students in the circle. Her mental map lacked detail, but she was confident in the placement of everyone.

A moment later, one of the spheres lit up with a bright flash—the one to Jason's right. Then the one by his feet. She watched the energy signatures flash around all the spheres, and then two at a time.

There was no way Raena would publicly admit that she was able to so clearly visualize the minute differences. Jason's perception was also well above normal, and Ryan's skills had grown quickly, as well, but they were anomalies among an already exceptionally gifted group. Most of the other students were doing well if they could just tell there was any sizable electromagnetic signature to an object.

"Very good, Jason," Michael stated. "You can open your eyes, everyone. Did you have any sense of the movement pattern?"

"Yes, there was some sense," Ryan volunteered. *"That was easy, right?"* he added privately to Raena.

"Oh, totally."

"It's all pretty fuzzy," Ned, one of Ryan's roommates, said. "I can't tell what I'm sensing."

Jason was eyeing the spheres, clearly apathetic about the exercise. "Is this an ateron coating?" he asked.

The question caught Michael by surprise. "Yes. How do you know about that?"

"I've spent some time looking over the specs for craft with direct telepathic relays," Jason replied. "Ateron absorbs energy, correct?"

"It can. Why do you ask?"

"Well, basic electromagnetic sensing is an important skill when you're just starting out and all, but that in and of itself isn't very useful. Shouldn't we be more concerned with detecting and manipulating energy signatures through an intermediary?"

Raena groaned inwardly. *"We agreed that we weren't going to jump ahead in front of them,"* she chastised him.

"It's been eight months. I'm sick of twiddling my thumbs," he replied.

She had to agree with him there. *"What do you have in mind?"*

"I'm still working that out."

"Intermediary relays are an advanced skill," Michael replied to Jason's question.

"Okay," Jason continued aloud, "but what, in theory, would a person do to practice those kinds of skills?"

Michael's gaze flitted from Jason to Raena and Ryan. *"Are you three conspiring amongst yourselves?"*

"Didn't I ask a valid question?" Jason countered.

Their instructor sighed. "One exercise would be networking the spheres—feeding energy into one and using it as a transfer conduit to the others."

Jason flourished his hand and rearranged the spheres into a roughly pyramid shape in front of him.

The other Trainees gasped at his controlled use of telekinesis.

"Now you're just showing off," Raena said with a mental tsk.

"Like you don't enjoy it yourself." He flashed a mischievous smile in her direction.

"So, something like this?" Jason asked aloud. He began feeding energy into the top sphere and it cascaded through the others until the six spheres were all glowing with subtle white light.

"Yes, exactly like that." Michael crossed his arms, his pale blue eyes slightly narrowed.

"But I imagine the next step would be to work together in a team," Jason continued.

Several students around the circle openly gawked as he

rearranged the spheres into a triad with one point near himself and the others in front of Raena and Ryan.

"Sorry," Raena offered privately to Michael and then sent a low-intensity telekinetic stream into her sphere.

She detected Jason and Ryan doing the same, and soon the group of spheres at the center of the triad was glowing brightly with the combined energy.

"Yeah, that would be the next step," Michael muttered. *"Are you finished?"* he asked the three of them.

Raena released her energy stream, and Jason and Ryan did likewise.

"Yep. Just working on our skills," Jason said.

"Well, that was a wonderful demonstration," Michael stated with thick sarcasm. "Now, if you don't mind, I'd like to get back to my actual lesson plan."

"Of course." Jason smiled as Michael returned him to his place in the circle.

Michael went over a series of exercises with the class for the next fifty minutes. It was all painfully simplistic as far as Raena was concerned, but she played along for the good of her team. When the time was up, Michael dismissed the class and helped the students toward the wall containing the gravity lock.

"Raena, Jason, Ryan, hang back," Michael requested.

The other Trainees piled into the gravity lock and the door sealed.

Michael looked over his star students. "I'm not sure what to do with you."

"What do you mean?" Raena asked.

"You're first year Trainees," Michael replied with a shake of his head, "you shouldn't be able to network the spheres like that."

The three of them looked at each other.

"But we can," Jason said slowly. "I thought the Primus Elites were all about pushing limits?"

"Yes, but..." Michael faded out. "It's obvious you're bored. I think we need to add in some training for you outside of the other group activities."

Ryan raised an eyebrow. "Instead of, or in addition to?"

Michael shrugged. "Not sure yet. I'll have to talk with

Command."

"Is it actually a question for Command, or for our parents?" Jason asked, crossing his arms.

"A little of both." Michael shook his head. "I know better than to insert myself into the middle of the dynamics at play here."

"We're not trying to be difficult," Raena said.

"I know. I just want to make sure you get what you need," Michael responded.

Raena glanced at her brother and boyfriend. "We're open to suggestions."

Their trainer nodded. "All right. Go catch up with the others."

They pulled themselves toward the wall housing the gravity lock—another feat that should not have been possible for them yet—and prepared to exit.

Raena checked the time on her handheld when they entered the gravity lock. "Practice ran late today."

Michael confirmed the late hour on his own handheld. "So it did. Sorry about that."

"No worries—it was a good session," Raena told him.

"Even though you had to share the spotlight?" Jason said with a grin.

I could do way more than him if I wanted to. Raena brushed off his comment with a shrug.

The gravity lock cycled and they slowly descended to the floor.

"Well, I'm going to get dinner ASAP so I can finish up that awful Taran politics homework before we leave on the trip," her brother continued.

"Good idea," Raena agreed, realizing that she'd forgotten the assignment was due the day after they returned from the trip. "I need to get on that..."

Michael cast her a sidelong glance.

"I'll get it done," she assured him.

"I have no doubts about your aptitude—academic or otherwise," he replied simply.

With the gravity equalized, they exited into the hall and took the elevator to the floor of Level 2 housing Initiates and Junior

Agents.

"Have a good night. I'll see you at 08:00 tomorrow," Michael said when the doors slid open.

Raena, Jason, and Ryan exited the elevator and bid their goodbyes.

"I didn't want to say it in front of Michael," Jason commented as he set off across the lobby, "but it's obvious what's distracting you from class assignments. You two aren't being nearly as sneaky as you think."

There was no point in denying it, since it was true, so Raena said nothing.

In the eight months since they'd begun training with the TSS, two things had become clear to her. The first was that she, Ryan, and Jason were mastering their telepathic and telekinetic skills far more quickly than their fellow Trainees. The second was that Ryan had come to mean more to her than she'd dreamed another person ever could in so short a time.

Given her unique position as a High Dynasty heiress—and Ryan's secret station as the lost heir to Dainetris—their relationship was simultaneously perfect and highly suspect. As far as any of the other TSS trainees knew, Ryan was just a former Ward—little more than an indentured servant after being abandoned by his parents. The truth about a Dainetris heir surviving the Dynasty's fall more than a century prior could not be revealed until the appropriate political pieces were in place. That was still potentially years away.

For the interim, Raena and Ryan had been careful with how others saw their relationship. They sat together whenever possible at mealtime, in class, and during social hours in the common area of their quarters, and occasionally would hold hands or lean up against one another. The subtle acts of affection had raised a few eyebrows, but it was nothing that couldn't be written off as casual flirtation.

In reality, though, their growing bond was the foundation for a lifetime together. They had remained true to their promise to one another to allow their relationship to develop slowly, given the numerous political complications. However, with their deepening emotional connection came the desire for physical intimacy—something that was all but impossible in their shared housing within the TSS.

Fortunately, the upcoming field trip to the Rift in two days would afford some time together in a different environment more conducive to togetherness.

Jason parted from them to go get dinner, but Raena hung back with Ryan when she noticed that they were alone in the hall for the moment.

"We have a few minutes before we need to get to the mess hall," Raena said and took Ryan's hand, drawing him to her. She gazed into his gray eyes.

He held back. "We really shouldn't be together out in the open like this."

"Why not? It's been almost a year of us having every meal together and hanging out in downtime. I don't think anyone would be terribly surprised to see us together as a couple."

"But they know who you are."

"So?" She reached a hand around the back of his neck and stretched up on her toes for a kiss.

After a moment of hesitation, Ryan gave into her advance—placing his hands on her hips and leaning her back against the wall.

Such stolen moments of closeness in study rooms or an empty hallway were hardly enough. The façade of innocent flirtation had been slipping for the past two months, and Raena had no doubt they'd be caught. However, she'd found herself inclined to intentionally press their luck with a kiss in a public place hoping that they would be. The entire notion that highborn should only date other highborn wasn't a tradition she was willing to support. If her family wanted a revolution, then she was going to do her part and take a stand by not hiding a relationship with someone who meant so much to her.

Ryan pulled out from the kiss. "We can't keep doing this."

"Stop worrying about what others think."

"That's not what I mean. I..." He searched for the words. "Every time we meet up like this, it's starting something we know we can't finish. I care about you way more than to have just a few minutes together like this."

"I know, me too. That's why I'd rather just come out with it."

"It's more complicated than that."

Raena searched his face. "We could tell them half of it—about your dad."

"That would raise a lot of questions."

"Nothing we can't handle."

Ryan cupped her face in his hand, pressing against her. "Once we take the next step, there's no going back—"

"Well fok! What have we here?" a voice said from down the hall.

Raena quickly separated from Ryan, dropping her hands to her sides. "Hey, Tiff."

Tiff crossed her arms, an amused smirk playing on her lips. "You two, huh?"

"Yeah, you know…" Raena said with a little shrug.

Ryan flushed next to her. *"There's no way she'll keep it to herself,"* he said to Raena.

"Well, I intend to keep you to myself, so that's all I really care about." She took a step closer to Ryan to close the gap he'd created between them. "It shouldn't come as that big of a surprise."

"I guess not." Her friend looked them over. "Does your dad know?"

"Eh…" Ryan began.

"Yes," Raena answered for them. "Not that I needed permission or anything."

"Yeah. Hmm." Tiff shrugged. "See you at dinner."

Ryan watched her depart. "Now we've done it."

Raena gave him a quick kiss. "Let them talk all they want. We know what's between us."

He entwined his fingers with hers. "Yeah, we do."

— — —

Cris surveyed the main administrative office for the Sietinen Dynasty. Work stations with holo interfaces were arranged in small groupings throughout the room, and the two-story ceiling made the space feel light and airy.

He had spent a good portion of his youth in the room as part of his 'education', and his impression had always been a bunch of attendants doing busy work. Now, as the Head of the Dynasty and being completely informed about the specific goings-on, his opinion hadn't changed at all.

"I still don't understand why we have this office," he commented to Marina while fiddling with the jacket of his new, regal attire. He couldn't bring himself to wear the traditional robes his father had favored, so he'd opted for a dark blue outfit with a cut closely resembling his former TSS Agent uniform—even if he hadn't been able to avoid the ridiculous silver embroidered accents.

His advisor sighed and evaluated him out of the corner of her green eyes. "It's what keeps everything in the Third Region running smoothly."

"Yes, but *what*?" Cris pressed. "Infrastructure is handled by local municipalities or corporate interests, transportation and the like is all managed by other corporations, and policing is under the jurisdiction of the Tararian Guard."

"Integration," Marina replied.

"That's not an answer."

She clasped her hands in front of her emerald gown. "This office is here to ensure synergy between the disparate parts."

Cris stared at her for several seconds in silence, slowly tilting his head questioningly. At Kate's urging, he'd also left behind his tinted glasses in favor of exposing his glowing cobalt eyes. While it seemed to unnerve many of the staff, he had found that he never had to ask for something twice.

Marina yielded. "All right, I don't know what they do, either."

"Thank you." Cris consulted his tablet. "And yet, they account for twenty percent of the annual budget for operations outside of SiNavTech."

"I don't have an answer for you, but I can look into it."

"Good enough." Cris sighed. "I'm all about making sure everyone in the city gets paid a living wage, but I'd hope that any work would be going toward some productive end."

Marina nodded. "I agree."

"All right, now what were you saying about the Aeris shipyard?"

"The facility is in need of a complete structural upgrade," Marina explained. "The local shield wasn't installed correctly and the main supports have been worn from radiation and solar winds."

"What about the workers? Are they okay?"

"Yes, everyone's fine," she assured him. "All work is performed in EVA suits or by bots, which all have their own plating. This is just about the outer skin on the facility itself."

"Then why haven't the repairs been made?" Cris asked.

"You asked me to flag any assets that were absorbed from Dainetris or DGE. This is one of them."

"Right, that." Cris hadn't yet told Marina about Ryan's lineage, but he'd bring her into the fold soon. After all, Marina's experience having her daughter, Saera, taken from her paralleled the circumstances of Ryan's childhood—courtesy of the Priesthood's meddling—and that would give her a unique affinity for the situation. Furthermore, despite Cris' differences with Marina when he was younger, she'd proved herself to be a trustworthy and capable advisor. At least that was one thing his father had gotten right.

Marina raised an eyebrow. "Is there something you'd like to tell me?"

"Not right now, but soon." Cris looked over the notes about the shipyard Marina had transferred to his tablet. The repairs were going to be a significant capital outlay—at least seventy billion credits. *We need to move forward with these upgrades. I can't hand over failing facilities to Ryan.* He turned to Marina. "Complete the repairs—don't cut corners."

She looked like she was about to question the decision but then inclined her head. "Very well."

"Next order of business?"

"Well, there's the SiNavTech board meeting in two days."

Cris groaned. "Right. The vote on the new advertising initiative."

"I've pulled everyone aside individually, I think we have majority support," Marina told him.

"That would certainly make things easier."

She nodded. "You've asked for them to change ways of thinking that have been ingrained for a very long time. But they are open to trying new things. You bring ideas to the table that no one has before."

Cris smiled. "Go me."

Marina rolled her eyes. "In some ways, you haven't changed at all."

He shrugged. "You might be surprised. Apparently, I'm pretty good at effecting change around me."

"You are." Marina set off toward the hallway. "That's why it's my job to make sure you don't make a mess of things."

CHAPTER 2

TO RAENA'S GREAT surprise, Tiff seemed to have kept her observances to herself. The morning freefall practice session garnered no sidelong glances, and her initial class in the morning with a quarter of the Primus Elite Trainees—Introduction of Navigation Theory—proceeded without any unusual comments.

Ryan seemed relieved, but Raena was annoyed. Everything had been lined up for them to finally get their relationship out in the open, and Tiff hadn't taken the bait. *Why did she have to pick* now *to start keeping secrets like a good friend?*

By the time Raena entered her first class after lunch, her annoyance had evolved into impulsive fantasies about making a dramatic announcement to settle the matter once and for all. The class's subject matter happened to be about strategies for information dissemination in sensitive political scenarios, but, in this case, she was inclined to disregard everything she'd learned throughout the term.

Due to the highly relevant subject matter, Jason and Ryan were also in the class. Their instructor, Agent Galin, was in the midst of discussing the finer points of vocabulary choice during negotiations while Raena's mind wandered.

"I can't believe Tiff didn't say anything to anyone," she commented to Ryan.

"Stop worrying about it," he replied.

Agent Galin looked at her, likely detecting the telepathic

exchange. She didn't say anything, but Raena took the hint and tried to return her attention to the class.

"Once you have a common vocabulary established," the Agent was saying, "you'll be able to enter into future discussions with a much better understanding of the subtleties in their phrasing."

"Don't we get that through telepathy, anyway?" Jason asked.

"We can readily tell if someone is being sincere," Galin replied, "but the motivations behind their thoughts will rarely be on the surface. I shouldn't have to remind you that anything beyond the highest level gleaning goes against our code."

"Then how is inferring meaning through vocabulary choice any different?" Jason pressed.

"Because one is a direct invasion of another's mind versus just that—inferring."

Jason leaned forward in his chair and rested his arms on the desktop. "And what if what's inferred points to some really critical revelation?"

Galin's eyes narrowed ever so slightly behind her tinted glasses. "Those situations must be taken on a case by case basis."

"What about—"

"Do you have a point you'd like to make?" Galin interrupted.

"Well, it's a little tangential to this class," Jason began.

"Like that's ever stopped you," Raena muttered.

Unfazed, her brother continued, "I've been reading up on Taran history as it related to the Bakzen War, and namely how there's been a marked division between those with abilities and those without. I guess it just got me wondering where all of these codes and conventions related to abilities came from. Because, it seems to me that most of those practices involve us ignoring a part of our innate selves. To achieve true integration and cultural advancement, shouldn't we all be working toward maximizing our potential—and training the general population how to form mental blocks rather than only teaching us not to look?"

Galin took a deep breath. "Thoughts from the class?"

"He makes a valid point," Liz offered. "Except, there's a problem with the numbers. There are far fewer of those with abilities than those without. When it comes to education, it's much easier to teach us restraint than it would be to properly educate every Taran citizen about mental guards—and what about children or people with disabilities who are unable to maintain proper guards? It's not practical."

"Then how would it work in a society where everyone had abilities?" Jason asked.

"Oh, I see what you're doing..." Raena said to him. *"Don't. We aren't supposed to talk about the Priesthood's genetic manipulation that led to the Generation Cycle."*

"Why not? A thousand years ago, no one would think about abilities being the exception, not the norm."

"Because we don't have any evidence yet. This isn't the time or place to broach the subject."

Jason rolled his teal eyes and sighed. "Just throwing it out there as a rhetorical question," he added aloud to his last statement.

Galin smiled. "Well, I'll take that as a segue into an interesting case study. One of our former Agents had her internship on Valdos III, which is one of the only worlds where abilities are still openly cultivated and exercised. In instances where both parties are equally proficient in mental guards and gleaning, that attention to wording choice comes into play in a big way."

The rest of the class session went into a study of some negotiations that happened during the Junior Agent's internship, and Raena soon realized that the trainee in question had been her paternal grandmother, Kate.

"I guess our grandparents left quite a legacy here in the TSS," she said to her brother while the lecture was wrapping up.

"It's a lot to live up to," he agreed.

Agent Galin began to dismiss the class, then stopped herself. "Some of you will be away on the trip to the Rift tomorrow. Remember your papers are due the following day."

Jason grinned at Raena. "Already finished."

"I'll knock out the rest of mine tonight," she replied with an inner groan.

"Same," Ryan concurred as he rose from the seat on her other side.

"Ugh, it figures the Primus Elites get to go on the first trip to the Rift," Liz grumbled.

"You're going next week, calm down," Raena told her.

Liz scoffed. "Easy for you to say as the High Commander's daughter." She turned to Jason. "And don't even get me started on you."

Jason made a dismissive flip of his hand. "I just voice what everyone else is thinking."

"Uh huh. Sure." Liz shook her head and walked out of the class.

"You *have* been interrupting a lot recently," Raena added. "Take it down a notch."

"How does it not bother you how they talk around everything? A little directness doesn't hurt."

"Maybe we can complete our first year as Taran citizens before deciding what's best for everyone." Raena patted him on the arm and then descended the steps from where they were seated in the tiered second row.

"Ryan, you grew up on Tararia," Jason said, loping down the steps past her. "Don't you agree that it's backwards how they handle the division of those with and without abilities?"

Ryan held up his hands. "I have a limited vantage. I couldn't say."

Jason cast him a sidelong glance. "You just don't want to disagree with Raena."

"I'm not disagreeing with you," Raena interjected. "I just think we need to practice some careful wording." She cast an appreciative glance in the direction of Agent Galin.

"At least one of you listens to me," Galin muttered under her breath while she deactivated the holoprojector.

"Just give Jason more work to do," Raena suggested. "He starts getting argumentative when he's not kept busy enough."

Galin grinned. "That can be arranged."

"All right, all right! I'll keep my thoughts to myself, geez," Jason groaned and headed out of the classroom.

"Thanks, Raena," the young Agent said with heartfelt appreciation. "I shouldn't really say this, but I'm still not sure how I'm supposed to be with you two, since you're… you know."

Raena smiled at her. "We're Trainees just like all the other first years here in the TSS."

"Yeah, there's that, and then who your parents also are in here."

"Jason likes to test boundaries. If you don't set them, he'll keep pushing," Raena assured her. "We can take critical feedback. I don't think our parents would want you showing us any special favor."

"Okay, sounds good." Agent Galin nodded. "Have a good trip."

"Thanks, see you in a few days."

Raena and Ryan said their goodbyes and exited into the hall. The next block in the afternoon was study time before their afternoon freefall training session, but this particular day was Raena's monthly Lead Agent check-in—which, of course, meant a one-on-one with her mother.

"See you soon," Raena bid to Ryan as they parted ways.

She took the elevator to Level 1 and entered the administrative wing. Her mother's Lead Agent office was at the end of the long hall lined with other Agent offices, and she found that the outer glass wall was on the transparent setting.

Inside, her mother looked up from behind her desk. "Come in, Raena."

"Hey."

As Raena took a seat in one of the guest chairs, Saera used controls on her touch-surface desk to adjust the tint on the glass wall to an opaque gray for privacy.

"These formal check-ins still feel weird," Raena commented.

"A necessary part of the Lead Agent-Trainee relationship, I'm afraid," Saera smiled. "Once a month isn't so bad, right?"

"I guess not."

"How are you doing?" her mother asked, eyeing her through her tinted glasses.

Raena shrugged. "Good."

"Classes going all right?"

"Yeah, I think so. I'm getting a handle on the differences from back home."

Saera smiled. "I remember feeling comfortable by this time in my first year, too. It all started to click." She paused. "And what about things with Ryan?"

The question caught Raena off-guard. "Yeah, it's all good."

"I'm asking that part as your mom, not Lead Agent."

Raena looked down.

"What's wrong?"

"Nothing with him," Raena hastily replied. "He's great! It's just… tough to get any time as a couple."

"Ah." Her mother nodded with understanding. "Yeah, I've been there."

"How did you and Dad manage?"

"Well, he was an Agent by the time I was finishing my first year. We always had his quarters."

Raena's eyes widened. "Sneaking into the Agent's wing?"

Her mother smiled. "I got very good at it."

"I guess we're out of luck, then."

"Don't be silly. We'll figure out a place where you can get alone-time together—maybe some quarters on one of the Militia Levels."

They'd really set up a place where we can… Raena felt her face flush slightly. "That just seems so… I dunno."

"Relationships are complicated enough without having to worry about where you can even have a private conversation when you need to," Saera replied. "Keep in mind, I was almost a year younger than you when your father and I bonded."

"How did you know that was the right thing to do?"

"There's not an easy answer to that—we just felt it." Her mother paused. "I don't think most people would be prepared to commit at that age, but we'd both been through some fairly profound life experiences that made us grow up fast."

"I'm pretty scared by the whole thing," Raena admitted. "Not because I don't think Ryan will be a great partner, but just… having to give up a part of myself."

"No, it's not like that at all. It's more like your sense of self expands. You're still all of you, but you gain this extension that can make you feel more fulfilled and stronger than you ever thought you could be."

I hadn't thought about it that way. Raena looked up at her mother. "That actually sounds really nice."

"It's a feeling that can't be put into words. But it does go both ways—happiness is shared between you, but if one of you is hurting, you both do."

Raena noticed a subtle grimace flit across her mother's face, as if recalling a painful memory. "Have you ever regretted bonding with Dad?" she asked.

"No, but that doesn't mean it's always been easy. Especially after the war, he—" she cut herself off and forced a smile. "Don't rush into anything, but don't hold back only because you fear the unknown. You'll know what to do when the right time comes."

"Okay, thanks." Raena smiled back.

"I know there have been a lot of major life changes in the past several months. I'm impressed by how you've taken everything in stride."

"Eh, it's not like I've had a choice."

Saera nodded. "Well, if you have this kind of poise at seventeen, the other politicians on Tararia need to look out."

"Shouldn't they already be on high alert?" Raena asked. "I mean, we control both SiNavTech and the TSS now."

Her mother grinned. "Oh, yeah. It's taken fifty years, but all the pieces are in place. No one can stop us now."

— — —

After showing off the previous afternoon in spatial awareness training, Ryan made a point to be on his best behavior. Even Jason seemed to be taking Raena's advice, as he took a more agreeable attitude with the instruction than Ryan had seen in the past several months.

Despite Raena and Jason growing up on Earth and being unfamiliar with things like freefall maneuvering and Taran math, they'd quickly picked up everything that had been thrown at them. Oftentimes, Ryan was concerned he'd be left behind. What had been considered exceptional aptitudes among the servant ranks on Tararia were fairly average within the TSS, and he found that he had to push himself much more than he ever had before. He was keeping up, though, and Raena was both encouraging and supportive in the efforts.

The afternoon training session concluded on time and the Primus Elite Trainees returned to their quarters to unwind for the night. They were set to depart for the Rift at 07:00—an hour earlier than their normal start time—so most wanted to get to bed ahead of their typical schedule.

Ryan decided to take a quick shower before dinner so he could come home to finish his Taran politics paper after the meal. When he emerged from the bathroom, he found Raena lounging in the common area with some of her friends.

"Tell them," she said to Ryan when she spotted him.

His heart skipped a beat. "Tell them what?"

"That my family isn't a bunch of power-hungry dictators bent on taking over Taran civilization," Raena clarified.

"Uh..." His brow furrowed. *"Where is this coming from?"* he asked her. *"Has this come up before and I missed it?"*

"Apparently, Jason's stunt in class today got out and people are talking about us wanting to telepathically control the rest of the population if they don't agree with us."

"That's not what he meant at all."

"I know that, but they don't believe me," she said, her mental tone strained.

Ryan looked around the faces of those in the common room. "You might consider my opinion biased, but I've spent time with the Sietinens, and their interests are very much rooted in increasing equity, not totalitarian control."

Tiff evaluated Ryan from her place on the couch next to Raena. "His opinion is biased, all right."

Great, is she going to pick this moment to reveal what she saw yesterday? Ryan's supposition was immediately confirmed.

"Those two are a thing." Tiff pointed at Raena and Ryan.

All eyes turned to Raena and then shifted to Ryan.

"Seriously?" Liam asked.

"It shouldn't be that surprising, given all the time we spend together," Raena said. *"I don't want them questioning my parents' plan,"* she added privately to him. *"This will distract them."*

"Should we really *give them a distraction?"* he asked.

She smiled. *"Go for it."*

Ryan sat down on the edge of the coffee table closest to where he was standing. "It's fitting that we'd develop a relationship—with her dad being High Commander now and all."

Adaline looked confused. "How do you mean?"

"Well, my father used to be a TSS High Commander," Ryan said casually.

Ned's mouth dropped open. "Come again?"

"Yeah, Jason Banks," Ryan continued like he was doing nothing more than reading off a homework assignment. "I mean, that's how he was known around here. Back on Tararia, he was from the Bankris Dynasty."

Liam blinked at him with disbelief. "Your dad was High Commander and from a dynasty?"

"That's right." Ryan nodded.

"And you didn't think to mention any of that when that asshole was giving you shite about being a Ward when we first got here?" Ned questioned.

"It was beside the point in that instance," Ryan replied. "I guess it just never came up again. Our positions outside the TSS don't matter, right?"

"But that…" Liam breathed.

Ryan shrugged. "No one asked."

Tiff's mouth dropped open a little and she gave Raena a questioning look under raised eyebrows. Raena just smiled and gave her a coy shrug in response.

"Well shite," Tiff breathed. "I guess that explains why your dad was okay with it."

Jason emerged from his bedroom at the tail end of Tiff's statement.

"Dad's okay with what?" he asked Raena.

"With Ryan and me, since Ryan's dad is your namesake and all that," she replied.

"Oh, yeah. Small universe," Jason said and continued on his way to the back cabinets to grab a snack bar.

"You're not exactly helping your case for this not being a friendly takeover," Ned muttered.

"On the contrary," Raena said, "it's a bunch of old friends whose lives have intermingled. I know it looks like a crazy political scheme, but my dad has the highest CR on record—of course he'd take over as High Commander. And my grandfather was the sole Sietinen heir. Yes, they so happen to hold two key positions of power, but so what? My mom was raised on Earth, Ryan was raised as a Ward—I'd say, all in all, that makes for a pretty diverse group as far as potential power-holders go."

"Oh, so you and Ryan are *really* a thing?" Tiff said, her brown eyes getting even wider.

I'd say that distraction is in full swing now. Ryan feigned assurance. "That's between us."

Pensive looks of speculation washed over the faces of the other Trainees.

"I don't know about you," Raena stated as she rose from the couch, "but I'm going to dinner. All this attention is making me hungry."

"Fok… I have so many questions!" Tiff followed her.

Ryan stood and Liam came up to him with Ned.

"Dude, seriously, how'd you even…?" Liam asked.

"It's a long story," Ryan replied, thinking back to the convoluted truth he could never share with them. "The short version is that Wil saw me around the estate and realized I had telekinetic abilities. When they ran a search of my records, they found a genetic match with my real dad—Banks—who was killed in the war before I was even born. Being the lost son of a family friend, they brought me under their care. When Raena and I met, we just… clicked."

Ned shook his head. "Crazy."

Ryan smiled. "You're telling me. I still can't believe it."

Raena glanced back at him from by the door. "Coming?"

"On our way," he said. *"You know I'll always follow you."*

She took his arm. *"Not following. We're in this together."*

They hung back while the others went ahead.

"Thank you for revealing everything like that," Raena told him when the other Trainees were beyond earshot. "I know you didn't want to."

"It was going to get out one way or another," Ryan replied. He dropped his voice to a near-whisper, "You were right—we couldn't have people asking about how the Sietinen Dynasty is positioning."

"I know it's for the greater good, but it does look all creepy overlord-y, doesn't it?"

He tilted his head the slightest measure. "Yeah, kinda..."

Raena frowned. "I really hope my grandparents know what they're doing. This has major potential to backfire."

"And we'd be the first to go down—especially me."

"If it wasn't simultaneous, I'd only be milliseconds behind you," she said, keeping her voice low. "But if Sietinen were to fall, too, that's a whole other situation."

"It won't come to that," Ryan assured her. "We'll pull this off, whatever 'it' is, exactly."

"I believe that, too."

CHAPTER 3

AS THE PRIMUS Elite trainees prepared to board the TSS *Vanquish*, Jason was surprised to see his sister and Ryan suddenly being so open with their relationship.

He'd been watching them with interest for the last eight months. At first, he had been wary of Ryan's intentions—plenty of guys had taken an interest in Raena over the past couple of years on Earth, and almost none for the right reasons. He'd initially expected Ryan to be like them, taking advantage of the situation when he caught Raena's eye. But as Jason had observed them during their time at TSS Headquarters, he realized that it was nothing like he'd suspected. It was the kind of relationship like his parents shared, and something that Jason had never come remotely close to having himself.

Since he didn't have direct understanding of what was between them, he observed and tried to dissect it from a scientific perspective.

From Raena's brief account of her time behind the scenes with the Priesthood, Jason knew there was a genetic component to their attraction. His parents had been reticent to say anything, but Jason had taken it upon himself to do some digging. Buried deep in the Mainframe, he'd found reference to a nanoagent carried in the bloodlines of the High Dynasties and select other familial lines. What he saw in the couples around his family might very well be genuine attraction, but it might also be nanotech that had messed with their neural chemistry. It made him wary, but it also fascinated him to see others so taken with each other.

Beyond Jason's ties to Raena as his twin, he had few other friendships he'd consider significant. Remaining somewhat of a loner had the advantage of agility. When they were forced to suddenly leave Earth, for instance, there were few he was sorry to leave behind—as much as he'd protested, it was mostly for show.

In truth, he was far more drawn to what the TSS had to offer. It combined the appeal of a military lifestyle with the opportunity to intellectually challenge himself. He had yet to come close to doing so, but at least the potential was there.

Even so, all the attention was on Raena and Ryan—the Sietinen heiress and lost Dainetris heir, such a perfect pairing that it could be nothing short of engineered.

The fact that no one was concerned about such obvious orchestration worried him. If his parents knew about some master plan, they hadn't indicated anything beyond the pertinent points for the revolution they were planning.

Jason continued to watch and wait, pushing the boundaries here and there to see what topics solicited a reaction. One such topic was certainly the Rift, and he was anxious to visit it for himself. He might finally get some answers about the deal his father had struck with the mysterious Aesir when they'd come on the day of his and Raena's Awakening, and what their true future might hold. There was more on the line than just the Priesthood's removal from power, that much was clear. How much more, and Jason's potential part in it, remained to be seen.

Jason's introspection was interrupted by Liam plopping down onto the couch next to Jason in the lounge area of the *Vanquish* set aside for transporting the group.

"Hey," Liam greeted. "I can't believe we're about to go to the mythical Rift."

"It's hardly a myth," Jason replied. "It's where they fought most of the Bakzen War for five hundred years."

"The war itself seems almost mythical. No one who was actually there will talk about it."

Jason shrugged. "I don't blame them. A lot of people died. I wouldn't want to remember that, either." *It was enough to mess up Dad. I can't even imagine what leading that would be like.*

"Your dad is coming with us, right?" Liam asked.

"Yes, being the first educational tour about the Rift, he wanted to set the tone, or something."

His classmate nodded. "I guess he'd be able to do that better than anyone."

"We're lucky we get to see the Rift while it's still around," Jason said. "They'll have it closed eventually."

Liam shook his head. "The scale of it is still mind-blowing."

"And it's now two-thirds the size it was at the end of the war."

"And no more pathways to the civilized worlds."

The Bakzen's almost undetectable backdoor for attacking us. It's brilliant and terrifying at the same time. Jason nodded. "The loose threads have been tied off and they're healing the biggest wounds."

Liam chuckled. "Talking like that makes it sound like space is a living thing."

"From the way my dad talks about it, maybe it is. The energy pathways follow an ancient order we have no way of understanding from our vantage."

"Dude, that is way too mind-boggling to think about this early in the morning."

Jason smiled. "Never mind. I'm sure we'll have all sorts of perfectly boring explanations during the tour."

Raena grinned as she approached with Ryan. "With who's coming on this trip, there's no way it will be boring." They took seats across from the couch where Jason was sitting.

"I might take your advice and keep my mouth closed for once," Jason replied. "We'll see how resourceful people get to generate excitement without my generous inputs."

"First off, I don't believe for a second you could go on a field trip and not make at least one scene," his sister stated. "And secondly, I'm pretty sure traveling to a super-energized habitable pocket between subspace and normal space qualifies as excitement enough on its own, with or without your antics."

She may have a point. It's too unique a place for there not to be something interesting—especially with our luck. His mind flashed back to the Aesir and the Priesthood's bold move to apprehend Raena and Ryan. *I'm actually surprised they're letting us out of Headquarters at all.*

He sent Raena a telepathic hint of the latter point and she nodded solemnly. "I think that's why Dad is coming along," she stated. "It's not a coincidence that he's going on the tour at the same time as us while other Primus Elite Agents are leading the tours with other groups."

"In this case, the favoritism toward you works out to all our advantages," Liam commented, unaware of the subtext to their conversation. "It's cool getting to learn about the Rift from the former Supreme Commander himself."

Jason was about to tell Liam how much his father hated the use of that title when a low vibration began to emanate through the floor.

Raena's face lit up. "Oh! We're about to head out."

"Do you recall how long of a jump it is?" Ryan asked.

"A good five hours, I think," she responded.

Ryan groaned. "I guess that's why they gave us this digital binder of reading materials this morning."

She scowled. "Do you really think they're going to quiz us?"

"I always take the threat as a serious possibility," he said.

Jason shrugged. "With Dad, you never know."

Outside the viewport, the space surrounding the *Vanquish* began to take on a blue-green hue as a spatial distortion formed around the ship.

"I'll never get tired of that view," Raena breathed.

Jason cast her a sidelong glance. "Too bad you agreed to be heir. I doubt you'll get much chance for interstellar travel once you're stuck in a life of politicking on Tararia."

"I'm sure I can invent a reason or two for travel," she said with a smirk.

Jason noticed that Ryan remained strangely quiet during the exchange, careful to avoid eye contact with anyone while the discussion of Raena's political future was on the table. Though others now knew they were dating, Jason realized that most of the trainees would assume the relationship was just a fling while both were trainees within the TSS. The truth about Ryan's true lineage and future place within the Tararian elite would surely come as a shock.

"Well, I'm going to stay in the TSS for as long as they'll let me," Jason declared. "Touring the stars and doing fancy things with my mind sounds like the life."

"And here you thought you were going to be a beach bum college student in California," jested Raena.

He sighed. "In retrospect, I should have known that was never going to work out."

"We had no way of knowing just how different things would be."

This time, Raena and Ryan did make eye contact, and Jason detected a brief telepathic exchange between them.

"Well, we should probably get to all that reading," Raena continued.

"Right." Ryan stood with her. "We'll see you when we arrive."

They headed out of the common room.

Liam watched them depart, his eyebrows raised. "That's a hookup in the makings if I ever saw one."

"I don't care," Jason said truthfully.

Liam sighed and leaned back on the couch. "I guess we really *should* do that reading."

"Yeah, you're right." Jason pulled out his handheld and began absently scanning through the materials.

Most of it was information he'd already come across in his previous research into the Bakzen War. The refresher was useful, but he allowed his mind to wander.

Why are they so intent on sealing the Rift? he wondered. *And why show it to us now?*

— — —

Despite what others might think they were up to, Raena had stepped aside with Ryan simply so they could have an uninterrupted conversation out loud.

"Thanks again for helping with that distraction last night," Raena said as soon as they were alone in a small conference room near the common area housing the rest of the students.

"Of course." Ryan embraced her. "I do have to say, it was nice getting to have breakfast together without needing to pretend like I wasn't looking specifically at you."

She smiled. "Yeah, it was."

He released her. "Where... do we go from here?"

The question didn't need any elaboration. They cared about each other a great deal—and had for some time—but their circumstances had maintained a degree of physical and emotional boundaries. There were moments where Raena had desired to be with him more than anything, but she also took comfort in things being just the way they were—much more than friends, but not a proper couple, either.

"I've never had a serious boyfriend," she said after a slight pause.

"I've never really had a serious girlfriend, either."

She eyed him. "Maybe not in a proper relationship sense, but you've been with other girls."

He nodded.

"Well, I haven't."

"I know. And that's why I'd never push you into anything."

"It's not pushing me," she clarified. "I care about you, and I want it. But I also know there's more to it..."

"Bonding," Ryan supplied.

"Right."

"For what it's worth, I already can't imagine my life without you." He took her hands. "I want you to know that I'm ready to take that step whenever you are—whether that's tomorrow or years from now. I'm not going anywhere."

She stretched onto her toes and kissed him, releasing his hands so she could reach around his neck. They savored each other for a minute before parting, slightly breathless.

"I'm not gonna lie," Ryan said into her chestnut hair, "it's becoming increasingly difficult to stop here."

I know that feeling. She smiled up at him. "I do love you, Ryan. It'll be soon—I just want to wrap my head around a few more things first."

"I love you, too." He gave her another light kiss.

The words of affirmation they had first exchanged several months prior weren't spoken aloud often due to their shared quarters, but Raena always felt the adoration in his mental tone. She considered herself incredibly lucky to have such a caring and attentive partner.

Ryan took a step back from her. "So, right, I think we were supposed to be reading something."

"Yes, that." Raena sighed. "All right, let's dive in."

They settled into the chairs around the conference table—with Raena opting to prop up her feet on one of the empty seats—and began reading on their handhelds.

The reading materials provided a survey of the years following the Bakzen War and the attempts to seal the Rift. Teams of Agents had been working together for more than twenty years to re-weave the fabric of space where threads had been rended from their natural pathways. The Rift was a wound that needed to be healed. What the materials did not cover, however, was how the Rift was created in the first place, and why, if it was such a ghastly mar on their reality, they'd take students to tour it.

"Something doesn't add up," Raena commented to Ryan after she'd finished reading.

Ryan glanced up from his handheld, apparently not quite to the end yet, but he nodded. "I'm guessing there's no profound conclusion that wraps everything up with a nice bow."

"Quite the opposite. I'm frankly not sure why this many resources are being dumped into sealing the Rift. Based on everything I'd heard before and what's reiterated in these materials, spatial rifts do exist naturally, though on a much smaller scale, and they'll self-correct over time. If we just left it alone, it's not going to get any worse."

"And traveling into it doesn't seem like it'd help the healing process."

"It actually actively sets it back," Raena said. "I checked one of the citations in the last chapter, and that pointed to a report about how subspace jumps near a newly repaired rift corridor can re-tear the spatial fabric. They'll send a team in after us to re-stitch the frayed threads caused by our presence."

Ryan frowned. "That makes zero sense why we'd take a field trip here."

"It has to be more than just viewing a war monument."

"But what?"

Raena thought about it. "Maybe there's something that can be done or seen in the Rift that's not possible anywhere else?"

"Such as...?"

"Something with our abilities, maybe? With the heightened energy in the Rift," she speculated.

"That's as good an explanation as any," Ryan replied. "I guess we'll find out soon enough."

They returned to the common room and found that the chairs near Jason were now occupied by his roommates, so they selected a pair of plush chairs with a good vantage out one of the viewports along the back wall of the common room.

Fifteen minutes later, the scene outside the viewport changed from the light of subspace to the most bizarre sight Raena had ever witnessed.

At first, it appeared to be a normal spacescape with an expanse of stars in every direction. But upon closer inspection, everything was... off. It was almost like looking at an old double exposed photograph with a ghost image, where the stars were only an echo of their full form.

Her brow knitted. "This is so weird."

"And do you feel that?" Ryan asked.

Raena nodded. The air around her almost hummed, charged with much more energy relative to the environment of normal space. She tested herself ever so slightly with nudging one of the empty chairs nearby, willing it to shift position on the floor. It responded to her silent will as if she'd given the action her full attention. *"This is incredible,"* she said to Ryan.

"I feel like I could do anything," he agreed.

Raena was about to test a scaled-back version of that theory when the room suddenly silenced. She looked over at the entry doorway and saw her father standing with Michael.

"Thank you for accompanying us here today," Wil said. "As I'm sure you've surmised, we're now inside the Rift."

"Why does it look so strange?" Nora asked.

"It's a product of the Rift's position between subspace and normal space," Wil explained. "What you're seeing are elements of our physical reality bleeding through to this plane. You won't ever be able to witness people or ships, but something on the scale of a star or planet has a powerful enough signature that its presence can be detected here. The gravity wells aren't as pronounced as in normal space, but any pilot needs to be careful when navigating through the Rift."

"Why did you bring us here?" Jason asked from his seat, jumping straight to the point, as usual.

Wil nodded. "I know it doesn't seem like there's a lot to see here, but the Rift has some unique properties. We won't always have it at our disposal, so I wanted to take advantage of it while it's still here."

"If it's so handy and special, then why are you trying to get rid of it?" Liam asked.

"Because as great as it is, it's also a poison," Wil replied solemnly. "You can spend some time here now with no long-term ill effects, but prolonged time in the Rift will make it nearly impossible to feel fulfilled in normal space. The power is intoxicating. We need to seal it while we can, because sooner or later someone would try to possess it and rip it wide open again. Doing so has the potential to cause a cascade effect throughout the fabric of space, and we can't begin to speculate about the negative effects that might cause."

"Our presence here isn't helping with that healing," Jason pointed out.

"No, but it does yield invaluable information about your future as Agents." Wil smiled slightly. "You see, while in the Rift, you'll be able to glimpse your future abilities."

Except I've already witnessed some crazy things in normal space, Raena thought to herself. *What more will I be able to do here?*

"So, we're here to be tested?" Jason clarified.

"Not a test, exactly," Wil replied. "It's more to gather some data about how we can best guide you in your advancements."

"How will you evaluate us?" questioned Raena.

"That," her father replied, "requires a bit of a demonstration."

The echoed starscape outside shifted while the Vanquish changed position. As the ship turned, Raena saw a darkness at the edge of her view into the surrounding space, where the stars suddenly ended.

"What's that?" she asked.

"The edge of the Rift," Wil explained. "The easiest way to view your inner abilities is to link with the energy you manipulate when exercising those skills—and what better way than to directly interact with that fundamental energy network underlying our reality?"

He gazed out the viewport. "The aim here is to join in the healing of the Rift. You must detect the frayed threads and return them to their natural state. The approach you take to this task will reveal much about your innate aptitude."

Liam and Ned exchanged glances. "Isn't that normally done in groups?"

"Yes, in groups of four, typically," Wil confirmed. "You'll be attempting it just with me."

"All right.... How do Agents work together to make the repairs?" Adaline asked.

"It's easiest if I just show you," Wil replied.

Raena expected him to call on her, but to her surprise, he said, "Ryan, care to join me?"

Ryan glanced at Raena, then rose from his chair and stepped forward. "Sure."

"Now, I know not all of you have experience focusing telekinetic energy, but my understanding is that you've been over the basic principles of observing the use of abilities?" Wil said, casting an eye toward Michael.

"Yes," Michael stated. "But I think it's now time for the big reveal."

Raena perked up. *Reveal of what?*

Wil smiled. "Very well. This would be an easy exercise with Junior Agents, but without advanced visualization skills in electromagnetic patterns, it'd be challenging for you to see how the threads are woven together. For that reason, we have devised a bit of a visual aid."

Michael walked over to a storage cabinet in the side wall of the common room and produced a domed object the size of a dinner plate. He approached the bank of viewports along the back wall with Wil and placed the dome on a low table between two chairs.

"This is a specialized holoprojector," Wil explained. "Back during the war, we came up with a method to relay telepathic perceptions back through a ship's computer and use it for visualization. The device here is a simplified version of that visualization processor."

"It will let us see what you see?" Raena asked.

"Yes." Wil's attention lingered on her for several moments longer than the reply warranted. He then turned to Michael. "At this early stage in your training, it's unfair to draw direct comparisons in capability. Your abilities will emerge at different rates, and that has no bearing on your future potential. For that reason, we'd like to meet with each of you individually."

I don't think that's the only reason, Raena realized. *They don't want the others to know what I can do—or what Jason can do.* Suddenly, it made sense why Ryan had been selected.

"Still," Wil continued, "it's easier to only have to explain the process once. Are you still okay modeling the activity?" he asked Ryan.

Ryan nodded. "No problem."

"Good." Wil waved his hand over the dome on the table and it lit up with a blue ring around the base of its perimeter. "Join me over here," he instructed.

When Ryan was standing on the other side of the device from Wil, a telepathic connection formed between them, viewed as a silver conduit in Raena's mind's eye. She detected a telepathic conversation but was unable to listen in.

A moment later, both of them stared out the viewport and a holographic image materialized above the dome, depicting a grid of silvery blue threads against a black backdrop. Several threads were gathered together in a tight bundle with frayed edges.

"This is a visualization of a segment of the spatial tear we know as the Rift," Wil explained. "The task is to return the threads to their natural place, which will, in turn, seal the Rift in the designated area."

"Is that really a good idea to do while we're, you know, *inside* the Rift?" Jason asked, his arms crossed.

"The remaining Rift still encompasses the equivalent area of three Sol-sized systems," responded Wil without turning from the viewport. "You don't have to worry about it collapsing around us."

On the projector, a bright point of light flashed just outside the center of the thread bundle. In response, several of the threads began to unfurl, gravitating toward where the flash had been. Several more flashes appeared in the ensuing seconds, which resulted in the coarse bundle distributing into a more uniform grid pattern. The frayed edges remained, though—the ends of broken threads swaying as if eddied by an unseen current.

"What you just witnessed is a technique of sending focused energy pulses toward where you want the grid to move," Michael explained while Wil continued to work with Ryan. "Spatial fabric naturally wants to right itself, but sometimes it needs a little push in the right direction. We offer that guidance."

As he spoke, the ends of a broken thread moved into alignment, and a new, silvery connection formed between them. Tendrils slowly wove together between the two pieces until they were re-joined.

"Once the grid is close enough to its preferred state," Michael continued, "the real repairs can begin. The key is to offer enough—shall we say, coaxing—to break apart the damaged sections without causing additional damage. It's a very slow process, but the technique works."

"Except for nearby spatial jumps," Jason interjected.

"A repair does take about two days to fully take," Michael added. "So, the team will typically move deeper into the Rift before jumping out."

"Why not perform the repairs from normal space?" Raena asked.

"We can," Michael said, "and sometimes do. But after experimenting with all the methods, it's easier to work in here. Once we get close to the end, we'll make the final push from normal space."

Wil and Ryan had worked their way along the visible length of the former knot, and now only four unsecured thread lengths remained. Several more flashes lit up, and those final pieces wove together. Out the viewport, the blackness at the edge of their view seemed to advance closer to the ship.

As Wil pulled his attention to back inside the common room, the holographic projection vanished.

"That was amazing," Ryan breathed. "I've never felt anything like it."

"You're a natural," Wil said with a smile. "You had very good intuition for where to direct the pulses."

Ryan smiled back. "Thanks. It just felt… right."

"Much of what we do is driven by intuitive feeling," Wil said with a nod. "Learning to listen to your instincts is just as important a skill as actual mastery of the telekinetic manipulation." He looked out over the Trainees around the room. "Any questions before we proceed with the one-on-ones?"

No one spoke up.

"All right. Let's get to it."

Michael gathered the holoprojector from the table and explained that the one-on-ones would take place in a conference room down the hall. Tiff was the first student, with Ned up next, and Michael stated that the next two people in the queue would be summoned by the returning individual.

Given the unknown time until her turn, Raena settled back into her plush chair and Ryan returned to the adjacent seat.

"What was it like?" she asked him while they waited.

"This is going to sound weird, but it was almost like looking back in time."

"What do you mean?"

He shook his head. "It was as though I was witnessing something ancient—and beautiful. There's something timeless and enduring under what we see in everyday life, and making those repairs was returning order to that ancient web. When everything fell into place, there was this feeling of profound happiness."

Raena smirked. "Like the universe was thanking you?"

He laughed. "Hey, I won't turn down some good cosmic karma."

Across the room, Jason was talking with Liam, who showed him his handheld. Jason scowled at the device and then approached Raena and Ryan.

"Looks like we'll be the last two up," her brother said. "No surprise."

"I'm curious to see how your experience differs from mine," Ryan commented.

Jason glanced at the other students nearby and then perched on the broad arm of Raena's chair. *"I think they brought us here for different reasons,"* he said telepathically. *"I've been reading some accounts from people who lived in the Rift for extended times. They've talked about chance encounters with the Aesir."*

"They told the Aesir to leave us alone for five years," Raena pointed out. *"Why would they go out of their way to force an encounter now?"*

"Because that was Day One for us. Now they know we're not fragile newbies. It's no secret between the three of us that we should not be able to do the things that are already second nature for us," Jason countered.

Raena frowned. *"But still, what would be gained from another brush with the Aesir?"*

"They have that place where you can see things," he replied. *"Like, a glimpse of your destiny, or something. I bet they have no idea what to do with us and are looking for some direction."*

"And this hypothesis is based on… what?" Ryan asked.

"Intuition, of course." Jason grinned.

Raena rolled her eyes and gave him a playful shove. *"You're impossible. These sorts of guessing games aren't productive."*

"Maybe not, but I'd rather be prepared than caught by surprise," her brother replied.

She eyed him. *"How can you possibly prepare when we don't even know what we'd be getting ready for?"*

He shrugged. *"Fine, then I'm prepared to be prepared."*

"Good luck with that," Raena said with a mental chuckle. But she knew he was right. There had been far too many unexpected developments to assume that past decisions would hold. She needed to be ready for anything.

CHAPTER 4

IT WAS TWO hours before Jason was finally called for his one-on-one evaluation, and Raena was left to wait in anxious anticipation with Ryan.

"Why do you think Dad left me for last?" Raena pondered aloud.

Ryan cast her a sidelong look. "You really have to ask?"

She didn't, but it was habit for her to try to downplay her uniqueness. Growing up on Earth, she'd always had trouble blending in. Only after she learned her parents had spent most of their lives on another planet did it make sense that she'd never quite felt at home on Earth. She belonged elsewhere, and not just in terms of a physical place—she'd been born as an heiress to help lead an entire civilization, and her profound telekinetic abilities made her an even greater rarity. She and her brother were the children of the prophesied Cadicle. A little special treatment was sure to come with the territory.

Raena shrugged off her original question and waited in silence for Jason to return. After seven minutes, he appeared in the doorway to the common room, looking shaken.

"You're up, Raena," he said.

She walked over to him. "Are you okay?"

"Yeah, I'm fine," Jason replied. *"Dad will explain,"* he added telepathically.

Raena nodded and left the common room with a parting

smile back to Ryan. She traversed the hall of the *Vanquish* leading to the conference room that had been set aside for the private meetings with her father.

Inside the room, Wil was staring out the viewport. He turned around when Raena entered. “Hi.”

“Hi,” Raena replied, then noticed that Michael was also in the room, standing along the front wall out of view from the hallway.

Michael looked Raena over when she entered. “I’ll leave you to it, then.” He departed, closing the door behind him.

“Dad, what’s going on?”

Wil clasped his hands behind his back. “We’re in a difficult spot. I’d expected you to need time to train like most students, but in a matter of months you’ve progressed easily to the level of a Junior Agent—and with very little coaching.”

Raena felt her face flush. “I guess.”

“This isn’t the time for modesty,” her father said. “Honestly, have you been holding back?”

She met his gaze. “I haven’t even tried to push myself.”

He nodded. “That’s what I suspected. However, my hope is that your fellow trainees—with the exception of Ryan and Jason, of course—don’t realize just how talented you really are.”

“I thought you didn’t want us to hide our abilities?”

“In the end, no. But right now, it’d make things easier on Tararia if you appeared to be on a more traditional training path.”

That makes sense. She glanced out the viewport. “You didn’t bring us all the way out here to tell me that.”

“Correct. But I wanted to establish that before we got to the real reason for this trip. I needed to make a show of it with a large visitation group so it didn’t call attention to one individual. But truthfully, Raena, this was all so you can help me.”

Her breath caught in her chest. “Me help *you*?”

He inclined his head. “You see, I reached out to the Aesir.”

“Why?”

“Because I wanted to make sure that we’ve accounted for all the variables. I have reason to believe that you can help me see something I haven’t been able to see myself.”

Raena shifted on her feet. “How? I don’t understand.”

"The Aesir's test," Wil explained, "offers a glimpse of some universal truth specific to you and your life. There's a place they call the nexus that makes this vision possible. But I think the Rift—and these properties that heighten our abilities—serve a similar purpose, on a smaller scale. The Aesir won't allow me to look into the nexus again, as I already learned my truth—the true nature of the Bakzen. However, there's something else they want me to know, and they made it sound like you could help me see it."

He's the most powerful Agent there's ever been. What does it mean that he's turning to me now? Raena took an unsteady breath. "Of course, I'll help. What do I need to do?"

Wil smiled with relief. "Well, I need to teach you astral projection."

"Isn't that a bit… metaphysical?"

"No more so than telepathy or telekinesis," her father pointed out. "Consciousness is energy, too. Disconnecting from your physical self is quite freeing."

"Yeah, I bet." Raena took a step toward him. "How does it work?"

Wil beckoned her the rest of the way to him and gestured for her to sit on the ground cross-legged as he did likewise. "It's easier in freefall, but this will have to do," he stated. "Close your eyes and focus on the energy of the Rift around you. Clear your mind. I'll find you."

Raena did as she was instructed. The sweet power of the Rift called to her at the edge of her consciousness. She wanted to reach out and touch it, but her physical self was holding her back. It was so tantalizingly close, and yet the power was just beyond her grasp.

Then, a presence appeared at the outer reaches of her mind. *"I'm here,"* her father said.

She sensed a power that she'd never experienced in person—a force that was both comforting and terrifying. Other Agents always appeared as bright spots in her mind, but her father's presence was like trying to look at the sun in comparison to a full moon. Her instinct was to withdraw into herself, but she resisted. She knew he would take care of her and there was no need to be afraid.

"I sense the energy of the Rift," Raena said when her breathing had settled. After taking some time to adjust, Wil's presence was no longer so overwhelming.

"Good. Now follow my lead."

Raena was aware of the room around her and Wil seated a meter in front of her. However, the presence of her father began to move away from his physical form.

"Wait, where are you—?" Instinctively, she followed him, focusing only on his presence within the emptiness of her mind. He raced ahead of her, just beyond her grasp but not so far ahead that she lost track. After what felt like several seconds, his pace slowed and she caught up with him.

It was then that she realized she was no longer attached to her physical form.

Behind her, she saw the *Vanquish*. At least, she knew it was the TSS ship she had been on moments before, but her vision wasn't the same as when she viewed her surroundings using her corporeal eyes. Rather, everything was an outline of its main physical form, but she could simultaneously detect each object's energy signature down to a subatomic level. The details were too much to reconcile in her mind at once, so she didn't even attempt to delve deeper than the surface.

Her father appeared in her mind as the version of himself she knew in day-to-day life, but she recognized that was only for her benefit—really, neither of them were floating in space outside the ship.

Whoa! It's like I'm on a spacewalk without a suit, she realized when it occurred to her that she perceived the echoed starscape of the Rift behind her father.

Looking at the *Vanquish*, she spotted the conference room where their physical forms were waiting for them. An invisible thread bound her to herself—the tether she could use to trace back no matter how far she roamed.

"This is incredible," she said to Wil.

His image smiled back at her. *"I thought you'd enjoy it. But this is nothing."*

He extended himself to her, as though taking her hand, and

then raced into open space. The *Vanquish* became a tiny speck in a split-second, and within moments, even the echoed image of the nearest star was just a distant dot.

Wil stopped at the far edge of the Rift. "*We can go as far as you can imagine in normal space, but this task requires us to stay here.*"

"*I see what you mean about it being freeing,*" Raena said, feeling an elation like she'd never experienced before.

"*Yes, but now we must evaluate,*" Wil said, his tone turning serious. "*There's something the Aesir want us to see, but I don't know what it is.*"

He fell into silent meditation in the near-empty blackness.

Next to him, Raena probed around herself, willing an answer to come to her. She could detect the ancient energy and felt the discord within the Rift where the Bakzen had unnaturally altered the pathways to create their home.

Then, she sensed a different energy signature. It beckoned her, and she heeded. Wil followed behind at a distance, letting her set the path.

She raced across the expanse until a black pit came into view.

Behind her, she felt her father tense.

"*What is this place?*" she asked.

"*It was the Bakzen homeworld,*" he stated, his mental tone pained. "*I destroyed it.*"

Raena was moved by the hurt emanating from him, but she couldn't allow herself to become distracted by the past. There was something about the site that had drawn her in.

She probed the blackness, seeking the origin of the call. And then she saw it—a minute tear within the fabric of space, not to subspace or normal space, but to somewhere else entirely.

"*This,*" she told her father. "*I think this is what we were meant to find.*"

Wil assessed the tear, and she sensed his worry.

"*I was afraid of this,*" he said eventually.

"*Do you know what it is?*"

"*A doorway—to a reality other than our own.*"

Raena didn't know what to make of the statement. "*Like… another dimension?*"

"Yes, something like that." Wil stared into the black pit, his cerulean eyes glowing in the darkness. *"Come. We've seen what we needed to see."*

He led them back to their bodies on the *Vanquish*, and Raena found it fascinating to see herself from the outside. She lingered just a moment to observe herself and then returned her consciousness to her physical form.

Her eyes opened with a start. Everything around her seemed so flat and plain after the depth she'd seen around her while in the state of astral projection.

Wil rose from the ground and ran his fingers through his chestnut hair. "Don't speak of what we saw to anyone—not even Ryan or Jason."

"Why not?" Raena stood across from him.

"Because there's absolutely nothing we can do about it," he replied. "As long as that tear exists, there's no way we can completely close the Rift. Maybe the Aesir know a way."

She nodded. *I don't like the idea of keeping anything from Ryan, but worrying about something we can't control doesn't help anyone. I hope I can forget about it myself.*

"How did it feel out there?" Wil asked.

"Incredible. I'm surprised you aren't out there all the time."

"I do venture out occasionally," he said with a slight smile, but it didn't hide his worry over what they'd seen.

"So, Dad," Raena began after a slight pause, "what you said about me meeting with the Aesir… Do I need to wait four more years to meet with them?"

"Were you any less Gifted, I'd advise waiting as long as possible. But as things stand, you may meet with them whenever you feel ready. Honestly, the sooner we have your vision to guide us, the better off we'll be."

Her heart leaped at the prospect of meeting their mysterious Taran brethren. "Then I'll go. Soon." *I want to know what I'm supposed to do, too. There are so many potential paths…*

Wil placed a hand on her shoulder. "You're incredibly talented, Raena. I have no doubt you'll succeed, no matter what's ahead of us."

"Thanks." She smiled.

He pulled her into a quick embrace and she hugged him back. "Your mom and I will support you in any way you need."

Raena released him and stepped back. "Thank you."

Wil smiled. "All right. Now, you should probably get back. You've been gone for at least twice as long as anyone else."

"Okay." She headed for the door. "And Dad?"

"Hmm?"

"You'll tell me if I should worry about what we saw, right?"

He nodded. "I promise. But if it does become an issue, I suspect that will be a whole other saga."

"All right," she agreed. "I'll focus on taking care of the Priesthood."

Wil chuckled. "That's the spirit. One fight at a time…"

— — —

The conversation with his father hadn't quelled any of Jason's concerns. He stared into the meditative, swirling light of subspace while the *Vanquish* returned to Headquarters, allowing his mind to wander.

He'd expected his father to offer some alternate explanation or to refuse commentary when Jason brought up evidence of the nanotech he'd discovered in the High Dynasty bloodlines, but instead his statements had been met with affirmation.

When Jason had gone on to question about the true nature of the field trip to the Rift, his father had made no effort to hide that it was about Raena and her abilities. It was no surprise, then, when her meeting lasted twenty minutes, compared to the seven minutes others had spent in the conference room. What concerned Jason, though, was that Raena wouldn't discuss what had transpired during the meeting.

As twins, they'd told each other nearly everything. In their time since joining the TSS, though, they'd drifted apart—not much, but enough that Jason knew he couldn't rely on Raena to tell him everything she might know.

For that reason, he'd elected to keep his own discovery to himself. The orchestration of their lives ran far deeper than anyone had admitted before his father's confirmation today. Jason wasn't about to let it slide.

I know we were made, and I know they're not finished with us yet. If they wanted his help, he'd need to be let into the inner circle.

— — —

Wil relaxed on the couch in the center of his office facing the viewscreen on the side wall. The trip to the Rift hadn't gone quite how he'd imagined and there was a lot to process.

As if his conversation with Jason hadn't been enough, both of his children's growing abilities were going to complicate matters more than he'd anticipated.

He'd known for several months that Raena was significantly more proficient than even he had been after an equivalent amount of time following his own Awakening. What she had been able to do while in the Priesthood's custody would have been considered remarkable for even a seasoned Agent, but for an untrained first year student… It was the reason he hadn't told her about her true potential. That degree of power was more than any one person should tap. But now that she knew, it remained to be seen what she'd do.

Then there was Jason. His abilities had grown at a more measured rate, but he had already outpaced most Junior Agents. He would need to be kept busy if that exceptional ability was to be channeled productively. But moreover, his son had started digging into matters that Wil had hoped would remain buried in the past. It was a longer-term concern, though, so Wil set it aside while he focused on more pressing issues.

I hate being in this position. My life was orchestrated behind the scenes and now I'm about to do the same thing to my own children. This isn't right. He took a deep breath and ran his fingers through his hair. There had to be another way.

He'd vowed to let his children choose their own path. When he and Saera moved down to Earth, that was the driving force behind their decision. He needed to remain true to those original wishes.

Given that mandate, there was only one course ahead in the immediate future.

Raena needs to visit the Aesir. The notion scared him more now that it was an imminent event. His own encounter with them had changed his life. The truth that Raena would undoubtedly see would certainly change hers, as well.

A light knock sounded, and a moment later Saera cracked open the door. "Hey. I thought you might want to talk," she said, stepping inside.

"Good timing, as usual."

"Well, that brief telepathic exchange when you got back on the *Vanquish* made it clear something significant happened."

Wil patted the couch next to him. "Yeah, that's one way to put it."

"So…? Details." Saera removed her tinted glasses and plopped down on the couch.

"In short, Raena is too advanced to stay here in the TSS," Wil stated, removing his own tinted glasses. Hearing the words out loud, it sounded even less real than it did in his head. *I didn't think anyone else's ability could actually worry me. But it does.*

Saera raised an eyebrow. "I didn't expect to hear that."

"I think whatever we throw at her, she'd just do it intuitively. I took her out with me."

His wife's eyes widened. "You mean astral projection?"

"Yes, and she picked it up immediately. She has a true gift for seeing… And if she has a limit, I think it would be beyond mine—and I don't think she'd need years of training to get there."

His wife took a minute to process the revelation, tugging on the end of her braided auburn hair. "Then what do we do?"

"She's asked if she can visit with the Aesir sooner than later, and I see no reason to stop her."

"A year ago, I would have refused, but I think you're right."

"I have no worries about her passing the test," Wil said. "They've already established that she has great value to them, so they won't risk harming her. I genuinely believe that they'll be able to tell us the best path forward. We ultimately want the same things—to fix the Generation Cycle and to restore balance to the Taran Empire."

Saera nodded. "We need powerful allies beyond a handful of High Dynasties on our side. A relationship with the Aesir might give us a measure of insurance we can't get anywhere else."

Wil searched her jade eyes. "I expected you to be resistant to the idea."

"Don't get me wrong—I'm not happy about the notion of Raena, or you, getting wrapped up with the Aesir. We hardly know anything about them. But I do know that Raena is special, and if ever there was a time to go outside our comfort zone, it's this."

"Agreed." Wil took a deep breath. "And then there's Jason."

"Is he as strong as her?" Saera asked.

"That's still unclear. It's possible he's a fair match for me, but since I don't rightly know my own limit, I can't make an accurate comparison. What I *do* know is that he's already bored with the pace of the training program, and he's going to start making trouble if we don't give him something to do."

Saera groaned. "I was afraid of that."

"But moreover, I learned that he's digging into some of the darker truths surrounding our lives. He's already made some connections I was hoping our children would never know."

"Like what?"

"About the degree of genetic engineering that went into our creation. He's been researching nanotech."

Saera's face drained. "How did he find out?"

"I have no idea. A lot of information was declassified after the war. He's smart, and determined. I'm sure there was something out there waiting to be found and he dug until he found it."

"That didn't take long! It hasn't even been a year."

"Precisely," Wil said. "So, we either allow him continued free rein, or we give him so much structure that he falls in line with our larger plans."

"Knowing him, he'll see the manipulation for what it is and rebel even harder."

"Not if we tell him the truth."

Saera eyed him. "And what truth is that?"

"Something I haven't wanted to admit to myself," Wil replied. "We say we're in this final fight with the Priesthood so there can be peace. But there's never going to be peace—not completely. There will always be conflict of some sort because it's the nature of our species to push boundaries and drive change. Not everyone in a population of trillions is going to want the same thing, and without a doubt there are going to be arguments that escalate beyond innocuous political spats. Someone needs to be there to keep things from getting out of hand when that happens."

"The TSS needs to remain a police force," Saera concluded.

"Yes. The notion of being just an academic institution is shortsighted. I hate to say it, but weaponized telekinesis shouldn't go by the wayside."

She sighed. "So much for that vision of living a quiet life without any drama."

"When did we *ever* think that would actually happen?" Wil laughed.

"Okay, maybe that was all in my head for, like, a second."

He smiled at her. "You agree, then?"

"I do," she admitted. "I don't like it, but I'd rather be on the side holding all the cards than the other way around."

"All right. I'll talk with Jason and we'll figure out a plan. I'll have to play it by ear, but I think we can work out a new training program that will keep him occupied and get us where we need to be."

"And Raena?" Saera circled back.

"I'll contact the Aesir. It's time we learn more about what they have to offer."

"I have always wondered where they live."

"Me too," Wil said. "Years ago, they said I was always welcome among them. I hope that means I can come just for a visit."

"Any chance I can tag along?" she asked.

"Doubtfully, but even if you could, I'd feel better knowing that you were watching over Headquarters here. It's one thing for us to take a trip to Tararia together, but there…"

"Yeah, I know what you mean." Saera looked down. "Do you

think they'll test Raena the same way they did you?"

Wil nodded. "It seems to be their standard induction. It's actually why I'd like for her to meet with them sooner than later."

"Why?"

"I want to know what truth she sees," he replied. "It very well may shape our future."

CHAPTER 5

THE MORNING AFTER the field trip to the Rift, Raena had made up her mind. *I need to meet with the Aesir right away.*

She'd considered waiting longer, but after mulling it over as she had lain in bed unable to sleep, she realized there was no point in delaying the meeting. Whatever information could be gleaned from the Aesir would be best to get as soon as possible.

After breakfast, Raena fiddled with her tablet in the Primus Elite's common room while she tried to think of the best way to broach the subject with Ryan. She had just adjusted her positioning on the couch when a buzz sounded at the entry door.

"I'll get it," Nora offered, being the closest.

When the door slid open, Raena was surprised to see her father.

Nora startled. "Sir, what can—?"

"Good morning," Wil greeted and then spotted Raena. "Raena, may I speak with you?"

"Is this about the Aesir?" she asked.

"Yes," he confirmed.

"Sure. Let me grab some shoes," Raena said aloud and ran into her bedroom. She returned to the common area and slipped on her boots before following her father into the hall.

He led them to a meeting room several doors down.

"I reached out to the Aesir yesterday and told them what we'd seen," Wil said as soon as the meeting room's door was sealed.

"They confirmed that's what they'd wanted us to witness."

"But why? What does it mean?" Raena asked.

"I don't know, but they're worried. They don't want the Priesthood to learn about it—it's made them want to accelerate the plans."

Raena crossed her arms. "The political pieces aren't in place yet for an overthrow."

"No, they're not. So, I don't know what to do," Wil admitted.

"I need to look into the nexus," Raena stated. "That will reveal my path, right?"

Her father nodded. "I hope so. But are you sure you're ready to do this?"

Raena smiled. "I was just about to come find you and say I want to go."

He let out a sigh of relief. "Good, because they're standing by to send a ship. I was also able to convince them to let me come along. After your test, they're allowing us to go see their home."

"Really?" she asked incredulously.

"I'm not sure if there's only one place—and if it's a space station, or a planet, or something else entirely—but they have tech beyond anything the Priesthood allows anyone to possess these days. It sounds like they might be willing to share some of it with us."

Raena's face lit up. "I can't wait to see it!"

Wil grinned. "Me either. Their ships alone are incredible."

"Cool." Raena thought for a moment. "What should I tell everyone?"

"Jason and Ryan know about the Aesir already, so you can tell them the truth. For the others, it's probably best to say that you've been summoned to Tararia for some urgent business for the Dynasty."

She nodded. "All right. Any idea how long we'll be gone?"

"A day or two, I imagine. But honestly, I have no idea."

"Okay."

Wil checked the time on the viewscreen inset in the wall of the meeting room. "It will take them two hours to arrive. So, meet me in my office in ninety minutes—we'll go up to wait for them at the main spaceport."

"All right." Raena took a deep breath. *I can't believe I'm about to meet with an ancient order of people with advanced telekinetic abilities. This is crazy!*

"See you soon."

They parted ways, and Raena returned to her quarters.

Nora looked at Raena questioningly as soon as she returned.

"I need to take a brief trip to Tararia," she replied to the unspoken question. Telepathically, she reached out to Ryan and Jason, *"Have a few minutes? I need to tell you something."*

Within seconds, her boyfriend and brother appeared in their respective bedroom doorways. Raena headed for her room and they followed.

Tiff and Adaline were lounging on their beds reading.

"May we have the room?" Raena requested.

Tiff and Adaline exchanged glances. "What's up?" Tiff asked.

"We need to discuss some things in private. Please?"

Her roommates eyed her suspiciously but got up from their beds.

"Whatever," Adaline said.

They evaluated Ryan as they passed, probably trying to figure out just how much impact his relationship with Raena was going to have on his standing.

Tiff's gaze lingered on Jason, as well, but she walked past without commentary.

Raena rolled her eyes as soon as they were behind her and she slid the bedroom door closed.

"Why the secret meeting?" Jason asked.

"All right…" Raena took a deep breath. "You know my extra-long meeting with my dad yesterday? Well, one of the reasons it ran so long was we were discussing the Aesir."

Jason's brow knitted. "What about them?"

Raena swallowed. "I'm going to meet with them today."

Ryan's face paled and Jason's eyes widened.

"Why would you do that?" Jason exclaimed. "Dad freaked out when they came for us before!"

"Yeah, but that was before everything that happened with the Priesthood," Raena replied. She looked at Ryan. "It's pretty clear I don't need those five years to train."

"You can do fancy shit without trying, we know," her brother said. "That doesn't mean you should go hang out with a bunch of creepy space people who would just as soon let you die or go insane if their test doesn't go as planned."

"I don't like it, either," Ryan murmured. *"Are you sure they won't hurt you?"*

"Dad is going with me," Raena added, hoping that would set them both at ease. "If anyone asks, the cover story is that we had to take care of Dynasty business. But we're really going to see if some kind of partnership is possible."

"Partner with the Aesir?" Jason shook his head and crossed his arms. "That'll be the day."

"You don't know any more about them than we do," Raena shot back. "We have no reason to believe they won't help us. They want the Priesthood gone as much as we do—maybe even more."

"But they also stood by and did nothing during the Bakzen War," Jason pointed out.

"Regardless of their motivations now or before, you're walking into a big unknown," Ryan interjected. "Still, it sounds like you've already made up your mind." Worry filled his eyes.

"I'll be fine," she assured him privately. *"I know this is what I'm supposed to do."*

"This is crazy," Jason said, shaking his head.

"It's the only way we can get new insights beyond what we already know," Raena insisted.

After several seconds, her brother nodded. "I can see that. I still think it's crazy, but I guess I can't disagree with the plan."

Ryan looked less confident, but he nodded, as well. "We'll be waiting for you to get back."

Jason glanced between the two of them. "I'll give you two a minute." He gave Raena a quick hug and wished her good luck before leaving the room.

Ryan embraced Raena as soon as they were alone. "You'd better come back to me in one piece."

"I will, I promise." She took a slow breath and pulled back to look at him at arm's length. "We might be gone for a few days, so don't freak out if I'm not back right away, all right?"

"Me freak out? Never." He smiled at her.

"When I come back, I'll know what we need to do," she said. "No more wondering what's right."

"That's a lot of faith to put in one, brief meeting."

"Yeah, like that's never happened before," Raena jested, sending him a telepathic reminder of when they first bumped into each other.

He chuckled. "Point taken."

"I'll be back soon." She reached her hand behind his neck and they kissed. It might be a while before they were back together again, so she made it count.

— — —

Ryan hated the idea of Raena going off to stars-know-where to meet with the Aesir, but he recognized she was in a challenging position. To balance responsibilities to the TSS and Tararia would be difficult enough for someone groomed to fulfill those roles, but to have grown up on Earth without even knowledge of the Taran civilization made it an overwhelming proposition.

She had borne it well thus far, but her apprehension in recent months belied her underlying self-doubt.

Ryan couldn't blame her—most days he wound up chastising himself at one point or another for saying or doing something unbefitting of a dynastic heir. Constant second-guessing was exhausting.

He was skeptical about Raena being able to gain any direction from the Aesir, but if it would make her feel more confident, he needed to support her in that mission.

When Ryan returned to the common room after his parting discussion with Raena, he noticed Jason's glum expression. He was seated in one of the single lounge chairs along the back and side walls of the common room, typically used for private study. His headphones were in, but Ryan could tell he was thinking more than reading.

"Hey, she'll be fine," Ryan said to him telepathically.

Jason looked up from his tablet and located Ryan. *"I have no doubt about that. I'm just wondering why I wasn't asked to go along with them."*

"You haven't yet done what she has."

"Different circumstances," Jason replied. *"That doesn't mean I couldn't."*

"I'm sure you'll get your chance soon enough."

Jason nodded solemnly and returned his attention to his tablet. *"I'm curious to hear what Raena has to say."*

"Me too." Ryan just hoped that whatever she saw, he'd still have a place in her life.

— — —

The concourse of the TSS space station was sealed off from other travelers while Raena and her father waited for the Aesir to arrive.

"Should I say anything special to them?" Raena asked.

"No, this isn't like when you met your great-grandparents on Tararia," Wil replied. "They'll read anything they want to know directly in your mind."

Her brow knitted. "Even through mental guards?"

"They seem to… network, somehow. Their collective consciousness is too much for one individual to block."

"And I guess trying to block them out would just make it seem like we had something to hide, huh?"

Wil nodded. "We need to be as open with them as possible."

"I'll try," Raena replied.

Five minutes passed in silence while they stared out into the starscape. Then, a blue-green spatial distortion formed two thousand meters from the spaceport as a ship dropped out of subspace.

The vessel's delicate, arched form and sweeping lines were unlike any of the ships Raena had seen, civilian or military. It was only half the size of the *Vanquish*, but its presence demanded attention. The hull seemed to glow against the blackness of space, and as it neared the space station, Raena was able to make out numerous viewports lining the upper decks, and a panoramic dome at the aft of the vessel hung beneath the forked jump drive.

She stared at it in awe as it maneuvered into the open berth.

"The aesthetic is truly unique, isn't it?" Wil commented as he looked it over with more reserved awe.

"Is it just me, or does it feel different, too?"

He nodded. "Their ships seem to be tuned for telepathic operation. You'll notice a more pronounced hum on the ship."

The Aesir ship completed docking, and the hatch at the end of the gangway opened.

"Here we go," Wil said with a rueful smile.

Her stomach knotted with nervous anticipation, Raena ascended the gangway with her father. As soon as they passed through the open hatch, she sensed the hum of energy her father had referenced.

The interior of the ship resonated with a warm glow of power that washed over her and made her feel completely at ease. She extended herself toward it, and the ship responded with a gentle pulse of acceptance.

Physically, the ship reminded her of the *Vanquish*, though the details were less military and more luxurious—like what she might find in a well-appointed home on Earth. The carpeting underfoot had more cushioning, and the crystal coverings over the inlaid lights gave an impression of sophisticated elegance.

Raena was so caught up in examining the ship that it took her a moment to notice the figure robed in iridescent black standing down the hall. He was gazing at her with intense interest, his pale eyes glowing slightly. His skin was pale and almost translucent, as though he'd never been out in the sun or under UV lights like those found throughout TSS Headquarters. The most mesmerizing thing about him, though, were his ageless features; his level gaze was one of mature wisdom, yet there were no lines or other distinguishing marks to suggest he was older than thirty.

"Hello, Dahl," Wil stated. "I shouldn't be surprised you'd come."

"I remain the Aesir's ambassador for matters involving the Cadicle," Dahl replied. "This must be Raena."

A shiver ran down Raena's spine as a powerful mind

skimmed the surface of her own, indistinct whispers flitting by in an instant. Her chest constricted.

"She is as powerful as we expected. Maybe more so," Dahl stated. "It was wise to bring her to us now."

"Raena has come on her own accord," Wil said.

"Yes, hello," she managed at last. "I wish for you to test me, so I may see my path."

Dahl inclined his head. "We are anxious to know that path, as well. So much has become unclear with recent events."

The hatch to the gangway swung closed and locked with a hiss.

"Come," Dahl stated, and headed down the hall.

He led them to a lift. As they were stepping inside, Raena felt the subtle vibration of a jump—much more muted and smoother than she was used to experiencing, but the slight elongation of time at the moment of transition was unmistakable.

They took the lift down five levels and then traversed a hall toward the aft of the ship. The hall terminated in a set of double doors, which parted to reveal the interior of the rounded observation room Raena had witnessed while the ship was docking. The curved windows around three sides of the room and transparent floor provided a breathtaking view of subspace while they traveled toward their destination.

"We have never tested someone so soon after Awakening," Dahl admitted. "But we suspected, when we came for you before, that you would be different. I am pleased to see that we were right."

"Should Jason have come, too?" Raena asked.

Dahl shook his head. "While he could survive the test in his current state, he is not ready to see his truth. That is for a future fight."

Raena looked to her father for an interpretation of the statement, but he just gave a slight shake of his head in response.

"Today is about you," he said privately—or at least as privately as was possible in the Aesir's presence.

They gazed into subspace while the ship completed its jump. Raena wasn't sure how much time passed, but it felt like only ten or fifteen minutes.

"Where are we?" she asked when the ship dropped into normal space.

"The nexus," Dahl replied, making a sweeping gesture with his hand to encompass the black pit in front of them.

Raena was drawn to the blackness, but she remained focused on the room around her. "But where is it?"

"Near the core of the galaxy," Dahl replied.

Wil perked up with interest. "How could we travel that far so quickly?"

"Our jump drives are not like yours," the Aesir Oracle stated. "But right now, that is not your concern." He inclined his head toward the nexus, bidding Raena to look into its depths.

She took a deep breath to center herself and then gazed into the blackness. As she stared, she found herself drawn outward, and she disconnected her consciousness from her physical form, just as she had while exploring the Rift with her father only the day before. She checked the thread that anchored her to herself, and then ventured into the depths of the blackness.

Once inside, the energy pattern making up the universe around her began to take shape—silver threads across the infinite expanse, forming a web of pathways between people and worlds. She drifted outward to observe it from a higher vantage, seeing all pathways ultimately leading back to her people's roots on Tararia.

Raena looked for her own place in the web, and she was pulled toward Tararia. Her perspective zoomed and morphed until the planet took up the entire view of her mind's eye. Energy pathways looped around the world, connecting individuals through relationships that were so fundamental they were written into the patterns of the universe.

Her own ties led her to Sieten—to the Sietinen estate outside the city. As she focused on the location, a vision came to her.

She stood atop the cliffs on the northern coast of the Priesthood's isle. The sun shone down on her, warming her skin. While she gazed out over the sea, she detected someone coming up next to her, and she turned to see Ryan. He didn't appear as she knew him now, but could feel a bond between them and knew him to be the most important person in her life.

Ryan beamed at her and she was overcome with elation that radiated through her. They'd just accomplished something—something they hadn't dreamed possible.

Raena looked down at her feet and saw a brilliant, red flower swaying in the breeze. She recognized that it was a symbol but wasn't sure what it represented, only that everything was in its rightful place.

The vision faded and Raena once again saw Tararia, a glowing gem against the starscape. As she reveled in its beauty, a dark shadow appeared over the planet.

She recoiled with fear from the looming darkness. It wasn't her fight to lead, but it was there on the horizon. Others would unleash the threat if her intended future didn't come to pass. She searched around her, looking for the path she need to follow to quell that darkness, but she was lost.

The thread that bound her to her physical self was disintegrating as the darkness crept toward her. She fled in the only direction available—away from herself and her home.

No, I can't run. She stopped herself. *But how do I fight?*

She had no answer other than the certainty that her place was on Tararia. No matter what, she couldn't afford to let whatever loomed on the horizon interfere with her own path.

With newfound determination, she tried to trace the thread back to herself, to share what she had learned. But her tether was gone. There was only the darkness closing in around her.

— — —

Raena collapsed on the floor in front of Wil.

What happened? Wil rushed to her side while Dahl looked on with reserved surprise. "Raena?" He brushed his hand over her forehead but she was unresponsive. *Stars, no!*

Wil prepared to dive into the nexus after her—he had pushed her to come too soon. He'd thought she was ready, but…

"You cannot go," Dahl cautioned.

"She's my daughter. I'd do anything for her." Wil dove into the nexus despite another plea from Dahl. There was nothing the

Aesir could do to change his mind.

Darkness closed in around Wil. He couldn't see anything—not like the energy web he'd viewed his last time. He was alone, drifting. A chill seeped into his very core. Raena was out there somewhere, but he had no idea where to find her.

He raced into the darkness, willing for there to be some sign of where to go. His own tether to himself was so fragile without having any other sense of grounding.

Then, he saw the tattered end of Raena's tether. She'd disconnected—she could be out there anywhere.

"She's gone," Dahl said in the distance.

"No! She's too important—how could you just let her go without trying to get her back?"

Only silence was in the blackness for moments that felt like an eternity.

"You speak the truth. We must find her."

The warm presence of others filled the darkness. *"Find her,"* echoed a chorus of voices—more than Wil could count.

He ventured into the blackness with them, feeling a distant sense of others searching nearby. It had only been a minute—Raena couldn't have gone too far.

Except, they were searching the nexus near the ship. She could be anywhere. He thought to his own travels, how far he'd gone in just a matter of seconds.

Where would she have gone? Only one place came to mind. *"Tararia!"* he shouted to the others and raced across the expanse.

The Aesir followed his lead, but they stopped at the boundary to the Tararian System. *"This is not our place,"* they said. *"But we will help you find your way back."*

There wasn't time to argue. Wil forged ahead without them, expanding his mind as he had during the war to take in a heightened view of his surroundings. Raena's consciousness was out there somewhere. They were bound together as kin—he could use that tie.

He concentrated on the familial bond, calling out to her. At first there was no response, but then he detected a weak cry in the distance. She was alone and scared, but she'd heard him.

"I'm almost there!" he called out, and he felt her rally and

move toward him.

They closed the remaining gap in seconds, and he embraced her. She felt so very cold—weakening without the tether to her physical self.

Gently, he pulled her toward the Aesir waiting just outside the system. *"It'll be okay,"* he assured his daughter.

"So... empty..." she murmured in his mind. Her presence was fading.

"Hang on," Wil urged her, but she was too far gone to respond. *"You have to help!"* he pleaded to the Aesir just out of sight at the outskirts of the system.

Some of the Aesir protested, but others heeded to his call for aid, Dahl among them. He sensed the Oracles surround him and reach out to Raena. They latched onto the spark of her that still remained and restored it by giving up a small part of themselves.

As she stirred, another presence suddenly appeared—rooted on Tararia.

"Why have you come?" the voice demanded. After a moment, a low chuckle echoed in Wil's mind. *"Ah... That was quite a discovery to try to keep from us."*

Fear and concern radiated from the Aesir. *"It will never be yours."*

"And you'll die without our efforts," the voice replied.

Before Wil could question the exchange, the Aesir were guiding him back across the expanse, cradling Raena's consciousness in their collective grasp. Within seconds, he was back in his body on the Aesir ship by the nexus.

Raena was still in his arms, and her eyes fluttered open. "What happened?" she asked, sitting up.

Wil's chest heaved with relief. "You lost your tether."

She sat in silent contemplation for a moment. "There was something... it severed it."

Dahl's face was drawn. "They're more powerful than we realized... and now they know."

"Know what?" Wil demanded.

"About the tear."

"You mean what we saw in the Rift, at the site of the destroyed Bakzen world?" Raena asked. With Wil's help, she rose to her feet.

Dahl inclined his head. "The Priesthood has been searching for a means to make their power absolute and enduring. Such an energy source, combined with their other plans, could permanently shift the balance of power."

Raena crossed her arms. "That must have been the darkness I saw on the horizon."

"A new stage of the Priesthood's threat," Wil realized.

The Oracle nodded. "But the TSS has been guarding the Rift, so the Priesthood hasn't dared venture. But now they know what's there. They will seek to control the tear at any cost, because it can fuel them with what they need."

"Which is what?" Wil asked.

"The power to ascend—to leave their physical forms and dominate all living things."

Wil and Raena exchanged glances.

"Why would they do that?" questioned Wil.

"Because there are those among the Priesthood who always wished to be gods themselves," Dahl explained. "They have lived for thousands of years, seeking the power to truly ascend, but their means are flawed. We among the Aesir realized long ago that we weren't yet worthy of such ascension. If we are, it will happen of its own accord."

That's similar to what Banks told me, but he'd never hinted at the High Priests wanting to become gods! Wil's pulse pounded in his ears. "If the Priesthood is going to make a move to access the tear, then—"

Dahl shook his head. "They do not yet have the means to harness its power. But now they know where to go, and they will begin gathering their resources for the final stages of their plans."

Raena's face drained. "How long will that take?"

"A decade, perhaps? Less if they rush the process," Dahl replied. "But you can be ready before then. You already know how to win a war."

Wil swallowed. "I didn't think I'd have to go into battle again."

A smile touched Dahl's thin lips. "This is a different kind of fight. And last time, you didn't have us."

CHAPTER 6

RAENA STILL FELT woozy after her brush with death in the nexus. *I can't believe I lost my way like that...*

As she thought about the experience, though, she suspected that it wasn't some product of her mind where she'd stumbled and almost lost her life—the darkness that dissolved her tether wasn't part of her vision, but rather a real physical assault. She'd heard from her father that the Priesthood had made an appearance while she was unconscious, and she shuddered to think that they were behind the attack—that they had such power.

Dahl had taken her and her father up to a conference room as soon as she'd been able to walk unaided. The three of them were now seated at the table, with Wil and Raena facing out toward the panoramic viewport into subspace while the ship jumped to the Aesir homeworld.

If it's a planet at all, she realized, examining Dahl. "Where do you live?"

"The location is in the galactic core," he replied. "Or do you mean the habitation itself?"

"Both," she said.

"We have seven freestanding structures," Dahl explained. "Concentrating all our assets in one place seemed foolish, so we have spread out across several systems."

Wil tilted his head with interest. "How many Aesir are there?

I always figured there were only a handful of you."

Dahl cracked another subtle smile, much more at ease and natural than he had been upon first meeting Raena. "Approximately two thousand members of the Priesthood left Tararia and the surrounding worlds before the revolution over one thousand years ago. Our ancestors decided that those numbers would not sustain us, even with our technology to extend our lifespans, so they propagated. There are approximately one hundred million of us now."

Her father audibly choked. "One hundred million?"

"Yes. Is that surprising?" Dahl looked at him quizzically. "It is well below historical Taran population growth rates."

"You just didn't seem like the sort to have families," Wil tried to explain.

"Us Oracles do not," Dahl stated. "You would find many of the Aesir to be more like yourselves."

"Oh." Wil leaned back in his chair.

Everything I'd heard about the Aesir in the last few months made it seem like the Oracles were the extent of the Aesir order. If that's not the case, then maybe there is more of a chance for partnership than we'd hoped. Raena gazed out the viewport for a minute before returning her attention to Dahl. "You said you can extend your lives. How long do you live?"

The Oracle's eyes widened slightly like she'd just asked a ridiculous question. "As long as we wish."

Wil tilted his head, clearly intrigued. "Through… cellular rejuvenation?"

Dahl nodded. "It was one of the first technologies the Priesthood buried when they came into power after our departure. They wished for the Taran race to evolve as quickly as possible, so limiting lifespan so others may take their place was the best strategy to expedite that process. The High Priests themselves could use that technology to extend their lives and achieve the immortality they desire, but their thirst for greater power caused them to go down the path of genetic modification and cloning instead."

Raena was speechless. She looked to her father for commentary.

"Are you one of the original Aesir who left Tararia?" Wil asked after a moment.

The Oracle inclined his head. "I am."

Wil eyed him. "How old *are* you?"

Dahl gave a slight shrug. "Age becomes less relevant with time. By your measures, I am just over twelve-hundred years old."

Raena coughed. "Wow."

"I… was not expecting that," her father said from the seat next to her.

"Some choose to pass over after they've led a full life. Others of us are driven by a longer-term vision," Dahl said.

"So, this technology to extend lifespans—it's something that can be used on a broad scale?"

Dahl nodded. "Yes, as long as the genetic markers are in place."

"And what are those?" Wil questioned.

"The sequence that was corrupted in the Priesthood's interventions that resulted in the Generation Cycle." Dahl fixed his gaze on Wil. "You and your children are the only Tarans outside the Aesir with that genetic sequence. That is why we invited you to join us."

"But in two generations we can have a patch," Wil said.

Dahl shifted his attention to Raena. "Perhaps, but that solution is not as guaranteed as we'd hoped. There are many variables. We have not yet decided if the matter should be forced."

Raena reflected on what the Priesthood had said while she was being held in their underground lab—something about crossing back the genetic lines within her immediate family. "Yeah, no. Not if I have any say in it," she stated. *Immortality at stake or not, going to those extremes would just bring us down to the Priesthood's level.*

"That's off the table," Wil agreed. "We've been getting by just fine for the last thousand years without everyone living to crazy-old ages."

"A long lifespan is not for everyone," Dahl agreed. "Of more interest to you may be our ship and weapons tech."

"I wouldn't have thought military might would be your priority," Wil said.

"We suspected the Priesthood might come after us one day. We wanted to be ready," replied the Oracle. "The key point is that our databanks hold all the records of past Taran advancements the Priesthood has kept sealed for the last millennia."

"And let me guess… you've had an independent jump drive all this time?" Wil said.

Dahl cracked a smile. "Actually, no—you really were the first to piece together the necessary components. We have established a beacon network using the methods SiNavTech employs to scout new routes."

"Huh." Wil shook his head.

"If you have records, what about the fall of the Dainetris Dynasty?" Raena interjected.

"I should clarify," Dahl said, "all the data records from up until the time we departed Tararia. More recent history is as much a mystery to us as you, since we remained at a distance until the Cadicle's coming."

Worth a shot, Raena thought to herself.

"My biggest concern right now," Wil said, "is what the Priesthood will do regarding that tear in the Rift. The TSS has disarmed considerably since the war. We're not prepared for a full-on fight."

"Neither is the Priesthood," Dahl said. "They will use other tactics."

"Such as?" Wil prompted.

"We don't know."

Her father sighed. "Then without knowing what we're up against, that doesn't change the potential need for TSS' influence in a more military sense."

"No, it does not," Dahl agreed. "Whatever moves the Priesthood may make in the coming years, you must have a force standing by, ready to fight back."

"I had already arrived at that conclusion after our visit to the Rift. The TSS is less entrenched in everyday affairs than most other organizations—we're relatively autonomous. That puts us in the best position to mediate conflict."

Dahl nodded. "We were pleased to learn that your father severed ties with the Priesthood. If you had remained connected to them, this conversation would not be possible."

Wil studied him. "The way that voice—one of the High Priests?—spoke to you… Do you have an agreement with them?"

The Oracle waited several seconds before responding, seeming to choose his words carefully. "When we left Tararia, it was with the knowledge that we were condemning our people to the Priesthood's reign. However, our numbers were insufficient to make any headway without being silenced one way or another. Fleeing here, we were at least able to preserve a record of Tarans as we once were."

"Did you ever intend to go back to Tararia?" Raena asked.

Dahl shook his head. "No, but we also did not expect any influencers to decide to take a stand. The recent developments in Sietinen were quite unexpected and welcome."

"But you knew about Ryan, and Dainetris," she pressed.

"An unfortunate collapse," Dahl hung his head. "When we learned of your plans for Tararia, we knew an heir was needed."

Wil's eyes narrowed. "Wait… Earlier you said that recent Taran history is unknown to you and you don't have details about the Dainetris Dynasty's fall, yet you knew a member of their family survived and that Sietinen has been planning an overthrow of the Priesthood? That doesn't add up."

Dahl cracked a smile. "Our information is not in the form of official records, which is what you asked for previously, and those we do not possess. Our knowledge is more fluid—universal truths so profound they are written into the fabric of the universe around us. Simply put, the events unfolding now were destined to come to pass. Those are the insights we have gleaned in our study, and we have offered guidance where we were meant to do so.

"Ultimately, the final path is up to you. The truths we read are… guidelines. No matter what you decide—staying true to the universal pattern or making your own way—you will define the future of Tarans for generations to come."

Raena slumped in her chair. "No pressure."

Her father offered her a supportive smile. "Fortunately, this is bigger than just one person."

"Follow what you learned while gazing into the nexus," Dahl told her. "You will know what to do when the pieces are in place."

Raena took a deep breath and nodded.

"But now," Dahl went on, "we have almost arrived."

A moment later, stars began to show through the ethereal subspace cloud. When the cloud had lifted, Raena saw that the stars weren't completely solid, but rather appeared as an echo—just like within the Rift.

Her jaw dropped. "Are we in a rift?"

Wil tensed next to her as he, too, took in the view.

Dahl inclined his head. "We are. But unlike the Rift where the Bakzen resided, this rift is entirely natural. It is the largest of those we have come across in our travels, and where most of us now call home. The six others house smaller populations, scattered around the core."

"So, you don't live on a planet," Wil inferred.

"No, but our sect of the Priesthood hadn't called Tararian soil home since well before we left—we had a temple inside Denae, much like the one the TSS now has as their Headquarters."

"There are other facilities like that…?" Wil questioned with audible shock.

"Several. I expect the Priesthood sealed all of them, though."

Wil shook his head and let out a long breath.

Raena gathered herself. "I don't see anything out the window."

"The ring is ahead of us," Dahl explained. "Come, we will get a better view."

He led them down the hall toward the front of the ship. The corridor terminated in a door, which opened into a spacious room with seating and facilities resembling a kitchenette.

Mess hall or lounge, maybe? Her speculation was cut short when she looked out the viewports on the far wall of the room, curving around the room above the nose of the vessel. In front of them was a ring, as Dahl had indicated, but the scale boggled her mind. They were approaching it perpendicularly, showcasing an expanse of parks and urban development on the inner surface of the ring orbiting around a small, artificial sun.

Next to her, Wil was staring at it, mouth agape. "How did you build this?"

"Piece by piece, like anything else," Dahl replied cryptically.

"No, just like your temples—for the size of your population, construction like this shouldn't be possible."

Dahl chuckled. "I suppose I could not bring you here and not expect questions. Very well… We have certain nanotech that allows us to simply grow structures, if fed the proper raw materials. Our understanding is that the Priesthood suppressed this technology in favor of maintaining a population of workers too absorbed in their physical labors to pay much heed to the political environment."

Wil shook his head and scoffed. "No wonder. If you let everyone live a life of luxury, they'd start learning and thinking on their own. Educated people are much more difficult to control."

"And too short of lifespans for most to truly get ahead and change their lives," Raena added.

"Yes." Dahl inclined his head. "We, on the other hand, choose to work toward self-actualization, to be the best possible versions of ourselves through continual introspection and advancement."

"And there are families here, you said?" Wil asked. "Young people, children?"

"Of course," Dahl confirmed. "Almost sixty million residents live in this ring."

Her father shook his head. "It's going to take some time to get over thinking about you as just the mysterious people living on space ships somewhere out in the stars."

"You will adapt, I'm sure."

The Aesir ship glided toward the outer wall of the ring. As they neared, Raena noticed that there were ships docked along the outer edge in several ports that extended below the ground-level of the inner ring.

"Why the ring structure?" Wil asked. "You obviously have artificial gravity on this ship."

"Of course, but you know it's not the same. Centrifugal force makes for a most sustainable long-term environment," Dahl explained. "I'm sure you'll ask about the sun next. The technical specifications of its creation would take too long to explain, but it's stable. And yes, we have an electrostatic shield around the ring, which can be tinted to mimic night on the rings. We still honor the twenty-five hour Taran clock of our ancestry. Right now, it is mid-morning."

"It's incredible," Raena breathed.

"I would offer you a tour, but you must meet with the Council so that we may decide how to proceed. Visits such as this are unprecedented," Dahl stated.

"Of course," Wil agreed. "We'll follow your lead."

The ship docked in a berth just below ground level near one of the more urban-looking sections of the ring. Dahl led them off the ship and into the port.

Unlike a space station with long concourses and gangways, the port reminded Raena more of a train terminal. The aesthetic of the space was sleek and sophisticated, with the same crystal light fixtures she'd seen on the ship, but this time accompanied by hydroponic plants arranged around the support columns and holographic displays denoting departure details.

Raena took it all in, wondering at the incongruity of it all. "This looks like a functioning port," she ventured when her curiosity got the better of her. "That makes sense in the Taran worlds, but how often do you travel to and from here?"

"We are… around," Dahl replied. "Considering our limited facilities here—we have groups tending food crops on various planets outside our homes within the rift pockets."

"Yeah, I guess you'd have to," she realized.

"Our way of life is not the concern, though," Dahl stated. "We must come to accord about how to handle the Priesthood."

The Oracle led them to an elevator, which had controlled access through a biometric scanner. Though not registered in the system, Dahl had Raena and her father submit to the scan, which granted them temporary credentials.

The elevator ascended a tower on the interior of the ring. Once past the first four stories, windows in one wall of the elevator car afforded a view of the gardens and temples dotting the landscape within the city wrapped around the interior of the massive ring. Raena marveled at seeing the ground seemingly curve up to either side of her, where 'up' was really inward, and the sky wasn't really sky at all. Thinking about it started to give her a strange sort of vertigo, so she opted to keep her gaze focused at the base of the tower as much as possible.

After a minute of travel, the elevator came to rest on an airy level with a cantilevered section jutting out from the main tower. The result was both breathtaking and terrifying as Raena stepped onto a floor with glass block inlays, as though she was walking directly in the sky.

Her father also seemed unnerved by the architectural choice, but that wasn't too surprising, knowing he'd spent his formative years in windowless TSS Headquarters.

Four figures robed in black were waiting for them near the elevator, hands clasped at their fronts and pale, glowing eyes that revealed the age and wisdom of those who'd witnessed a millennium of history.

"We did not expect to have you here with us like this," a woman standing in the center of the group said.

Wil examined her. "We met when you examined me, didn't we?"

She inclined her head. "I am Jayne. Like Dahl, I am one of the original Oracles to have left Tararia. Whitney, Erron, and Kent are from our second generation once we had begun building our new home." She gestured to her companions in turn.

"That makes us a spry eight hundred," Kent said with a warm smile.

Raena was mesmerized by the power the Oracles possessed—an aura glowing around them even brighter than the most powerful Agents she'd witnessed. She'd expected them to look upon her as a pitiful, lower being in comparison, but she was surprised to see a hint of respect or even awe in their guarded expressions.

"We have much to discuss," Jayne continued. "Please, this way."

She directed them to a conference room that would put any other meeting space to shame. Whereas the other flooring had glass inlays interspersed with solid sections, the entire floor of the conference room was one seamless, transparent platform. Likewise, windows curved in a dome around the space, resulting in the room appearing like it was encased in a bubble—a bubble two hundred meters above the ground.

Raena glanced at her father, and he took a cautious step onto the transparent floor from the comfort of the solid walkway.

"Quite a place you have here," he said.

"If we cannot be directly in the stars, living in the sky is the next best thing," Dahl replied.

The conference table and chairs were well suited to the space, made of transparent plastic sculpted in minimalist, ergonomic forms. The Oracles took seats around the far sides of the oval table, leaving the two chairs closest to the entry door for Wil and Raena.

When everyone was seated, Jayne began, "We know Sietinen and Vaenetri have been planning a political overthrow of the Priesthood. While your methods are admirable, it won't work."

Wil folded his hands on the desktop. "And why's that?"

"Because you can't simply remove them from power—or even imprison them—and expect that to be the end of it," she elaborated. "Their labs are everywhere. If you remove the High Priests, they'll have their consciousness uploaded to a new form and begin again."

Raena's heart sank. "They can do that?"

"They will do anything to perpetuate their existence," Erron stated. "You've already witnessed what lengths they go to with the hopes of achieving their ends."

"Then how do we stop them?" Raena asked.

"You must strike all their facilities simultaneously," Dahl said.

"We don't have the resources to do that," Wil objected.

Jayne fixed him with a level gaze. "But we do."

— — —

The notion of trusting the Aesir with Taravia's future went against everything Wil had believed for his entire life. *They left their home knowing that people would suffer. How can we pin our hopes on a group who'd walk away like that?*

As Jayne laid out the tactical details of the Priesthood's labs and other outposts, though, he realized that the Aesir hadn't truly run away. They were hiding out and biding their time for the right opportunity to make a move. It was no different than what his own father had done when he'd left Tararia as a teenager, only to return when the pieces were almost in place for decisive action.

The Aesir would have been wholesale hunted down and killed had they stayed within the Taran civilization while the Priesthood made its power play during the revolution. Instead, they had gone to a remote location so that they could build up their resources without distraction or interference. For a thousand years, they had been increasing their numbers and their technology to offer a swift and decisive victory over any opposition the Priesthood could throw their way.

That's what they think, at least. It's tough to know if the Tararian Guard will maintain their allegiance to the Priesthood at any cost or if they'll listen to a majority vote from the High Dynasties. Wil searched the faces around the table. He didn't see any doubts.

Next to him, Raena looked like she was vacillating between excitement and terror while she learned about the reach of their foe.

"*We've got this,*" he told her.

"*I'll leave the fleet direction to you,*" she replied with a slight smile.

Launching a coordinated, interstellar strike wasn't high on Wil's list of things he wanted to do after the war, but at least he was confident that it was within his skillset.

He cleared his throat. "This all sounds great, but I need to ask the obvious question: you help us take out the Priesthood using your offensive forces, but then what do you want in return?"

The Oracles' eyes all turned to him.

"We want you to hand over the Bakzen's Rift to us," Dahl said.

"Whoa, wait a minute." Wil held up his hands. "You all but

told me that Rift was dangerous and unnatural and needed to be closed."

"It is, and it will be in good hands," Jayne replied.

"You just want the energy source of the tear—same as the Priesthood," Wil shot back.

She inclined her head. "But not for the same end."

"Then why?" he pressed.

"So that we may heal it and modify it into a new nexus point," Jayne said. "As skilled as you have become, you do not have the means to heal the Rift or dimensional tear. The Rift must be sealed as quickly as possible."

Wil shook his head. *Can we trust them?*

"You must," the Oracles replied in unison.

He recoiled from the words echoing in his mind—the force of the statement overwhelming him.

Next to him, Raena winced.

Wil gathered himself. "We need to work together because neither of us can do what must be done alone. I don't like your terms, but we'll have to trust each other to do what's right. We're on the cusp of bringing the Taran civilization into a new era."

"That we are," Dahl said. He looked to the other Oracles and they inclined their heads. "Now, Cadicle," he continued, "we must speak alone."

"I—" Wil began to protest at the thought of leaving his daughter with the Oracles.

"She will be fine," Jayne said in response to his unvoiced concern.

Raena nodded. "It's okay, Dad."

Reluctantly, Wil rose from the table and followed Dahl through the open elevator lobby area to another, smaller conference room without a terrifying transparent floor.

Dahl remained standing once they were inside, so Wil stood with his hands clasped behind his back, awaiting instruction.

"We must walk a difficult line," Dahl said after nearly a minute of silence. "The Priesthood has spent millennia controlling and filtering the information and technologies made available to the Taran people. We possess all of that knowledge that has been suppressed—it is something which we should freely give in the interest of the openness we wish to foster with you. However, not all of these technologies belong in circulation."

"I can appreciate that perspective," Wil replied.

"Then you also understand how challenging it is to make a call about where to draw the line of what is shared versus what is locked away."

"We have faced similar dilemmas within the TSS."

Dahl nodded. "It is one thing for leadership to shape the beliefs of subordinates, but it is quite another to shape the collective consciousness of an entire civilization. That is not a responsibility to be taken lightly."

"I don't," Wil said. "But I'm not the one who'll be making those decisions. You should really be talking to Raena."

The Oracle tilted his head questioningly.

"I thought I'd done my part when we won the war with the Bakzen. Then I realized that I'd have a role to play in taking out the Priesthood. The next generation can deal with the political implications from the decisions regarding lost technologies and—"

"No," Dahl cut in. "This isn't just a matter of political implications. You have the power to change the very form of the Taran race."

"You mean the genetic patch for the Generation Cycle."

"Yes, and where that leads. It's not only a repair, but also a step forward. The Aesir have been waiting for you since the Priesthood was founded nine thousand years ago."

Wil frowned. "Well, you're welcome to take blood samples or whatever you want, but the Priesthood had some twisted ideas of next steps, and as I already said, that's not going to happen."

"The kind of cross-back they've suggested offers the most certainty, but it is not the preferred way."

"What's the other option?"

"To trust that everything will work out as it should," Dahl stated simply.

"If the alternative is to just sit back and watch, then why are you being so insistent I get involved?"

"You misunderstand. We trust the genetic line to run its natural course. We wish for your involvement because you are the only one among your people to have seen what happens to the pattern when it is forced to diverge from the course—the way the Bakzen ripped it apart. There are those in positions of power who would again try to force an unnatural outcome."

"So… you want me to make sure that no one does anything to meddle?" Wil eyed the Oracle with skepticism. *It sounds like they're trying to bait me into something, but what?*

"We only wish for you to embrace who you are," Dahl said. "You've begrudgingly accepted your responsibilities for your whole life—first in the Bakzen War and now in the future of Tararia. Your instincts and insights, though… you were made for these roles. Those skills don't vanish just because a single task is complete."

" 'Single task' is a bit of an over-simplification, I think. And moreover, that whole 'made' part… I've never much appreciated how a pre-determined future was dropped on me without the slightest bit of choice in the matter. I've always done what's asked of me, but it's never enough. When do I get to live my life like a normal person?"

Dahl shrugged. "You took the opportunity to raise your family on Earth away from the TSS and Taran concerns. Arguably, sixteen years is a much longer sabbatical than someone in your position could ever expect to take."

"And what is my position, exactly?"

"To guide Tararia, of course—to be the moral compass that the Priesthood has failed to be."

Wil laughed. "Yeah, I don't think anyone wants me in that role. I've made some incredibly selfish decisions that I wouldn't hesitate to make again. You've got the wrong guy."

"You speak of Cambion."

They know about that? Wil swallowed.

"We watched the war from afar. You are right to stand by your decision—it was in the best interest of Tarans as a whole. It only seems selfish from your vantage, but knowing what we know, there wasn't another option."

"Because of Saera's importance to the genetic master plan?"

Dahl shook his head. "No, because if you had blocked the Bakzen from taking Cambion, they would have gone for Ryla.

And once they captured Ryla, they would have discovered it housed the Genetic Archive. Having access to that…"

"So, *that's* where the Archive is!"

"Yes," Dahl acknowledged. "And it's best you secure it before you make your move against the Priesthood."

"Yeah, I'll say." Wil thought for a moment. "So, by making a completely selfish decision, I inadvertently kept the Bakzen from gaining access to data that could have changed the momentum of the war?"

Dahl nodded. "Indeed. With the information contained in the Archive, the Bakzen would have had the key to make targeted biological warfare infinitely more effective than the neurotoxin they employed to control the minds of civilians."

"Shite!" Wil exclaimed. "Why didn't I think of that? Fok!" He ran a hand through his hair, teeth clenched.

Dahl looked at him with alarm.

"The Priesthood has access to all that information, right? Well, the TSS reverse engineered the Bakzen's neurotoxin—that means the Priesthood has that, too," Wil explained.

The Oracle's face drained beyond his already pale complexion. "That is what they will do in retaliation—the unknown move we were not sure how to predict."

"The when or how are still complete unknowns." Wil sighed. "Stars! This is bad. They could kill billions with a minute's notice."

"We feared they would resort to… extreme measures," Dahl murmured.

Wil scoffed. "They proved long ago that the lives of innocents mean little to them."

"We must begin making our final preparations for an offensive. We'll be ready whenever the political structure is in place to fill the vacuum from the Priesthood's absence."

"That will take longer to complete. We're still several years away," Wil cautioned.

"Then there is no time to waste." Dahl stepped toward the door, then paused. "Think on what I have said today. I hope you will come to embrace your role."

"Let's just take care of the Priesthood first."

They returned to the conference room, where Raena was still seated with the other Oracles.

"It is time for you to return to your people," Dahl stated.

Raena stood up. "All right." She glanced at Wil. *"Is everything okay, Dad? They started saying some pretty cryptic stuff—I don't know what they mean."*

"We'll talk once we're back home," he told her.

"We are glad to have met with you today," Jayne said as she and the other Oracles rose from their seats. "We hope this is the beginning of great things to come."

"Likewise," Wil replied. "I will reflect on your words."

The Oracles inclined their heads.

"Until we meet again," Jayne stated.

Dahl led Wil and Raena from the conference room back to the elevator. "You must expedite your activities on Tararia."

"I suppose it has changed things now that the Priesthood knows we're working with you," Wil said.

"Indeed. They'd hoped we would sympathize with their position after having had time to meditate on the possibilities, but we are more convinced in our approach than ever."

Wil nodded. "That we can agree on."

Raena's face was drawn with concern, and Wil offered her a telepathic hug. *"This is moving more quickly than I expected, but we'll figure it out."*

She relaxed the slightest measure, but he knew there was no quick fix to what they were facing.

They returned to the Aesir ship, where they went directly to the cafeteria-style room for the voyage home.

Wil hadn't expected a day trip, but he supposed that Dahl was right—they didn't have any time to delay putting the next phase of their plans into action. He didn't like that those plans involved placing demands on his children that were only slightly less onerous than the responsibilities he'd been given. The concept of birthright had taken on a whole new meaning.

Consistent with previous travel in the Aesir's ships, the return to Headquarters took a fraction of the time it would have with a conventional jump drive. When the ship arrived at Headquarters, Dahl directed them to the exit hatch.

"I'll need to get fleet specs from you so I can coordinate the offensive," Wil said to Dahl as they walked down the hall.

"I'm afraid that's not possible," the Oracle replied.

He has to be kidding! Wil groaned under his breath. "Didn't we just agree that we need to work together?"

"Indeed, but the specifics of our fleet are not necessary at this time. Once we know which information will be shared with the broader Taran population—after the Priesthood is no longer in power—then we can discuss the extent of our forces. Suffice to say for now, our fleet is sufficient when combined with the TSS' resources."

"I can't make plans without specifics," Wil objected.

Dahl fixed him with a level gaze. "Tell us where to be and when and we'll be there."

"If you don't show up, we'd be screwed."

"We are true to our word. I assure you," the Oracle replied.

The future of the entire Taran race is at stake and all we have to go on is a vague promise? Wil sighed and shook his head.

"We spoke of trust earlier. You must believe," Dahl said when they reached the hatch, which had been swung open.

"There's a lot at stake to just go on faith."

Dahl cracked a smile. "Isn't so much of life?"

"We don't have a choice," Raena reminded Wil.

He glanced at her and nodded. "Very well."

The Oracle inclined his head. "We will see you at the agreed upon time to test Jason."

That's right! I'd forgotten about that. Wil nodded. "And then we can finalize our plans as the time for action nears."

"Be well. Stars be with you," Dahl said with a bow, and they parted.

The TSS spacedock felt empty after the energy within the Aesir ship and structures. Wil evaluated Raena as they descended the gangway and saw that she was uncharacteristically sullen.

"That was an intense few hours," he said aloud. "Why don't we chat before going back into Headquarters?"

She nodded, and Wil led her to a small conference room near the junction of the concourse with the core of the station.

"I'm still trying to process everything I saw in the nexus,"

Raena said as soon as the door was closed.

"It took me some time to come to terms with my vision, too." He examined her. "What did you see?"

"Everything pointed to Tararia," Raena said.

"That's not surprising."

Raena shook her head. "No, I mean, I think… I think I'm supposed to be there."

"There's still your training to finish—" Wil started to protest.

Raena fixed him with a calm, steady gaze. "Dad, we both know I don't need the TSS to master my abilities."

Wil took a deep breath. "That's true, I don't think you do."

"You said that training with the TSS beyond the first year is optional. I can leave at the end of this term."

"And what about Ryan?" Wil asked.

"He's integral to Tararia's future, too—he should come with me. We could keep training together, like we have been."

"Without instruction?"

She thought for a moment. "Couldn't grandfather teach us?"

"Yes... But that doesn't change the fact that practice of telekinesis outside of the TSS is still illegal on Tararia."

"He was High Commander."

"And needed to give up his official TSS commission when he assumed the role of Head of the Dynasty," Wil pointed out. "I doubt he plays by all the rules—you can't spend your whole life with abilities and not occasionally use them—but we need to position you as a proper, law-abiding heiress."

"There *has* to be some way!" his daughter insisted.

"Maybe…" Wil said after a moment. "If an active Agent in the TSS went with you to Tararia as an official instructor, the case could be made that you were on an extended internship."

"Sure. Then why do you sound so hesitant?"

"Going to Tararia puts you so close to the Priesthood. They came for you once—I have no reason to believe they wouldn't try again."

"Didn't Grandfather do all sorts of security upgrades when he moved back there?"

"He did, but…"

Raena smiled. "Dad, I think you're just making up excuses for me not to go because you'll miss me."

Wil softened and pulled her into a hug. "I'll miss you like crazy."

After several seconds, Raena pulled back and looked up at him. "You know this is the best way forward."

He nodded. "I do. The TSS was never your path."

"There's something on Tararia for me to find. I can feel it."

"We'll make the arrangements for you to go as soon as the term wraps up."

Raena gave him another hug. "We're going to finish what you started. And we'll win."

CHAPTER 7

THE HOURS PASSED slowly while Ryan awaited Raena's return. He knew he shouldn't expect her for at least two days, but he couldn't help thinking about having her back in the relative safety of Headquarters.

Since their kidnapping by the Priesthood eight months prior, they hadn't departed the TSS facility aside from a brief trip down to Earth and the more recent field trip. Considering how cautious Raena's parents were about being out in the open, Ryan had taken that to mean there was an imminent danger, from the Priesthood or otherwise. To willingly go with the Aesir—who were questionable allies, at best—was directly contrary to the behavior he'd seen Wil exhibit in prior months. Either the Aesir were not as unpredictable as Ryan had been led to believe, or there was much more urgency for action than he'd realized.

Ryan holed up in his bedroom after dinner, trying to lose himself in some assigned reading while lounging on his bed. His eyes were scanning the words on the screen of his tablet, but he wasn't absorbing the content.

There was so much that could go wrong while Raena was out with the Aesir—from another capture, to failing their test, or even her realizing that she didn't want to stay among Tarans. Though Ryan trusted in their relationship, he wasn't positive that their connection would win out if she was faced with alternatives. After all, they weren't officially bonded and she had been somewhat unsure about doing so. That might simply be a product of her age—she was almost four years younger than him, after all—but when combined with his own self-doubt regarding his social position, he easily went to a dark mental place of feeling unworthy of her affection. Those thoughts had come much less frequently in recent months, but they still surfaced in stressful times like his present situation.

After half an hour of trying, and failing, to concentrate while his thoughts continued to turn toward negative outcomes, Ryan gave up and began playing a puzzle game involving the arrangement of 3D blocks using the holographic interface on his tablet. He had just completed the eighth level when a soft voice filled his mind.

"I'm back. Grab Jason and meet me in our usual study room."

Ryan's heart leaped as he reveled in Raena's mental presence. They were always able to find each other through the din of other minds throughout Headquarters, even without a formal bond. *"I'll be right there,"* he replied as he rose from his bed.

Thank the stars she's all right! He dashed into the living room to find Jason before another thought surfaced. *Why does she want to talk to both of us now? Does she have something bad to say and wants Jason there as backup?*

Anxious to get some answers, Ryan continued through the common room and into the other bedroom.

Jason was lying on his own bed, as were two of his roommates. He glanced up when Ryan appeared in the doorway. "What's up?"

"I was hoping we could go over some of the homework questions before class tomorrow," Ryan said to him aloud, then added, *"Raena's back."*

"Already?" Jason rose from the bed. "Sure."

The other Primus Elite Trainees hardly paid them notice as they departed the shared quarters and headed for the meeting room.

"That was fast," Jason commented. "I didn't think they'd be back until tomorrow at the earliest."

"Same. I hope everything's all right," Ryan said.

Jason cast him a sidelong glance. "You worry too much."

"Maybe you don't worry enough."

His friend shrugged. "I try not to get worked up over things I can't control."

They arrived at their destination in short order and found Raena waiting for them. She smiled when they entered the room and closed the door.

"How are you?" Ryan asked, wishing Jason wasn't there so he could give her a proper greeting.

"Good. Tired," she replied.

"What happened?" questioned Jason.

"Things, uh…" Raena faded out, seeming to search for the words. "I don't think things are going to be quite how we planned."

Ryan's heart dropped for an instant, but when he searched her face, there was still the same love in her eyes as the last time they'd spoken about their future together. "What do you mean?"

"We now have a ticking clock," she explained. "We know what the Priesthood is after."

Raena proceeded to give an abbreviated account of her time with the Aesir, from her brush with the darkness outside of Tararia and the Aesir's incredible facility within another rift. Ryan and Jason were completely captivated while they listened to the account. Only when Raena reached the point of her return to Headquarters did they relax enough to react.

"Well shit," Jason said after a few seconds to process the story. "I didn't think an interstellar battle was on the table."

"Hopefully, it won't come to a firefight," Raena said. "There are so many civilians… we need to stop this before it comes to that."

"Where do we go from here?" Ryan asked.

Raena looked at Ryan and then her brother. "Well, there are two things—getting everything squared away on Tararia, and getting the TSS ready for another fight. We're kind of in a 'divide and conquer' situation at the moment."

Jason shook his head as though he'd picked up on something in her words that was lost on Ryan. "I'll go talk to Dad." Without another word, he departed.

"What'd I miss?" Ryan questioned when they were alone.

"We need to go to Tararia," Raena stated bluntly. "It was fun to think about training here with the TSS, but we're needed elsewhere."

The statement caught Ryan off-guard. "Like, *now*?"

"End of the term."

"That's…" He didn't know what to say. The TSS had been a safe transition place for him to come to terms with his lineage and learn how to be the person he'd need to become for the trials ahead. To go to Tararia now and cut that time short would mean diving into a new life he was not yet ready to lead.

"As much as I'd like to grow my abilities, that will need to take a back seat to learning about politics and all that," Raena continued. "My grandparents are in the best position to teach us what we really need to know."

"I suppose they are."

"I want to continue training, though. We have a plan to have an Agent come tutor us in telekinesis while we're on Tararia—we won't officially be leaving the TSS, just… going on an extended internship."

Ryan nodded. "You know I'll follow you anywhere."

Raena gazed into his eyes. "I do." She stepped forward and took his hands. "Now, when I told you about my time with the Aesir, I didn't say everything…"

— — —

It didn't take much for Jason to pick up on the meaning of Raena's statement: if they were going to divide, Jason would stay with the TSS and Raena would go to Tararia.

He didn't like the idea of being apart from his sister—they'd been almost inseparable for their entire lives—but she'd been drifting away from him for some time. With Ryan now in her life, she had other priorities, and nothing was going to change that from this point forward. Jason needed to focus on finding his own place in the challenges to come.

As soon as he left the meeting room, he sent a message to his father asking to meet. Given the late hour, Wil was in his quarters rather than his office, but Jason figured that talking to both his parents—in their capacity of High Commander and Lead Agent—at the same time was the most expeditious route.

He headed up one floor to their quarters and pressed the buzzer by the door.

His mom answered several seconds later. "Hey. Is everything all right?" she greeted.

"Yeah, Raena just filled me in on the trip," Jason replied.

Saera nodded. "Right. I just heard an account myself. Come in." She stepped aside to allow Jason through the door.

Wil came out from the bedroom. "Hi. I thought you might be by after you heard what happened."

Jason nodded. "Yeah… Honestly, I'm not sure why you took Raena and not me, too."

His father released a slow breath. "That was a calculated move." He stepped toward the couch and chairs arranged at the center of the living room and gestured for Jason to have a seat. Saera sat down next to Wil.

"You see," his father continued, "we're only allowed to look into the nexus once—whether that's just custom or by some unknown necessity. What we see is not a certain outcome, but rather a truth in our own lives at the time it's witnessed. What we do with that information will determine if the truth comes to pass."

"Okay…" Jason wished he'd jump to the point.

"Right now, Raena's truth is what we needed to see. Given her relationship with Ryan, we know her path leads to Tararia—or the political side of our ventures. What I've learned, though, is that we aren't yet in a place where the TSS can be a peaceful academic-focused institution. We still need to be warriors."

Jason glanced between his parents. "All right. So, what does that have to do with me being tested by the Aesir?"

"By delaying your view into the nexus, you'll get to witness a truth of the coming battles far closer to the time of action, giving a much more accurate impression of what we'll face," Wil explained.

"That… makes sense, in a weird way," Jason admitted.

"I haven't actually tried to deviate from the paths ahead," Wil went on, "but the more insight we can have going in, the better off we'll be."

"To that end," Saera added, "we need to change the way we think about training in the TSS. We need to be prepared for a fight."

"Weaponized telekinesis?" Jason guessed.

Wil nodded solemnly. "Something I thought we'd left behind."

"I'll learn," Jason agreed. "And so should the rest of the Elites—maybe others, too."

"It's not that simple," his mother cut in. "We've already made public statements that the TSS is disarming. If the Priesthood suspects we're rebuilding our forces and capabilities, it might prompt them to take action sooner than we're prepared to address."

"Then we'll do it in secret," Jason replied. He met his parents' eyes in turn. "I wasn't crazy about getting involved with your plans when it just involved politicking in Tararia, but I also didn't like the idea of sitting back and doing nothing while Raena gets to save the day."

Saera smirked. "Are you really going to make this about sibling rivalry?"

Jason grinned. "Whatever motivation works, right?"

"I won't argue," his father said with a chuckle. "But if we do this, it's serious business."

"I know." Jason nodded. "Just tell me where to start."

— — —

Raena's heart pounded in her ears as she stood with Ryan in the small meeting room. The things she'd seen in her vision were so vivid she could still feel them, and she wasn't sure how to put the experience into words.

"I…" She squeezed Ryan's hands and looked into his eyes. "I know I've been taking things slow—cautiously, even—with us, and you've been so patient with me. I guess with everything going on, I didn't want to jump into anything for the wrong reasons."

He nodded. "I know what you mean. How could we know how to be a couple when we were still trying to find our own identity?"

"Yeah, exactly." She took a slow breath. "Honestly, I'm still figuring that out. But I do know what I saw."

"And what was that?" The longing was there in his voice, hope that her words would affirm the feelings that ran deeper than what they'd dared express to one another.

"I know we're meant to be together," she told him, finally allowing herself to relax. "I can't explain how, but when I looked at my path, it led to you—to us on Tararia. And we'd won. We were standing on a hillside of the Priesthood's isle with these red flowers at our feet under the heat of the sun, and we were happy. We were in love and only good things were ahead of us."

Tears formed in her eyes as she spoke, reliving the elation she'd experienced that morning as the vision had unfolded before her.

"Raena…" Ryan wrapped her in his arms and held her close.

In his embrace, the rest of the world faded away. It was the only place she wanted to be.

"No more hesitation," she murmured into his chest, then pulled away just enough to look up at him. "I want to be with you."

"I do, too, but," Ryan looked around the room, "not like this."

"There's somewhere we can go," Raena said as she took his hand and led him from the room to the central elevator.

He gave her a quizzical look when she selected Level 5 as their destination. "Militia?"

"My mom figured that would be the least conspicuous."

"Wait, you asked your mom for a place where we could…?"

Raena shrugged. "Not for anything in particular. She spent years hiding a relationship with my dad and understands the need for private couple-time."

Ryan was clearly not convinced by her statement, but he let it slide while the elevator descended to their destination floor.

There were too many competing thoughts swirling through Raena's mind for her to have a clear vision of how the following events would play out. The only certainty was that she wanted to spend time with Ryan without the prying eyes of her roommates and to be in a place other than a conference room with only a table and chairs.

When the elevator doors opened, they dropped their hands to their sides and strode across the lobby toward the designated residential wing like they were on an official assignment. The Militia officers paid them no more than a glance as they passed by.

Raena stopped outside the door to the quarters her mother had reserved for them and waited for the hallway to clear before she palmed open the door.

She could sense Ryan's nerves as they entered the room, also well aware of her own anxious excitement.

The Militia quarters were similar to the Agent housing on the upper levels, with a well-appointed common room consisting of a couch, chairs, and coffee table, and a sliding door to a separate bedroom.

Raena silently took in the space as she closed the door to the hallway. *Relax. No one is expecting anything.*

She didn't believe her own lie. She knew exactly what she was expecting, and what Ryan likely was, as well. The process of getting to that eventuality, though, remained a total mystery to her.

They stared at one another, standing an arm's length apart. There had never been any doubt about their attraction to one another, but there had always been a reason to keep those feelings in check. Now, standing in a room alone together without those boundaries, Raena wasn't sure what to do.

"So…" they both began at the same time.

Ryan stopped and looked down.

Raena sighed. "I didn't mean for this to be so damn awkward."

"No," Ryan said, meeting her gaze. "It shouldn't be awkward." He took a step forward and placed his hands on her hips.

His touch grounded her, reminding her of the times they'd shared in their months together that had led them toward this moment.

"I love you," she told him. It was the only truth that mattered.

He smiled. "I love you, too."

As their lips met, all uncertainties disappeared. Their paths would be forever entwined, but neither of them would have it any other way.

CHAPTER 8

THE FINAL TWO months of the term passed quickly for Raena. Her new bond with Ryan solidified the connection that had been between them since they first met, offering a much needed sense of stability to help offset the upcoming transition.

Her parents, brother, and Michael knew that she and Ryan would be leaving for Tararia at the end of the term, but the other Primus Elites had no idea. However, with their departure now imminent, she could no longer keep them in the dark.

After much deliberation, Raena decided it would be better to tell her roommates before making a broader announcement to the whole group. She waited until her four friends had retired to their room for the night and then scooched down to sit cross-legged at the foot of her bed.

"So, I have an announcement."

Tiff glanced up from her tablet. "Relationship drama or something else?"

"Option B," Raena replied. "Well, mostly."

Adaline set down her own tablet. "All right, spill."

Raena waited until she had Nora's and Susan's attention, as well. "I won't be continuing in the TSS beyond this first year."

Nora's eyes widened. "Wait, you're leaving us?"

"I wish it wasn't one or the other, but I have to go to Tararia. I'll miss all of you," Raena told them.

Tiff stared at her. "That's it? You're just leaving with no

warning?"

Raena's face flushed. "People treat you differently when they know you won't be around soon. I didn't want anything to change."

"Blindsiding us isn't any better," Susan said.

"I'm sorry," Raena responded, but she had no regrets. "You should also know that Ryan is coming with me."

They all stared at her with surprise.

"Now, *that* I did not expect," Tiff said after several seconds of silence.

"I'm telling you that as my friends," Raena said. "It's not exactly public yet, but we're officially together."

"Like, bonded?" Adaline questioned.

Raena nodded. "But for now it's better if the rest of Tararia still thinks I'm… unattached."

"Well, shite." Tiff crossed her arms. "I really didn't expect your relationship to last."

"Why not?"

Her friend shrugged off the question. "Just figured you'd end up with someone High Dynasty, I guess."

"Not everything is about that," Raena said. *Even though this is. Except, what's between us has always been much more.*

"When do you leave?" Susan asked.

"The term officially ends tomorrow, so the morning after," Raena revealed.

"Bomax, that *really* isn't any warning," Tiff said. "I thought we'd at least get a week or two."

Raena tried to sink into her bed. "This seemed best."

Nora sighed. "Nothing we can do about it now."

"Too true," Adaline agreed. "But you do realize this means we're going to demand to spend our midterm break next year on Tararia with you, right?"

Raena smiled. "I think that can be arranged."

They chatted for a while longer, reminiscing about their time together over the last year. Living and training together had made them into an extended family with relationships that would not be easily eroded by time or distance. Raena would miss their companionship, but as long as she had Ryan she would never feel alone.

Word of her departure spread through the group over the following day, and she held one-on-one goodbyes with friends as she prepared to leave.

Ryan, likewise, exchanged parting words with the teammates who'd had his back. Everyone would be in for quite a shock in a few years when they'd learn Ryan's true identity and why a relationship with Raena should never have been questioned. For now, though, everyone just thought the Sietinen heiress and a lost Bankris heir were returning home to learn about operating a company and managing political negotiations.

Raena was content to have them think just that.

As the time for their departure grew near, there were still final goodbyes that Raena wished she didn't have to make. She knew it was more of a 'see you later' than a true farewell, but to leave her brother and parents while she journeyed to another world meant a complete change in the family dynamic that had been the underpinning of her entire life.

With her personal effects packed into three bags and only an hour before the transport ship was set to depart, eventually Raena could delay the conversations no longer. She dragged her luggage into the common room and then approached the doorway to Jason's quarters.

One of Jason's roommates, Liam, was working at his desk, but he quickly left when he saw Raena.

"Safe travels," Liam said as he passed by and gave Raena a quick hug.

"Heading out?" Jason asked as he stood next to his bed.

She nodded. "I know we've only been in the TSS for a year, but it's so much harder to think about leaving here than it was to leave Earth."

"That wasn't breaking up the family," her brother said. "God, it'll be so weird not having you around."

"You're telling me." Her eyes began to sting. "Who's going to keep you out of trouble when I'm not here?"

"I'll try to behave myself, but no promises."

Raena shook her head. "Gah, come here!"

They embraced each other and laughed.

"I'm more worried about you," Jason jested. "I mean, you're outright going to Tararia to *make* trouble."

Raena grinned. "You've been a terrible influence."

Her brother chuckled. "Try not to blow up the planet. I'll try to keep things in line around here, too."

"Deal."

They exited into the common room, where Ryan was saying his final farewells. He nodded to Raena as she approached with Jason.

"I guess this is it," Raena said. "Thank you, everyone. Know you'll always have an open invitation to come visit on Tararia."

"You better come back here at some point, too," Liam said.

Ryan smiled. "I'm sure we will."

"Look after each other," Jason told Ryan, shaking his hand.

"I will."

Before anyone could initiate another round of goodbye sentiments, Raena and Ryan telekinetically gathered their bags and exited into the hallway.

"I can't believe we're leaving," Ryan said as soon as the door to the Primus Elite quarters was closed.

"Neither can I." Raena shook her head. "I've never been away from my family before."

"You'll have a chance to get to know your grandparents, at least."

"True. I am looking forward to that part."

They walked in silence down the hall with their luggage levitating behind them.

"Honestly, though," Raena said after they'd passed by six doors, "I thought I'd be more upset about leaving. I guess I'm not because I'll still have you."

Ryan smiled. "We are pretty stuck with each other now."

She nudged him. "Good."

He grasped her hand. "I never really had a sense of family before, but I do with you."

"And you won't have to be alone again."

Raena could hardly believe how close they'd become in just a year together, though it was also crazy for her to think about there ever having been a time when they weren't in each other's lives. She didn't expect anyone else her age to understand how she could be so certain and make that kind of commitment already, but it wasn't anything she needed to justify. The love and bond between them was as real and certain as anything ever would be.

When they approached the elevator lobby, Raena spotted her parents standing in the center of the space—nearly empty at the mid-afternoon hour. Even through their tinted glasses, she could tell they were on the verge of tears.

"You better not make me cry," Raena said, trying to swallow the lump in her throat.

"Us? Never." Her mother pulled her into a tight hug and rocked her back and forth. "I'll miss you so much."

"I'll miss you, too, Mom."

As soon as Saera released her, her father hugged her, in turn. "You have only great things ahead of you. We're just a call away if you need us."

"Thanks." She gave him a final squeeze and stepped back. "I love you both. Thank you for not putting up a fight about me going."

"It's the smartest move," her father said. "We love you—you'll do great."

Her mother nodded and looped her arm around Wil's, taking a deep breath.

"Stay vigilant," he added.

"We'll have each other's backs," Ryan said.

"Good." Wil nodded. "Well, the transport is ready for you. Kalin will be there in a few days to resume your training."

Knowing that training wouldn't end just because they'd no longer be living in TSS Headquarters had also eased Raena's anxiety about departing for Tararia. Kalin, one of her father's former Primus Elite trainees, had volunteered to relocate to Sieten and serve as their instructor—an offer they'd readily accepted. Presumably, two new trainees would be pulled from one of the other Primus cohorts to take their places in the Primus Elites. Raena was skeptical that her friends would fully accept new arrivals after a year of bonding, but she was trying to be optimistic about everyone getting along well enough.

"Thank you for everything," Ryan said. "I'm truly indebted to you."

"Taking care of our daughter will be thanks enough," Wil replied.

"We'll see you soon," Saera said.

"See you soon," Raena replied, though everyone knew it would be months, at least, until they could even visit. Likely, they'd never be living under the same roof ever again. *This isn't the end—it's just a new beginning.*

With final waves for farewell, Raena and Ryan gathered their bags and boarded the elevator, which took them to the port on the surface. Ryan wrapped his arm around her as soon as they were alone in the elevator car while Raena fought back tears.

"Tararia is just a few hours away," Ryan soothed her. "It's not like we're going to another galaxy."

She nodded. "Pretty soon, we'll be too busy to even think about what we're missing here."

"Exactly."

Steeling her resolve, she traversed the rest of the way to the transport ship with him.

They settled into a lounge room on the ship for the subspace voyage, selecting chairs in the center of the room. The time passed quickly while they played on their handhelds during the subspace jump, paying little attention to their surroundings. After becoming absorbed in a game, Raena was surprised when she looked up and saw a starscape outside with a partial view of a sprawling spaceport.

She took a deep breath. "Home sweet home."

"For one of us, it actually is." Ryan grinned.

"True. I suppose it will be soon enough for me, too."

They gathered their things and departed the TSS transport ship. A complement of guards met them at the foot of the gangway, to Raena's surprise.

"I guess they're not messing around," she said privately to Ryan.

"Two heirs walking around on their own... It doesn't surprise me. I don't think we'll have a lot of privacy out in public settings."

"This whole 'being someone of importance' thing is going to

take a lot of getting used to."

Ryan chuckled. *"Tell me about it."*

A shuttle took them from the spaceport to one of the centrally located landing pads on the Sietinen estate. While they were landing, Raena spotted her grandfather waiting for them.

The pilot told them their luggage would be brought to their new quarters, and they exited the shuttle out the side door.

"Welcome to your new crazy life of Taran politics," Cris greeted with a smile.

"Oh, can't wait," Raena smiled back.

"And don't worry," Cris continued. "We've augmented security across the entire estate, and we ran a thorough scan for any hidden TSD arches or other secret entryways. You're safe here."

Raena nodded her thanks. She'd assumed as much, but it set her at ease to have confirmation that she wouldn't have to worry about a repeat of her last time staying in the manor.

"Stars, it's so weird to be back here," Ryan murmured.

"You're not who you were before," Cris told him.

Ryan hesitated. "Are you sure it's okay for me to say I'm a Bankris heir?'

Cris tilted his head. "It's true, isn't it?"

"I guess…"

"It's half the truth, and it will carry enough weight for us to begin moving forward," Cris said. "The rest will be revealed when the time is right."

"And when will that be?" Raena asked.

"When all the pieces of our plan are in place," he replied. "Right before we put the two motions to a vote with a council of High Dynasty delegates."

"But you need to make sure you know how that vote is going to go ahead of time?" Raena prompted.

"Exactly." Cris nodded. "The information you brought back from the Aesir makes a compelling case, so we're on the right track."

Raena crossed her arms. "I need to figure out what my vision was pointing to on Tararia. There was something beyond just us being here."

"We'll figure it out," Cris assured her. "Now, come on. Let's get you settled in."

He led the way to the main Sietinen mansion and took them to the residential wing for family.

The corridor was airy and ornately decorated like the rest of the estate, but portraits of past family members gave the passageway a homier feel than any other portion of the manor Raena had encountered.

Cris stopped outside a door in the middle of one of the halls. "Raena, this is my former suite—it has one of the best views in the whole estate, so I thought you might like it."

She beamed. "Sounds great!"

Ryan shifted on his feet next to her.

"What about…" Raena began.

Cris smiled. "I thought you'd be concerned about that." He continued down the hall to the next door. "Now, it's important we keep up appearances—*I* know you two are together, but from a political perspective, it's premature to announce any sort of betrothal."

At the next door, Cris gestured for Ryan to palm open the biometric lock. The door clicked open.

"So," Cris continued, "as far as anyone is concerned, I have taken the son of my dear friend under my care as one of the family." He entered the quarters.

The common area was arranged with a couch, entertainment center, and terrace overlooking the lake. On the wall adjacent to Raena's quarters, there was a door, which Cris approached.

"It just so happens," he said, "that these two rooms have internal access." After physically unlocking a deadbolt, he swung the door inward, revealing that a matching door in Raena's assigned quarters was already open. "Some might consider it one, big suite—but how that space gets used is entirely up to you."

Raena and Ryan smiled at each other. "I'm sure we can figure it out."

Cris smiled back. "I thought you might." He showed himself back out to the hallway and paused at the door. "Oh, and now that I'm running things around here, dinner doesn't call for formal eveningwear, unless you want it."

"Yeah, no, I'm good," Raena replied.

"Thank the stars!" Ryan breathed.

Cris looked them over. "I'm really happy you're both here."

Raena took Ryan's hand. "Me too. It was tough to leave my parents and Jason, but I believe this is where we're supposed to be right now."

"I believe so, too," Cris affirmed. "Well, I'll leave you to get settled in. Are you hungry?"

"I could eat," Ryan said.

Raena nodded. "Same."

"All right, I'll have the kitchen prep some dinner. Half an hour?" Cris asked.

"Perfect." Raena smiled.

"See you then in the usual spot," her grandfather acknowledged and departed, closing the door behind him.

Ryan let out a long breath. "Okay… we're really doing this."

Raena grinned. "You bet we are."

— — —

There was a somber tone in the common room of the Primus Elite's quarters following Raena and Ryan's departure. Jason was certain that some of the mood was projected from his own sense of loss, but that would be temporary. New ventures would soon demand his full attention.

As he passed through the common room on his way to the main door, Tiff emerged from her bedroom and jogged over. She intersected with him in the front corner of the common room away from the other Trainees.

"Hey, how are you doing?" she asked him.

He shrugged. "Fine."

"I already miss Raena. I know you two were close…"

"Yeah, I'll adjust." He forced a smile.

"Well, if you're feeling lonely and ever want to talk, or," she tilted her head and looked him over, "anything else, you know where to find me."

Did she just proposition me? The statement caught him by

surprise. "I'll keep that in mind."

She glanced at the other Trainees in the common room, but no one was paying attention to them. "The three of you were always together, so I didn't want to butt in before." She lowered her voice, "Sorry if I'm being too forward, but I got the impression you're not quite as prim and proper as your sister."

"You could say that." Jason looked down. *I guess I am on my own now. But introducing new attachments now won't do me any favors.* He swallowed. "Look, I don't know what you're after, but—"

"No agenda," she hastily replied. "Sometimes it's nice to just have the company of a… friend."

He couldn't argue with that. It had been entirely too long since he'd had that kind of company. "Yeah, thanks. I'll think about it."

Tiff nodded. "All right. I'll, uh, see you around." She slinked back toward her bedroom.

Well, that was unexpected. Jason shrugged off the encounter and filed the proposition away as something to consider at a future time. For the present, he was late for a meeting with his father.

Since their discussion two months prior, Jason had only spoken with Wil twice regarding the plan to implement a new weaponized telekinesis training program. With Raena and Ryan now on their way to Tararia and a new TSS term about to begin, this was the prime opportunity to put those initial plans into action.

He arrived at the High Commander's office and pressed the buzzer next to the door. Two seconds later, the door clicked open.

Wil was seated behind the desk toward the back of his room, seemingly in a contemplative state.

"Hey," Jason greeted.

"Hi," his father replied. "Close the door and take a seat."

Jason complied. "So, how's this going to work?" he asked while settling into one of the chairs across from the desk.

"That's what I've been trying to figure out for the last two months. I don't have a definitive answer yet."

"Last time we spoke, it sounded like an urgent timeframe."

"It is," his father said. "We should have been underway by now, but I wanted to make sure things get done right. I've been through a war—I know how quickly things can go sideways if the wrong people get involved."

Jason nodded. "And you're trying to figure out screening?"

"Not exactly. More who to approach directly. This isn't a matter where we can put out a general call for volunteers."

"Why not?"

Wil's brow furrowed. "Well, it's a similar issue we ran into while I was trying to train the first round of Navigators to use the independent jump drive. It's not just a matter of enthusiasm, but also competence."

"Aren't all the trainees and Agents pre-vetted?" Jason questioned.

"To an extent, yes. But weaponized telekinesis goes beyond basic telepathic aptitude. When we restructured the TSS over the past few terms, we began taking some Eighth and Twelfth Generation students with abilities present, but at levels far below our historical guidelines for Agent trainees—in the 4 range of potential."

"Some of the Trion Agents are around 5, right? It's not *that* much lower."

Wil exhaled heavily. "When taking the number at face value, no. Except, the intensity measures are exponential. You can't tether a 4 with a 9 and not have it be completely overwhelming for the weaker Agent."

Jason crossed his arms. "Then Trion is out completely."

"That's what I've been trying to decide," his father continued. "I'm toying with the idea of different units or teams—grouping people by ability level so all skills can be maximized without risking burnout."

"Makes sense."

"Yes, but the issue is which teams to assign to which kinds of tasks. Not to mention, the broader the categories we open up, the more likely it is that people will start talking, and eventually someone will say the wrong thing to someone."

"Hmm." Jason slumped back in his chair. "Well, if the teams

were to follow existing groupings, then it might be possible for each to function independently—and they wouldn't have to know there were any other groups."

"That's the solution that came to the forefront for me, too. It's practical, given our present needs, but it also goes against everything I've tried to stand for as a leader. My tenets of command are openness and honesty whenever possible."

"Maybe this is one of those times when it's *not* possible to be so transparent."

Wil scowled. "I figured you'd say that."

Jason raised an eyebrow and leaned forward slightly. "Were you just looking for someone to agree with you?"

His father cracked a wan smile. "I've had to make some tough calls, many of which I've questioned for many years after the actions. Sometimes it's nice to hear that others also feel it's the right course, even when you already know it's the best option. Fewer recriminations that way."

"I could see that. So, let's say completely independent secret training groups are the best way forward—there's still the question of how to select the members."

Wil inclined his head. "I'm afraid that also means breaking some of my other rules—most notably, playing a lot of favoritism with my friends."

"Your first round Elite trainees?"

"Precisely. When I installed Ethan and Ian as division heads, a secondary function was to have trusted colleagues in place in the event some need like this arose in the future."

Jason smiled. "You probably figured that'd be a little further out than a year after the promotion."

Wil chuckled. "Stars! I stopped having any clear expectations about the future when I was younger than you. If I hadn't gotten used to going with the flow by now, I would have lost my mind years ago."

"Agility does have its perks."

"Indeed it does." Wil folded his hands on the desktop. "It'll be easy enough to insert some more team leads in key positions at the start of this next term. I guess my main question for you right now is where you want to specialize."

"I… hadn't really thought about it," Jason replied after several seconds. "I'd always thought of it as 'weaponized telekinesis' in a general sense. What are the options?"

"In broad strokes, offensive, defensive, and support," Wil explained. "Within those classifications, there are several possibilities ranging from one-on-one engagements, use of small craft, and teamwork using larger vessels. Or, there's healing."

"Regardless of the options, something tells me you already have something in mind for me."

Wil smiled. "It's almost like you've known me for your whole life, or something."

Jason laughed. "Yeah, so weird…"

"But yes, I do have something in mind. The difficulty is that it's something I swore to myself I'd never do."

His father's suddenly somber tone wiped the smile from Jason's face. "Which is?"

"To tap into power on the scale that can protect—or destroy—a planet."

Jason's heart leaped. "What do you mean?"

Wil looked down. "I know before the field trip to the Rift you went over the end of the war in your classes—and how the Bakzen's main planet was broken apart."

"Yeah, it must have been a hell of a firefight."

"It was," his father said, still keeping his gaze downcast, "but that's not what destroyed the planet. I did."

A chill gripped Jason's chest. "What do you mean?"

"I focused a strong enough charge through the *Conquest* to implode the planet."

The statement was too bold to possibly be true. Jason shook his head, dismissing the absurd claim. *No one person could handle enough energy to destroy an entire planet.*

"I'm serious, Jason. That's why I'm not taking this lightly."

"You're talking about literally destroying a planet with raw telekinetic energy?"

Wil nodded, finally meeting Jason's gaze. "Up until I did it, no one thought it was possible. But I know what it took, and I have a sense of your potential. I no longer think I'm the only person capable of feats of that magnitude."

Jason's chest felt like it was trapped in a vise. "Dad…"

"Now, I don't think it will come to that. I just need you to understand that this is serious business—billions of lives may be in your hands one day."

What can I possibly say to that? Jason searched for the right words. "I know I'm not ready to make those kinds of decisions, but I think with time, and the right guidance, I could."

Wil nodded. "I'm glad to see you're a little reluctant—I'd be concerned if you were overly eager to take that on."

"You'd have to be insane to be excited about that. I might be a little crazy when it comes to some things, but I try to keep it in line."

"I think that particular brand of crazy runs in the family."

"Considering what Raena's already signed up to do, I'm inclined to believe it's genetic."

The concern finally faded from Wil's face. "Very true. I'll leave the politicking to others."

"Meanwhile, we'll just be building a secret special ops force."

"Yep."

Jason grinned. "That sounds like way more fun, not gonna lie."

Wil smiled back. "I hate to admit it, but part of me is a little excited by the prospect."

"It does make sense," Jason replied. "I mean, it's unfinished business. I can't imagine you felt a real sense of resolution after the war, knowing the Priesthood is still at large. After positioning to do something for twenty years, I think I'd be pretty excited to finally take out the bad guys."

"Well, when you put it like that…"

"Whoa! Maybe dial back that devious glint in your eyes a notch or two," Jason said with a grin.

Wil laughed. "All right, you got me. But we're going to get them."

"Let's get started."

— — —

Ryan admired Raena asleep in bed next to him—watching the rise and fall of her exposed back, her flawless skin and refined features the very image of perfection. Even more than her external beauty was her brilliance and heart he'd first fallen in love with when they met.

He still couldn't help feeling a sense of awe to be in the same room as her, let alone knowing that they were now bonded to each other. This incredible young woman—amazing in her own right, even without the credentials of her family—was one day going to be his wife.

Nothing about that prospect seemed real. Ryan still saw himself as the Ward he was in his youth, without family or anything to his name. For everything to have changed so dramatically in a year's time was still too much to fully process. All he could do was trust in the love he shared with Raena and that they'd be able to navigate the upcoming challenges together.

My past showed me what needs to be different in my future. I'm no longer alone. He took a deep breath and slipped out of bed.

Raena stirred as he got up, but she quickly settled back into her quiet slumber.

Ryan pulled on pants, a t-shirt, and shoes before stepping out into the hallway. He didn't have a particular destination in mind, but taking a walk outside in the nighttime air sounded refreshing. There were too many thoughts churning through his mind and he needed to re-center himself.

The common areas of the estate were empty at the wee hour, and Ryan wandered slowly through the halls on his way out to the gardens. Even when viewed with only the dimmed nighttime lights and moonlight streaming through the windows, the details of the architecture spoke to the Sietinens' wealth and level of opulence in their lifestyle. *I wonder if it was like this for Dainetris before the fall?*

He had no way of knowing, since all but the most public information about the Dynasty had been sealed. Cris mentioned that the eastern expanse of the Third Region used to be the Seventh Region, but no maps in the digital archives outlined that political boundary. It was frightening to think that so much information could be suppressed over the course of one hundred fifty years.

Directions to strike discussion of the Dynasty from the oral history, passed from parents to their children, took care of common knowledge, and the Priesthood's complete control of the central data repositories ensured that digital records were scrubbed to paint whatever picture they desired. With that information altered and no one left alive to have experienced another political structure firsthand, for all intents and purposes there had never been a seventh High Dynasty. Ryan couldn't help but wonder if people would even accept his claim, however valid it was.

No, they will… because Raena and I aren't like the others. They'll accept us because we're as close to being one of them as anyone with this level of influence ever has been. His self-assurances offered temporary relief from his worries, but deep down he knew he wouldn't feel confident until their task was complete.

Ryan wandered downstairs and was about to exit into the gardens when he heard light footsteps in the hall. He turned around and was surprised to see his former friend, Tony, about to enter into one of the many hidden servant passageways.

"Stars! Ryan?" Tony exclaimed in a whisper.

"Hey!" Ryan greeted with a smile. He kept his voice at just about a whisper, as well—he was confident any nearby bedrooms were soundproof, but the darkened surroundings called for hushed speech, it seemed.

"What are you doing back?" Tony asked. "I thought you joined the TSS?"

"I did. I mean, I'm still in the TSS," Ryan tried to explain. "It's complicated."

Tony eyed him suspiciously. "Yeah, I'll say. You're a guest at the Sietinen estate as a TSS trainee? I know Cris Sietinen was TSS High Commander, but still…"

"He's been very gracious welcoming me here."

"Uh huh." Tony crossed his arms and looked Ryan over. "C'mon, what's up?"

Anything I tell him will be common knowledge by tomorrow

afternoon. But they'll see me with Raena... May as well control what story they tell. Ryan took a deep breath. "I'm here because when I joined the TSS, I found out who my father was."

Tony cocked his head. "Really? Who was he?"

"It's a little crazy." Ryan tousled his hair. "He was the TSS High Commander before Cris. And, apparently, he was also a secondary heir to the Bankris Dynasty in the Second Region."

"Whoa! So, you're a dynastic heir?" Tony's eyes were filled with disbelief and envy.

"Yeah. Crazy, right?"

"I'll say." His friend shook his head.

"So, anyway, the Sietinen heiress, Raena, is here to get educated on Taran politics and be groomed to take over as Cris' successor. Since I know nothing about being highborn, they decided to send me along, too, as a shadow—sort of an early TSS internship."

Tony's brow wrinkled. "I suppose that explains why that TSS Agent is with you."

"Exactly."

"Wow..." His friend took a step back toward the servant passageway. "Well, I guess you have your new highborn life to live now."

"Tony, it's not like that."

"Really? Because it sounds like you're keeping company with the Sietinen Dynasty heiress these days—and on a first name basis, no less."

This is just like when I left before... he'll find fault in everything I say just because it's something he can never have for himself. It's easier to keep me as the outsider. Ryan composed his reply, "Raena has been a good friend to me, and she's going to make an excellent leader. She's not like most highborn—she grew up on Earth living a normal life with regular people. Bringing that perspective will mean changes around here. Good changes."

His friend brushed it off. "Yeah, whatever you say, *my lord.*"

"Seriously, Tony, finding out about someone's birthright doesn't change who they are as a person—I'm still the same guy who used to sneak cake from the dessert cart with you and who swapped the ringtone on Laura's handheld."

Tony finally cracked a smile. "That was a good one."

"Come on. Don't assume I'm some stuck-up outsider now that I have a family crest. I'd like to think our friendship had more to it than just convenient proximity."

"Yeah, you're right..." Tony looked down.

"I know it's weird, and I don't expect us to be close like we used to be. I just want you to know that if we pass each other in the hall, you can—and should—say 'hi' to me like we're old friends, because we are."

"Okay, sure."

Ryan smiled. "All right. Well, I'll see you around."

"Yeah, see you." Tony slipped into the servant passage and closed the door.

It was unlikely any of Ryan's old friends would ever regard him like a personal acquaintance again, but at least he'd made an effort.

The conversation left him feeling even more restless than he had upon waking up, so he continued on his path out into the gardens.

Everything was quiet in the world outside. The moonlight cast the lush foliage in a blue glow, augmented occasionally by amber accent lighting lining the paths. Ryan ambled along the paved trail past a babbling fountain and down to one of the scenic overlooks above the city of Sieten below.

Unlike the residential wing of the estate, the city was alive even in the dead of night—responding to the ongoing needs of the Taran civilization. Sieten had it easier than some cities, being relatively close to the time zone of the Priesthood's isle that set the clock observed as common time throughout the disparate worlds. Ryan wondered what it would have been like to grow up in a place where the accepted business hours were always in the middle of the night.

He brushed off the notion and all its ripple effects that would only serve to make his head hurt. Managing a civilization wasn't his responsibility.

Except, it will be... he realized.

In a matter of years, he was expected to assume the role as Head of the Dainetris Dynasty. With all likelihood, the divisions of the former corporation operated by the family would be returned to his purview—at least those absorbed by Sietinen—and he'd have to be both businessman and politician.

Dainetris had been responsible for ship manufacture and other infrastructure projects before their fall. Those activities were more important than ever as the Taran civilization continued its expanse. Ships needed near-constant upkeep in the harsh, irradiated environment of space. Old vessels needed to be decommissioned and recycled, and new craft with the latest technology advances were always under construction in massive shipyards throughout the worlds. If any of the production was mismanaged, repair parts wouldn't make it to where they were needed and interstellar commerce would grind to a halt.

The same went for an issue with the SiNavTech network, VComm communications, or Makaris Corp food shipments—or the services delivered by the other High Dynasties, for that matter.

That's why they are core services. That's why Cris and Kate recognize the High Dynasties can't rule from a place of greed, but must uphold an interest in the common good. As Ryan stared at the city below, he gained a new appreciation for the revolution that was about to take place. He had a chance to be a leader, to set a new standard for resource management and allocation. If the other dynasties were willing to see the big picture of where Tarans could go as a collective people, so much more would be possible.

All the same, the thought of getting to that point was daunting, to say the least. He knew nothing about running a civilization, but he was willing to learn.

A cool breeze swept up from the lake, and Ryan's skin prickled from the sudden chill.

There's still time to grow into the person I need to be, he decided. *And I'll have Raena with me. We'll figure it out together.*

Ryan took a brisk pace back along the garden path as the wind continued to pick up. His mind was still too active for sleep when he made it back to the manor, so he decided to wander toward the administrative wing.

The lights were at full brightness in the corridor leading to the operations center, as SiNavTech employees worked around the clock to monitor the critical transportation network. The scent of brewing coffee wafted through the halls.

Unlike the daytime hours Ryan had witnessed as a maintenance tech, the halls were sparsely populated. He was able to stroll through the corridors looking at the holopaintings and memorabilia displayed on the walls and pedestals, encountering only the occasional passersby, and they were all too concerned with their own tasks to pay him much attention.

Eventually, he arrived at a dead-end hall tucked away from the main activity. It housed a collection of artifacts characterized by old-world craftsmanship from a previous era where wood, stone, and metalwork were vogue rather than the digital art popular in recent decades. Such fluctuating aesthetic tastes changed with every generation, but Ryan had always been drawn to art with a physical presence.

He approached a carved, three-dimensional relief map of Tararia mounted on one of the walls, at least two meters high and four wide. The entire model was painted with stunning realism, and he noted how even mountain peaks were detailed with the location of stream headwaters from ancient glaciers.

Examining the location around the city of Sieten, Ryan noticed that a green serpent resembling the Sietinen crest was situated in the hills to the north of the city, corresponding with the location of the estate. Likewise, in the First Region, he spotted a Falcon in the outskirts of the city of Vaentar. Curious, he scanned over the rest of the map and noticed the icons from other crests he recognized throughout the world.

Then, he saw it: a red flower identical to the painting his mother had given him at their brief reunion. It was along the southeastern coast of what was now the Third Region—squarely in the territory he was told used to be the Seventh Region, the seat of power for Dainetris.

Was this the capital city? No modern database had identified the location of the administrative complex—the Priesthood had destroyed those records in their information purge. But a map such as this, something that would have been dismissed as stylized art, had never been seized. Knowing where to look, they might be able to find more information about the Dainetris Dynasty's fall.

Heart racing with excitement, Ryan snapped a picture of the map with his handheld and raced back to the adjoining quarters he was sharing with Raena. Middle of the night or not, he was anxious to share his discovery.

"I found something," he told Raena telepathically as he entered the bedroom, going to sit next to her on the bed.

Raena roused, pulling the sheet around her chest as she rolled over. "What time is it?"

"I dunno—02:00? I couldn't sleep so I took a walk. Look at this." He showed her the image of the map on his handheld.

She rubbed her eyes. "Is that Tararia?"

"Yes, look." Ryan zoomed in on Sieten. "You see the serpent?"

"Yeah, that looks like my family crest."

He smiled. "Exactly. So, look at this." Scrolling the image to the side, he centered the coastline containing the red flower icon.

Raena stared at it blankly. "What am I supposed to see here?"

"The flower, that—" Ryan took a calming breath. "I think that flower is the Dainetris crest."

Her eyes met his. "Why do you say that?"

"My mother's holopainting—it's this same species. It can't be a coincidence."

She caught on, shaking off the grogginess of sleep. "This may mark the location of the former Dainetris estate."

"Yes, and maybe will give us a lead about how and why the Dynasty fell."

Raena shook her head. "That explains what I saw."

"Hmm?"

"When I was with the Aesir. I saw the pathways leading to Tararia, and a red flower at the top of a cliff. Maybe this is what I was meant to find."

Ryan examined her. "Did you see anything else in that vision?"

Her brow wrinkled. "No, it was just the flower motif."

So no easy answer. He turned off the handheld's screen. "You don't think anything survived the Priesthood's purge, do you?"

"I don't think I can take anything I saw in the vision at face value," Raena replied.

"Well, regardless, we need to go to that city."

"Absolutely." Raena laid back down and reached one arm around Ryan's back to draw him to her. "But that can wait until morning."

CHAPTER 9

RAENA BURST INTO the dining room with Ryan to find Cris and Kate seated at the table midway through breakfast. "We figured it out!" she announced.

Cris raised a quizzical eyebrow. "Pardon?"

"My vision," Raena clarified.

Ryan nodded. *"The red flowers—I think they're the Dainetris Dynasty crest,"* he explained telepathically, glancing at a servant in the corridor leading to the kitchen.

Kate and Cris exchanged glances. "What makes you say that?" she asked.

"I found this map." Ryan showed them the picture he'd shared with Raena the night before.

"That's the same flower I saw," Raena insisted. "I think we should go to that city and check it out."

Cris took a slow breath, then gestured for the servant down the hall to give them some privacy. "If this is true, our friends may be watching."

We can't ignore a lead just because the Priesthood is after us. Raena sat down across from Cris and folded her hands on the tabletop. "We're going."

Her grandfather eyed her. "I'd think you were an only child, if I didn't know better. You seem used to getting your way."

"Yes." Raena grinned. "We'll leave in an hour." She rose from the table.

"Maybe we should think this through…" Kate suggested.

"Agreed. I appreciate your enthusiasm, Raena, but it's unlikely we'll find anything worthwhile there at this point. If there was anything incriminating, I'd think our friends would have taken care of it by now."

"Unless they didn't know where to look," Ryan offered.

"And you do?" Kate asked.

"I don't know for sure," Raena interjected, "but I do know my vision is pointing me there. I don't think it would unless we'd know what to find when we got there."

A hum of energy passed between Cris and Kate while they conducted a telepathic exchange.

"All right," Cris said after ten seconds. "I still don't fully understand where these visions come from or what they mean, but I always trusted what Wil saw, and I should pay you the same respect."

Raena nodded. "Thanks."

"I'm concerned, though," he continued. "I don't like the idea of you being out in the open."

"If our ultimate goal is to send a message of strength, we can't always hide behind these walls," Raena stated.

"I agree. And that's why I'm coming with you," Cris said.

Raena frowned. "Our chances of being recognized go way up with you as an escort."

"And the likelihood of anyone trying to mess with you also goes way down," her grandfather countered. "I may not be an official TSS Agent anymore, but I can certainly put up a compelling telekinetic fight if it's needed, legal or not."

"And that'd be a great way to undermine all our plans—dragging the legality of ability use into things," Kate stated.

"True," Cris conceded. "Then no telekinesis. Even without that, it still makes sense for me to go. I haven't conducted a proper tour of the Third Region since becoming Head, and a visit to the east coast is fitting."

Kate gave a slight shake of her head. "It's still risky."

"Like almost everything else we do," Cris replied. "I think Raena's right, though—we need to take a chance and see if we can get some answers."

"I'd really like to understand where I'm from," Ryan added.

Cris smiled. "And I hope we can give you that."

"Then it's settled," Raena said. She grabbed a pastry from a basket on the table. "See you back here soon."

Before her grandparents could change their minds, she withdrew from the dining room with Ryan and headed back toward their quarters.

"That was strange seeing someone talk to the Head of a High Dynasty like that," Ryan commented when they were halfway down the hall.

Raena laughed. "Oh, yeah. Whoops."

"I guess you don't really see him that way, though."

She shrugged and took a bite of the pastry she'd snagged from the breakfast spread. "Yeah, they're my grandparents. But I should probably 'respect my elders', or something."

"Like he said, you're just used to getting your way."

She grinned. "That I am. Sorry."

"I'm doomed, aren't I?"

"I'll be a benevolent dictator."

Ryan chuckled. "I should have figured I'd just be along for the ride."

"But it'll be a *good* ride," Raena replied. "I can't help it if I'm always right."

"One of these days… One of these days *I'll* be right, and you'll never hear the end of it," Ryan joked back.

"Good luck with that."

"Oh, just you wait…" His eyes glinted with faux challenge.

"I'll believe it when I see it."

They ducked into the respective doors to their adjoined suites to get ready for the day. After showering, Raena selected a plain street clothes outfit consisting of black pants and a form-fitting red top with a cowl neck. She checked the weather in their destination city and saw that its climate was kept somewhat cooler than Sieten due to some sensitive crops in nearby agricultural lands, so she also grabbed a black jacket.

Ryan was ready around the same time, and the two of them returned to the dining room. When they arrived, Kate was absent, but Cris was waiting for them with Marina.

"The three of you are incredibly reckless," Marina stated as soon as Raena and Ryan entered the room.

Raena froze. *"Does she know?"* she asked her grandfather, including Ryan in the exchange.

"Yes," Cris replied aloud. He gestured for Raena to close the door behind them.

She complied. "So, Ryan…"

Marina nodded. "Cris had to tell me three times before I believed him." She looked at Ryan. "It's an honor."

Ryan flushed. "I'm…" he faded out and shrugged.

"Everything made a lot more sense after Cris told me," Marina continued. "I always found it odd that they took you in so quickly during Raena and Jason's first visit here. I never could have guessed the real reason."

"I knew you were one of the only people who'd understand," Cris said to her. "You were also manipulated by the Priesthood."

A grimace flitted across Marina's otherwise serene face. "Your poor mother," she said to Ryan, shaking her head. "I had the same thing done to me with Saera."

He looked down. "Yeah."

"Anyway," Cris continued, "given the maneuvering to come, it seemed prudent to bring Marina into the fold."

Raena nodded. "That'll definitely come in handy."

Marina gathered herself. "Yes, and of course now that I know, I realize just how delicate and dangerous this situation is, and how the last thing you should be doing is gallivanting around. However, I also know better than to fight your hard-headedness."

Cris smirked. "See? Progress."

His advisor rolled her eyes and sighed. "I took the liberty to investigate that map you found. I believe I have a lead for you."

Raena perked up. "Oh?"

"According to the imprint on the back, it was made by a sculptor in the city of Dain approximately eight hundred years ago," Marina explained.

Cris' brow wrinkled in thought. "I won't profess to know every town in the Third Region, but that doesn't sound familiar—aside from the obvious name similarity to the High Dynasty."

"That's where things get interesting: there is no city of Dain," Marina replied.

"Name change after the Dynasty's fall?" Cris asked.

She nodded. "That's my best guess. I did some digging, and the best candidate is Shorlaen. The city's records are… incomplete in a suspect way. Certain documentation points to a well-established metropolis going back thousands of years, but other records suggest new development only two or three generations old."

"Sounds like a data purge to me," Cris said.

"Indeed," Marina agreed. "It's nothing that would jump out unless you were searching specifically for evidence of such an occurrence."

"How is it even possible to change the name and history of a city without anyone knowing?" Ryan asked.

"It can't be done overnight," Marina replied, "but give it a generation or two, once no one living can offer a firsthand account, and official records become the most reliable source of information—supposedly." She sighed. "It's a monumental undertaking, but the Priesthood's reach is sufficient to pull it off."

We already know the Priesthood is all-powerful. Finding some artwork hardly seems like a solid lead. "All right, so what about the sculptor?" Raena prompted.

"Right." Marina pulled her handheld from a pocket in her gown and set it on the dining table. She used its holographic projector to display a series of relief murals similar to the one Ryan had found in the hallway. "Looks familiar, right?"

Everyone nodded.

She smiled. "Well, these were produced within the last thirty years by a craftsman in Shorlaen."

"Descendent of the original?" Cris speculated.

"Or at least connected to an apprentice in some fashion," Marina said. "While I don't expect this individual to know anything, they may have information regarding the original craftsman's studio. It seems that the Priesthood overlooked this craftsman during the purge, otherwise they would have had complete records regarding the artwork and where it was distributed. We wouldn't have the map here in the Sietinen estate if they knew to come looking for it."

Why didn't I think of that? Raena lit up. "So, there might be untarnished records with concrete information regarding Dainetris."

"Maybe," Marina said. "However, the original workshop may have been demolished and paved over years ago. Or it might be intact and have nothing of interest."

Ryan shrugged. "It's a place to start."

Cris nodded. "All right, let's go."

"Be careful," Marina told them as she picked up her handheld from the table. "If I'm right, the Priesthood made a mistake—and they'll correct their oversights at any cost."

"We'll try to keep a low profile," Cris assured her.

She scoffed. "You? Right."

Cris gave her a sheepish look. "Okay, maybe we won't exactly blend in, but I do like being alive and intend to stay that way."

Marina shook her head with exasperation. "Very well."

"Thank you for finding this," Raena told her grandmother. "I'm glad we'll be able to talk about things with you now."

"Me too."

Raena flashed Marina a parting smile and then followed Cris and Ryan out of the manor toward the main surface port containing transport ships. Her stomach fluttered with anxious anticipation. *I wonder what we're going to find?*

— — —

Ryan gazed out the shuttle viewport at the former home of his ancestors. The coastline jutted more than one hundred meters above the sea at the foothills of a coastal mountain range. Though the mountains were mere hills compared to the impressive Bethral Mountains to the east of Sieten, the topography made for an impressive approach to the city from the air.

Unlike the western coastline Ryan had known for his whole life—which sloped gently toward the water and had wide, sandy beaches—this land simply ended where it met with the water. It made for a dramatic sight, but he couldn't help wondering about what it would have been like to grow up here instead, without being able to swim in the water or bury his toes in the sand.

The metropolis of Shorlaen rolled across the hills, eventually turning into a terraced wall facing the expansive sea. The city mostly consisted of lower structures finished in shades of brown and gray, which was a harsh contrast to the white stone, glass, and gleaming metal featured in Sieten's towering skyline. Only three buildings in Shorlaen rose above ten stories, and their bland design features looked more suited to an emerging colony world than any place worthy of a High Dynasty seat.

My family may have been from here, but this isn't my home. Sieten is everything I know. Ryan tore his gaze away and returned his attention to Raena and Cris inside the shuttle. "How much do you think the city has changed in the last one hundred fifty years?"

Cris glanced back at him from the pilot's chair. "Tough to say. This really doesn't have the look of a capital city, does it?"

"Yeah, it's weird," Raena agreed from her seat across the narrow aisle from Ryan. "I'd have expected the city to either be in ruins or more like Sieten."

"Maybe showy architecture just wasn't important to them," Ryan speculated. *But where's any evidence of an estate? With a flower for the family crest, I'd at least expect a garden somewhere.*

"We'll see what we can find out," Cris said as he directed the shuttle toward a port on the northern outskirts of the town.

The craft touched down lightly next to a row of similar vessels, and they exited through the side door.

"One sec," Cris told them and jogged over to speak with the port attendant.

"If anyone recognizes him, everyone is going to be so confused about why the Head of Sietinen is playing tourist in some nothing town," Ryan muttered, crossing his arms to block out the cool, salt-laden breeze blowing across the hilltop. "I wish we could have come alone—I don't think you're well-known enough yet to stand out too much."

"I know," Raena agreed as she buried her hands in her jacket's pockets. "But he's right—if we do run into trouble, I'd rather have him with us than not."

"True."

The port attendant nodded understanding and gave Cris a slight bow.

Cris returned to where Ryan and Raena were waiting. "We're all set. I told him who I am but asked him to keep it quiet."

Raena looked skeptical. "Think he will?"

"Oh, stars no!" Cris laughed. "But if everyone in the town thinks they're supposed to be keeping it a secret, they may be more inclined to speak with us if they believe we're on a special mission and only those in the know on the inner circle can help."

"Tricky tricky," Raena said with a mischievous smile.

"Let me tell you, dealing with teenagers for as many years as I did as Lead Agent gave me all sorts of insight into group behavior. Except for you rational, mature types," he said with a grin to Raena and Ryan. "You defy all expectations by actually doing what's reasonable."

Raena laughed. "You got me—rationality is my weakness."

"Thank the stars! You can balance out my impulsiveness." Cris led them toward a paved path leading in the direction of the city. "Just don't forget, the sense of what's rational is influenced by perspective."

"And that's why we're here," Raena replied. "I want as close to the truth as we can find."

The path led to a parking lot with an assortment of sleek ground transportation vehicles for rent. Cris selected a white, four-passenger car with a domed roof and palmed open the side entry. The doors parted and they climbed in, with Raena and Ryan on the front bench seat facing back toward Cris.

Cris tapped on a console between the seats and brought up a map of the city. "All right, I believe the sculptor is in this block here." He pointed to an intersection within the central district of the city. "I say we start out by paying him a visit."

"Works for me," Ryan agreed.

Raena nodded.

Cris entered in the command to the automated nav console, and the doors closed. Within moments, the car was speeding down the roadway.

Single-family homes became more densely packed closer to

the city, eventually transitioning into low, multi-unit buildings mixed with commercial space. Up close, the city had the same bizarre combination of new and old Ryan had noticed from the air. It was almost as though the buildings had been transported and repurposed.

Except that's completely impractical. It's probably just what building materials mined from this region look like, Ryan decided.

The car slowed as it entered the city core, merging with other ground traffic on the automated transit grid. Eventually, it parked in a slot parallel to the street one block from the location Cris had identified.

"Shall we?" Cris hopped out from the car.

Amid the buildings, the breeze was much less pronounced and Ryan found he was able to walk without feeling chilled like up at the port. Few people were strolling down the streets at the mid-morning hour, but those who were varied in their reactions—some barely seeing the three of them and others watching with great interest. Ryan was pretty sure he heard at least one person whisper something about Cris Sietinen to their companion. *I hope he's right about those rumors being helpful.*

When they reached the location Cris had identified on the map, there was only a plain gray three-story structure that appeared to be more recent construction than the surrounding blocks.

"Hmm," Cris mused aloud. "I can't say this looks promising."

"No, it doesn't," Raena agreed.

"This building is new," Ryan observed. "Maybe something happened to the original and they moved the workshop?"

"Possibly." Cris crossed his arms.

One of the passersby noticed the group's consternation and stopped two paces from them. "Are you looking for something?"

Cris turned to address the middle-aged woman. "Yes, we—"

"Stars! My lord." The woman dropped to a deep curtsy.

"No, please," Cris insisted in a low voice. "We're not here on official business."

The woman hesitantly rose, adjusting her shawl around her shoulders. "If it's Elren you want, his shop is three blocks to the south and one east."

"How did you know that's who we were looking for?" Cris asked her.

She gave him a knowing smile. "When strangers come, it's often for him. He's something of a collector."

"Our thanks." Cris bowed his head.

"The honor is mine, my lord," she replied, then cast an evaluating look in Raena and Ryan's direction. "It's surprising to see you here."

"It was past time I visit the lands beyond Sieten," Cris replied with a smile. "Now, we should be on our way."

"Of course, my lord." The woman glanced again at Ryan, then inclined her head and continued down the sidewalk.

"Any bets on how long it is before the entire town knows we're here?" Raena said when the woman was beyond earshot.

Cris chuckled. "Twenty minutes tops."

Raena smiled. "So, Elren, huh? I wonder if that's our sculptor."

"One way to find out." Cris strode ahead in the direction the woman had indicated.

After two minutes of walking, he stopped outside a nondescript beige building, marked only by a carved wooden door.

"Much more promising," Raena commented.

"This must be it." Cris knocked.

A minute passed before a man spoke over an intercom, "Yes?"

"Hello, Elren? We're here regarding an old relief map created in this studio. We were hoping you could tell us some more about it," Cris replied.

"Where is the map?" the man asked, making no indication of his identity.

"In Sieten. We brought pictures," explained Cris. "This should only take a few minutes of your time."

The door bolt slid open and an elderly man with bushy brows peered outward. "Where in Sieten?" He looked Cris over.

"Within the Sietinen estate," Cris stated levelly. "I would appreciate your assistance."

The man's eyes widened and he took a step back, allowing the door to swing open. "My lord, I—" He noticed Ryan and Raena and he sucked in a startled breath. "Stars!"

Cris tilted his head expectantly.

"Come in, come in," the man urged.

Cris led the way, followed by Raena and Ryan. Once they were inside, the man closed and re-bolted the door.

The interior was cramped and chaotic, somewhere between a living room and a workshop. Though what little of the walls Ryan could see appeared newly renovated, the furnishings were well-worn. A couch had been overtaken by crates containing paints and decorative stones, and bookshelves along the walls were lined with an assortment of knickknacks. At the back of the room, where a dining room should have been, a work table supported a half-carved wooden mural nearly three meters on its longest edge. Wooden shavings littered the ground and the air bore an oaken mustiness.

Ryan inspected the artifacts on the bookshelves with interest, noting a bizarre mixture of electrical components and stone sculptures that looked like they could have been from another era. He was so engrossed in his study that it took him a minute to realize the old man was staring at him.

"What?" Ryan asked him.

"You look just like them," the man breathed.

"Who?" Cris prompted.

"The paintings in the Underground," the man replied like the answer was obvious.

"Does that sound familiar?" Cris telepathically asked Raena and Ryan.

"That's sometimes what we'd call the servant living area beneath the estate, but otherwise no," Ryan told him.

"Right," Cris said aloud. "But I think we skipped introductions."

The man's face flushed. "Of course, my apologies. I don't get many visitors." He clasped his hands and made a small bow. "I am Elren, yes. I inherited this studio from my master, Ulrich—he never had any children of his own."

Cris nodded. "I see. And do you happen to have any records of the art produced by the studio from before you were involved?"

"No, I'm afraid those were lost in a collapse," Elren said.

There goes that lead. Then Ryan caught himself. "Wait, what do you mean by a 'collapse'?"

"A cave-in," Elren said again like he was having to repeat the obvious.

Cris' brow furrowed. "I'm sorry, Elren, I understand the words but not the meaning. Can you explain the Underground and these collapses?"

Elren's bushy eyebrows rose. "You mean you don't know?"

"About what?" Cris asked.

"The original city," the old man stated.

Raena's jaw dropped. *"That's what happened!"* she exclaimed in Ryan's and Cris' minds. *"The Priesthood didn't remove the city of Dain—they buried it."*

Stars! Ryan's breath caught in his throat. "Can you access this Underground?" he stammered.

"Parts of it," Elren said with a nod. "It's dangerous, though, because of cave-ins."

"Do you have a map?" Raena asked tentatively.

Elren ignored her question, continuing to stare at Ryan. "Are you one of them?" he asked.

"I…" Ryan looked to Cris for help.

Cris took a step closer to him and addressed Elren, "We're here to seek the truth regarding what happened to this city."

The old man considered the response. "How did you find me?"

"A friend of ours researched the map at the estate. It was some lucky extrapolation," Cris replied.

"And who's he?" Elren nodded in Ryan's direction, not taking his gaze off him.

"Someone invested in Tararia's future," Cris said.

Elren nodded with understanding. "Some truths cannot be spoken aloud." He briefly turned his attention to Raena, shaking his head. "I never dreamed I'd live to witness such times."

"So, about the Underground…" Ryan said, bringing the conversation back to their objective.

"Right." The old man shuffled across the room to one of his

many bookshelves. He selected a chrome device the size of his palm and brought it to Cris. "This contains a map, but it must be charged."

Cris inspected the device. *"I should be able to tether it to my handheld,"* he told Ryan and Raena. *"You pick up a thing or two being married to a VComm heiress."*

"Thanks, Grandma," Raena jested back.

"Thank you, Elren," Cris said to the man. "Do you have a suggestion for where we should start?"

"That depends on what you're after," he replied.

"Evidence of unpopular truths that have been silenced for too long."

The old man smiled. "Then use the entrance on Mandelay Street. I think you'll find what you're looking for."

"How did you learn about all this?" Cris asked him after a pause.

Elren chuckled. "They think all of us have forgotten, but we haven't. We just know when to keep quiet."

"Does everyone here know?" Cris pressed.

Elren shook his head. "Just a few of us, but we preserve what we can. We take apprentices to the Underground so that they might gain necessary perspective."

"Well, we're indebted to you," Cris told him.

The old man brushed off the statement with a wave of his hand. "Truths can only be buried for so long. It's just a matter of finding the right people to listen."

"Why reveal this information to us now?" Raena questioned.

"Because if you have found your way here, you're ready to hear that truth. I have lived a long life and it does not take much to see who you are. I believe you can do what must be done—perhaps the first and only ones who would ever be in a position to do so."

Cris nodded. "We'll try."

Elren showed them to the door. "Be safe, and I hope you find what you need."

"Thank you," Cris said as the door unbolted and cracked open. He froze in the doorway.

"What is it?" Ryan questioned, taking a step sideways so he

could get a better view.

Gathered around the shop door were at least six dozen city residents. They took a collective gasp when they saw Cris.

"You just had to go around announcing yourself," Raena muttered.

Cris hastily stepped back inside and closed the door. "Well, that backfired."

Elren peeked out the window. "They mustn't see you enter the Underground."

"Is there another way in?" Ryan asked him.

The old man nodded. "I didn't want to suggest it because it's blocked, but with the abilities they say you have, you should be able to make a way through."

"Show us," Cris requested.

Ryan exchanged a worried glance with Raena as they followed Elren toward a downward staircase. *Whatever truth we find in this Underground, I don't think I'll be able to see things the same way again.*

CHAPTER 10

DESCENDING A MUSTY staircase while being led by a stranger into an unknown situation went against most of Cris' training, but curiosity kept him moving forward down the dimly lit corridor.

"Where are we going, exactly?" Cris asked the elderly guide, whose glacial pace only heightened Cris' anxiousness.

"I believe she's already put the pieces together," Elren replied with a quick look back to Raena.

"When they covered up the city, several of the buildings were too tall to hide," Raena stated. "So, some of the structures we see on the surface now are actually the tops of those tall skyscrapers."

Elren nodded. "The floors below what's now surface-level were sealed, but construction projects here and there over the last century have opened up passageways to the Underground."

Cris' heart leaped. "There's an entire, intact city beneath us?"

"Much of it is now in ruins due to lack of maintenance and time, but many of the structures are there, yes," the old man replied.

How is that possible? The city spans at least two kilometers. That's a huge structure to erect over the top. And where did all the residents go? "Elren, you said earlier that some of you haven't forgotten. Do you have any record—written or oral—regarding how the city got to be the way it is today?"

The old man shook his head. "I don't know the details, but there was an event a century or two ago when Dainetris was condemned. The people loved our leaders. Anyone unwilling to denounce their loyalties met a swift end at the hand of the Priesthood, and those few remaining were sent away. When they were allowed to return a month later, the city was no longer at sea level." Elren's shoulders slumped further. "From what I saw in the Underground as a youth, Dain was beautiful. What you see now of Shorlaen is our punishment for disobeying."

Cris hurriedly dismissed dark thoughts about what the Priesthood would do to the four of them if they discovered this new quest to expose the truth. "Is it one continuous platform over the city below, or…?"

"It appears the structure was erected in modules," Elren explained. "I am far from an architect, but I know enough of design to see the seams between pieces."

"But you can get between the different sections of the Underground?" Ryan asked.

Elren nodded. "Most places, yes. I suspect your question is specifically about the Dainetris Estate, and most of that is intact. However, there is a cave-in between here and there—but I believe a former Agent would have the means to find a way through."

If I have to use telekinesis on Tararia, at least it will be somewhere hidden. "We'll figure out a way."

They reached the bottom of the staircase three stories down, which terminated in a metal door. A cursory inspection of the area revealed a broken weld around the door, and chips along the walls and floor suggested a layer of concrete filling in the room had been jackhammered away.

"Exit at Mandelay Street after you complete your task," Elren instructed. "That's closest to your destination. The map will show you the possible routes."

"Not all the cave-ins are noted on the map, correct?" Cris clarified.

Elren inclined his head. "It was current as of five years ago. I've heard there have been new collapses since then, but I no longer journey into the Underground."

"Thank you again for your assistance," Cris told him.

"A worthy cause. Good luck." Elren began a slow climb back up the stairs.

Raena and Ryan descended the remaining steps to stand next to Cris after Elren had passed by them.

"Lost city adventure time?" Raena asked.

"Oh, yeah." Cris tested the handle on the door and it pulled toward him with a metal screech.

The space was black beyond the reach of the faint light shining through the open door. Cris evaluated the dark depths with a telekinetic assessment, sensing walls and a ceiling similar to the stairwell. However, there appeared to be another door on the far wall and a double door that he suspected led to an elevator shaft on the right side wall. He took a step into the room and found the floor was covered in a layer of dust. The stale air assaulted his senses and he fought the urge to cough.

"Not the least bit creepy," Raena said with heavy sarcasm behind him.

Cris pulled out the storage device from Elren and activated his handheld. "We should probably figure out where we're going."

It took three attempts to wirelessly charge the storage unit enough to extract the data, but within five minutes Cris had transferred the necessary information to his handheld. He transmitted the map to Raena's and Ryan's devices, as well.

"Oh, we're in a parking garage," Raena commented when she examined the map. She pointed to the door in the far wall. "Once we go out here, we should be able to follow the ramps to the surface level."

Ryan activated the flashlight mode on his handheld and approached the door. He yanked on the handle and it swung inward with a groan, releasing a shower of dust. Waving the cloud away from his face, he shined the light into the dark space. "All clear."

Cris held out his hand for Raena to go first and then followed her through the doorway.

The open area beyond was the size of a city block with a gently sloping floor, up on one side and down on the other. Charging ports for vehicles lined each wall. The ground was covered in a layer of dust like in the elevator lobby, which masked all but a few of the painted lines between parking stalls.

They walked three abreast down the ramp, shining their lights ahead and to the sides as they descended. Though there were no other signs of life, Cris occasionally checked over his shoulder behind for good measure.

After fifteen stories, the switch-backing ramp finally leveled out and led toward a broad opening into the enclosed city beyond.

Cris scouted ahead of Raena and Ryan. Outside the garage, a four-lane boulevard stretched as far as his light reached in either direction, sloping down a hill to the left. An eight-story building across the street blocked his view straight ahead, but the other structures along the boulevard began to answer the mystery regarding the city's fate.

The ceiling consisted of a series of interlocking panels right out of a cargo ship manufacturing yard. Structural support columns had been erected alongside the tallest buildings to provide anchor points for the panels. The curved nature of the panels created the appearance of hills they had witnessed from the surface. Cris spotted a distinctive brand on some of the sections; with the aid of the camera zoom on his handheld, he was able to make out the identifier—DGE, Dainetris Galactic Enterprises.

They raided the Dynasty's own foking shipyard to bury the city. He shook his head with disgusted awe.

Ryan grimaced as he stepped into the street next to Cris. "This is a city built for a population ten times what it is today."

"I don't want to think about it." Cris' stomach turned over.

Raena walked up next to Ryan and took his hand. "We need to focus on making sure this never happens again."

Ryan gave a weak nod in response as the group headed down the boulevard toward the location of the Dainetris compound indicated on Elren's map.

The city reminded Cris of the commercial district in Sieten, with a variety of storefronts on the bottom levels of buildings and premium residential space above. After a century and a half, the glass no longer gleamed and foliage had long since died off, but nothing about the environment spoke to why Dainetris had met its sudden end.

Unlike the Sietinen manor that was positioned well outside the city, the Dainetris estate was within the city limits to the south. As they traversed the abandoned streets, though, it became clear why Elren had suggested an alternate entry point. Up ahead, one of the massive support beams had fallen over, taking out several buildings and scattering debris for blocks in either direction. The remaining support beams at three corners of the ceiling segments were enough to support the city above, but if another gave way in the same area, they might be facing a disaster.

"We need to get a repair crew in here," Cris said, his voice echoing slightly in the eerie stillness.

"Think we can climb over the rubble?" Raena asked.

"I'm hesitant to disrupt anything—there's no telling how precarious this structure is," Cris replied.

Ryan consulted the map. "Looks like we don't have another option. The beam and rubble are blocking the entire eastern side up to the wall, and a series of older, smaller building collapses are in this area to the east." He pointed at the image on his handheld. "With the estate here, we may as well take a direct path through this park."

The former greenspace he identified did make for the most direct route, and the smaller number of buildings in the vicinity would likely mean debris had scattered in that area when the column fell. Cris still wasn't crazy about the idea of using telekinesis in such an unstable environment, but they were already committed to the course.

"Okay, we'll try it out," he agreed.

True to the map, they reached the outer edges of the ruins four blocks ahead. Chunks of concrete were interspersed with metal supports and shattered glass.

Cris gingerly picked a path around the larger pieces. As they pressed onward, he had to negotiate a course over piles of rubble, and soon nothing of the ground below was visible. He halted atop one of the piles to survey the area.

Directly ahead, the support column lay at a low angle across their path. With a diameter of seven meters, it was too tall and awkward to easily climb over. The best way ahead was to pass underneath the column near where it was propped up on the base of a toppled building. However, there was presently no person-sized gap through to the other side.

"Looks like some excavating is in order," Cris commented.

"And avoid getting pancaked in the process." Raena flashed a daring smile.

Cris gave her a stern look. "You two stay back. I'll clear the way."

"We've spent plenty of time practicing telekinesis," his granddaughter objected.

Ryan sighed.

"She always likes to take the lead, doesn't she?" Cris said to Ryan, concealing a smile.

"You have no idea," Ryan replied, then hastily added, *"I mean, with this sort of thing. Er..."* He flushed.

Cris shook his head. *"Never mind."* He held up his hand to reinforce his spoken message to stay back and approached the rubble around the fallen column.

The opening was in the crack between two buildings that now braced the column at an angle. Cris reached out telekinetically toward the rubble pile between the buildings and lifted up some of the smaller pieces. Dust filled the air around the site, but the column remained in its resting place.

Next, he began dragging away some of the larger chunks. The other rubble shifted and smaller pieces cascaded down the piles as the concrete chunks came free. He moved slowly, testing the stability of the piles before removing anything completely. Soon, a tunnel was cleared beneath the column.

Cris peered through from a distance. "That should do it."

Ryan watched some fist-sized concrete pieces roll down one of the debris piles next to the new opening. "It's not stable."

"It just needs to hold for a few minutes." Cris hopped off the flat piece of concrete atop the pile where he'd been standing and approached the pathway under the column. "I'll make sure there aren't any barriers on the other side before you come through."

He raised a telekinetic shield around himself as a precautionary measure and moved forward, keeping the light from his handheld cast in front of him. His chest constricted as he stepped underneath the massive column. While its mass was well within his capabilities to manipulate, he didn't trust his reaction time to catch it before it closed the three meter gap above his head.

The tension released as soon as he emerged on the other side. "I'm through!" he called back to Raena and Ryan. "It's much clearer on this side. I can see the wall around the estate."

"We're coming!" Raena replied.

Cris heard footsteps and sliding rubble as the two youths descended the debris pile. Their lights were just beginning the shine through the tunnel when the sound of grating metal pierced the darkness.

The massive column shuddered and crashed toward the ground.

Dust filled the air, and Cris had only his telekinetic senses to try to catch the column.

He was too slow. By the time he had control of the column's mass, it was nearly parallel with the ground. He ran forward with horror, trying to get a better view. "Raena! Ryan!"

No response.

Stars, no! Cris reached out telepathically. There was a presence—strained, but alive.

He was about to call out again when the column suddenly lifted out of his telekinetic grasp, moving up and backward toward where they had come.

As the dust cleared, he saw Raena rising to her feet with Ryan next to her. She waved her hand and the column came to rest on the ground on the far side of her. Her breath was ragged, and Ryan put his arm around her for support.

"Are you okay?" Cris called out as he ran toward them.

"Yeah," Raena managed between breaths. "Wow, that was close."

"I didn't even see it until you'd already pushed me to the ground," Ryan said. "How'd you know?"

"Instinct, I guess." She brushed some dust off her hair and shoulders.

"I should have been holding onto it while you passed under," Cris stammered, his heart still racing.

"Don't worry about it," Raena dismissed.

"We're fine," Ryan said as he dusted himself off, as well.

Cris shook his head. "It was reckless to come here—"

Raena cracked a smile. "In all fairness, we probably would have snuck out and come here without you, so…"

"I don't know what I'm going to do with you two," Cris muttered wearily.

She stepped toward him and patted his shoulder, her breathing once again normal and eyes bright. "There, there. You'll adjust eventually."

Ryan offered a compassionate smile as he passed by Cris after Raena.

Still in the haze of shock, Cris followed them to the main street leading toward the estate. One block up, they passed by one of the few skyscrapers in their immediate surroundings, which reached all the way to the ceiling.

"That must be the Mandelay Street exit," Raena pointed to the building's lobby entry.

The doorway was clear and tracks through the dust indicated that others had traversed it in recent years. Once they had been through the manor, it should be a straight shot to the surface where they could summon the car to meet them.

"I have half a mind to get out now before there's another collapse," Cris said.

Ryan's brow furrowed. "We can't give up now."

He's right. The Priesthood will know we came here and might do another sweep. This is our only chance to see if they missed anything the first time around. "Okay," he yielded. "But take it slow and easy."

A five-meter-tall wall of veined, gray stone surrounded the Dainetris estate, topped with wrought ironwork. The main iron gate through the wall adjacent to the main road was ajar, and the three of them easily passed into the courtyard beyond. A driveway wide enough for two cars led straight through what looked to be former gardens with raised flowerbeds. After more than a century underground, only exposed soil and stone edging remained amid gaps where wood and vegetation had rotted away.

The driveway terminated in a loop around a dry fountain

three meters tall with delicate terraces stacked to give the illusion of a blooming flower. Beyond the fountain, the manor, surfaced in the same veined stone as the surrounding wall, stood three stories and looked to be surprisingly intact despite the fate of its residents. Broad windows and doorways with accompanying terraces patterned the upper level of the manor, and the roof appeared to sport a deck along its length.

"It doesn't even look like there was a fight," Ryan said. "Where did everyone go?"

"Maybe we'll find answers inside," suggested Cris.

They traversed the driveway and ascended a set of three broad steps leading to the entryway.

Cris tried the handles on the double doors and found them locked. There was a biometric scanner next to the door, which he'd normally be able to use his handheld to crack, but there was no power to the building. "I guess we're breaking in."

"Mind if I do the honors?" Ryan asked.

Cris stepped aside. "It's only fitting."

Ryan stood a pace back from the lock and outstretched his hand like a claw, telekinetically gripping the door handle. He pulled his arm back and the handle broke free, allowing the door to swing inward.

With a deep breath, Ryan stepped inside.

The light from his handheld illuminated a double staircase with steps curving around either side of the foyer before meeting on the second floor. An ornate chandelier made of dazzling crystal was suspended level with the second story from a domed ceiling painted in a sky mural above the third story.

Beneath the dust gathered on the floor, through footprints from visitors left by Elren or his comrades, Cris could see the emblem of a red flower inlaid in the white marble at the center of the oval entryway.

Raena brushed the dust aside with the toe of her shoe. "It's the same symbol as on the map."

"That confirms it was the Dainetris crest," Ryan said. "Wow… this is so surreal."

"This must have been gorgeous," Raena commented. "I bet some of this can still be salvaged."

"Maybe," Ryan murmured.

Cris strode across the entryway toward a passage through an inner set of double doors. "I'd love to take in the artistry, but we should get out of here as soon as possible. You can come back after all the structures have been cleared by engineers."

"Right." Raena followed Cris into the passageway, which opened into a reception room consisting of several couches loosely arranged in an arc facing a broad viewscreen on the side wall. "From the outside, this place looks like it's almost as big as the Sietinen manor. Where do we start looking?"

"And I imagine any obvious incriminating information regarding the Priesthood was taken during the purge," Ryan said. "What may be useful?"

I wish I knew. Cris looked around. "Library, maybe?"

"Seems like a good place to start. There's *something* here," Raena insisted. "I know it seems ridiculous to trust some random vision, but the Aesir take it very seriously. I don't understand where those insights come from, but I think we need to believe."

"Wil certainly does. Endorsements from both of you are all I need," Cris told her. "But to answer your question, Ryan, I don't know what to look for."

"Actually, something just occurred to me." Ryan walked up to the wall and felt around the frame of a landscape painting. He wedged his fingertips behind the frame and awkwardly lowered the large canvas to the ground. "This is just a hunch, but it seems like the Priesthood overlooked art during the purge, right? Dainetris didn't know those things would make it through the search, but if they did hide something somewhere that wasn't destroyed or taken, it might be with a painting or sculpture."

Ryan inspected the back side of the painting frame, then shook his head. "But there are probably hundreds of art installations around here. It'll take days to go through everything."

"If there's even anything to find in one of them," Cris said. "There may be a faster way."

"Please do share," Ryan encouraged.

"Well, any data archive of consequence will be digital, and this entire area is effectively dead, electrically speaking," Cris said.

Raena's face lit up. "All we have to do is search for an electromagnetic signature."

"Assuming the battery backups aren't dead, it'd stand out," Cris replied. "Except, there may still be interference from other devices on backup power."

"There's one way to find out." Raena dropped to the floor and crossed her legs. "Give me a minute."

"I can—" Cris began, but his granddaughter held up her finger to stop him.

Cris and Ryan stepped back a dozen paces from her and waited.

Raena's eyes were closed, but her other senses were heightened. Cris detected her consciousness brush past him as she searched through the halls, spanning out in every direction to sweep the manor more quickly than a team of four dozen individuals could accomplish.

I didn't realize she was already this advanced, Cris thought to himself as she worked. *No wonder Wil was okay bringing her to the Aesir.*

The ability to separate consciousness from physical self was a more common skill than the act of spatial dislocation known as 'stopping time', but it was still a rare feat. For her to be able to perform both acts without training and so soon after Awakening suggested a level of aptitude that defied expectations—especially when considering her handling of the fallen column. If Jason was anywhere near as gifted, Wil would have his hands full in the coming years.

After three minutes, Raena's eyes opened and she smiled. "All right, I have four candidate locations." She gracefully rose to her feet.

"Should I verify?" Cris offered.

"It's not like the locations are kilometers apart," she countered. "Let's just check them out."

Cris nodded. "Fine, we can investigate and if we don't find anything I'll try my hand at a search."

"Sounds good," Ryan agreed.

Raena led them down a hall to the left toward a wing

containing offices and conference rooms. The hall terminated in an airy, two-story room that reminded Cris of the main administrative center in the Sietinen estate. Raena's target was a desk in the center of the room.

"Something in here..." she said while crouching down to view the underside of the desk. She slid her hand along the back recesses with a frown. "This all feels like a factory finish."

Cris inspected the desktop, noticing the VComm logo and model information. "Ah, that's what's going on."

His granddaughter looked at him expectantly.

"This was the communications hub for the office," he explained. "They're set up for intensive data processing and transfer, even during a power outage, so the battery backup and capacitors can hold a charge for a lot longer than any other standard equipment—apparently for well over a century. There's nothing hidden around the desk, it's just the equipment itself you sensed."

Raena wilted. "Oh."

"There aren't many setups like this, though. Hopefully, one of the other three leads pans out," Cris said.

With a resolute nod, Raena led them back down the hall.

The next location was also a bust—what turned out to be another communications console with backup batteries for emergencies. Its charge was almost depleted, but there was just enough life left to have caught Raena's attention.

"I'm growing more concerned that the power reserves in a hidden data archive may also have run out," Cris said with a frown. "The theory was a long shot to begin with."

"I have a good feeling about the next one," Raena replied.

"Lead the way." Ryan extended his hand with a flourish.

Raena backtracked to the main foyer and took the staircase on the right.

Their footsteps echoed off the stone lining the room, dust swirling around their ankles. *It's like we've traveled back in time.*

"I'll really need a shower after this," Raena commented as she looked down at the layer of dust on herself.

"That's what you get for rolling around on the floor," Ryan jested.

She grinned. "You might want to look at yourself in the mirror."

Cris tuned out their banter as they walked, instead focusing on the artistic details in their surroundings. Rather than the ostentatious carvings and gold-leafing in the Sietinen estate, the Dainetris aesthetic was more streamlined and elegant. Motifs of sea waves and stars were worked into crown moldings, but in a subtle way that flowed seamlessly with the architectural features. Paintings along the walls depicted a combination of seascapes from dramatic vistas and nebulae. The way the art depicting home and distant worlds played off one another spoke to a balanced perspective about the Dynasty's role.

I think I would have liked them, Cris thought with a twinge of sadness. *I hope I can help guide Ryan to recapture that spirit.*

The hall eventually turned into a residential wing with lounge areas in between closed doors to quarters. Along the walls were several family portraits—Ryan did bear a striking resemblance to many of his ancestors, aside from his darker hair. After having some time in the TSS to move past his youth as a Ward, he was even beginning to carry himself in a manner suited for his birthright. A few more years of coaching and he'd fit the part.

"We're close," Raena said. She broke into a jog toward a door three down on the right.

The room appeared to be an office. Antique paper books had been carelessly strewn around the floor and the desk was overturned. Someone had definitely been looking for something.

Cris followed Raena and Ryan inside, and then he saw that the desk's hard drive had been extracted. A safe inset in the wall was also opened and emptied.

"Looks like they got what they came for," he said.

"That's what they thought." Raena dropped to her knees next to the overturned desk and smoothed some dust from the floor tiles with her hands. "Except there was something hidden in a place they'd never think to look."

She hovered her hands over the tile, telekinetically raising the twenty centimeter stone square from its place in the floor. After setting the tile down next to the opening, she shined the light on her handheld inside a recess.

"Whoa—" Her jaw slack, she reached inside with one hand.

Raena removed a small box twice the size of her fist. It was crafted from white metal, and ruby accents formed a delicate flower on the top.

Could this really be it? Cris rushed to her and she handed him the box.

Cris inspected the object. A compact biometric scanner was inlaid on top of the front latch, likely as a genetic key. "I think this is all you, Ryan." He handed the box over.

Ryan took it and placed his index finger on the scanner. The lid popped open.

Inside, a crystalline data archive was stored with a battery pack.

Cris' breath caught. "I can't believe it."

Raena shook her head with wonder. "If they hadn't put the batteries in there…"

"And that the charge held," Cris added. "A few more years and we'd never have found it."

"Can this be linked to a handheld?" Ryan asked, examining the drive.

"I think so." Cris gingerly took the box from him. "Let's find a table."

They exited to the hall and set up at a small dining table in an adjacent lounge. Cris scanned through the sync options on his handheld and tweaked the settings until he found the right frequency to connect with the archive.

He activated the holographic projector on his device and they waited for the data to load.

The projection morphed into a prompt for a security key.

"Bomax. Any idea what it may be?" Cris asked.

Ryan thought for a moment. "The flower motif is everywhere. What's the species called?"

Cris shrugged. "I have no idea. I'd never seen it before."

Raena stepped away from the table toward a landscape painting depicting the flowers. She positioned her handheld over part of the image. "CACI, what type of flower is this?" she asked the device.

"Stellam matutinam," the digital assistant on her handheld

replied, "a coastal flower native to regions in the northern hemisphere on Tararia. Commonly known as morningstar."

Raena shrugged. "It's as good a guess as any."

"Worth a shot." Cris entered 'morningstar' into the prompt field.

A second later, the projection morphed again. Rows upon rows of files appeared—images, videos, text records. As Cris scanned through the folder names and dates, he realized the entire history of the Bakzen and the Priesthood's interventions in the Taran population was laid out before him.

Raena stared at the projection. "What is all of this?"

"Stars!" Cris breathed. "That's what they were up to."

Ryan examined the file list. "The Dainetris Dynasty was gathering evidence against the Priesthood?"

"And a lot of it," Cris replied. "No wonder the Priesthood took them out so fast. Based on some of these file dates, it looks like one of your ancestors must have come across some overlooked records that survived the purge a thousand years ago. When the Priesthood discovered that they had this information and were planning a disclosure…"

Ryan's face drained. "The Dynasty fell because they were trying to set things right."

All the more reason to honor their legacy. A slow smile spread across Cris' face. "Their sacrifices won't be in vain. This is everything we need."

CHAPTER 11

"I CAN'T BELIEVE it was there the whole time," Wil addressed his father on the viewscreen.

"Clearly, the Priesthood didn't think so, either," Cris agreed. "But we have it now."

I wish I didn't know these things, but that's why we need to make things right. Wil nodded slowly and took a deep breath. "What's our next move?"

"I need to get all of the High Dynasties on board. With this and the other information we've gathered over the years, a unanimous vote is within our grasp."

It had taken two full days for Wil to sort through the information from the crystalline archive, but it was time well spent. Unfortunately, the story he'd teased out so far was grimmer than he could have ever anticipated.

The records traced back more than twelve hundred years, to before the Aesir split from the Priesthood and Tarans were set on their current path. The snippets of videos he'd watched in order to catalogue the data depicted a high-functioning society where telekinesis and telepathy were integrated into everyday life. Teenagers played games involving object levitation, couples shared private conversations in each other's minds even when in the middle of a crowd, and the power distance between the social strata was much lower.

Despite the apparent utopia, though, a sect within the

populace feared stagnation. Tarans were expanding to new worlds, but there had been no major technology advances in centuries and the physical form of Tarans themselves hadn't progressed in a meaningful way in millennia.

In accordance with their doctrine, the Priesthood embarked on a mission to achieve enlightenment. A collection of news articles spoke of ascending to the next state of being by unlocking hidden genetic potential—Wil knew from his conversation decades before with Banks that it must have been the start of the experimentation that led to the disaster of the Generation Cycle.

The Aesir must have left quietly, as there was no official mention of the Priesthood splitting. However, the dates—from what Wil could tell—matched up such that thirty years after the Aesir's departure, there was the first mention of the Bakzen.

Early video and images of the Bakzen showed they bore little resemblance to the hardened soldiers Wil had encountered during the war. These people were nearly indistinguishable from their fellow Tarans, a combination of the most desirable traits with above-average height and enhanced muscle tone. The main distinguishing feature was their sorrel eyes, which glowed as a telling sign of their telekinetic abilities.

Such abilities were where they departed from their fellow Tarans.

Though telekinesis and telepathy were the norm, the strength of those abilities was limited. From what Wil could tell, an average citizen was somewhere around a low-level Trion Agent in their potential. Like with any attribute, the abilities followed a bell curve, with some individuals possessing great potential on par with senior Primus Agents, and others having such weak abilities that rustling a pile of fallen leaves would be a challenge.

The Bakzen were different. Every one of them had four times the aptitude of the most gifted individuals, and they could do anything with those abilities. Many Bakzen were trained as healers to manipulate energy flows within the injured or sick to aid recovery in ways no machine could achieve. Others assisted in labor, moving heavy objects with precision far more economically than would have been possible with heavy construction equipment. And others became soldiers, trained in weaponized telekinesis and advanced telepathic techniques that could quell civil conflicts before a situation could escalate.

For a decade, everyone was at peace. Then, voices of dissent entered the media.

First came the objections to the Bakzen's abilities—speculation about how they could be a danger. The Bakzen replied only with shows of peace, assisting in civil service while refusing any form of compensation. They lived simply in shared housing with only the most basic amenities, grouped by their specialization. With their numbers in mere thousands, most didn't view them as a threat. Those with concerns, however, would not be silenced.

One of the news outlets that had been on the skeptical front since the Bakzen first became public made an offhand comment in an opinion piece about bringing the rest of the Taran population up to the Bakzen's level. Other sources ran with the story, and the pivotal moment seemed to have come in a follow-up interview with a representative from the Priesthood. The reporter asked if it was possible to enhance the abilities of Tarans, and the Priesthood confirmed it could be done.

What the Priesthood didn't say was that those experimentations had been underway since before the Bakzen ever became public knowledge.

The confirmation that the form of Tarans themselves could be changed was met with polarized reactions. Some demanded to be given immediate access to the gene therapies, while others were horrified by the idea.

News coverage only told one side of the story, though. The data archive held one critical piece of information that was more powerful than all the other anecdotal evidence. It contained a detailed accounting of how and where a genetic therapy had been disseminated to the entire Taran population and known worlds—even those no longer recognized as part of the empire—through food, water, and medicine. Self-replicating and transferrable, the nanotech behind the therapy had worked its way to every living and future person within a matter of a decade.

By the time anyone learned of the Bakzen, that process of dissemination was already complete.

The population was unaware of this intervention, of course. But the Priesthood was crafty—they knew some people would begin exhibiting stronger abilities as a result of the genetic therapy, so they instituted public screenings to identify candidates to receive trial treatments. Whenever someone was found to be on the cusp of new abilities emerging, they would be 'selected' for the trial and issued a treatment that was nothing more than a placebo.

This continued for five generations, until the first ability losses emerged as a result of the Generation Cycle. It was only then that the Priesthood realized their mistake, and so the cover-up began.

Everything Wil had learned from Banks lined up with the events that followed—the public disavowal of telekinetic abilities, the Bakzen being ostracized and ultimately forced out, and the new laws banning cloning of sentient beings.

Along with those policy changes had come a radical shift in Taran culture. Technology, language, etiquette—everything had pivoted to favor modes of communication that diminished telekinesis and telepathy rather than having them at the center of the civilization. The Priesthood had to ensure that there were no remaining cultural artifacts of the Bakzen or the abilities the other citizens had lost.

That fate of the Bakzen was much more poignant now that Wil understood that context and had seen footage of them living in peace among his people. They had been kind-hearted and eager to be accepted. Tarans had driven them away and forced them to become the hardened killers he'd faced in the war. The wish for peace the former Bakzen general, Carzen, had expressed had been the one lingering remnant from that shared past.

Now, though, the Bakzen and their culture that could have been was gone. But there was still a chance for overdue justice.

The duplicate of the data archive now in Wil's possession was the collection of everything the Priesthood had sought to destroy—everything that pointed to their selfish interests and disregard for the autonomy of Taran citizens. No one would be able to look at that evidence and still trust the Priesthood as the supposed moral compass for the civilization.

Wil returned his thoughts to the present and the task at hand. "With this information, a unanimous vote to unseat the Priesthood is the only possible outcome," Wil said to his father. "I know you'll be able to get Ryan and Raena positioned how they'll need to be."

Cris nodded. "I don't have any concerns about their political aptitudes. But about Raena…"

Has he figured out just how strong she really is? Wil's chest tightened. "What about her?"

"While we were in the Underground, she did some things."

Wil braced himself.

"One of the columns collapsed, and she caught it."

"What? You didn't say anything about a collapse before!" Wil exclaimed. "You all could have been killed!"

"We got kind of backed into a corner. I didn't realize how unstable things were until we only had one way forward."

Wil glared at him. "I didn't think I'd have to worry about their safety with you."

Cris slumped. "They would have just gone without me. The important thing is everyone's fine."

Arguing won't change anything. Wil took a calming breath. "All right, so what about it?"

"The columns are huge. Well within the capabilities of a Primus Agent, but for her to be so young and the reaction time—it surprised me."

Wil nodded. "She's quite advanced."

"And her aptitude for astral projection…"

"Yeah, the first time I took her out, I was shocked."

Cris evaluated him over the viewscreen. "Is that why you didn't resist when she asked to leave the TSS?"

There were so many things Wil wanted to say regarding his hopes and fears for his daughter, but he didn't know if this was the right time to reveal his suspicions about what the coming years would bring. "It made the most political sense."

His father wasn't convinced, shaking his head. "There's more to it than that. I haven't forgotten her score when you tested her a year ago."

I don't want to lie to him. If I can't be honest with him, then no one. "You're still the only person who knows about that, and I continue to think it's best that it stays that way."

"Kalin is going to figure it out pretty fast once he starts training with Raena and Ryan," Cris pointed out.

"If he has suspicions, he'll keep it to himself. It's one of the reasons I selected him over some of the other volunteers."

"And what about when Raena figures it out for herself?"

"You don't think she already knows?" Wil countered. "When we went to visit with the Aesir, I think that confirmed anything that hadn't already been said aloud."

"My biggest concern is that she thinks she's invincible," Cris said.

"She'll grow out of that with a little more time. That's why I've been much more careful with Jason."

"Any new assessment of if he's as gifted as her?"

Wil shook his head. "Still unclear, but I do think he'll at least be on par with me. I've… put some plans in place."

"What sort of plans?" his father asked.

"To launch a secret training program in weaponized telekinesis."

Cris released a long breath. "I didn't think we were back to that."

"We both know the Priesthood won't go quietly, regardless of the political case against them. We need to be ready," Wil insisted.

"I don't disagree. I just wish there was another way."

"They made this a contest of physical might, and I'll do everything it takes to win."

His father nodded. "You're right. The time for peace isn't quite here yet."

"But soon."

Cris smiled. "Yes, very soon."

— — —

Raena took in the morning view of Lake Tiadon from her terrace, reveling in the warm rays of the sun on her back. During her year in TSS Headquarters, she'd missed being out in the fresh air.

"Beautiful morning," Ryan commented from the doorway.

She looked over her shoulder and smiled at him. "There hasn't been a cloudy day since we got here. This weather control thing is pretty handy."

"Nighttime rain when it's needed and perfect temperatures, I can't complain." Ryan smiled back. He approached her and wrapped his arms around her waist from behind; the privacy of a terrace was one of the few outdoor places where they could risk such a clear demonstration of their relationship.

Raena leaned back against him. "It's still hard to believe that taking care of all this will be our responsibility one day."

"I know. But seeing the Dainetris estate—tangible proof of what the Priesthood did—it's made me all the more committed. I still have no idea how to be a dynastic leader, but I want to learn."

"Me too." She spun around to face him. "For what it's worth, I think you already do know how to be a good leader. You're selfless and kind. Those are the traits you can't readily teach."

"I think there's a little more to it than that."

"You'll do great," she assured him. "And besides, we're in it together."

He gazed into her eyes and tucked a loose strand of hair behind her ear. "How did I get so lucky to have you as a partner?"

"I was just wondering the same thing." She paused. "Too sappy?"

"Not for me." Ryan drew her to him for a kiss.

Raena savored the contact, thankful to be close to her favorite person.

When their lips finally parted, she placed her head on his chest. "We might feel unprepared, but like it or not, we're about to help lead a revolution."

"Yeah, that makes me feel *way* better."

She smiled up at him. "Oh, come on. You have to admit, that's a pretty cool claim to be able to make."

"All right, maybe a little," he conceded with a grin.

"Speaking of which, we should probably get ready to sit in on that SiNavTech board meeting. We've gots learnin's to do."

Ryan chuckled. "I dare you to talk like that in front of the board."

"You jest, but now I'll have to."

He shook his head. "I still can't always tell when you're joking."

"Good, that'll keep things interesting." She gave him another quick kiss. "Now come on—we have some conspiring to do."

— — —

Keeping his extracurricular training a secret was going to be a challenge, but Jason was prepared to do whatever was necessary in the years ahead.

He snuck into the elevator down to Level 11 using the special credentials his father had given him for their covert training. Select members of the Primus Elites would be gathered into their own training groups eventually, but Jason's private practice sessions would be different.

Without having Raena and Ryan around, it'd become even clearer to Jason just how advanced his skills already were relative to the other trainees. The activities in group training felt like childish exercises and he craved more. That wasn't to say his fellow trainees weren't talented in their own right and the activities weren't beneficial, he was just beyond them. He would always be beyond them.

I wish Raena were back here. This would be a lot more fun with someone else, he thought as he exited the elevator. A hollow persisted in his heart for the absence of his lifelong best friend. She had Ryan now, but Jason had been left alone.

It'd be one thing if he was still back on Earth, where he could be just any other teenager—dating, hanging out with friends, going off to college. But within the TSS, he was one of the Sietinen heirs, the son of the High Commander and Lead Agent. Despite Tiff's offer, he imagined it would be unbecoming for him to have a casual girlfriend.

The situation was incredibly unfair when he looked at it in those terms—Raena getting to have sleepovers with her dream guy while Jason was forced into celibacy just because he didn't want to make a lifelong commitment to someone at the age of seventeen.

He tried to suppress the thoughts and his frustration as he approached the designated freefall practice chamber where he was scheduled to meet his father. Bitterness wasn't productive and there was too much at stake to be distracted by such things.

Wil was waiting outside the door, leaning against the wall while he reviewed something on his handheld. "Hey," he greeted as Jason approached. He studied him. "Is everything okay?"

Jason found himself in a moment of weakness. *Should I tell him?* He hesitated. *Keeping these feelings bottled up won't solve the issues.*

"Jason, if there's something bothering you, let me know so I can help," Wil urged.

"Let's talk inside," Jason suggested, gesturing to the door.

His father activated the door and they stepped into the gravity lock.

"Missing Raena?" Wil asked when the hallway door was sealed. He activated the lock and it began to cycle to null gravity.

"That's part of it. We've never been separated for more than a few days before."

"I miss her, too."

"It's more than that, though. Things around here… If I didn't have this special training to look forward to, I'd feel like I didn't have anything to ground me." Just as Jason spoke the final words, the gravity had diminished enough that he began floating up from the floor. "I swear, that timing was *not* intentional."

Wil smiled. "I know what it's like to be an outsider among friends. It can be lonely at the top."

"I get that, and I accept it. Some days, it just kinda sucks."

"I hear ya." His father nodded. "If I hadn't had your mom, I never would have made it through."

The inner door to the practice chamber opened, and they swung inside.

Jason grabbed one of the handholds along the wall near the door. "That's just it—I don't really have anyone to confide in now that Raena's gone. You had Mom, and Raena was totally fine committing to Ryan right away, whether it's from that nanotech messing with her head or something else."

His father didn't quite hide a wince.

"Sorry, Dad, I didn't mean—" Jason tried to explain.

"No, it's a complicated issue. I'm glad Raena and Ryan took their time getting to know one another for that very reason." Wil released a slow breath. "For myself, my conclusion has always been that I love your mom, and now we've spent more than half our lives together. Regardless of what may have drawn us to each other initially, we have a love bond, and that wouldn't go away if the nanotech were to vanish."

"Yeah, I can see what you have together—I don't doubt that." Jason looked down. "I'm just not ready for that kind of commitment myself yet."

Wil's brow knitted. "I hope I never set the expectation you'd find a partner immediately."

"No, you didn't." Jason searched for the words. "More like… I feel I'm in a position where I can't be with *anyone* without it having to be more serious than what I'm looking for. There's almost this unspoken expectation in the family that there's either insta-love or nothing."

Understanding passed across his father's face. "Ah. Hmm."

"I know there's probably not a solution, but it's annoying."

Wil looked pensive. "I suspect the limitations you've established are more self-imposed than anything."

"Right, like you'd be totally okay with it if I decided to work my way through half the Primus Elites."

His father scowled. "Well, that—"

"Okay, that's an overly dramatic example. But it seems like you and Mom and your parents were only ever with each other, and from early on. I feel like I'd be disappointing you if I can't get it right the first time."

"Jason, no." His father looked him in the eye. "All I want is for you to be happy."

"What about expectations for the Dynasty?"

"Keeping alliances among the highborn and all that?" Wil waved his hand dismissively. "As far as I'm concerned, I think it would *help* our political case if you ultimately ended up with someone of non-dynastic birth. Or don't ever marry—not everyone does."

"Seriously?"

Wil shrugged. "Like I said, your happiness means more to me than anything else. If you want to date around, then do it."

That's not how I expected this conversation to go. "Well, thanks."

"Of course." His father smiled warmly. "I'm glad you spoke up. I'd hate to think you were miserable about something completely avoidable."

"Yeah, me too." Jason returned the smile. "I guess I'll see how it plays out." *Maybe I will take Tiff up on that offer, after all…*

"No need to rush anything," his father assured him. "But we do have a ticking clock on some other matters."

"Taking out the Priesthood."

"Precisely."

Jason nodded. "No worries, I know that's the most important thing going on. I won't let anything else distract me from that."

"You don't need to be that rigid. Don't stress out quite yet," Wil countered. "I've been there, and I wouldn't wish it on anyone."

"All right, I'll try to keep it in perspective."

"Good, because the entire Taran civilization is at stake," Wil said with a completely straight face.

Jason's heart leaped. "You just said—"

Wil cracked a smile. "That it's important to remember how to breathe and unwind, even when you're up against incredible odds."

"All right, point taken." Jason relaxed.

"Now, we have some practicing to do." Wil drew himself to the middle of the freefall chamber and Jason followed. "The first skill you'll need to master is astral projection."

"That's what you did with Raena, right?"

His father nodded.

Jason tilted his head. "What for?"

"To keep watch."

"Please tell me you don't intend for us to roam around keeping track of a quarter of the galaxy…" Jason said with a frown.

"It'll be a lot more localized than that. We need to keep an eye on the Rift. If you can become as proficient as me, we can watch over it without having to be physically present. Are you up for giving it a try?"

"Sure. I won't turn down a challenge."

His father smiled. "Good. Now, I find it easier to close my eyes. Clear your mind."

Jason did as he was told. Floating in the chamber, there was little to perceive beyond his own breathing. He could sense his father near him, but everything else was a muted background hum.

"I'm here," Wil's voice sounded in his mind. *"Follow me."*

The voice moved upward, and Jason lunged after it.

He could see again—not the vision of his corporeal eyes, but rather something more insightful. He was outside himself, still within the practice chamber, but looking down at his own physical form. A representation of his father floated nearby, also outside his physical body.

"This is so weird!" Jason exclaimed.

"But kinda cool, right?"

"Totally." Jason thought for a moment. *"Wait, why didn't you use this to check on Raena when she was captured by the Priesthood last year?"*

"Frankly, I was too upset to make an attempt. It requires calm and focus to achieve this state," Wil explained. *"But later on, I did try. They have some sort of shield. I haven't been able to see anything inside the island."*

"This is the ultimate spy tool."

"A skill we must use responsibly," his father lectured. *"Just like with telepathy, we have a code to follow for respecting privacy."*

"Of course."

Wil nodded. *"Now, we're going out. Give me your hand."*

It was then that Jason realized his other-self outside his physical body still looked like him in his mind's eye. He thought about reaching out toward his father's image, and his right arm extended.

Wil grasped it. *"Yes, you can alter how you appear in this state. It's your consciousness—pure energy that's not bound by physical limitations. The default is what's most familiar."*

Jason hadn't meant to share his wonder with his father, but he realized that in their elevated state, his thoughts were open.

"This way." His father led him upward through the Levels of TSS Headquarters, then into the central elevator shaft and out into space.

Jason took in the sight, in awe of the starscape and Earth as he viewed them with new eyes. Everything had a depth and clarity beyond his normal vision, with every feature vivid. It seemed impossible that he could take in so much at one time, but still he yearned for more.

"And there is much more to see," his father replied to the unvoiced request.

They set out to explore the stars, traveling faster and farther than any ship could while still taking in the sights of normal space. They skimmed the divide between physical reality and subspace, not bound to the mechanics of either, but truly free to roam. Star systems zoomed by, and nebulae in a rainbow of colors.

Eventually, their journey took them to the edge of the Rift.

Jason sensed fear and concern emanating from his father. *"The Priesthood will come for this place. We need to keep it safe,"* Wil said.

"Aren't we closing the Rift?"

His father shook his head. *"I thought we were, but when I came here with Raena, I learned something."*

Without warning, Jason felt himself being pulled—not up or over, but through. The stars faded and there was a flash of blue-green light. Then, motion ceased. The sensation disoriented him, but when Jason looked around, he saw the echoed starscape of being within the Rift.

"I'll show you," Wil said, drawing Jason further into the spatial pocket.

Curious, Jason followed.

They stopped just beyond a dark mar near the center of the Rift.

"What is this place?" Jason asked.

"It's the site of the former Bakzen homeworld," his father replied. *"I destroyed it. But when I did, it created a dimensional tear. Both the Priesthood and the Aesir want to control that tear and use it as a power source."*

"Where is it?"

"Look." Wil zoomed their vision toward the center of the darkness.

Jason didn't see anything except blackness at first, but then a point of light came into focus. A sweet well of untapped power called to him, beckoning him inward.

"Don't give in," Wil said. *"There's nothing for us there."* He froze. *"Stars!"*

"What is it?"

Wil shook his head. *"It shouldn't be… The tear has grown. It's only been two months since I last saw it, but this is noticeably larger."*

Jason sensed his father's worry, and he recoiled from the tear. *"What happens if it keeps expanding?"*

"I'm not sure, but I suspect it will become an even greater target—the larger the opening, the more power that can be drawn from it."

"What can we do about it?" Jason asked.

"Train and prepare as best we can," his father replied. *"Only the Aesir could hope to close it, if that's even possible, but they won't come near until the Priesthood is eliminated."*

"And if the Priesthood gets ahold of it instead?"

Wil gazed at the point of light before them. *"They might ascend, and then there'd be nothing we could do to stop them."*

PART 2: REVOLUTION

CHAPTER 12

WIL REVIEWED THE latest reports from the head trainers responsible for the covert training groups within the TSS. The independent units were all progressing ahead of schedule, and most of the Agent cohorts were nearing graduation.

Four years had passed since Raena and Ryan departed for Tararia, and Wil had been busy training Jason and the other Primus trainees with the weaponized telekinesis skills they'd need to hedge their bets against the Priesthood's likely retaliation. Though he'd begun the exercise unsure if they'd be able to engage in the training activities without catching unwanted attention, they hadn't run into any trouble—yet. And since no opposition had presented itself, Wil had decided to not go looking for conflict before they needed to make a definitive move.

Now, they were close to being prepared. When Cris was ready to make his political power play on Tararia, the TSS would be standing by to enforce the High Dynasty's mandates. With their unified force, nothing would stand in their way.

He leaned back in the chair behind his desk in the High Commander's office and smiled. *We might actually win this thing.*

A buzz sounded at his door and Saera entered a second later. "Have a few minutes?" she asked.

"For you, always." He smiled at her.

"Romantic privilege for the win." She grinned and took a seat in one of the visitor chairs across from him.

"What's up?"

"I was thinking about the upcoming CR tests and graduation," Saera said, drumming her fingers on the armrest. "Should Raena and Ryan participate?"

The arrangement for them to continue training on Tararia under the auspice of a TSS Agent—Wil's former Primus Elite trainee, Kalin—had placed the duo in an unusual position. They hadn't been full members of the TSS for the past four years, but they also weren't civilians. TSS custom would dictate they go through the testing procedure, but that wasn't something Wil could allow to occur. If Raena were to be tested, she would no doubt smash the 10 barrier in a matter of seconds, and it was unlikely the testing sphere would fare any better than when Wil had cracked it during his own test decades prior.

Cris remained the only person aside from Wil who was aware of Raena's test from when she first joined the TSS. Now, with his wife eyeing him questioningly, Wil was unsure if this was the right time to come clean.

"You're keeping something from me," Saera said. "Out with it."

I did promise no more secrets. I should have told her years ago. Wil took a deep breath. "I tested Raena—before her first term began."

His wife sat in stunned silence for several seconds. "Why didn't you say anything then?"

"Because your position as Lead Agent would ethically obligate you to making it official record. As it stands now, we can invoke the clause to assign a suitable CR without formal testing."

Saera's brow furrowed as she glared at him through her tinted glasses, then she softened. "I guess that's valid. This is where things get tricky with the division of wife and fellow officer."

"If it were just you as her mother, I would have said something."

She nodded. "It must have been significant for you to want to keep it secret."

"I stopped her at 9.8."

"Whoa! And before classes even started?"

"Exactly."

"Huh." Saera slumped back in her chair. "What can she do now?"

"Kalin kept things by-the-book with the training. I suspect, however, that she'd be able to do anything Jason can with very little coaching."

"I guess that's not bad backup to have."

"No, we're not tapping her for this fight. I didn't tell her what she scored because I want her to focus on Tararia. The three of us can handle the TSS."

Saera inclined her head. "All right. Then, like you said, we'll assign a rank. What do you think?"

"I say we give both Raena and Ryan 9.3s and call it good."

She looked surprised. "That's all?"

"It's more about sending a message than factual accuracy at this point," Wil replied. "A 9.3 is advanced without overstepping the current senior officers."

"Raena will know she's being under-scored," Saera pointed out.

"But if my father has done his job, she won't care."

"That's true," his wife conceded.

"Besides, the moment she's sworn into an official political role, a TSS commission will become nothing more than a résumé entry."

Saera shook her head. "I can't believe we're this close. Finally!"

"We've done our part," Wil replied. "Now we wait."

— — —

Long shadows stretched across the landscape outside Raena's office window as she completed her tasks for the day.

The office was four meters square, making it cozy enough to work alone while not being cramped when she had visitors. Her wooden desk was parallel with the side wall, affording her a view out the back window and of the door. She enjoyed staring out at the lush gardens of the Sietinen estate whenever she had the opportunity to take a break from the affairs of politics and business that had become her day-to-day life. While she had no regrets about following that path, there were days when she wished for a vacation to journey amongst the Taran worlds.

When everything is in order here, we'll have to take a trip. It will give us a chance to connect with the people in the Outer Colonies who've lost faith in Taran authorities. The thought brought a smile to her lips and she gazed up into the sky. *That future isn't so far off.*

She was pulled from her reverie by a knock at the door. Before it opened, she knew it was Ryan—a happy tingle running through her core as their bond responded to the proximity.

"About time," she greeted. "When you said it was going to be a quick meeting, I thought it would be fifteen minutes, not five hours."

He came into view as the door swung open, appearing confident and assured compared to the young man she'd first met. His dark gray suit was more formal than his usual daily attire, but his movements were fluid and natural. "Apparently, there are way more models of robotic welders than you would ever imagine." He swung the door closed behind him.

"Why am I not surprised?" She rose from her desk and smoothed the jacket of her dark blue pantsuit as she walked over to meet Ryan in the center of the room. "I'm sure you made an excellent selection."

"And I'm also sure it would have been just fine no matter which one we picked." He gave her a light kiss.

"Come, now, that's no way to talk about your future company!" she jested. "Picking your robotic minions is a very important business decision."

"It's not mine yet. That'll still have to be negotiated." He sat down in a chair across the desk from her as she returned to her seat.

"It'll happen," she assured him.

"I guess we'll know soon enough."

Raena perked up. "Wait, you have an update?"

"Your grandfather should be here any minute."

Right on cue, there was another rap on the door and Cris poked his head in. "Is this a good time?" he asked Raena.

"Sure is. I've just been informed there might be news," Raena replied.

"Indeed." Cris swung the door open the rest of the way and Kate followed him inside.

"Hi, pull up a chair," Raena greeted, gesturing to the extra seating around a small conference table in the corner by the window.

Her grandparents gathered around her desk next to Ryan, looking somewhat more drained than their typical energetic demeanors.

"So, what's the news?" Raena prompted.

"I just had an interesting chat with my brother," Kate said. "He heard that Byron Monsari might be retiring early."

"That's good, right?" Ryan said. "He publicly detests people with abilities."

"Unfortunately, not good news," Cris replied. "He may detest us, but his successor, Celine, loathes, abhors—"

"I'm not sure if those words really have a hierarchy on a hate scale," Raena cut in.

"Well, whatever it is, it's worse," Cris concluded. "Byron is in the 'avoid us whenever possible' category and Celine is 'execute them all for being abominations'."

Raena scowled. "People like that really exist?"

"They are few in number but mighty in conviction," Kate said with a sigh. "Either way, if we want any chance of a unanimous vote, we should try before Byron leaves office."

"Even with all our evidence, you think Celine would still vote in favor of the Priesthood?" Ryan asked.

Kate scoffed. "Considering that the Priesthood's interventions, regardless of the underlying motivations, resulted in fewer people with abilities—she'd probably laud them and ask for more."

"Except the High Priests themselves have abilities and want to grow that power," Raena objected.

"Hypocrites turn a blind eye when it suits them," Cris said. "This wouldn't be the first time."

Raena groaned. "Fair enough. What's left to do?"

"We've laid all the groundwork we can with the other High Dynasties," Kate said. "The biggest outstanding item is restoring Dainetris' voting rights."

"Meeting with the citizenship council," Ryan supplied.

Cris nodded. "We simultaneously present a case for restoring the Dainetris name and joining the Dynasty with Sietinen."

What a terribly romantic way to think about getting married. Raena's gaze flitted between her grandparents and Ryan. "I take it we're talking about a private, civil ceremony rather than a big party?"

"The more secretive, the better," Cris replied. "Once we move ahead, things are going to progress very quickly."

"You ready to get hitched?" Raena asked Ryan privately.

"I have been for a long time," he replied. *"It feels like it happened years ago."*

"All right, we're ready when you are," Raena acknowledged.

"Okay," Cris agreed. "I'll make the final arrangements."

— — —

Jason slipped out of the study room a minute after Tiff. It wasn't the most becoming for two Junior Agents—especially members of the Primus Elites—to be sneaking around for random hookups, but over the last four years, either no one had noticed or they simply didn't care.

The relationship was exactly what Jason had hoped to find—a companion to help release the tensions of a difficult training day without emotional entanglements to cloud his judgment. He cared about her, certainly, but in the same way he regarded all his closest friends in the TSS. She felt the same way, as far as he could tell, and so what had begun as a fling had turned into an ongoing arrangement. They'd both spent time with other people in the first year or so of their relationship, but they kept coming back to each other. Now, while they were still free to see others if they wished, Jason was far too busy with training to take an interest in anyone else.

He returned to the Primus Elite quarters at a slow pace, providing ample time for Tiff to get settled in before he arrived. While he strolled, he took the opportunity to run through his to-do list for the evening, including an update on the dimensional tear for his father.

Over the years, they'd developed a system to measure the size of the tear to track its progression. Fortunately, the initial expanse rate his father had observed hadn't continued, and it was still small enough to not pose an imminent threat beyond its obvious appeal to the Priesthood. TSS guards posted around the Rift would make sure no one could get close enough to gain access.

With his task list mentally organized, Jason closed the final distance to his quarters and palmed open the door. Inside, half a dozen of the Primus Elites were watching a video on the main viewscreen. Tiff was perched on the arm of one of the couches chatting with Adaline, and she bobbed her head in acknowledgment as he entered.

"Hey," Liam greeted from the couch. "Have you checked your email in the last half-hour?"

"No, why?" Jason replied.

"Better look." His friend returned his attention to the video.

Curious, Jason hurried through the common area to his bedroom.

Gil was in the room, and he looked up with excitement from his tablet when Jason appeared in the doorway. "We're graduating!"

"We are?" Jason pulled out his handheld from his pocket as he sat down on the foot of his bed.

There was a message from the Lead Agent addressed to the Primus Elites as a group that they had become eligible for graduation and would soon complete formal CR testing.

"This doesn't make sense." Jason shook his head. "What about internships?"

Gil shrugged. "Beats me, but I won't complain."

Jason opened a chat feed with his father via his handheld. >>Graduating? Seriously?<< he wrote.

A reply came back several seconds later, >>If you want to

chat, come to my office.<<

>>On my way,<< he wrote back and stood up. "I'll be back in a few," he told Gil while heading back toward the door.

"Getting the inside scoop?" Gil asked.

"What good are perks if you never use them?" Jason smiled.

Tiff raised a questioning eyebrow as Jason walked back through the common area but said nothing.

He took the elevator up to Level 1 and traversed the familiar hall to his father's office.

The door was ajar when he arrived and Jason let himself in. "What's the deal?" He closed the door behind him.

Wil rose from his desk and walked around it to lean against the front. He crossed his arms. "In short, we're out of time."

"Things are ready on Tararia?"

"Almost," Wil acknowledged. "A matter of weeks, if that."

Jason released a long breath. "Okay then."

His father nodded. "This means it's probably time for you to have that overdue chat with the Aesir."

"I guess it is."

"Are you ready?"

"Yes." Jason smiled. "Let's do this."

CHAPTER 13

"JASON, IT'S TIME."

His father's words pulled Jason from his reverie in the TSS spaceport above the moon. The Aesir had arrived and his test was about to commence.

"I'll come with you," Wil offered again.

Next to him, his mother's face was lined with concern, but Jason could tell she already knew his answer wasn't going to change.

"Like I said before, you need to finish getting everything ready here," Jason insisted. *I'll finally get to see the Aesir face-to-face. Years of preparation and anticipation for just a few hours with them...*

His father wrapped him in a warm embrace. "See you soon."

As soon as he was released, his mother hugged him. "We're anxious to hear about what you see. We'll be ready to act."

"Save me some dinner," Jason said with a smile, giving them a wave while he turned to walk down the concourse.

His smile faded as he caught sight of the Aesir ship pulling into docking position, his expression transforming to serene contentedness. Even from a distance, he could sense the soothing energy of the vessel his sister and father had spoken about. It resonated with him and set him at ease.

"Join us," a chorus of voices sounded in his mind. Their power struck him, but they were also welcoming. *"We have been*

waiting for you."

More excited than nervous, Jason ascended the gangway as soon as the ship had docked. Its side hatch was open, and a figure robed in black was waiting for him at the entry portal.

"Hello, Jason Sietinen. I am Dahl," the robed man greeted, inclining his head. "At last we meet."

"I wished to come when you tested my sister," Jason replied.

"The time had not yet come for your vision," Dahl replied. "We hope you will now be able to guide us in what must be done."

"I hope so, too." Jason swallowed. *No pressure—just everyone counting on me.*

"You will only see what is written in the pattern," Dahl stated. "If it was not meant to be seen, then it won't be."

"And if I see nothing?"

Dahl hesitated. "Then we will take that as it comes."

The Oracle led Jason through the ship to an observation room that matched his sister's description. The transparent, curved walls and floor made Jason feel like he was walking amongst the stars, though after experiencing astral projection, it was still a far cry from the real thing.

Half a dozen other Oracles were already in the observation room, standing in a semi-circle. Jason bowed his head in greeting, but the robed figures didn't acknowledge the gesture, their faces hidden in the shadows of their hoods.

A vibration underfoot was the only warning before the view outside the viewport transformed into the ethereal blue-green light of subspace. Jason watched the swirling colors while trying to study the Aesir. The entire transit time, they remained motionless and impassive. Dahl seemed calm and unworried, so Jason took it as a good sign that everything was going to plan.

After fifteen minutes, the Aesir ship dropped out of subspace. Looming outside the ship was a dark maw in the surrounding starscape. *The nexus.*

It was every bit as awe-inspiring as Raena had described. He felt its pull—drawing him to see his truth that must be shared.

"You are aware of the procedure," Dahl stated, breaking the silence. "Proceed when ready."

Jason took a deep breath and cleared his mind. *This is easy. I've done it hundreds of times.*

He stared into the black maw and released his consciousness from himself, keeping a single thread connected to his physical form. The blackness surrounded him. He was a single spark within the void.

Light extended from him, illuminating the silvery threads underlying the fabric of reality. The threads wove through one another and shivered as energy coursed through them.

Jason zoomed outward to gain a better vantage of his surroundings, revealing that the nexus was near the core of his home galaxy. A presence he identified as the Aesir had been woven into the energy pattern in that place, though their signature was still new compared to the ancient fabric itself. Yet, it fit—there was a path for their future.

As he took in the sight, Jason felt content. Things were as they should be.

However, a chill began to seep throughout his being. He looked to the distant horizon along the threads of the energy network and saw a darkness creeping forth. It twisted and corrupted the threads as it advanced, breaking down all that was peaceful and good. Nothing could stop it, and it would all happen too quickly for anyone to act.

Jason tried to trace the darkness back to its source. He strained, searching, but there was no origin in sight.

Then, it came into focus. The darkness was seeping through the dimensional tear—but not just from the tear, corruption had also begun to overtake the Aesir's position that had once been in balance.

No, but the Priesthood are the enemy! Jason's heart raced in his body somewhere far away. *We need the Aesir to help us. They can't be a threat, too!*

The darkness continued to advance, consuming everything in its path. Worlds along the thickest corridors of the energy network disintegrated, energy tendrils dissolving into nothingness as the pattern was undone. The universe was dying.

Jason searched for the meaning in his vision. *If the Aesir are allowed access to the dimensional tear, will that lead to all our destruction?*

That didn't make any sense. They had lived in such harmony, had such respect. And moreover, granting them access to the tear was the key condition for gaining their help to take down the Priesthood.

There has to be another way. Jason yearned for an alternative, willing some alternate path to emerge.

The vision faded into darkness yet again.

Silvery tendrils illuminated in the darkness. Again, he saw the Aesir in harmony, but this time, there was another presence on the horizon. The tear remained, but it was controlled. A sentry guarded it. The sentry seemed so familiar, but Jason couldn't place an identity.

The order and natural integration extended beyond the Aesir's realm to the rest of the Taran worlds. Energy channels between even the Outer Colonies had been strengthened into lasting connections between the worlds. Tarans were unified and prosperous.

Unlike the previous vision that had a sense of imminent danger and urgency, this new vision was of a far future—what could be if all the right actions were taken.

How do we make this future? The outcome was everything Jason hoped to achieve. To have the result placed before him without knowing the means to reach it was torturous. He clawed at the vision, trying to rip it apart and see what lie underneath.

The vision distorted like a reflection on the surface of a pond as he stripped through the layers to find answers. *How do we take out the Priesthood? Where will they attack us? We need details for the here and now!*

No hidden truth was buried beneath the vision—only a vague pattern of the interlocking energy conduits. The threads were meaningless to his eye and he cried out silently in his mind with frustration. *I've failed… I haven't seen what we need.*

Jason returned to his physical body, leaving behind the nexus and its cryptic secrets. He'd need to find another way to discover the path ahead.

Dahl and the other Oracles were watching him expectantly when Jason opened his eyes.

"What did you see?" Dahl asked.

Jason's heart skipped a beat. *I can't trust them. I can't say anything.* "Take me home," he demanded. "I finished your test, I made it out. You can't keep me here."

"Why do you now fear us?" questioned Dahl.

Jason tried to suppress his thoughts, but the vision was too raw on the surface of his mind. "You make your intentions sound so honorable, but you crave power just like anyone else."

Dahl raised his eyebrows with surprise. "None have spoken about the Aesir in such a manner."

"I have a habit of calling things like I see them," Jason replied. *Anyone is tempted by power. There is no pure intent.*

"And is this your own conclusion or something the nexus revealed?"

"A little of both."

"This perceived truth makes you wary. Why?"

"I know my father had an agreement with you," Jason said. "I'm not sure that was the right call."

"You now want to change the terms?"

Jason stared down the Oracle. "I want what's best for the Taran civilization as a whole. I don't know you, so I can't trust you."

"I have lived sixty of your lifetimes. Do you question that wisdom?"

"Age doesn't automatically make you wise. You've hoarded technology and hidden away in a rift. Now you seek to possess an energy source that you claim is too powerful for the Priesthood to get their hands on—but it's totally okay if you do? Yeah, I'm going to be a little skeptical."

The slightest smile touched Dahl's thin lips. "This gives us much to reflect on."

"That's all you have to say?"

"Perhaps I am too old and my mind moves slowly," Dahl replied. "I will withhold comment until I know the right words."

With that, Dahl and the other Oracles spun around and left Jason alone in the observation room.

They're just going to leave me in here? He had a momentary flash of concern that there was a hidden airlock in the room, but then he felt the telltale vibration of a jump initiating and the vessel slipped into subspace.

He kept an eye on the door throughout the jump in case one of the Oracles returned, but there was no sign of movement.

The ship dropped back into normal space after fifteen minutes and maneuvered into docking position with the TSS spaceport. As soon as a shudder ran through the ship, indicating the docking clamps were in place, a chorus of voices in Jason's mind finally broke the silence.

"You are home. Leave us."

He stood his ground. *"I shouldn't doubt you,"* he replied. *"We need to work together."*

"You spoke your truth." The presence of the voices vanished.

A moment later, the door to the hallway slid open and Jason felt a shock behind him, driving him toward the door. He took the hint and followed the corridor to the lift up to the exit.

No Oracles were to be seen.

If I messed this up for us… He took a shaky breath. "Be well," Jason said in parting and left the ship.

He descended the gangway slowly, thinking through how to recount the events to his parents. They would no doubt be eager for a full report of good news from him about precise plans for defeating the Priesthood and all the answers to the questions that had gone unanswered for the last four years. Instead, he had nothing but some vague feelings and very well may have ruined the one alliance that could save them if it came down to a full-on firefight.

Wil was waiting for him on a bench midway down the concourse, but Saera must have gone back into Headquarters.

"How'd it go?" his father asked.

"I'm sorry. I think I pissed them off," Jason replied.

"What makes you say that?"

"I questioned their motives. Dad, something isn't right. They're keeping something from us."

"What?"

Jason shook his head. "I don't know, exactly. It had something to do with the dimensional tear. We can't trust them with it."

"I don't know that there's anything we can do about it. My

instinct tells me that closing it is beyond my capability."

"Maybe yours alone, but with Raena and me…"

His father nodded. "Maybe."

"I dunno. I can't point to a specific vision, but there was this feeling… If we hand over the Rift to the Aesir, something bad will happen."

"All the same, things might be ugly if we cross them," Wil said. "Maybe there's some compromise that will rise to the surface and we just can't see it at the present."

"I hope so." Jason took a calming breath. "I should have just kept my mouth shut. If this makes them back out from helping us with the Priesthood…"

Wil's face paled. "I can't even consider that possibility."

"Me either." Jason groaned. "Now I get what Raena meant when she said it would take time to process the visions. I always expected it to be one, clear image."

"Well, what did you see?"

Jason explained his series of visions as best he could while Wil listened silently, nodding on occasion. When he was finished, Jason let out a long sigh. "I've let everyone down."

"This test of the Aesir's is hardly an exact science. It was a shot in the dark to think you'd be able to give us all the answers," his father replied.

"Now I've just raised more questions."

"You alerted us to a potential concern," Wil assured him. "If Dahl said it was something they'd think about, I have to trust that they will reflect on it with good intentions."

"And if they don't show up to help us when we need them?"

"Then it wasn't a very strong alliance to begin with. I'd rather be on our own and need to work out a solution than find ourselves in a more dangerous situation long-term. Whatever you saw when looking into the void, you saw it because it's what needed to be seen."

It doesn't feel that way. Jason only shook his head in response.

"The most important thing is you made it back unscathed," his father continued. "We'll take the rest as it comes."

"You're surprisingly calm, considering what I just said."

Wil chuckled. "When you've been through what I have, it's

easy to keep things in perspective."

Jason shrugged. "I guess you'd have to."

"And with that said," Wil crossed his arms and eyed Jason, "there's the matter of what to do about your graduation."

"There are standard procedures..."

"Yeah, for typical Agents. You may have noticed, but you're not exactly at the same level as everyone else."

"Well, *you* went through standard CR testing," Jason pointed out.

"And I broke the testing sphere in the process—and let me tell you, those things are *expensive* to repair. I've always felt a little badly about that." He paused. "We have two options. One, you can go through the testing and I'll stop you at a 12.0 so the sphere doesn't break. Or two, we can agree on a number and you can skip testing."

"What are you doing for Raena?" Jason asked. "At least, I assume she's still getting a rank since she never officially left the TSS."

"The Lead Agent and I agreed she and Ryan will both receive 9.3s. Raw strength aside, they haven't been through the training program to justify senior placement in the command ranks," his father said. "You, however, have."

"So, what, you'd just assign me a... 12?"

Wil smiled. "I was thinking more like 13.7, same as me. Near as I can tell, we're evenly matched—I know that number isn't exactly accurate for me, but comparable is comparable."

Jason eyed him with skepticism. "In other words, if I don't get tested, I'll actually have a higher score on record?"

"Correct."

"Fine, I'll take it." *No one else will be happy about it, but whatever.*

"You get automatic seniority regardless, so this way is safer and easier for everyone."

Jason nodded. "I don't want to usurp you and Mom, though."

"Well, that's good, because we're not quite ready to retire."

"Have at it."

"Very well." Wil extended his hand. "Congratulations, Agent Sietinen."

CHAPTER 14

STEPPING INTO THE chambers of the Taran Citizenship Council may as well have been walking into another world. Ryan sensed the elders' eyes on him, wondering about the reason behind this secretive after-hours meeting called by the Head of Sietinen.

Cris and Kate appeared calm as ever, but Raena at Ryan's side emanated nervous energy.

"I should be the nervous one, not you," he said to her.

"You were at least born on this planet. They still have legal authority to refute my claim."

Ryan tried not to think about the fact that the council was technically an extension of the Priesthood—the section of the government outside of and superseding the High Dynasties, which was intended to serve as a neutral third party in disputes. Regardless of their failure to act in that capacity, they still held the power to stop any motion in its tracks if they deemed it prudent.

"Thank you for granting us audience," Cris spoke to the council.

"Your request was quite unusual," the council leader at the center of the semicircle of the five members replied. They sat behind a raised podium, faced with dark-stained wood. She eyed Cris with interest. "We have gathered, as you wished, without public notice. What is the business you bring?"

"There are two matters," Cris began. "The first entails the

ratification of my granddaughter as my legal heir to Sietinen."

The man on the right end of the semicircle raised an eyebrow. "You have already named your son, Williame, as your heir."

"That was before Raena's birth," Cris replied. "Raena is now twenty-one years of age, old enough to be legally confirmed."

"This act would bypass Williame's rights to be named Dynastic Head," the lead councilwoman stated. "Are all parties in agreement on this?"

"I have spoken with my father," Raena jumped in, "and he has expressed a desire to focus on the TSS. I came to Tararia four years ago to begin learning about the Taran people and how I might be an honorable and worthy leader for them. I wish to commit to that path."

"And you would name her as your sole heir?" the councilwoman asked Cris.

"Yes," he replied.

The councilwoman looked down at her desktop. "The official filing is in order. My only reservation regarding this revised succession plan is if it's in the Taran civilization's best interest."

"I'm inclined to agree," the councilman to her left chimed in. "There is no doubt about Raena's legitimacy as a Sietinen heir, only her readiness to be in direct line for succession. She's of legal age, yes, but still highly inexperienced—both in terms of leadership and our culture."

"While her upbringing may have been unconventional, she's proven herself in the last few years. She has shadowed me for hours every day for the last four years, and I feel confident she has the knowledge and aptitude to be successful in that role, should she unexpectedly need to assume the position," Cris countered.

"A moving testimony, but it does not change the facts of the matter," the lead councilwoman stated.

"Then how must I prove myself?" Raena asked.

The councilwoman was silent for several seconds. "It is not a matter of proving worth, in my mind, but rather a question of why—why do you seek this change now, so formally? Is it connected to your other secret business?"

Ryan swallowed. *Having Raena confirmed before presenting*

my case was always the crux of our plan. Without that, everything will fall apart if they try to deny me.

"I would rather address the two matters independently," Cris replied on Raena's behalf.

"This is all rather suspicious," the councilman on the right said. "I move to withhold vote of Raena's confirmation until all pending business has been openly stated to the council."

"Seconded," the woman on the left end said.

The two other council members cast their affirmative vote.

"The motion passes," the councilman declared. "Now, what is your second order of business?"

"We don't have a choice," Kate told everyone. *"We have a solid case. Just state the facts."*

Cris cleared his throat. "Several years ago, before I assumed the position of Head of Sietinen, I came across some information with the potential to dramatically change the course of the Taran political system."

"Such as?" the councilman on the right prompted.

Cris fixed him in a level stare, then swept his gaze across the council. "That the Dainetris Dynasty has a living heir."

The woman on the left audibly gasped, and the others' eyes widened with bewildered shock.

"That's hearsay without physical evidence," the lead councilwoman said after taking several seconds to recover.

Ryan's heart raced. *If they're questioning Raena's readiness to lead, what will they have to say about me?*

"We have all the evidence we need," Cris replied. He gestured to Ryan for him to step forward. "Ryan Pernelli, as he's been known, was born to Marie Pernelli and a traveling merchant almost twenty-five years ago. At the age of five, the Priesthood took him from his mother and he was assigned as a Ward of the Sietinen estate. However, when we met five years ago, his genetic analysis told a very different story. Ryan's father was, in fact, Jason Bankris, and Marie Pernelli was a direct descendant of the Dainetris Dynasty."

The council members looked to one another.

"Step forward," the councilwoman said. "We must verify these claims."

I have nothing to worry about. I'm exactly who I claim to be. All the same, Ryan's gut clenched. Ever since he had been informed of his true birthright, part of him had still held onto his old identity. Through this formal presentation of himself as a Dainetris heir, that entire past would truly become a distant memory—no more moments of being an anonymous former Ward who could blend into the background. He'd be front and center, both as the Head of his own High Dynasty and soon-to-be husband to the heiress of another.

His knees felt like they were about to buckle as he stepped forward to address the council. "I…" The word was barely audible. He took a deep breath. "I present myself to you as Ryan Dainetris, heir to the seventh High Dynasty and rightful executive of DGE and all its assets."

Under the intense gaze of the council members, Ryan held out his right hand, palm up.

The lead council woman inclined her head, and a compartment in the front of the podium opened. The metal implement had a sharp, gleaming tip, which Ryan recognized as a mechanism to extract a blood sample for genetic analysis.

He placed his hand on the device. It pricked his finger and drew a drop of blood, then a cool tingle replaced the sting and the wound was instantly healed.

Ryan removed his hand. "Once you receive confirmation, I wish to receive an official Mark."

"Two minutes," the councilwoman replied.

The seconds passed by at an excruciatingly slow pace. Behind Ryan, the three Sietinens stood rigid and alert, ready to take defensive action should the council turn against them for any reason. On paper, duty as a neutral third party was one thing, but these individuals could have more loyalty to the Priesthood than the moral good.

Finally, a soft tone sounded and the council members all turned their attention to the desktop displays in front of their stations.

The lead councilwoman looked from her desktop to Ryan slowly, her face painted with wonder and confusion. "It appears you do speak the truth."

"How is this possible?" the man on the left exclaimed. "Trickery!"

"The test is infallible," the previously silent man next to him countered. "Despite the odds, this young man is genuinely a rightful Dainetris heir. Since his mother has not put forth an official claim for the title, all rights of ascension pass to him as the first claimant."

"The laws are clear," the lead councilwoman concurred. "Ryan Dainetris, you are hereby entitled to all rights afforded as a Head to one of the Taran High Dynast—"

"I object!" the man on the right shouted. He bolted to his feet and leaned forward on the desktop, glaring at Ryan. "Dainetris fell for a reason. Living heir or not, that Dynasty no longer exists."

"Councilman, that is not the way of the law," the woman in the center said in a calm but firm tone. "Return to your seat."

"I answer to a higher order." The man began to reach inside his robe.

Before he'd moved more than an inch, he flew up into the air, his arms and legs spread to the sides. A pulse gun fell from a hidden holster within his robes.

Members of the council looked on with slack jaws as the man struggled against invisible telekinetic bonds. "Put me down!" he demanded.

Raena stepped forward to stand next to Ryan. "What orders are higher than Taran law?"

"You shouldn't be using abilities like this!" Ryan exclaimed in her mind. *"It's illegal."*

"Regulations state that any TSS Agent trainees facing physical threat may legally take defensive action," she replied. *"You're welcome."*

The councilman squirmed in the air but made no attempt to reply.

Raena took another step toward him. "What orders do you follow?" she repeated.

"I only serve the Priesthood," the man said at last.

The other council members studied him for several seconds, and the man closest to him leaned over in his chair to pick up the dropped weapon. He handed it to the lead councilwoman.

She stared at the object with distaste. "Our duty is to answer to no one but the law," the councilwoman declared. "If you're unable to remain an objective interpreter of the law, then you have no place on this council." The woman turned to Raena. "Please lower him. I will have him escorted from the premises."

"Before that," Cris interjected, "we must present some other critical information regarding the Priesthood. I fear the corruption we have just witnessed on this very council extends throughout our government and traces back centuries."

The councilwoman looked to her counterparts and they nodded. "You have spoken nothing but truth to us thus far. Please, present your evidence," she stated, then looked at the former councilman still floating awkwardly in the air. "Could you detain him elsewhere?"

Raena levitated the man from the central dais and gently set his feet on the ground in the front corner where it would be easy to keep an eye on him. "Each of the four of us could stop you in a millisecond, so don't try anything," she said.

He glared at her but remained motionless.

Ryan released an unsteady breath he hadn't realized he was holding. *"Thanks,"* he told Raena.

She flashed a smile back at him. *"Anytime."*

"Now, your evidence?" the councilwoman prompted Cris.

"Right. I have a list of charges and documentation of the acts for you here." Cris produced four of the five small-scale tablets he'd brought in a travel bag and handed one to each of the council members.

They spent five minutes scrolling through the information before the councilwoman on the left broke the silence. "These are very serious charges of subterfuge."

"Indeed, and charges I do not take lightly," Cris replied. "However, as Head of Sietinen, I have a responsibility to care for my people's best interests. Restoring the voting rights of Dainetris will remove the Priesthood's position as a tie-breaking vote and offer a chance for addressing these persistent issues."

"We can restore the Dainetris name," the lead councilwoman said, "but the assets are a matter for the High Dynasty's corporations to address. This council has no power to demand redistribution."

"SiNavTech is prepared to hand over our ship manufacturing division to the rightful ownership of DGE," Cris stated.

"And I have authority to speak on behalf of my brother, Head of Vaenetri," Kate added, "VComm has committed to return the assets gained through capital sale of DGE holdings—with interest. The current cash value of those assets is approximately twelve percent of VComm."

"Those are significant contributions," the lead councilwoman replied. "Are these agreements in writing?"

"They will be as soon as this council affirms there's a Dainetris heir to receive them," Kate assured.

The councilwoman nodded. "Very well. Ryan Dainetris, step forward to receive your Mark."

At the front of the podium, the machine that had extracted Ryan's blood sample folded back inside and was replaced by another contraption with a curved acrylic platform the size of Ryan's forearm and another metal component arching above.

"Place your left hand on the device, palm up," the councilwoman instructed.

Ryan put his wrist in position. A needle plunged down from the upper arch into his skin, and then other components began to whir as a purple light passed over his wrist. With the passing of the light, the emblem of a flower began to take shape, glowing slightly just above the surface of his skin. Within seconds, the imprinting was complete and the light deactivated. The Mark was completely invisible to the naked eye. He removed his arm from the device.

The councilwoman folded her hands on the desktop. "Congratulations, Ryan Dainetris. May you have a long and prosperous reign."

"Thank you," he responded. *That's it? I'm an official Dynastic Head now?*

"Regarding the previous matter," the councilwoman continued, "I vote to confirm Raena's nomination as Sietinen heir."

Next to Ryan, he could see Raena fighting to keep a grin at

bay.

The other council members confirmed the nomination, as well.

"The request has been ratified," the councilwoman stated. "Do you have any other business to present?"

"No, that's all. When will these changes become public record?" Cris asked the council.

"Meeting minutes will be filed in the morning," the lead councilwoman replied. She looked to the councilman standing in the corner. "I suspect other news will travel more quickly."

"I hadn't anticipated a Priesthood mole on the council. We'll have to act fast," Cris said to Ryan and the others. *"Faster than we'd planned."*

Ryan placed his right hand over his wrist bearing his new Mark. *"Then let's do it—tonight, before the Priesthood has all the details."*

Raena nodded. *"I agree."*

"Your parents are going to hate we're doing this without them..." Cris said.

"They'll understand," Raena replied.

Ryan took a deep breath and addressed the council. "Thank you. I'll try to be a good leader for Tararia."

The council members inclined their heads and the councilwoman smiled at him. "May the stars be with you."

— — —

As soon as Raena had handed over custody of the rogue councilman to a complement of Tararian Guard soldiers, she raced with her grandparents and Ryan back to their shuttle.

"I can't believe a councilman would be stupid enough to pull a gun on us!" she exclaimed while they ran. *"Was that all him, or was he acting directly on the Priesthood's orders?"*

"No way of knowing," Kate replied. *"But I'm certain I don't want to be anywhere near here."*

Cris grimaced. *"If we weren't already, we're now officially at the top of the Priesthood's hit list. Once we get back to the estate, we'll have to hunker down and ride this out."*

The shuttle was parked on the roof of the administrative building in a government-dominated district of Sieten along the northern shore of Lake Tiadon. At the late evening hour, the other stalls for visitor craft were empty, granting Raena a clear view across the flat rooftop. She glanced at the Sietinen estate perched on the hillside above and was surprised to see half a dozen craft circling.

"Should those be up there?" she asked aloud, pointing toward the ships.

"Stars!" Cris breathed. "Those look like Tararian Guard."

"Why would they be circling like that?" Ryan asked.

"No idea." Cris pulled out his handheld from his pocket and initiated a call using its holographic video projector.

Marina answered after three seconds. "Bomax, Cris! What did you say during that meeting?"

"Just what we planned—except for the part where one of the councilmen tried to pull a gun on us," he replied. "Raena took action."

"Well, the four of you are wanted for questioning," Marina explained. "If that's how it happened, then there shouldn't be a problem."

"If a councilman was compromised, then we can't trust the Tararian Guard, either. There's no way I'll risk a meeting with them," Cris told her.

"Is Ryan confirmed?" Marina asked.

"Yes, all the documentation will be filed in the morning," Kate said from next to Cris. "We just need a day. Try to get the Tararian Guard to back down."

"You think I haven't been trying that?" Marina groaned. "Hold on, let me see if I can get any more details about what they want, specifically." The holographic image went dark, replaced by a small VComm logo.

"It's probably me," Raena said. "I did openly use telekinesis—while it was valid under the regulations, I technically hadn't *seen* the gun at the time I acted."

"I believe the members of the council will back up our story,"

Cris assured her. “My worry is that the Tararian Guard’s presence now is an excuse to get close to us rather than them just doing their due diligence.”

“Agreed,” Kate said. “It’s only been ten minutes since we left the chamber. For them to already be assembled means that they were on their way before we even entered the council chambers. This is a setup.”

“What do we—”

Before Raena could finish, the ships circling the Sietinen estate broke from their flight paths and began heading straight for the administrative building.

The holographic projection sprang to life. Marina’s face was flushed. “Go for the hidden entrance,” she instructed and the call disconnected.

“Fok!” Cris exclaimed and ran full-speed for the shuttle.

What’s going on? Voicing her question wouldn’t get them any closer to safety, so Raena kept it to herself.

She reached the shuttle a second after Cris and sprinted up the ramp, followed by Ryan and Kate.

“Strap in,” Cris instructed as he secured his own flight harness in the pilot’s chair. “This may get dicey.”

“They wouldn’t actually fire on us, would they?” Ryan asked while he snapped the buckle on his harness. “The city—”

“Nothing is out of the question,” Kate replied stoically from the co-pilot’s chair. “But we won’t let it come to that.”

A hum filled the air as the shuttle powered up. Cris directed the craft from the ground and pointed it toward the oncoming ships.

Raena gripped her flight harness with both hands, trying to keep her breathing even.

“It’ll be okay,” Ryan said in her mind.

She forced a nod.

“Brace yourselves—I need to dial back the inertial dampeners to get full flight controls,” Cris said.

Sudden G-forces pinned Raena against the back of her seat as her grandfather accelerated the shuttle to arc over the oncoming Tararian Guard ships.

The ships scrambled to intercept, but Cris quickly dove the

shuttle downward, causing Raena's stomach to rise into her mouth. She felt herself lifting off her seat, then a moment later lurch to the side as the shuttle entered a barrel roll. Wincing, she squeezed her eyes shut as the harness dug into her shoulders, willing the spinning to subside.

When the sensation of tumbling ceased, Raena opened her eyes to look out the front cockpit viewport. They were headed straight for the side of the hill.

We're going to crash! A cry caught in her throat. She reached out through her bond to Ryan, sending him one final message of love.

The hill rushed toward them, details of tree limbs and leaves coming into focus—and a door, slowly sliding open beneath the foliage.

Raena's heart leaped. She looked over to Ryan and saw him shaking his head with relief.

But they weren't safe yet. The door had not yet fully retracted, and the final meters were closing fast.

The nose of the shuttle cleared the opening, but halfway inside, the narrow wing on Raena's side clipped the door.

Raena lurched forward in her seat, then was slammed to the left as the shuttle spun sideways and skidded to a halt.

No one moved.

"Ugh," Raena groaned, reaching up to her head. She felt intact, if somewhat sore and dizzy. "Is everyone okay?"

"That's the last time I let you pilot," Kate said to Cris, releasing her harness.

"Fine up here," Cris replied to Raena's question.

"Yes, are you all right?" Ryan said, alarm pitching his voice.

Raena followed his gaze to the right and saw that a gash had opened up in the side of the shuttle, ending a mere meter from her seat. "Wow, that was close."

"We need to get out of here," Cris said, joining them in the main cabin. He forced the side door open using the emergency release. "I'm not sure if the outer door will close properly after that impact."

"I'm sorry for snapping at you," Kate told him. "I know there wasn't any clearance."

"No worries." He hopped out of the shuttle and held out his hand to help his wife down.

"Where are we?" Raena asked as she followed her grandmother out.

"Emergency access—or exit—for the estate," Cris explained.

"I heard about these tunnels," Ryan commented when he was on the ground. "They never gave us any specifics."

Cris smiled. "Secret in the strictest sense of the term." His smile faded when he looked down the tunnel toward the entry. "Shite, the door *is* still open. I don't know if the shield is up yet. Let's move." He took off at a quick jog into the darkness.

"Shield? Raena questioned telepathically, as not to disrupt her breathing at the brisk pace.

"We have a defensive shield around the estate," her grandfather clarified. *"It's offline most of the time, but when Marina told me to head down here, I think it's because she was in the process of activating it."*

"How effective is the barrier?" questioned Ryan.

"Enough that the Priesthood won't be able to get in without an express invitation. But that also means we're not getting out," Cris replied.

Raena's brow knitted. *"But what about meeting with the other High Dynasties? We were supposed to call a session tomorrow."*

"It doesn't have to be done in person," Kate told her. *"That would have been ideal, but a video call will have to do."*

They ran in silence for the remaining kilometer before the tunnel broadened into a bay with berthing for a dozen shuttles and a set of double doors at the back, which appeared to be for an elevator.

Cris stopped outside the doors. "True loyalties are about to be shown. That display with the Tararian Guard was quite public—some may question us. Make no assumptions about our friends."

"What about Marina?" Raena asked. *I can't imagine my own grandmother would turn against me, but…*

"There was a time when I wouldn't have been sure," Cris said, "but now I trust her with my life."

Kate nodded her agreement.

Ryan cracked a smile. "The five of us against the world."

"Or universe, but who's keeping track?" Raena jested back.

"And on that note, we have one more important order of business." Cris activated a panel next to the large metal doors, which parted.

Rather than the elevator Raena had expected to see, there was a room filled with crates, obscuring the side walls. Along the back wall, however, the bottom steps of a switch-backing flight of stairs extended into the room.

"Stairs, really?" she sighed.

Cris grimaced. "I figured there was an elevator, but I've never actually been down here before. It's only forty flights. But hey, I'm the old guy here—*I* should be the one complaining, not you young people."

Kate shook her head, then sighed as she crossed the room and began jogging up the stairs. "Stop dilly dallying."

Raena rubbed her hands on her quads and began the long ascension up the stairs. After ten flights, her legs were feeling the burn from scaling the taller-than-normal steps. By the halfway point, she was starting to feel winded, but she was relieved to see the others were also slowing down. The last fifteen stories were a grueling haul.

"Almost there," Cris encouraged between labored breaths.

"I hate stairs," Raena moaned.

Cris chuckled. "We've all earned some extra cake for dessert."

Ryan smiled. "Why didn't you say so sooner?"

Panting and exhausted, they finally reached the door at the top.

"I swear, if this is locked…" Kate reached out for the handle. She gave it a yank but it didn't budge. "You *have* to be kidding!"

Cris laughed. "No, that'd be too perfect." He stepped up next to her and sent a low-intensity telekinetic probe. "Well, fok."

Raena leaned against the smooth concrete wall of the stairwell, thankful for the cool surface. "No way I'm going back down those stairs." She telepathically reached out to Marina, searching throughout the Sietinen estate for her.

Her grandmother's consciousness was far above the subterranean tunnels, busy in a heated engagement with an administrative aid.

"We need your help," Raena implored, looping her paternal grandparents and Ryan into the telepathic link.

Marina cut her in-person conversation short. *"Where are you?"* she formed the question in her mind for Raena to read.

"The stairwell at the top of the back entrance tunnel. It's locked."

Surprise filled Marina's mind. *"Oh, I unlocked the elevator access. I thought you'd take that."*

Raena shook her head with disbelief and glared at her grandfather.

Cris groaned. "It must have been hidden behind the crates."

"Awesome." Kate crossed her arms.

"Hey, but extra cake," Ryan reminded everyone.

"I'll override the door lock, give me a minute," Marina told them and severed the connection.

By the time the lock released, Raena's breathing had normalized and her legs felt considerably more stable.

The door opened into a corridor in what appeared to be the underground servant passageways.

"I know this place," Ryan said. "It's a straight shot to the residential wing that way, correct?" He pointed to their right.

"Sure is," Cris confirmed.

They jogged down the halls and were fortunate to encounter no one in the seldom-used corridor. To Raena's displeasure, they had to scale two more flights of stairs up to the main level of the manor, but after the forty flights earlier, two was a breeze.

Single file, they slipped out from the servant passage into the main corridor.

"I hate to even see what's going on outside…" Cris walked over to the nearest window and peered through the glass. "Oh, this'll be fun."

Raena joined him and looked out. The Tararian Guard ships had resumed their circling over the estate, but they were now kept at a distance by a shimmering dome encompassing the entire Sietinen estate and extending a kilometer down the hill.

The click of brisk, heeled footsteps sounded from down the corridor, and Raena turned to see Marina approaching. Her face was still flushed, but her shoulders rounded with relief when she saw the four of them.

"You stirred up quite the mess," she said. "I didn't think it would escalate quite this quickly."

"Now the Priesthood knows what we know, and come morning, everyone will learn there's a Dainetris heir. We have to make our move," Cris said.

Marina nodded and turned her attention to Raena and Ryan. "Are you two ready?"

Raena swept back her sweat-damp hair from her forehead using the back of her hand. "I feel so incredibly bridal."

Her grandparents smiled.

"We'll have another event and make a proper spectacle of it later," Kate told her. "Not to be un-romantic, but right now we just need the legal proceedings."

"That doesn't change that I love you," Raena said privately to Ryan.

"And I you."

"Lead the way," Raena said. She took Ryan's hand as she followed Marina back toward the administrative wing of the manor.

"Kaiden just called me in a panic," Marina said as she walked. "Apparently, footage of what's happening outside has started making it to the major news outlets."

"At least we'll have witnesses," Cris muttered.

"I'll call him as soon as we're done here," Kate replied to Marina. "What time should we call the assembly?"

Cris shrugged. "As soon as possible, I'd say. 09:00?"

"Can the TSS mobilize in time?" Kate asked Cris.

"Knowing Wil, a two-hour lead time would be enough—thirteen should be more than sufficient. I'll speak with him while you chat with Kaiden."

She nodded agreement.

Marina led the group to a conference room just outside the core of the administrative center. Inside, a middle-aged man wearing a black robe was waiting for them.

Raena recoiled when she saw him. *Marina is handing us over to the Priesthood, after all?* Then, after giving herself a few seconds to study the man, she realized that he had no trace of abilities and his physical resemblance was not that of the red-eyed High Priests. Rather, this man was a judge.

"Good evening," he greeted in a warm, deep tone. "I understand a wedding is in order."

Raena looked down at her disheveled appearance. "Sure is."

"We're keeping this brief and to the point, yes?" the judge questioned.

Cris nodded. "We have a few other things to get to."

The judge smiled. "I noticed." He looked over Raena and Ryan. "Do you two come here today of your own freewill to be joined in marriage?"

"I do," Raena and Ryan said in unison.

"Do you swear to be true to each other and to act in the best interest of the Taran people?" the judge asked.

"I do," Raena and Ryan replied.

The judge held up a tablet, projecting two beams of purple light underneath. Raena and Ryan both pushed up their left sleeves to expose their Marks under the beams. The screen on the tablet lit up with the serpent crest of Sietinen and the flower emblem of Dainetris.

"Your commitment has been recorded and ratified, the Dynasties of Sietinen and Dainetris are now joined," the judge stated, his tone taking on a hint of wonder as he uttered the name of the long-lost seventh High Dynasty.

That's it? Raena glanced at the others in the room, but no one moved. "Okay, then."

"Are they waiting for us to kiss, because having three of your grandparents staring at us…"

"Yeah, not gonna happen," Raena agreed. She took Ryan's hand and nodded to the judge. "You heard him, the wedding is a done deal. Let's get to those conversations that need doing."

"Right." Cris agreed. "We have less than thirteen hours until the assembly. We'll check in at 06:00."

Marina and Kate came forward and gave Raena and Ryan hugs, wishing them congratulations and officially welcoming Ryan into the family. While they were exchanging words, the judge showed himself out of the room.

Cris lingered after the two women left to attend to their tasks.

"Take some time for yourselves tonight. All the action items are on us—just meet up with us at 06:00."

"Are you sure?" Raena asked.

"Positive. Get some cake and enjoy the moment. You just got married, for stars' sake!"

Raena smiled at her new husband. "I won't argue."

Ryan squeezed her hand. "Thank you," he said to Cris.

"Gladly. See you in a few hours." Cris hurriedly departed to speak with Wil about the final preparations.

When they were alone, Raena gazed into Ryan's eyes. "I'll be the best partner I can be to you. I'll love you always."

"And I to you. I love you."

With no audience present, there was no reason to hold back with the next kiss.

— — —

Cris' capacity to appear calm was nearing its breaking point. *Restoring the Dainetris name, crash-landing after a would-be aerial assault, a wedding… This has been one foking night so far.*

And it was far from over.

Cris took a series of calming breaths as he traversed the hall to his office. He hoped his statement earlier that Wil would only need a couple hours was, in fact, true. He also hoped Wil would forgive him for making him miss his own daughter's wedding.

The central administrative office was abuzz at full staffing levels despite the late hour. As Cris passed through the room, he overheard snippets of video conversations with reporters asking why the Tararian Guard had encircled the estate. As yet, no word about Dainetris had leaked, but it was just a matter of time.

Pretty soon, it won't just be a handful of ships surrounding the estate. The TSS and Tararian Guard might have to go head-to-head. He hated the idea of having to engage in a civil war, but anyone who still stood with the Priesthood after all evidence became public would demonstrate a disregard for ethics too dissimilar for them to coexist peacefully. The opposition would either have to leave the Taran worlds or would be forcibly removed—lethally, if it came to it. Such were the grim realities of war.

Cris spotted Marina in her office next to his, and she paused her video call. "Assembly time is set," she affirmed.

"Good. I'll come find you when I'm finished here."

Marina resumed her conversation and Cris entered his office, closing the door behind him.

The space was largely unchanged since when it had been his father's, aside from some updated furnishings. Cris had always enjoyed the view out the arched window at the back of the room, and even at night it afforded a spectacular view of Sieten below.

After taking a few minutes to gather his thoughts while staring out the window, Cris initiated a call directly to Wil's handheld, figuring he'd likely be in his quarters at that hour.

It took a full minute for Wil to answer, voice only. "Hey, Dad, what's up?"

"It's started," Cris said. "Everything's been accelerated."

"*How* accelerated?"

"Ryan's position has been ratified, and the two Dynasties have been legally joined," Cris replied, bracing for his son's reaction.

"You had the wedding without us?" Wil exclaimed.

"They *what*?" Saera shouted in the background.

"I know, I—" Cris cut off as the voice call switched to holographic video.

Wil and Saera sat on the couch in their quarters, glaring at the camera.

"Having the wedding tonight wasn't part of the plan," Wil said.

"You had no right to move ahead without telling us—you could have at least had a video feed!" Saera added.

Cris was relieved she couldn't reach through the holographic projector and attack him. "I would have, but things have been a little hectic. The Tararian Guard decided to pay us a visit on our way back home. Everything's about to go public. Marina grabbed one of the judicial chancellors and he conducted the quickest wedding I've ever seen—it was over and done in a minute."

"And still, you didn't call us," Wil glowered.

"You missed nothing more than signing a legal document, I

assure you. We can have a proper celebration when all this is over," Cris insisted. "Now listen: as soon as the Dainetris reinstatement becomes public record at 08:00, things around here are going to go from chaotic to a total shiteshow. If the Tararian Guard is already up in arms, you better bet things will turn nasty really quick once they learn what's going on. People will pick their loyalties and we won't have a lot of time to sway the public sentiment in our favor."

"The facts will lead people in the right direction," Saera said.

"I have no doubt about that, but the Priesthood might not allow it to come down to rational choices," Cris countered. "We still have no idea if they have a neurotoxin in play that could turn the entire population against us in an instant. Are the Aesir standing by to assist?"

Wil hesitated. "That's the plan."

"The Aesir *are* still on board to help us, right?" Cris questioned.

"Let me worry about that," Wil evaded. "The TSS is ready to mobilize. We'll be standing by to respond if there are any uprisings."

Saera nodded. "We'll have an eye out for signs of a neurotoxin. Our teams have been trained in how to control groups under such influences, as best as we can prepare."

"All right, I'll leave you to it," Cris agreed. *What's going on with the Aesir? I thought we could trust that alliance. Stars, I hope we're not on our own!* "The High Dynasty assembly is set for 09:00. We'll take the official vote then."

"Good luck," Wil said. "We'll talk to you on the other side."

"Good luck to you, too." *We're all going to need it.*

CHAPTER 15

BY 06:00, CRIS was feeling the lack of sleep from working through the night. However, his efforts had paid off and the final groundwork was in place for the High Dynasty assembly in three hours' time. His fellow conspirators would be arriving for their check-in at any moment.

A stim strip dissolved on Cris' tongue as he leaned back in the chair around the conference table, savoring the sudden surge of energy and clarity as the chemicals worked their magic.

Soft knocking sounded on the door, and Raena and Ryan entered.

"Hey, newlyweds," Cris greeted. "Sorry to start your married lives with such drama."

Raena grinned. "Are you kidding? I can't think of a better wedding present than ousting the Priesthood."

There is no doubt she was born for this role. Cris beamed. "That is a gift I will happily give you."

"And here I was going to settle for a few days on Alushia," Ryan jested.

"That can be arranged, too," Cris told him.

"Oh, goodness, yes—please spend some time on Alushia together after this is over!" Kate said as she entered, catching the tail end of Cris' offer. "You've earned it."

"When we're successful, we'll have way too much to do in the coming months to get a vacation anytime soon," Raena replied with audible regret. "But it's nice to know it's there when we can get away."

"It's going to take some time to get used to traveling in style," Ryan said. "Or vacations at all, for that matter."

"Hearing you say that makes me realize we need to take a look at the Ward program," Cris reflected.

Kate nodded. "Back to the present now, though. I had a productive conversation with my brother."

"Right, yes. What did he have to say?" Raena asked.

"I explained what happened with the council and our surprise to find the Tararian Guard after us. He was shocked about the Dainetris revelation, of course, but he told me he'd make some calls on our behalf in advance of the meeting this morning," Kate replied.

"He's always come through for us—and his word is respected," Cris said.

She gave him a hopeful smile. "Now we need him more than ever. Last night's events have painted us as aggressors. That is not an ideal public opinion environment in which to broach the kind of topics we must."

"We work with what we have," Cris stated. "Now, where is Marina?"

A moment later, the door swung open and his chief advisor entered. "Sorry I'm late," Marina said. "These reporters won't let up. I think one of the staffers let word of the High Dynasty meeting slip. The news networks are running with every possible theory you can imagine."

"Anything we should worry about?" Cris asked.

"The prominent voices are leaning toward a revelation about some major political upset—the leading theory is that you're resigning," Marina said.

Cris chuckled. "Well, won't they be sorely disappointed."

"Doubtfully," Marina replied with trained composure. "Public opinion of you was high until things went sideways last night."

"Then we can hold out another three hours until the formal release of our findings regarding the Priesthood," Cris concluded. "Any other loose ends we need to tie up before then?"

"Let's go over the logistics for the assembly," Marina suggested. "We'd planned on the dramatic reveal of Ryan bursting into the room in person, but it's a little different now that it will be a holoconference."

"I'm more concerned about if they'll take me seriously," Ryan admitted.

"Once we show them that Mark and the attestation from the council, they'll have to," Cris said. "So, let's make it the best foking show we can."

They dove into planning the final details and dramatic cues to heighten the impact of key statements. Whether it was the stim or just pent up anticipation from decades of planning, Cris felt more energized than he had in years. He'd accomplished many things in his life, but if the coming hours proved successful, he would look back at these times as one of his greatest moments.

By 08:30, the group was as rehearsed as they were going to get. They took a short break to eat and hydrate before the madness that would be the rest of their day.

Cris found himself alone in the conference room with Kate as she reviewed her talking points one more time.

"Can you believe this is finally happening?" he asked her.

She looked up and shook her head. "Barely. Between the lack of sleep last night and all the build-up, I feel like I'm in a dream."

"I know the feeling." He leaned back in his chair. "When I first proposed this idea to you all those years ago, I didn't think we'd actually do it."

"We had to do it," Kate said. "If we didn't, no one else would."

"That's true."

"Besides," she gave him a coy smile, "the audacity of you even suggesting such an idea is one of the things that made me fall in love with you in the first place. And you knew it—you had to follow through."

"I also can't argue with that." He gazed at her, nothing but love in his heart for everything they had done and would continue to do together. "I never would have done this without you."

"Nor I without you."

Cris chuckled to himself. "Despite all the planning, nothing is going to go how we imagined, is it?"

Kate scoffed. "Not a chance."

Raena and Ryan returned in short order. They'd changed into professional business attire suitable for the presentation.

Ryan still seemed a tad uncomfortable in such clothing, but he was assured and relaxed as long as Raena was nearby. Now that he had aged to his mid-twenties, Cris occasionally caught him at an angle that reminded him of his father, Banks. Cris wished his mentor could have lived to see everything as it was today. He would have been so proud to know what a fine young man his son had grown up to be. And even more than that, he would have loved to see Tararia finally on the cusp of a renaissance. Without Banks' contributions, many of the efforts now underway would have been impossible.

Marina was the last to return from the break, but when she did, she brought with her an air of determination that restored everyone's focus to the task at hand.

"We have our assignments, we know our talking points, and we have the facts on our side. I have no illusions that this won't get ugly, but we stay the course and push through," Cris said.

Raena nodded. "Game on."

"All right, initiating the holoconference." Cris manipulated the controls on the touch-screen desktop and a simulated room appeared on the far side of the table.

They had programmed the settings so viewers on the other end of the conference would see Cris seated at the head of the table with Raena to his left and Kate to his right. Marina and Ryan remained out of view for the time being.

The three Sietinen representatives sat with their hands crossed on the tabletop while they waited for the other attendees to arrive.

"Would a little punctuality hurt anyone?" Cris griped telepathically as the clock passed 09:03.

"Everyone thinks they are the most important," Kate replied with patience that only went as deep as the surface of her mind.

At 09:05, a flurry of notifications appeared around the simulated table as the attendees began to arrive. Vaenetri and Talsari first, followed by Baellas, Makaris, and finally Monsari.

"Hello," Cris greeted the attendees when all were present. "Thank you for agreeing to meet on such short notice. It was critical for us all to convene."

"We're eager to hear what you have to say," Kaiden Vaenetri replied. "Especially considering the show last night."

"Yes, allow me to address the Tararian Guard's presence at our estate," Cris continued in response to the planned segue from his brother-in-law. "But the explanation is tied to the larger matter we have gathered to discuss today: a pervasive corruption within the ranks of the Taran government, which must be rooted out if we're to move forward as a people. The presence of those guards was in direct response to the parties in question being made aware that Sietinen was preparing to have this very conversation with you."

"We have no time for riddles," Liam Makaris interjected.

Cris had anticipated either he or Eduard Baellas would be impatient and want to jump ahead. "Very well, then let me speak plainly. We have asked you here to this meeting to present irrefutable information regarding the Priesthood's corruption and the need to immediately and permanently remove the organization from power."

Byron Monsari burst out laughing. "You really have lost your mind!"

"May I remind you," Cris countered, "that we have evidence to support these claims. I am transmitting the relevant data packets now. I trust you will each have your staff validate the materials."

He paused while the High Dynasty representatives took time to scan through the list of charges against the Priesthood listed in the Executive Summary.

"This is preposterous," Eduard Baellas muttered. "Conspiracy, abduction, murder—genocide? The scope of these charges is inconsistent and, frankly, a reach."

"I would agree, if the evidence did not support each of these claims," Kate replied. "Please, send the packet for verification. I assure you, it's all genuine."

"I've submitted mine," Ellen Talsari said to Cris' relief; it wouldn't have looked good for Kaiden to be the first adopter at each juncture.

The other Heads grumbled their consent and relayed the packets to their staff.

"While that validation is in progress, I'll give you some highlights," Cris continued. "The story begins a little over a thousand years ago, back when the Priesthood was still a proper theological institution. They thought about things like the future of our race and how we could become our fullest selves. Well, some members of the Priesthood decided that the secret to advancement must be in our genetic code. They started experiments to see how we could become even better."

"There's nothing illegal about that," Liam stated.

"No, agreed," Cris replied. "But what you might find interesting is precisely which aspects of Tarans the Priesthood wished to advance—namely, strengthening telekinetic abilities."

"So, that's how you came into being," Byron sneered.

"Oh, you misunderstand," Cris shot back, glaring at the Monsari Head. "Back then, *everyone* had abilities. But the Priesthood's experimentations didn't go how they expected, and those abilities disappeared from all but a few."

"Good riddance," Byron muttered under his breath.

Cris ignored him. "Rather than admit any wrongdoing, they decided to make everyone forget. Just like they made everyone forget about the Bakzen. Just like Dainetris. And just like all of us if we don't stop them right now."

"Are you suggesting the Priesthood is connected to the Bakzen and to the fall of the Dainetris Dynasty?" Ellen questioned.

"That's exactly what I'm saying," Cris confirmed. "I know it sounds preposterous, but the evidence is right there in front of you. The Priesthood made the Bakzen, then cast them aside and forced them to fight us when we threatened their way of life. When the Dainetris Dynasty uncovered this evidence of the wrongdoings we are now reviewing, the Priesthood condemned them to death and buried their city in an attempt to make the rest of us forget they ever existed.

"The acts of deceit and manipulation haven't ended. We have learned through personal accounts that the Priesthood has continued their genetic experimentation. Hundreds of women have been captured over the years and held in labs within the Priesthood's island as surrogates for clones." Cris paused to let his words sink in.

"What personal accounts?" Kaiden asked. The last bit of information was news to him as much as the other representatives.

"I was there," Raena broke into the conversation on cue. "I saw all of it, and they would have done the same thing to me."

The Heads studied her with interest. Most had interacted with Raena in some capacity over her four years on Tararia, and as far as Cris knew, she had a positive reputation. Or, she *had*—everyone may now think she's crazy.

Ellen was the first to speak. "I have always found you to be reliable and wise beyond your years, Raena, but claims of that magnitude require more than one person's eye-witness account."

"Of course." Raena inclined her head. "In the matter of captives, I can offer nothing other than my word at this time—aside from missing person records, which could be dismissed as circumstantial. What I can do, however, is provide a detailed account of systematic violations of the Taran laws related to genetic modifications, and trace those activities directly to the Priesthood."

"I'll hear the case," Eduard said. The other Heads nodded their assent.

Raena walked through the use of nanotech in the bloodstreams of the dynastic lines, and then spoke of Marina and her mother. Revealing that information placed Sietinen at the center of the Priesthood's plans, but trying to downplay that fact wouldn't do them any good. If anything, the more they could establish their authority, the better off they'd be.

Cris watched the Heads as they absorbed Raena's words, nodding with understanding and wincing with disgust as she took them on a journey through centuries of manipulating their lives from behind the scenes. *We have them!* He was filled with relief and joy as the Heads began to squirm in their seats. *With us united against the Priesthood, they'll have nowhere to run.*

"The question is," Raena passed her gaze around those at the simulated table, "do you want to continue to take direction from an organization that's so willing to lie to you at every turn? These actions have been in the best interest of the Priesthood, not of the Taran people. As leaders, more is expected of us. We must hold ourselves to a higher standard, and we must take corrective action in the face of injustice." She folded her hands on the tabletop and leaned forward. "Consider the evidence. Is that the kind of future we want for generations to come?"

"Well done," Cris told her. *"They're squirming in their seats."*

"Drive it home," she replied.

Cris took a deep breath. "There you have it—generations of lies and covert manipulation. I move we end it now. I hereby introduce an official motion as a Head of the Sietinen Dynasty to abolish the Priesthood and remove the organization, in its entirety, from power."

"How dare you make such a proposal!" Eduard exclaimed.

"It's treason," Byron echoed, looking rather pleased that Cris had finally placed himself in such a compromising position.

"You really feel that way, after everything we've presented?" Kate looked around the faces at the table. She locked eyes with her brother, and even he seemed unsure now that he was surrounded by others so adamant in their opposing opinions. "For the last thirty years, we've talked with you about every aspect of Taran life. You've agreed that conditions are far from ideal. This is our chance to set a new course."

Eduard scoffed. "Saying things could be better and suggesting an overthrow of our most respected leadership institution are two very different things."

"Respected?" Kate shook her head. "How can you have *any* respect for the Priesthood after what's been laid out in front of you?"

Byron scowled. "There's justification for every action."

No! We can't lose it like this. Cris swallowed. "I introduced a motion. Is there a second?"

The Heads around the table fell silent.

Cris focused on his brother-in-law, willing him to take a stand. *We just need Vaenetri and Talsari. Hopefully, one of the others will follow…*

But Kaiden said nothing. He looked down.

A moment later, a private text message popped up on the tabletop in front of Cris, from Kaiden: >>I can't second a motion that's sure to fail. Bring Ryan in, then we'll have a chance to sway them.<<

Cris hated to admit it, but Kaiden was right—there was no way a vote was going to pass.

We have one more chance. Cris looked at his wife and granddaughter; they nodded. He addressed the Heads, "If having your very genetic code modified without your knowledge isn't enough, consider the fate of Dainetris and how the same could happen to you."

"They violated Taran law," Liam interjected. "Of course they fell. Your treasonous accusations will land you in the same place."

Cris cocked his head. "*Did* they violate any laws, though? All the records surrounding the fall were purged, so it's all hearsay—or it was. The information we transmitted about the creation and destruction of the Bakzen won't be found in any existing records, but by now your data forensics experts will have concluded that the records are all genuine. How is that possible? Because the Priesthood was the one to wipe those files and change history to suit the narrative they wished to tell. The Bakzen War was kept a secret for so long because they didn't want anyone to dig into where such a powerful enemy had come from.

"The last people to launch such an investigation were the Dainetris Dynasty. As leaders of the corporation responsible for ship manufacturing, they were the first to realize that something was going on beyond the Outer Colonies. They kept quiet for years, supporting production when help was needed beyond the TSS' private facilities. Eventually, though, someone got curious and looked into the secret enemy, and they discovered the truth. The Bakzen used to live among us in peace, and the Priesthood turned them into killers. Thousands—millions—died, all because the Priesthood had tried to cover up their mistakes rather than make one, honest admission in their entire history.

"Instead of making any admission of wrongdoing when faced with the evidence, the Priesthood decided to eliminate Dainetris. They invented charges and sentenced them to execution—wiping out an entire genetic line. The corporate assets were divided, the city was buried, and everyone was told to move on like it'd always been the Big Six. The seventh High Dynasty was no more."

Each of the Heads had their gaze fixed on Cris as they thought through their own lives and what could be taken from them. The threat of having their power stripped away was as terrifying a future as death, but both were unthinkable.

Kate surveyed the group. "Whether you admit it or not, the Priesthood has already been controlling your personal and corporate interests. Liam, can you account for all of the food supplies distributed to the Outer Colonies during the Bakzen War? And Ellen, how were those deals with the Priesthood structured for providing ores through TalEx's mining operations?"

"Well, it—" Liam began.

"The supply chain checks out fine on the surface, but we all know those supplies never made it to the Outer Colonies," Kate stated. "Most of the shipments were diverted to the TSS to support the secret war. We'd be happy to share that official documentation with you, if you need a reminder."

The two Heads stared at their hands resting on the tabletop.

Kate turned her attention to Byron. "And don't think Monsari didn't play its part. MPS' power generators are integrated into everything from ships to planetary shields. We know your investigators glossed over what happened at Grolen with the shield failure leading up to the Bakzen attack. And don't even get me started on—"

"Enough!" Byron cut in. "What's your point?"

"That you know the records have been manipulated," Kate shot back. "You claim to be in control of your company's operations, but when the Priesthood asks you for a favor or to turn a blind eye, you have no choice but to comply. We've all been in that position at one time or another. Can we in good conscience allow that to continue when we know that those actions are hurting the people who rely on us to provide a quality life?"

"Is there really anything we can do about it?" Ellen murmured. "The Priesthood has final authority on all matters."

"Their power isn't absolute." Cris stood up slowly and leaned forward with his hands on the table, passing his gaze across the attendees. "The Priesthood thinks they control everything, but those of us present here today hold the real power. You see, the assumption has always been that when Dainetris fell more than a century ago, all was lost. But as of last night, the seventh High Dynasty has returned."

Sharp breaths sounded around the table.

Ryan walked over from where he had been waiting along the side wall and stood to Cris' right so he was by Raena. "I am Ryan Dainetris," he stated clearly. "As my first official act, I second the motion to abolish the Priesthood."

"Dainetris isn't a voting member!" Byron objected.

"You may want to check the official registry," Cris replied with a concealed smirk.

"I ask you again, what kind of future do we want?" Kate asked the group. "We can continue playing into the Priesthood's hands, or we can take the necessary actions to make sure our people can prosper."

The room fell silent.

"In light of this development," Kaiden said at last, "I must also cast my vote in favor of abolishing the Priesthood."

Cris breathed an inward sigh of relief and waited for Ellen Talsari to follow.

"I vote against," Byron declared. "I'll have no part of this."

"I also vote against," Liam concurred.

Ellen took a slow breath. "You've made a compelling case and shined a light on serious issues we've all been too willing to overlook. However, a change such as this would alter the course of our civilization. Even when faced with this evidence, I must consider if the cost of that change might result in more harm than these past acts alone. To refine is one thing, but to abolish the Priesthood entirely… I'm afraid I must also vote against the motion."

Cris' heart dropped. *We had always counted on Talsari. Getting a unanimous vote was ambitious, but we were sure to get a majority. If they are against us now…*

Only Baellas remained, and it was clear where the direction that vote would swing. As soon as the final vote was cast, it'd be over.

I've done everything I can and it still wasn't enough. Next to him, Kate looked like she was about to be sick. *What else can we do?*

— — —

Raena stared with appall at the images of the High Dynasty representatives in the holographic conference room around her. *How can they still support the Priesthood after everything we've presented?*

The evidence was right there in front of them, all the atrocities laid out in perfect detail. If anyone wasn't outraged by the information, they were lying to themselves.

"If what the Priesthood has done in the past isn't enough, then you better think about what they'll do in the future—what all of their plans have been working toward," Raena said to the room, rising to stand next to Ryan. She glared at the Heads. "Any guesses? Well, they want to become gods."

"That's absurd," Liam snickered.

"You may think that, but look at the evidence," Raena implored. "For the last thousand years, they have been trying to perfect a physical vessel to allow them to ascend to a higher state of being. They recognized that the Taran people might find that plan a little suspect, so they have also developed a neuro-control agent to telepathically command planets' worth of people. It may have already been disseminated out there in the population and none of us would be the wiser.

"The Priesthood seeks to control. You herald them as a moral compass, but how can you blindly follow leaders whose actions are purely for their own benefit? Judge them by what they have done, not by what they espouse. We can't let them have even more power. We must take action now, while there's still a chance to fight back. The seven of you can make a new future for all Tarans. *You* can be the leaders rather than just the puppets dancing on the Priesthood's strings. Take a stand for what's right."

The Heads sat in silence.

Ellen let out a slow breath and met Raena's gaze. "We take comfort in familiarity, but sometimes what's necessary is not what's safe and easy." She paused, a slight smile touching her lips. "Maybe it is time for a real change. I reverse my vote to be in favor of the motion."

That's it—that's the majority! A grin spread across Raena's face as she looked to Ryan and her grandparents.

"Better than I could have said it," Cris said to her. *"You're a natural."*

The remaining Heads slumped in their chairs as they realized the motion had carried.

"We have a majority vote in favor," Cris stated. "What happens next is up to you. We can start a civil war or you can join us and make this a unified front."

Eduard sighed. "Fine, I'll change my vote."

Liam and Byron glanced at each other.

"And if we don't join you?" Byron asked.

"The TSS will take your assets by force for non-compliance with a majority ruling by the High Dynasty assembly, the only recognized legal authority as of this moment forward," Cris replied.

"I'm in favor of the motion," Liam hurriedly stated.

Byron shook his head. "The motion is carried by unanimous vote."

Raena's and Ryan's eyes met. *"We did it,"* she said to him.

"Now for the hard part," he replied.

"The official vote is recorded," Cris said and submitted the log to the Council. "Things might get a little crazy. If a TSS warship happens to show up, just follow instructions."

"But—" Eduard started to object.

Raena looked down at an alert on her desktop. The Tararian Guard had just quadrupled their numbers around the Sietinen estate and all known military installations across the Taran worlds had been activated. "Well, that didn't take long."

"Shite," Cris swore under his breath. "Transmitting these vote records to the Tararian Guard now."

Raena took a slow breath. "Let's hope they listen."

CHAPTER 16

"FOK! THIS IS IT." Wil took in the reports of the Tararian Guard's activities across the empire. The TSS had superior firepower and the telekinetic skills of Agents gave them another edge, but it'd make for heavy casualties on both sides if it came down to a firefight.

"They'll back down when they see the vote results," Saera assured him.

"Some will side with the Priesthood, regardless," Wil replied.

"Old ways die hard."

"And people with them."

His wife nodded solemnly. "We've practiced non-lethal techniques. This won't be like the last war."

"I hope not." Wil sighed. "Let's get to it."

Wil and Saera jogged from their quarters on the path to the administrative wing of Level 1 of TSS Headquarters. The halls were abuzz as word of the Tararian Guard's offensive spread.

An Agent flagged Wil down as he and Saera entered the elevator lobby. "Sir, is the TSS taking an official stance?"

"I'm about to make an announcement," Wil replied. "You bet we're taking a stance."

The Agent nodded her understanding and Wil and Saera entered the elevator.

"Hopefully, everyone agrees with the side we're taking," Saera said as soon as the elevator doors were closed.

"I have no doubts about anyone in the TSS. It's the rest of the population that worries me."

"If this turns into a civil war…"

"It won't," Wil told her. "It can't."

The doors opened on Level 1, and Wil was immediately bombarded by a wall of Agents and administrative personnel tripping over each other with questions.

He balked at the sight of them. "Just hang on!" he called over the din. "I'll make a statement as soon as I make it to the conference room. Stand aside."

To his relief, the crowd parted and allowed him through with Saera.

They reached the main conference room at the end of the hall next to the High Commander's office and found that the other senior Agents had already gathered.

Wil gave a nod to Michael as he and Saera entered the room, and he assumed his normal chair at the head of the table.

"Ryla is secure," Michael told him telepathically.

Thank the stars! As long as the Archive is protected, we'll have some leverage. Wil nodded his thanks and took a deep breath. "The people in this room have a much better idea of what is about to happen than most others," he began, "but what I'll share with you now will cast your understanding in new light.

"We have been preparing for a fight for the last four years. We've spoken of a political revolution and needing to have a military force in place to help ease that transition with as little harm to civilians as possible. Well, the time for action is now.

"Each of you has been involved in training a team to perform specific tasks in these efforts—what you likely didn't realize is how many teams there are. Eighty percent of Agents in the TSS are now attached to one such team, and we're about to mobilize."

Ian chuckled and shook his head. "I should have known you were up to something."

Ethan nodded. "Yeah, a disparate handful of teams didn't make sense. What you've arranged, though…"

Wil swallowed. "I didn't like concealing it from you, but we wanted to keep the operation as compartmentalized as possible. That probably now makes sense after the rumors that have been circulating about a vote on Tararia. I will confirm that information: the Priesthood has officially been voted out of power and asked to step aside."

Exhales of surprise sounded around the room.

"About foking time!" Scott declared.

Wil smiled. "I agree with you there. But the Priesthood isn't going quietly. We knew they wouldn't. That's why we've been preparing and that's why the TSS needs to step up. Our abilities grant us the means to offer policing without the use of weapons that may harm the innocents.

"Our job is to keep this situation from escalating further. We'll help escort the Priesthood out and put temporary management in place to ease the transition.

"As of right now, the Tararian Guard is still under the Priesthood's influence. They are not our enemy, but they aren't friends, either. We will use our specialist teams to assess and control our opponents and adjust our strategies, as appropriate."

Wil paused to look around the room at the faces of his old friends. The expressions were a mixture of worry and excitement, but all of them had commitment in their eyes. *They trust me to see us through this. I have to deliver.*

He placed his hands on the tabletop. "Many of us have been into battle together before. We came out victorious then, and we will again now. The coming hours will test us, but stay true to yourselves and each other and we'll come out on top."

The other Agents smiled back at him.

"I've been itching for a good challenge," Ethan said.

Wil smiled back. "In that case, all your assignments have been transmitted. I'll make the all-staff announcement. Let's finish this."

— — —

The TSS *Conquest* was the last ship Jason expected to get for his first command, but it was the only vessel capable of supporting his mission in the Rift.

He sat in a pedestal chair at the center of the round

Command Center. Though four similar chairs surrounded him, all were empty. Only a single officer, Rianne, was with him in the room. She had served on the *Conquest* during the war, and Wil had trusted no other to accompany Jason.

"Looks like the rest of the TSS is mobilizing," Rianne commented as she monitored subspace communications from her console at the front right of the room.

"CACI, bring up a map of current TSS fleet positions," Jason instructed the ship's computer.

The spherical viewscreen wrapping the ceiling and transparent floor transitioned from a representation of the echoed starscape surrounding them into a high-level map of the Taran Empire, accounting for approximately a quarter of the galaxy. Even after five years with the TSS, Jason was still in awe every time he saw the civilization depicted in those terms. Crazier was the notion that his family controlled so much of that empire. Being a TSS officer was enough responsibility, as far as he was concerned—Raena could do her thing on Tararia.

Jason studied the map around him, identifying TSS outposts represented by green icons and offensive vessels indicated by blue dots. Red dots representing the Tararian Guard ships dotted the map in far greater quantity than the TSS.

Based on his review of records from the Bakzen War, Jason knew the TSS fleet was a fraction of its former size. However, the task at hand was not battle, but rather to function as a police presence to keep anything from getting out of hand. If it came down to a firefight between the Tararian Guard and the TSS, there'd be bigger problems than just fleet numbers.

In addition to those already stationed at outposts, TSS offensive vessels were en route to the thirty foremost Taran worlds. The move was precautionary, in the event the Priesthood did have a neurotoxin in their game plan that might pose a threat to the civilian population. The teams of TSS Agents who'd trained for the last four years in suppression techniques and the use of technological aids would, hopefully, be able to keep the situation under control, but any incident on a planetary scale would likely be too much for the specialist teams to handle. If that neurotoxin extended to control of the Tararian Guard fleet, the TSS would be out of luck.

Jason gulped. *We need the Aesir. But will they show up?*

He couldn't allow himself to be distracted by what might happen on the other worlds, though. His task was to protect the spatial tear within the Rift. The Priesthood would undoubtedly come to claim it, and only Jason and his skeleton crew on the *Conquest* stood in their path.

"The fleet is stretched so thin," Rianne commented while examining the map on the viewscreen. "No wonder we're here on our own."

"Not a lot of ships to spare, for sure," Jason agreed. "But if it comes down to us against enemy forces, it'll be better if no one friendly is nearby."

Rianne nodded somberly. "Been through that before." She paused, turning around to look at Jason. "Your dad didn't do it alone, though."

Jason swallowed. "His officers had pulled back by the end, but that doesn't matter. I won't need to focus that much. If it comes down to me needing to do something similar, ships will be a whole lot easier to take out than a planet."

The Militia officer turned back around in her chair. "Right."

"I don't want it to come to that."

She glanced back over her shoulder. "I know."

They waited in silence, watching the TSS fleet move into position. Groups of the blue TSS dots paired with the red of the Tararian Guard. As movements ceased, there was no doubt the TSS was greatly outnumbered. Even with superior firepower at individual ship levels, they wouldn't last long if it came to blows.

Jason slumped in his chair. *Let's hope we can wait it out here in peace.*

"We have incoming!" Rianne exclaimed.

So much for that idea! Jason straightened to attention. He waved his hand to minimize the map on the viewscreen, returning the view to their immediate surroundings.

A cruiser, three warships, a dozen destroyers, and two carriers dropped out of subspace around the *Conquest.*

Well, shit. Jason frowned. "Does that seem a little overkill for taking on one ship?"

"Clearly, they haven't underestimated you."

He cracked a cocky smile. "I'm not so sure about that."

Rianne tensed in her seat. "Incoming communication from the flagship."

"On screen." Jason turned his attention to the front of the domed viewscreen.

The view of the Rift surrounding the dome dissipated in the front center, replaced by the image of the Tararian Guard cruiser's Command Center and a very stern-looking middle-aged man who appeared to be none too happy with his present assignment.

"I'm General Allen Lucian of the Tararian Guard, acting on direct orders of the Priesthood. Stand down at once."

Jason evaluated the man. "You do realize, General Lucian, that as of 09:26 this morning, the Priesthood is no longer a recognized authority."

"I swore my allegiance to the Priesthood, and I will carry out my duty."

"Yeah, about that…" Jason leaned forward in his chair. "See, we figured you'd say something to that effect, so we looked at the specific wording of those oaths. Turns out that you actually swore allegiance to serve the Taran people. Since the Priesthood is, you know," Jason swiped his hand across his neck in a cutting motion, "it's kinda now treason to keep doing things in their name."

The general stared at him with shock and confusion. "Who *are* you?"

"Oh, right. Sorry, I left out the introduction there. I'm Jason Sietinen. You may know my dad, Wil. This is the ship he used to blow up the Bakzen homeworld."

General Lucian stood his ground, but the staff behind him in the Command Center visibly shrank into their chairs.

"Sir, maybe we should—" a woman next to the general whispered.

General Lucian ignored her and glared at Jason "You have no authority to be here." The woman took a step back, staring at the floor.

Super charismatic leader, this one. "Yeah, I'm gonna have to disagree with that assessment," Jason replied. "I suggest you take your little fleet and leave. The Rift is in TSS jurisdiction."

Rianne muted the comm channel. "Their weapons systems just activated. I'm not sure how many direct hits we could take. Is this a fight we can win?"

"Not without blowing up their ships," Jason replied in her mind without taking his level gaze off the viewscreen. *"The point is to limit loss of life."*

"You're provoking them," Rianne muttered.

"They won't fire on a Sietinen heir... I don't think."

Rianne sighed and unmuted the comm channel.

Jason smiled at General Lucian. "So, why don't you just head on back to Tararia, or wherever."

"I'm afraid that's impossible," the general replied. "I must insist you stand down now or we'll need to use force."

"Really? That's a shame."

General Lucian shook his head. "Are you actually in charge here? You're a kid."

"I'm twenty-one, so technically I'm not really a 'kid' anymore," Jason said. "In fact, I'm actually a TSS Agent. And a dynastic heir. So... even if I were a kid, I'd at least be an *important* kid. I really don't think you want to attack my ship."

"Listing off your titles won't keep me from completing my mission," General Lucian insisted. "We—"

The comm channel muted on the other end.

"Difference of opinions?" Jason speculated to Rianne.

"Maybe, but you should probably be aware that their weapons are now fully charged," she replied after muting their own mics.

"Well, that's just fantastic."

— — —

Cris was pulled back to the present by Marina waving a hand in front of his face.

"Cris, you with me?" she said, her tone pitched with urgency.

He nodded. "Right, sorry. The Guard fleet..."

"They've mobilized on all the major Taran worlds and all

their docks have been emptied. If we can't get through to leadership, it looks like they're prepared to carry out the Priesthood's orders even if it means attacking their own."

"And the TSS?" Cris questioned.

"Almost in position, as well. We should have the full complement in orbit of Tararia within ten minutes. But you know the numbers..."

Cris drew a slow breath. "Their backup is better than not having it, even if their presence in and of itself won't be much of a deterrent."

Marina crossed her arms. "Do you think this will turn into a firefight?"

"Well, this wouldn't be the first civil war the Guard has fought," Cris muttered. He leaned against the wall outside the conference room where the High Dynasty assembly had recently adjourned. "We need to let Wil focus on the other worlds. Our immediate concern is what's happening right outside our window."

"Oh, this is very, very bad!" Raena shouted as she ran up to him from down the hall. "A destroyer is in geosynchronous orbit right above us."

"There's *what*?" Cris exclaimed, coming to full attention. "They wouldn't possibly..." *What am I saying? Of course the Priesthood would issue that kind of order.* He groaned. "Well, shite! What can we do about that?"

Raena frowned. "How good is that shield around the estate?"

Cris tossed up his hands. "Will it hold up to an orbital bombardment? Maybe. But the deflected weapons fire would completely vaporize the city."

"So, weathering the storm is a no-go," Raena concluded.

"Not if we want to have anything left of our home when this is over." Cris ran a hand through his hair. "Wait, where's Kate?"

"Talking to Kaiden, I think," Marina replied. "Things over in the First Region are looking a bit grim, as well."

"And Ryan?" Cris asked.

"Adding his seal to all the orders regarding the Priesthood's dissolution," Raena replied. "Why?"

"We need to divert that ship," Cris stated.

Raena eyed him. "That'd be great, but how?"

"Between the four of us, I think we could send a powerful enough telekinetic beam to make them move away," Cris suggested. "It wouldn't buy a lot of time, but I'll take however many minutes we can get until the TSS arrives."

"Yes, that could definitely work." Raena perked up momentarily, then drooped. "Except, we'd have to drop the shield to launch the assault."

"Even better—it'll look like we're cooperating," Cris said.

"I guess it's really the only play we have right now. Let's get outside," she agreed.

"I'll hold down the administrative center," Marina told Cris. "Good luck."

"We'll do our best." He flashed a smile, but doubt was creeping in. *This has already turned so much more violent than I ever anticipated. Was this the right move for us to make?*

Cris and Raena dashed toward the gardens of the Sietinen estate, sending telepathic messages to their respective partners about where to meet.

"I now understand where my dad and Jason get their crazy streak from," Raena commented as they ran.

"Me? I'm subdued and practical," Cris replied.

"Tell that to the crew of the destroyer we're about to knock out of orbit."

Cris smirked. "Okay, maybe 'subdued' isn't the right word. But practicality does apply."

They reached an empty spaceport Cris had identified as the rendezvous point. At four hundred meters away from the manor, their telekinetic exertion shouldn't cause any damage to the structure.

Coming down the path, Cris spotted Kate and Ryan running to join them.

"It figures that the *one day* I wear heels, I end up sprinting around the estate," Kate grumbled once she was within earshot.

"Ah, I miss my TSS uniform..." Cris lamented while staring up into the sky, attempting to identify the exact location of the destroyer. The craft would be invisible to the naked eye, but his telekinetic senses would allow him to home in on its signature with a little focus.

His initial search was ineffective. However, Kate picked up on his goal and assisted.

"I think I feel it," Kate said after several seconds. "Right up there." She pointed.

Raena and Ryan joined in the telekinetic assessment.

"That's definitely it," Raena agreed. "Those things look big up close, but that's a tiny target from this distance."

"So are we." Cris took a slow breath. *"Marina,"* he relayed telepathically to the other side of the manor, *"we're in position. Drop the shield."*

A moment later, a shimmer passed along the boundary of the massive dome that had provided transparent protection for the estate.

Cris nodded to his family. "Follow my lead."

The four of them linked their minds in preparation for the assault. It had been years since any of them had performed a significant telekinetic feat, and Cris sensed a shared elation as they each drew energy into themselves. Unbridled power coursed through Cris, waiting to be unleashed.

When he could hold no more in himself, he focused the energy into a beam, targeting the signature of the destroyer in orbit above them.

Beams from the others joined in, blending into a single ray of pure energy. They fed the beam as it shot upward toward the ship, true to its course.

Cris winced as the beam hit its mark and was partially absorbed by the shields. He sent one final burst of energy, enough to knock the ship from its fixed location. A flash was just barely visible in the daytime sky as the craft's shield lit up to protect the hull from the force of the blast as it careened out of orbit.

Raena let out a relieved laugh. "That actually worked!"

"Wow…" Ryan breathed.

"Well, I bet that royally pissed them off," Kate said.

Cris smiled. "Indeed. That was surprisingly satisfying."

"Better get that shield back up," Raena advised.

"Right." Cris sent the requisite message to Marina and took a deep breath. "The TSS fleet should be in position any moment. We'll either be safe, or things are about to get a whole lot worse."

— — —

Wil studied the fleet positions on the holoprojector in the Primary Communications room of TSS Headquarters.

A broad viewscreen spanned half of the back wall, and consoles filled with Militia and Agent tactical personnel wrapped around the sides. Two curved consoles occupied the center of the room, leaving a clear pathway to a table with a holographic display of fleet positions beneath the main viewscreen.

The room was abuzz with support personnel coordinating logistics and optimizing fleet distribution in response to the Tararian Guard's shifting movements.

Accompanied by Saera, Michael, and a handful of his other most trusted TSS friends, the scene was too eerily similar to the Bakzen War for Wil's liking. *Except rather than a sworn enemy, these are our own people ready to fight us.*

The conflict would, hopefully, diffuse on its own accord once everyone learned of the Priesthood's treachery and removal from power, but that information took time to disseminate and many wouldn't trust the first wave of reports. The TSS would need to keep a full-on civil war from breaking out until all the facts were public knowledge. But at the rate the Tararian Guard was ramping up their offensive, he wasn't sure they'd be able to hold out for that long.

There was no doubt the Guard was acting on direct Priesthood orders. Though the TSS had once reported to the Priesthood, that relationship was always kept need-to-know, and once Cris had taken command of the TSS, the ties were officially severed. It meant that the TSS had autonomy, but their actions now might be perceived as a coup—which wasn't exactly inaccurate, but not in the way people would assume.

"I don't like the way this is going," Michael commented from next to Wil, his brow knitted as he examined the number of Guard ships versus their own.

"It won't just be us out there," Wil tried to assure him.

But the truth was, there had been no sign of the Aesir. All of their preparation had been with the assumption that they'd have the Aesir as allies to step in and diffuse the situation. Wil hadn't taken Jason's concern about their follow-through seriously, but now he found himself questioning if that had been the right call.

"They'll come," Saera murmured, sensing his thoughts. She rose from the work station in front of Wil and placed a reassuring hand on his arm.

"But when?"

"When we need them most," she replied.

Does every rescue have to be at the last minute? Wil groaned.

"I won't let myself freak out yet," Michael said. He eyed his daughter, Corine, busy at the controls of the right station in the center of the room. Though she hadn't been born with the Gifts of her parents, she'd already proved herself to be a highly capable Militia officer. Fatherly pride filled his gaze as he watched her work. "And, I'd rather be in here than out there."

Wil forced a smile. "Of course."

Michael immediately realized his misstep. "Sorry. I know Raena and Jason are…"

"They can hold their own," Wil replied. "I wouldn't have sent Jason to the Rift if I didn't think he could handle it."

All the same, Wil sensed a wave of worry emanate from his wife. *"Something's wrong,"* she said privately in his mind.

"I feel it, too, but it could be any—"

A red warning light flashed across the main viewscreen.

"Some kind of shot was just fired from the surface at the Guard destroyer in orbit of Tararia," Michael reported.

"It wasn't a weapon," Corine corrected. "That was a telekinetic blast."

Wil ran over to Corine's station. "What was the point of origin?" *I hope that wasn't the Priesthood's doing…*

"The Sietinen estate," Corine replied, her eyes wide with wonder.

Wil sighed. "My parents taking matters into their own hands, no doubt."

Saera inspected the scene. "No wonder. That destroyer was in geosynchronous orbit."

"The Tararian Guard wouldn't—" Wil started to object, but his wife pointed at the screen. "Oh, shite."

Alerts lit up across the board as the Tararian Guard ships moved into combat positions against the TSS fleet.

"Well, that escalated quickly," Wil muttered.

The communications officers shouted to Wil, "Sir, you need to see this."

Fok! What else? Wil directed his attention to a screen on the officer's console to the left of the central pathway.

A live video feed was playing of a crowd gathered on Crydael—everyone moving as one entity while they advanced on the TSS Militia guards sent to keep peace.

It's the mind control agent! They're actually using it on their own people... Wil's stomach turned over.

The officer gave a grim nod. "Reports are coming in from every major world. Dozens of accounts."

Wil turned to Michael and Saera. "Send in the teams—divide them up as best you can. We need to diffuse the riots before anyone gets hurt."

"Teams are in transit," Michael confirmed. *"I don't know if we can handle this scale,"* he added privately to Wil.

"That's the least of our worries. If civilians are being controlled, it could just as well be influencing the Tararian Guard."

"What about the TSS?" Michael asked.

"Let's hope that antidote from the war we proactively distributed is effective against this variation of the neurotoxin."

His friend nodded. *"We'll take samples from a few civilians and see what we can learn."*

"Shite!" the communications officer exclaimed.

"What?" Wil demanded.

"All Tararian Guard ships now have weapons locked on the TSS fleet."

Fok! So, the Priesthood is *using the neurotoxin against them, too—they wouldn't have one hundred percent compliance if it was only orders. Reasoning won't work.* Wil took an unsteady breath. "Michael, tell our fleet to defend itself. Target enemy weapon's systems and jump drives, but try to keep the rest of the ship intact."

"I'm on it," he acknowledged.

Wil set his jaw. *There has to be a way to end this without casualties… Enough people have already died for the Priesthood.*

CHAPTER 17

WHILE THE *CONQUEST* was a formidable vessel in its own right, being in the weapon's lock of more than a dozen warships had left Jason feeling rather outgunned—but that was almost certainly the intent.

Jason maintained his façade of calm. "General Lucian, are you preparing to fire on my ship?"

"This is your final warning to stand down," the general replied on-screen. His narrowed eyes accented angular features lined by years of scowling.

"I'm not going anywhere," Jason replied. "I don't want to hurt you, but I will if it comes to it."

Rianne took a shaky breath at her station in the front of the Command Center.

"Then you have forced my hand." General Lucian ended the transmission.

"We should probably brace for impact…" Jason suggested.

"Shields are up," Rianne confirmed. "They'll target weapons first and then our jump drive."

"In that case, we should probably make it a difficult target to hit." Jason gripped the handholds at the podium in front of his command chair. "You trust me, right?"

Rianne glanced back at him over her shoulder. "I barely know you."

"Well, you trust my dad, at least."

"I do."

Jason nodded. "Then trust that he trained me well."

"What are you—"

Before she could complete the question, Jason linked with the ship. He felt the bioelectronic interface respond to his inputs, becoming an extension of his physical self. All the ship's systems were accessible in his mind.

But what he had planned was not through the ship itself. He used the neural interface to link with the ship only so that it would be a closer part of him, to make it easier to grasp. With it held firmly within his mind, he initiated a spatial distortion—drawing the ship with him to the edge of subspace.

Rianne gasped when she realized what he was doing, but otherwise remained motionless and quiet.

Jason concentrated on holding the ship, a much larger object than he was used to pulling into a distortion with him. He'd practiced with his father using this very vessel, but it was different having someone else there for backup. This was all on him.

Hovering in that state at the edge of subspace, the ship was only an echo in the physical world—impervious to weapon's fire. Telekinetic energy discharge, however, was not confined to a single physical plane.

Jason maneuvered the ship outside the sphere of enemy ships and lined up with the flagship. The motion took minutes from Jason's vantage, but the spatial distortion meant real-time would be advancing much slower outside the distortion field. To General Lucian, it would appear the *Conquest* moved in the blink of an eye—and without the use of its jump drive.

I can't wait to hear what he has to say about this. Jason smirked as he brought the TSS ship into a broadsiding position only fifty meters from the flagship. As soon as he dropped the *Conquest* back into Rift space, the Tararian Guard would be hit with a barrage of proximity alerts and be far too close to the TSS vessel to fire. *Here it goes.*

Jason returned the vessel to the Rift.

For five seconds, the Tararian Guard fleet made no move. Their weapon locks had broken when the *Conquest* suddenly shifted from its former position, and it would take some time to reestablish the locks at the new position. However, no locks came.

Instead, an incoming communication request illuminated on the front viewscreen.

With a smug grin on his face, Jason answered the call from General Lucian. "Hello, General. It looks like your ship could use a fresh coat of paint."

"You're foking insane!" the general exclaimed. "How did you do that?"

"You maybe should have led with the second part. I don't think I want to tell you after you opened with an insult—or maybe it's not an insult. I'll have to think about it."

The general's face flushed with rage. "Stand down!"

Jason gazed back at him, unflinching. "You know, since you seem so intent on talking down to me like a child, I may as well play the role. If you want me to stand down: make me."

"Smooth…" Rianne muttered just loud enough for Jason to hear without the mics picking it up.

"Oh, come on—this guy's the worst."

General Lucian sputtered and deactivated the comm channel.

"Rianne, if he moves his ship, match it. Keep him uncomfortably close," Jason instructed.

"A stalemate never lasts forever," the Militia officer replied.

"I don't intend for it to. We just need—"

"Oh, shite!"

Red lit up across the screen as a volley of energy weapon's fire struck the *Conquest*'s shields.

"What the f—" Jason cut off when he saw the sea of fighters swarming around his ship.

The small craft were designed for stealth and had done their job—sneaking up for a precision strike where the larger warships had failed. At that proximity, it didn't matter that the flagship was so close. Their shots were true and packed a serious punch.

"I count one hundred eighty fighters," Rianne reported. "We can hold our own against a handful, but this many will wear us down fast."

"I can't hold us in a distortion indefinitely. Maybe if I just augment the shields…" Jason linked with the ship once more.

Each impact of the energy weapons with the shield felt like he'd been shot himself—a searing heat and electric shock that zapped his senses. He tried to feed energy through himself into the shield, but processing the rapid bombardments soon clouded his mind and he was forced to pull back.

He took in the sight on the viewscreen surrounding him. The fighters were everywhere. Even if he moved the ship, they would be there in an instant.

"Do we retreat?" Rianne asked. "We can come back with more ships and retake the Rift."

Jason shook his head. "And what if one of those ships is carrying some of the High Priests? We can't let them access the tear, even for a moment."

Rianne consulted her console. "Shields are down to forty percent. We'll be facing complete collapse in three minutes."

"We can't stay here." Jason gripped the podium and linked with the ship. *We have to defend the tear! Every other TSS ship is already subscribed to the other worlds. I have to find a way.*

He initiated another spatial distortion around the ship and began moving the vessel further into the Rift. Perhaps if he could get closer to the tear, he could tap into some of that power himself—just enough to stave off destruction. A little draw from it wouldn't hurt.

Jason could hear the sweet energy within the tear calling to him from a distance. He drew the *Conquest* toward it, eager to have a taste of the power. It would be the only way for them to stop the Guard fleet. Just a little bit of help and he'd be able to stand up to them.

They approached the site of the tear. It was invisible to the naked eye within the blackness, but Jason could feel it beckoning him.

"What are you planning?" Rianne asked cautiously.

"We have to defend this position," Jason replied. "They'll follow us. I need to be ready."

The Militia officer shook her head. "We're defending this location because that tear isn't safe. You're not planning to… tap into it, are you?"

"What other choice do we have?"

She shook her head. "No."

Jason ignored her continued protests. The tear sang at the edge of his consciousness. He returned the *Conquest* to the physical plane of the Rift and then reached out toward the tear, extending a tendril of energy from himself to sample the power within its depths. It was so close, he could almost reach it. *Just a taste...*

"Wait!" Rianne called out. "Subspace distortions all around us."

Jason pulled back, just shy of touching the tear.

A smile spread across Rianne's face. "It's the Aesir."

Three dozen ships came into focus all around them. The vessels shined like pearls in the blackness, the refined lines and arching forms of the ships a spectacle at the scale of a warship. As the subspace cloud dissipated around them, the ships all oriented to face the direction from which the Tararian Guard would advance.

Jason released the telekinetic tendril he'd extended from himself. He realized his heart was racing. *This power really is intoxicating. I almost gave in...* He shook off the spell. *I'm here to protect, not be consumed myself.*

"Open a comm channel with the Aesir," Jason instructed.

"Declined," Rianne replied after five seconds. "Oh, stars!"

The Tararian Guard ships appeared jumping from their previous locations. They opened fire on the Aesir fleet.

Rings rippled along the Aesir ships' shields from the impact sites. Volley after volley launched from the Guard ships, and yet the Aesir did nothing in retaliation.

"Pull back," Jason instructed Rianne. *What are the Aesir's plans here? Are they going to help or just sit there and take a beating?*

Rianne seemed equally confused by their actions. "No sign of weapons initiation on the Aesir ships. Their shields are holding at full power, though." Her brow furrowed. "Hold on... I'm actually not picking up *any* sign of weapon systems on the ships."

Jason smiled. "Oh, that is brilliant."

"Care to enlighten me?"

"I'd wager those ships," he swept his hand to encompass the fleet depicted on the viewscreen before them, "are all like a super-advanced version of the *Conquest*. The weapons are the ship itself—one, giant energy amplifier. And with the Guard ships firing on them, they're just charging the batteries."

She chuckled. "Well, that'll be a problem for the Guard ships."

"Indeed. Any second..."

Each of the Aesir ships flashed with pure white light. Beams arced between the ships, sparking with electrical energy. The brightness of the beams intensified, and then rays branched out toward the Tararian Guard fleet.

The Guard ships shuddered as each was simultaneously struck by a ray. As the ray passed over each, lights on the Guard ships extinguished for a moment before flickering back on. When every one of the ships had been struck, the white beams dissolved.

"That's incredible..." Rianne breathed. "Weapons and propulsion have been knocked out, but all other systems remain intact."

"Conscious control," Jason said. "Wow."

The screen illuminated with an incoming communication request from the Aesir, which Jason accepted.

"Nice timing," he said. "That was an impressive show."

The man on the other end of the call was not someone Jason had seen previously. He had the same ageless appearance of the Oracles, but his skin was much closer to a standard Taran tint and his eyes were warm brown. "When we asked the TSS to defend the Rift, we thought you'd subscribe more than one ship to the task."

Jason shrugged. "We're a little tied up at the moment."

"I see." The man frowned. "You are Jason Sietinen, correct?"

"I am. And you are...?"

"You may call me Adam," the man replied. "I could be considered a general for the Aesir fleet. However, such titles are not part of our culture."

"Well, Adam, you have a flare for theatrics and I like your style. I'm very pleased to welcome you to the Rift."

"We will place fortifications around this site," Adam stated. "I hope our actions will prove to be a sufficient deterrent for other Guard ships."

Jason nodded. "I wouldn't mess with you, that's for sure. I don't suppose you have any more ships to spare?"

"The Rift is the most important site to protect, so we are only the first wave. Reinforcements for the rest of the TSS fleet are in transit," Adam confirmed.

"That's a relief! I was afraid you weren't going to show up."

Adam inclined his head. "Your statement to the Oracles resulted in a long debate. I was not privy to the deliberations, but I do know Dahl was struck by your words—enough to alter our plan."

"Really?" *Do those alterations help or hurt us?*

"That conversation is not my concern, though. My only mandate is to protect this place."

"We have that in common," Jason replied. "You got us out of a tough spot, so you're more than welcome here. Make yourselves comfortable." *If they make a move toward the tear, though, they'll have another thing coming.*

— — —

Wil shook his head as he took in the scene unfolding on the holoprojector before him. The Tararian Guard fleet was weapons-hot across the board and there was no way for the TSS to pose any kind of opposition without a major loss of life.

"Maybe we should just pull back?" his wife suggested.

"And let the Priesthood carry out their plan, whatever it is? No," Wil objected.

"Saera has a point," Michael interjected. "Perhaps we should pull back and focus the fleet in larger numbers at a few worlds at a time."

"We wait it out," Wil insisted. *The Aesir will come… they have to.*

"Sir, we just got a proximity alert," Corine announced from her station. "Guard vessels: two battleships, a carrier, and four cruisers just dropped out of subspace at Headquarters."

Wil groaned. "Please tell me it's at least in the blind spot from Earth…"

"Yes, just barely," she confirmed.

That's one bit of good news. "Any message from them?"

Corine listened to her comm. "Same blanket transmission as to the rest of the fleet—'surrender at once or else' gist."

Michael sighed. "Well, now we're stuck in here."

"Not that we were planning to go anywhere." Wil's mind raced. "Okay, we know the Guard and the civilian population are being controlled by the neurotoxin, right?" His friends nodded. "What about the dynasties? Has Sietinen reported any odd behavior from the other leaders?"

"No," Corine replied. "And it's not *all* civilians—just concentrated clusters in the main population centers."

"In other words, the places that will most effectively draw the TSS' resources. We'd never try to intervene at a dynastic compound, so they haven't bothered to activate anyone there," Wil concluded.

Saera eyed him. "That suggests that they *could* if they decided it would be worthwhile."

"I'm not ruling out any possibilities."

"All right," Saera conceded. "But what can we do about it? We have warships knocking on our door and mass hysteria is about to break out on dozens of worlds. Do we sit on our hands, walk away, or…?"

"We're not backing off," Wil reiterated.

"Then what?" she pressed.

"I'm thinking." Wil wished there was a clear answer, but any action—or inaction—would have ripple effects for the rest of their plans. "All right," he said after another minute of contemplation. "As things stand, the most immediate threat is the Tararian Guard. They have the big guns. The civilians might get into fistfights, but on the whole, any injuries or other damage will be minimal compared to what a warship can inflict. Instruct all TSS teams to shift their focus to disabling the Tararian Guard. They're fewer in numbers, so there's a chance that the suppression nets will have full effect at scale."

Michael nodded. "I'm on it."

"Good thinking," Saera said privately.

"It's the best I've got right now." He hoped it would be enough.

Michael set about relaying the new orders to the rest of the fleet. The suppression nets were designed to deploy an electromagnetic field that would dampen telekinetic and telepathic abilities. Since the Priesthood's orders were delivered telepathically, the field would, in theory, negate that telepathic influence and result in a person's behavior returning to normal. Tests on the neurotoxin used by the Bakzen had been effective, but the Priesthood's variation was new. If the nets were ineffective, the TSS would be at the mercy of the Tararian Guard.

"The first wave is deploying the nets now," Michael reported.

Stars, I hope this works... Wil's gaze was glued to the viewscreen as a grid of video feeds appeared from the TSS ships.

The suppression nets were invisible over the camera feeds, but Wil could sense the one cast over the Guard ships outside TSS Headquarters, even through the mass of the moon. It generated a low hum that pestered the back of his mind. He tried to block it out and focus on the video footage.

Ten seconds passed with no indication of success. Then, the weapons on the Guard ships powered down.

Wil breathed a sigh of relief and ventured a smile. "That's a good sign."

"Only ships at half the sites have started to stand down," Michael reported. He paused. "We're getting a communication request from the lead ship outside Headquarters."

"Put it through," Wil instructed.

The videos on the main viewscreen shrank and moved to the border of the screen, making room in the center for the new communication feed.

A woman dressed in dark gray with slicked-back hair appeared, sporting an expression of concern. "I'm Commander Rysa of the *Valkyrie*."

"Hello, Commander," Wil replied. "I'm High Commander of the TSS. I request your ships withdraw from our jurisdiction immediately."

Rysa frowned. "That's just it... None of us have any

recollection of jumping here."

"So, the telepathic influence also results in amnesia? That complicates matters," Wil said to the Agents present.

"It's consistent with the Bakzen's technique. Nolan didn't remember what he'd done, either," Saera pointed out.

Wil returned his attention to the viewscreen. "Well, Commander, I regret to inform you that the Tararian Guard and a number of civilians are currently under telepathic influence via a neurotoxin administered by the Priesthood. We have deployed a suppression net as a countermeasure, but it has not been as effective as we'd hoped."

Rysa raised an eyebrow. "Pardon, the Priesthood deployed a neurotoxin?"

"I trust you haven't seen the new mandate," Wil continued. "The Priesthood has been removed from power. They have been less than honest with the Taran people."

"Excuse me for a moment." The video feed changed to the Tararian Guard's emblem, which represented Tararia and its two moons set against a black background. Thirty seconds later, the feed reinitialized. "I've confirmed the new directive that all previous orders issued by the Priesthood are to be disregarded, but there's no way to authenticate that command. Everything has always borne the Priesthood's digital seal."

Wil nodded. "We anticipated concern about the new mandates. You'll find attached an official order ratified by all High Dynasties."

Rysa appeared to be reading through something off-camera. "This is ratified by *seven* High Dynasties… with a seal from Dainetris."

"It was a busy morning," Wil said with a slight smile.

"I need to verify these instructions with the Guard leadership," Rysa stated. "Thank you for your assistance." She ended the communication.

"Uh oh…" Corine murmured from her station. "The Guard ships are on a vector that will take them beyond the suppression net in six seconds."

Please tell me they're just going to jump away… Wil held his breath.

"They're slowing down," reported Corine.

An electric flash lit up the viewscreen.

"What was that?" Wil demanded.

Michael closed his eyes while he filtered through incoming telepathic reports from Agents at the various sites. "The suppression nets are down. The Priesthood must have figured out a way to counter the frequency."

Fok! Wil's heart raced. "Can we cycle the frequency… anything to make it effective?"

Saera shook her head. "That will take time—"

"Weapons are locked on the TSS spaceport!" Corine exclaimed. "I need—"

She cut off as dozens of subspace signatures appeared on the viewscreen.

Wil's breath caught in his chest. *A fleet that size could easily blow up the whole moon!*

Ships appeared within the subspace distortions, slowly resolving into solid forms. The design was unmistakable—the elegant styling of the Aesir.

Saera sighed with relief. "I thought we were done for."

"I knew they'd come." *At least, I hoped they would…*

On the viewscreen, similar subspace distortions appeared at all the sites populated with Tararian Guard warships. In each instance, the Aesir vessels were a match for—if not outnumbering—the opposition.

"Incoming communication," Corine reported.

"Accept," Wil acknowledged.

Dahl's image appeared on the main viewscreen. "Hello, Cadicle. May we offer our assistance?"

Wil beamed at him. "Please! I can command a fleet in battle, but politically fueled stalemates are beyond me."

"I believe you would have found a way. All the same…" Dahl nodded to someone off-camera. An instant later, engines and weapons on all the Tararian Guard ships simultaneously deactivated. "Now you can focus on the real task at hand."

"Thank you," Wil said. "But the last suppression field failed."

"We are actively controlling this one," Dahl replied. "The mind is much more powerful than technology."

Wil bowed his head. “Indeed it is. We are indebted to you.”

“You already know our terms,” Dahl stated.

Except, if Jason’s right, we may be trading the Priesthood for an even more powerful opponent. “Yes, and we will hand over the Rift to you when the Priesthood is secure.”

“We will take it now,” Dahl said. He paused, realization flitting across his face. “If you are concerned about us accessing the power contained in the tear, you needn’t worry. We reflected on your son’s words, and we have seen that we are not yet ready to follow that path.”

Can I really take that statement at face value? He glanced at Saera and she looked equally skeptical.

“We must trust one another,” Dahl continued. “You may not believe my statements are genuine, but you must have faith.”

“We’re out of options,” Saera said privately in Wil’s mind.

“I guess we really are.” Wil inclined his head to Dahl. “I’ll have Jason withdraw the *Conquest*. The Rift is yours.”

“In good faith, we will withdraw, as well,” Dahl told him. “With the Tararian Guard fleet disabled, there is no need for an active patrol.”

“Thank you,” Wil acknowledged.

Dahl gave a single nod. “Now, you must subdue the High Priests. Even without their fleet, they are not powerless.”

“We’ll have them soon.”

“We will make sure the Guard is not a threat. End this.” Dahl terminated the communication.

Wil released a long breath.

“Talk about timing…” Saera murmured.

“Last possible second, for sure.” Wil sighed. “Let’s call up Jason and get his side of things.”

Corine initiated the communication, and Jason picked up in the Command Center of the *Conquest* five seconds later.

“Hey,” he greeted with a smile. “The Aesir showed up, after all.”

“Thank the stars!” Wil breathed. “You all right?”

“Unscathed,” his son reported. “I think a particular Tararian Guard officer might now have it in for me, though.”

“I’m sure we can smooth things over when we’re finished

here. Is the Rift secure?" Wil asked.

"Well, there are three dozen Aesir ships. The Tararian Guard doesn't stand a chance against them, but can we trust them to be left alone with the tear?" his son replied.

I wish I knew the answer, but we're out of options. "They claim they'll withdraw when you do. But if they can't be trusted, I don't want you there without any backup. I could use your help on Tararia."

Jason took a slow breath. "All right, I'll head right over."

"I'll let Raena know to expect you," Wil said. "Be safe." He ended the call. "Michael, now that the Aesir can keep the civilian and Guard forces in order, reallocate TSS resources to eliminate any suspected Priesthood lab sites. No more clones."

"Consider it done," Michael responded and got back to work.

"I'm glad we have the Aesir on our side," Saera said. "If they'd turned against us…"

Wil shook his head. "I can't help but think how different things would have been if they'd assisted us in the war."

"Well, we're united now. This is our chance to start over."

"It is," he agreed. "And to that end, I should be there."

Saera's expression made it clear she wasn't thrilled with the idea of them separating, but she nodded. "It's a conversation to be had face-to-face."

"This is almost over." He kissed her. "We have them cornered."

"Finish it," she told him.

"That's precisely what I intend to do."

CHAPTER 18

CRIS DASHED THOUGH the marble-lined halls of the Sietinen manor with his family in tow.

"Again with the running!" Kate moaned, and she paused to slip off her shoes before continuing to jog barefoot on the tiles.

"The Tararian Guard ships are dormant. We need to make a move on the Priesthood's island while we have an opening," Cris replied.

"Isn't that the TSS' job?" Raena ventured.

Ryan nodded. "I'm inclined to agree. We're in no position to get in the middle of that fight."

"I didn't spend almost two decades as TSS High Commander just to sit on the sidelines for this," Cris said. "You don't have to join me, but I'm going to do anything I can to help."

Kate shrugged. "I guess there's no point in removing the Priesthood from power if we aren't going to change the rules around telekinesis."

"Actually, that's a great point... Ryan, how do you feel about changing that law?" Cris asked.

"Sure, I'm for it."

Cris pulled out his handheld from his pocket and halted in the middle of the hallway. He initiated a call to Kaiden.

After several seconds, his brother-in-law answered. "Cris? I thought we'd handled everything for today."

"One more item," Cris replied. "I move we lift the ban on

telekinesis."

Kaiden sighed. "What are you planning?"

"Nothing specific. It'd just be nice to have some… flexibility." *And to retroactively dismiss that stunt we just pulled.*

"All right, I'll ratify it. You'll need a fourth vote, though," Kaiden said.

Cris smiled. "That's my next call."

"Good luck. Now, if you'll excuse me."

"Of course. Thank you." Cris ended the communication.

"Talsari?" Kate asked.

"They're our best bet," Cris agreed. He brought up Ellen Talsari's contact information and opened a call.

This time, however, there was no answer.

Cris groaned. "Not helpful."

"Let's get to the administrative center and find out what's going on," Kate suggested. "We didn't run all this way to stand around in the hallway."

"Sorry." Cris resumed jogging down the corridor.

"You know," Raena began after a minute, "we should try Baellas instead of Talsari."

"I don't think Eduard is very fond of us after this morning." Cris countered.

"I doubt he's that displeased. He did cast his vote in favor early," Raena pointed out. "Besides, Baellas is extremely dependent on SiNavTech—and now DGE—for transporting their goods. This would be a great chance for them to earn some favor."

Cris admired her. "When did you become such the politician?"

She grinned. "I was always a good student."

We do need to solidify alliances while everything is up in the air. A strong additional partnership would serve us well. Cris nodded. "I like it. We'll make it happen as soon as Marina fills us in."

They reached the administrative center soon thereafter. Staff members were looking worn after a night and morning of solid work, but the frenetic energy from earlier had mellowed—either due to things being more under control or sheer weariness.

Marina spotted them as soon as they entered the room and rushed over. "The Aesir just dropped into orbit," she announced. "People are asking questions. We need to release a statement."

"All right." Cris sighed. "Raena, want to call Baellas?"

"Sure," she agreed.

Cris nodded. "Okay, I'll draft a quick statement and then head for the Priesthood's island."

Marina raised an eyebrow. "No."

"I—"

His advisor shook her head. "We'll make a thoughtful, live broadcast and conduct a Q&A afterward. You need to make a stand as an authority figure—you can't get tied up in the thick of things."

Cris groaned inwardly, knowing she was right but also hating that after all the years of planning his part would come down to a few choice words.

"TSS reinforcements are on their way," Marina continued. "By the time we've made a statement, they should be able to move in without civilian resistance."

"Then let's go reassure them," Cris agreed.

— — —

Raena's heart pounded in her chest as she entered the conference room with Ryan. "When did we become so important?"

"Probably right around the time we agreed to run a civilization."

"Oh, right. That."

He took her hand. "Hey, you've got this. We've already done the hard part."

Raena took a slow, even breath to calm herself. "You're right. Thanks for being here with me."

"As long as I'm in here, I don't have to deal with all that." Ryan gestured toward the door.

"Good point." Raena composed herself and then entered the communication request on the main holoprojector in the room.

Twenty seconds passed, and then an image of Eduard Baellas resolved on the holoprojector, as though he was in the room with them.

"Hello, Eduard," Raena greeted. "Sorry to bother you so soon after our meeting this morning."

"Is something wrong?" Eduard asked.

"More of a follow-on request," Raena stated. "Sietinen has introduced a proposal to overturn the telekinesis ban on the central worlds."

Eduard's brow knitted. "Is that so?"

"I'm calling to request your vote in favor," Raena continued. "Given the… evolving dynamics with SiNavTech and DGE, this seems like a prime opportunity to secure a mutually beneficial relationship between our three families."

The Head of the Baellas Dynasty stroked his chin. "What do you propose?"

"We could forfeit Baellas' interest in DGE," Ryan proposed. *"SiNavTech's and VComm's shares are more than enough to get the company off the ground."*

"Good thinking." Raena smiled. "Well, with the return of Dainetris, you're facing a potential ten percent loss of your assets, due to what was—as it turns out—illegally absorbed from DGE. We are prepared to allow you to retain all of those assets Dainetris would otherwise claim."

Eduard cocked his head, a smile touching the corners of his mouth. "Is that so?"

"It is," Ryan confirmed. "I hope that your vote of confidence in what we have to offer in non-business matters can carry over to a new professional relationship."

Eduard looked between the two of them. "I would be foolish to not recognize what a partnership between Sietinen and Dainetris means for our future. I welcome the chance to begin this new relationship on good terms."

"So, you'll ratify the vote?" Raena confirmed.

"Indeed. Provide the official order and we'll make some more history."

Raena smiled. "Our thanks to you."

"I look forward to our future business dealings," Eduard said.

"Anything else?"

"That's all. Thank you," Raena said.

"Best of luck." Eduard ended the call.

Ryan leaned against the table. "Well, that was easy."

"It certainly is when you have exactly the right leverage."

"What do you think your grandfather has planned?" Ryan asked, concern creeping into his voice.

"Well, we did just launch the assault on the destroyer, so getting a pass on that will be handy," Raena replied. "But beyond that, we have no way of knowing what kind of final stand the Priesthood might take—this means we can defend ourselves. Now that we're married and you're a Dynastic Head, we can't technically be in the TSS anymore."

"This all happened so fast, I hadn't even thought about that," Ryan admitted.

Raena took his hands. "Being with you is more important to me than use of any abilities, even if the laws weren't overturned."

"All things being equal, though…"

She cracked a smile. "Opening doors telekinetically to make badass entrances?"

He grinned. "Exactly."

They exited the conference room and found an aide to draft the resolution to overturn the telekinesis ban. The language was significantly more complicated than Raena had anticipated, and they soon found themselves deep into the nuances of appropriate telekinesis use. In retrospect, Raena realized it wasn't just overturning a ban—they actually needed to establish the new law of what was allowable and when.

"*We really should be consulting others about this,*" she said privately to Ryan.

"*We can always change it after the fact. As long as it's broad enough to cover what we might encounter over the next day, we'll be fine.*"

Reluctantly, she agreed and they hammered out the details as best they could.

Just as the finalized document was being distributed for official signing, Raena spotted Cris waving to them from across the room.

"Wil and Jason just got here," he told them.

Raena and Ryan jogged over to him. "That was fast," Raena said as they approached.

"It's been almost five hours," Cris replied. He cast them a quizzical look. "What have you been up to?"

"Uh, rewriting the laws on acceptable practices for civilian use of telekinesis?" Raena said sheepishly.

Cris chuckled. "Well, that figures. I was just busy giving a public address about how things are changing for the better, so I suppose that's appropriate."

Raena rubbed her eyes. "I can't believe it's been five hours. That explains why I'm hungry."

"We can grab a bite to eat with your dad and brother. Let's go meet them," Cris suggested.

They didn't need to go beyond the porch. Wil and Jason were coming up the path and were already almost to the manor, looking travel-worn.

Though she and Ryan had gone to visit TSS Headquarters several times in the intervening years since she left the official training program, she hadn't been with her family on Tararia for five years. It'd been eight months since their last visit, and it took her a minute to get over seeing Jason dressed as an Agent.

"Wow, look at you," she murmured.

Jason grinned at her. "You're one to talk! Wow, you've gone native."

Raena looked down at her business attire. "You should see the evening gowns."

Before she could say any more, her father had wrapped her in a warm embrace. "I wish we had been here for the wedding. Your mom—"

Raena patted his back. "It's fine, Dad. It seriously wasn't that big of a deal."

Ryan flashed a sheepish smile. "We'd sorta just crash-landed and run up forty flights of stairs."

Cris shook his head. "It's a long story."

Wil released Raena and scowled. "Uh huh…"

Jason took the opportunity to give Raena a hug. "I missed you."

"I've missed you, too." She squeezed him.

"Congratulations." Wil shook Ryan's hand while Raena parted from the embrace with her brother.

"Thanks," Ryan replied. "It'll be nice to have some time to process everything."

"Soon enough." Wil took a deep breath. "First, we take the High Priests into custody."

They're not the only ones on the island. "We also need to get those women out of there," Raena insisted. "Once the High Priests know they're cornered, they might… try to destroy evidence."

Her father considered the statement. "You're right. We should send in a team. We might be able to use that vent you escaped through as an entry point."

"I'm going," Raena stated.

"No way." Wil chuckled.

She stared him in the eye. "I'm going. I left them behind once, I owe them now."

"It doesn't have to be you—" her father tried to protest.

"But it should be. If I want to prove myself as a leader for the people who've been taken advantage of, then this is the best way to show it. I may not have been training in Headquarters, but I can hold my own."

Wil sighed. "You'll just sneak aboard a shuttle if I try to stop you, huh?"

She shrugged. "Probably something along those lines."

"I'll go with her," Jason volunteered.

Wil eyed them. "What are you thinking in terms of a team?"

"Just the two of us," her brother suggested. "Raena knows the layout. The two of us are stronger than a team of a dozen Agents—or more."

Their father shook his head but then nodded his agreement. "Fine, but you need to promise to play it safe."

"We will," Raena assured him. "I just… I need to make things right."

"I know that feeling." He looked to Jason. "Take the lead on getting everything prepped. Don't take any unnecessary risks."

"I'm on it."

"While you take the back entrance, I'll lead a team on the surface. I have some unfinished business with Quadris," Wil said.

"I guess Ryan and I get to hold down the fort here," Cris muttered.

Wil cast him a level gaze. "You're High Dynasty leaders—leave the dirty work to others."

Raena interlocked her fingers and flexed her hands. "I'm just going to forget about that title for a few hours, if you don't mind. This is personal."

— — —

I really don't like Raena and Jason going in on their own… Wil tried to suppress his misgivings. He knew his children were more than capable of handling whatever they may face, but sending loved ones into a dangerous situation was always difficult.

However, Wil also knew he'd insist on going in, himself, were he in Raena's position, so it was unfair to have any other expectations for her. The best thing he could do was secure the upper part of the facility to give Raena and Jason a clear exit.

To that end, he needed to get his team in order.

Wil reached out over the telepathic network between the TSS commanders, *"Michael, I need a team to infiltrate the Priesthood's island. Who do you have for me?"*

"All the Elites aside from Kalin are on other worlds, but we have a Primus team and two Sacon units on cruisers in orbit. You have your pick of Militia," his friend replied.

"Send the three Agent teams and a full battalion of Militia soldiers. I don't want to mess around."

Michael's surprise carried over the telepathic network. *"All right. What should I set as the staging point?"*

Wil thought for a second. "We'll go directly to the island. Meet at 17:00."

"You've got it."

That gave Wil less than an hour to get into position, but it would be enough. The faster they got there, the less time the High

Priests and their acolytes would have to plan an escape past the TSS and Aesir ships. He had to hope their strong drive for self-preservation would be enough to keep their captives safe until they knew they were truly cornered and had no way out.

"We move in at 17:00," Wil informed his children.

"We'll be ready," Jason confirmed.

Next, Wil reached out to Kalin with orders to meet at the surface port to the west of the Sietinen manor.

His friend was waiting for him when Wil arrived. Wil smiled. "It's been a long time."

Kalin clapped him on the back. "Going on two years, huh? I guess I'm used to life planet-side now."

"I was surprised when you didn't come back to Headquarters the last time Raena and Ryan came to visit."

"I still stay in touch with everyone," Kalin replied. "But now, one of the admin staffers here and I are… closer."

Wil cast his friend a quizzical look, but Kalin just gave a coy smile in response.

"I'm glad to hear it," Wil said. "I hope you're up for one final mission."

"Absolutely."

They went to the kiosk at the port and coded in access to one of the shuttles.

"I'm glad it worked out for you to be here," Wil commented as they got settled in the craft. "I appreciate you leaving Headquarters to train Raena and Ryan."

"They were exceptional students. It was a privilege." Kalin paused. "I was surprised when you only assigned Raena a 9.3."

"That was more political than an attempt at accuracy."

His friend nodded. "Clearly."

When pre-flight checks were complete, Wil directed the shuttle from the ground and set a course for the Priesthood's island. "While you were training her, she didn't—"

"Wil, we can be honest with each other. We both know I didn't actually do any 'training'; I was here to make everything look legit on paper. She was beyond me before we ever left Headquarters."

He wasn't sure how to respond to that. "She's very gifted,

yes."

Kalin chuckled. "Yeah, that's what we'll call it. What I think you're asking is if others know she's at least as strong as you? No, I doubt it. She's never made any grand, public display."

"She made a conscious choice to serve Tararia."

"Well, something tells me that in the years to come, those Gifts and politics will no longer be mutually exclusive."

"Of that I have no doubt," Wil agreed.

The flight path took the shuttle over the river flowing from Lake Tiadon to the ocean, passing by suburban residences and the occasional commercial center. Eventually, the river fanned out into a wide mouth that spilled into the ocean, bisecting the pristine coastline extending in either direction.

They crossed the expanse of the ocean in silence, staying low in the hope of appearing to be a sightseeing craft admiring the sea life below. When they were twenty kilometers from the destination, Wil received an encrypted communication.

"This is Agent Gaedon," a woman said. "We're ready to move in on your order."

Wil gauged the timing. "Do it. Send teams to secure the complexes on the southern shore. I'll land at the northern port to take the main structure."

"Aye," Gaedon acknowledged and ended the call.

"How many people do you think are in there?" Kalin asked.

"My guess is maybe two to three hundred, but I really have no idea."

"Well, we can take 'em."

Wil smiled. "You bet we can."

They made the final approach to the island just as two dozen TSS transport shuttles dropped through the cloud cover in one dramatic assault front. The craft dispersed across the island, and Wil arced to the north to land on the cliffs near the main administrative building.

He powered down the shuttle as soon as they landed and jumped out the side door with Kalin.

Agent Gaedon ran up. "Are you coming in with us?"

"I wouldn't miss it. I already have our first stop in mind," Wil replied.

Five years prior, when Raena and Ryan were captured by the Priesthood, Wil had identified the location of High Priest Quadris' office. The Priesthood leader might not be in the room after seeing an assault force arrive, but that wing was as good a place as any to start.

Wil broke into a jog toward the castle-like structure, accompanied by Kalin, a team of five Agents, and thirty Militia soldiers.

Four of the Militia soldiers scouted ahead with pulse guns. When they reached the main door into the buildings, two simultaneously swung open the double doors and the others rushed in to sweep the room. Though he didn't detect anyone aside from the soldiers, Wil couldn't be sure that the Priesthood didn't have defensive tech to mask their presence.

The soldiers gave the all clear signal and Wil moved in.

Inside, the building was the same as he remembered it from his brief visit as a teenager. Polished stone archways adorned the interior corridors, with mosaics inset in the floors.

Though beautiful on the surface, the space had the same emptiness Wil had sensed on his previous visit. Knowing what he did now, he realized it was because the Priesthood lacked the heart and spirit that brought other places alive. This was a place fueled by selfish ambition. It sent a chill down Wil's spine as he moved further into the space.

Ahead, the scout soldiers suddenly halted and aimed their weapons.

"On your knees!" one shouted.

Wil rushed around the corner to see a group of ten acolytes dressed in light gray lowering themselves to their knees with their hands behind their heads. Their expressions were eerily calm considering the guns pointed at their faces.

One of the acolytes spotted Wil. "You'll never stop us."

"Think again," he replied and nodded to the guards to secure the Priesthood members. Privately, he reached out to Michael. *"Are all the Priesthood's labs under TSS control?"*

His friend took ten seconds to respond. *"Everything we and the Aesir know about. We'll do another sweep once you have access to the Priesthood's records to make sure we didn't miss anything."*

"Good. We're moving through the facility now."

Four Militia guards escorted the acolytes outside while the rest of Wil's team moved forward. They encountered one other group, which was also easily subdued.

At last, they reached the wing containing the office Wil had identified as belonging to Quadris. The halls were empty and offices darkened. However, a single, powerful presence waited up ahead.

It's him. The power was the same Wil had sensed coming from the hidden elevator as a teenager. It reminded him of what he felt while with the Aesir, but dark and twisted. Greed and hate swirled beneath the power.

"I'll take the lead here," Wil said and slipped past the Militia soldiers.

He telekinetically blasted open the door.

Inside, Quadris stood by the window, his back to Wil. Black robes covered him from head to foot. His pale hands were clasped behind his back. "I'm surprised it took you this long to come for me."

"Wanted to get everything else in order first." Wil gripped him in a telekinetic hold and spun him around.

Quadris stared unblinkingly at him with his glowing red eyes. "The irony… Our organization's namesake turned against us."

Irony or not, they brought this on themselves. Wil advanced on High Priest Quadris, tightening his telekinetic hold on him. "It's over. You lost."

"We will be born anew," Quadris forced out through the telekinetic vise around his chest.

"We've destroyed your facilities. Whatever backups you think you have, they're gone. This current form is all you have."

Quadris' face remained calm, accepting. "You could have become so much more."

"Well, looks like we'll just have to advance the old fashioned way," Wil told him. He released the hold enough for Quadris to breathe without laboring.

The old man gasped as his lungs were able to fully fill again. "You've learned the secrets of our past, but that doesn't change anything. Tarans are still weak. This species would wither without us."

"You know, I think we're going to be just fine."

Quadris glared at him. "You'll be cast as the villains for attacking us like this."

"Again, I don't think that'll be an issue." Wil took another step closer. "You see, while we've been chatting here, that data packet we shared with the High Dynasty Heads earlier has been transmitted to all the major news outlets—it even came with Vaenetri's official validation. Every member of the Taran civilization is now learning just what you've been up to for the past millennia or so. They'll all come to understand exactly what you've done and why you needed to be stopped. We've freed them."

"We…" Quadris' tone shifted, sounding genuinely contrite. "We were trying to save our fellow Tarans, too."

"You manipulated people's genetic code without their consent!"

"It was to help them. Many wished they could have more, and we tried to give that to them."

"But it didn't work." Wil fixed him in a level stare. "You didn't help them—you took away a core part of their being. Our entire culture changed when those abilities were lost. I've spent time with the Aesir—seen how fluidly they move between the spoken word and thought. I've felt how they interact with technology that's tuned to respond to those with abilities. It's the only place I've felt whole. When you took telekinetic abilities away, you condemned everyone to live an incomplete life, and worse yet, to not even know anything was missing."

"It's true," Quadris replied. "It was our greatest mistake."

The confession had come too easily, but Wil needed to capitalize on the opportunity. "Then admit it!" Wil shouted at him. "For once in your pathetic existence, own up to your mistakes! Tell the people what you did—that you made the Bakzen, that you villainized them to hide your own wrongdoings, that you've been capturing innocent daughters to serve your own selfish ends. How many lives have you ruined? You made me do so much of your dirty work, but no more! Admit what you've done and take some accountability."

Quadris quaked in Wil's presence, for once appearing only as a frail, elderly man. In that instant, gone was the all-powerful High Priest who would have had himself be a god. "I'm sorry," he murmured.

"Don't tell me—tell them." Wil activated the holoprojector and brought up a blank communication. *Even if it's not a genuine apology, a public admission of guilt will go a long way to promote peace.* "Confess what you did," he said to Quadris, staring into his sorrel eyes. "This is as close as you can ever come to making things right. It's your choice now what kind of legacy you want to leave—one of honesty in your final moments, or selfish and deceitful to your dying breath."

"You'd kill me now? An old, defenseless man."

Oh, now he's just playing me. Wil scoffed. "I honestly haven't decided what to do with you. But I suggest you treat every moment as though it's your last, because it very well may be."

His eyes narrowed, Quadris wrote out a message to the Taran people. He admitted their wrongs, and their deception, and he apologized for the pain they had caused. The words couldn't bring back the dead or undo the genetic manipulations, but they were the first step toward reuniting a divided people. The organization that had for so long been heralded as a moral compass had for once made a public statement that everyone could follow: to accept one another as they were and to find a path forward together.

When the message was sent, Wil released Quadris from his telekinetic grasp. Wil expected to feel more relief now that the Priesthood had finally taken responsibility, but he knew Quadris had caved too easily. Something wasn't right.

They still have some move planned. Wil studied the High Priest. "If I kill you, I'd be no better than you. No… I'll let that imperfect, cloned form you took for yourself slowly disintegrate. A swift death is too merciful."

"It doesn't have to be this way," the High Priest stated, far too calm. "There's still a way—you still have the genetic key to restore what was lost."

"We're done with manipulations," Wil shot back, growing increasingly concerned. *Quadris isn't acting like a man facing certain defeat.*

"It would only take two generations to be absolutely sure. Raena and Jason, with—"

Wil laughed at him with disbelief. "You really don't get it, do you? We're people, not walking, talking genetic samples for you to analyze and cross back until you arrive at a form that pleases you. Have you truly lost touch with what it is to be an individual with uniqueness and desires?"

"I seek knowledge and power."

"But that means nothing if you don't really *understand* and *feel.*" Wil shook his head. "You know, I don't think there's anything in the multiverse that would truly make you happy. You lost that capacity when you stopped respecting life." Wil was struck by an unexpected pang of pity. "We'll create that society you dreamed about—build it up the right way—and you'll never get to see it."

Whatever he thinks he has planned, I won't let him follow through. Wil turned from the High Priest and nodded to the Militia guards.

They prodded Quadris toward the door.

Wil watched them go. "I hope you're able to find some meaning, Quadris, because this will be your last life."

"I only need this one," Quadris replied. "It's not over yet."

What does he mean by that? Uncertainty gripped Wil's chest. The Priesthood's offworld labs may be secure, but there was no way of knowing what might still be inside the Priesthood's island.

Wil tried to send a telepathic warning to his children, but it was blocked by the interior shield. *Quadris seemed so certain. What does the Priesthood have planned?*

CHAPTER 19

THE SHUTTLE CUT through the strong sea winds as it looped around to the cliffs at the northwestern edge of the Priesthood's isle. Raena's gaze was fixed out the viewport while the pilot moved the craft into position.

Next to her, Jason was seated with his forearms resting on his knees, appearing surprisingly calm despite what they were about to do. He'd changed since she'd last seen him—the Jason from her youth would have been complaining about the lack of a plan and suggesting some alternate approach that may or may not have been better. Now, he was simply ready for anything.

Jason gave her a questioning look when he noticed her studying him.

"Sorry, it's just been a long time since we've spent much time together," Raena said.

He smiled. "Yeah, look at you—married to the Head of a High Dynasty."

"And you a senior Agent."

"A lot has changed, for sure," her brother agreed.

The shuttle inched closer to the cliffs.

"This is about as close as I can get it," the pilot said from the cockpit. "These winds are strong, so I suggest you move quickly."

"Thanks." Jason leaped into action, sliding the side door of the shuttle open.

Across from them, a solid five meter leap away, was the same vent through which Raena had escaped five years before. Their recon indicated that the shaft was still open, but the exterior grating had been reinforced.

Raena looked to her brother and he nodded.

With a hum of telekinetic energy, the metal grating began to vibrate and bits of rock fell away from its anchor points. Jason gave a yank with his mind and the grate came free. He dropped it into the ocean below.

"I'll go first," he said. Without hesitation, he leaped toward the narrow opening.

The distance was too far to jump unaided, but he used his abilities to pull himself toward the destination. Raena could sense the wave of telekinetic energy as he appeared to fly across the distance.

He landed lightly inside the opening and turned to face her.

"Show-off!" she shouted over the engine rumble.

Getting in is one thing, but will we have a way back out? Raena suppressed thoughts about what might be happening on the surface while she lined up her own jump, giving a quick check that the pulse gun in her waistband was secure. *They have their task, we have ours.*

Before she could psych herself out, Raena made the leap. She anchored herself to the destination and pulled herself along, exhilarated by the sea air blowing through her braided hair and the sensation of weightlessness as she all but flew from the ship into the tunnel.

Raena landed next to her brother and grinned. "Okay, why don't we go flying around all the time?"

"Well, it's not *really* flying," he countered.

The shuttle pulled away, leaving them alone in the tunnel.

"Besides," Jason continued, "astral projection is way more fun because we get to go through space."

"You have a point there," Raena agreed. She set out down the tunnel into the darkness.

Jason followed her. "Do you think they're expecting us?"

"I hope they are. I'd like to give them a piece of my mind."

They traversed the rest of the tunnel in silence, listening and sensing for any Priesthood soldiers lying in wait. The path ahead was clear of enemies, but three meters from the entry into the inner hallway of the Priesthood's lab, they were met with a force field.

"That's new," Raena muttered.

Jason smiled. "They really don't know much about us."

"I take it you have a plan?"

He raised his eyebrows and tilted his head. "Everything else must have you distracted, because this is an easy one. A little 'time stoppage' and we can slip right through."

"Oh, right." Raena blushed.

"Don't worry, sis, that's why I'm here."

Raena rolled her eyes, but deep down, she was happy to have him with her. *I might have an Agent rank on paper, but he's actually trained for that life. I can't compete with that.*

In unison, they initiated a spatial distortion around themselves. Time appeared to slow to a crawl around them, and the once solid force field began to flicker. Solid to open, back and forth with more time extending between each change. As the distortion fully materialized, the flickering settled with the force field on a fully deactivated position. Raena and Jason stepped across the barrier.

The moment they dropped the spatial distortion, the force field rematerialized behind them.

"I'd forgotten how much fun that is," Raena smiled.

"Now all you think about is political sway and balance sheets," Jason jabbed.

"Well, there's a little more than that. You might be surprised how enthralling a good political debate can be."

Jason looked like he was about to make a snide response when he suddenly ducked down, holding his finger to his lips. *"I think I heard voices,"* he said in Raena's mind.

She listened. Sure enough, there were at least two individuals speaking—and close.

"The outer grill was destroyed," one voice said.

"They have to be nearby," said another.

"Looks like we've been found out," groaned Raena.

Her brother cast her a sidelong glance. *"Like that's any surprise."*

Raena crept forward toward the vent opening she remembered from her escape. Unlike the addition of the force field down the tunnel, there did not appear to be any security augmentations at the grate itself. *"In here,"* she said to her brother.

Jason examined the tiny opening. *"Not really a way to enter into the hallway with an authoritative stance, is there?"*

"Like we need it," Raena replied. *"We can take all of them laying on our backs blindfolded."*

"Fair enough."

Raena telekinetically reached out to the bolts on the grate and loosened them. As carefully as she could, she lowered the bolts to the ground, and once all were out, tilted the grate away from its fastenings.

The voices had faded from audible range, so Raena poked her head into the hall. It appeared vacant, and she signaled to her brother to move forward.

Raena slipped through the narrow vent opening into the hall, all her senses alert for signs of the enemy.

Once she was on her feet, Raena was struck with a wave of nearby telekinetic energy. *The captives—* She caught herself. *The imprisoned women… the people I left here five years ago. Now is the time to make things right.*

She beckoned Jason to join her in the hall and began jogging lightly in the direction of the telekinetic signature.

"We'll need to free them quickly so we have some backup," Jason said. *"If things aren't going well on the surface, we may need to fight our way out."*

Raena gave a grim nod in response. *"I doubt any of them know how to control their abilities. Another big unknown will be any babies. They could be anywhere—some of the women might not leave without their child."*

"Is it really theirs?" her brother asked.

"Moral questions to be answered at another time."

Voices once again sounded down the hall and Raena froze. *"No taking chances,"* she said. *"Let's slip by."*

Without the need for further explanation, Jason initiated another spatial distortion field.

Raena followed suit, and the two of them dashed forward down the hall unseen in their bubble on the edge of subspace. They reached two acolytes robed in gray, seemingly frozen in time, and gingerly sidestepped them.

"Others are sure to be close," Jason cautioned.

"We're almost there. The Priesthood's numbers won't matter as soon as everyone is free." At least, she hoped that would be the case. There had been too many examples in history of captives becoming reliant on their captors for her to have absolute certainty that everyone would come freely, but she also couldn't imagine that anyone could be bred against their will and not want to get away as quickly as possible.

With the passage of time slowed to a crawl, they ran through the hallways toward the collection of holding cells Raena had passed through during her brief time in the Priesthood's custody.

When they reached their destination, Raena slowed to a walk but kept the distortion active while she took in the sights.

She recognized many of the women being held, though some she remembered were missing and there were at least two new additions. In that moment, she couldn't bring herself to think about where the others might have gone and how things would have been different in these new women's lives if she'd been able to free everyone like she'd wanted after she herself escaped. Regrets would get them nowhere.

As Raena had witnessed before, the imprisoned women were in various stages of pregnancy, ranging from barely showing to late-term. She hoped those nearing birth would be able to travel, but at this point, there was little choice.

"My god..." Jason uttered with horror in his mind.

"This is why we had to come here," Raena told him.

"Some of them won't be able to move very quickly."

"Then we'll help them along," Raena insisted. *"Just the two of us came on this mission because we could slip in and would have the power to get them out. We can't let them down."*

"I'd never think of it," her brother replied. *"Ready?"*

"Whenever you are."

With that, Jason dropped the spatial distortion and raced toward the nearest cell to deactivate the lock.

As soon as Raena and Jason were back in the normal flow of time, the women in the nearby cells startled to attention.

"Who are you?" the young woman nearest to Raena asked. She looked to be a year or two older than Raena and appeared to be around five months along.

"A friend," Raena replied, knowing the details were too complicated to get into at present. "We're here to get you out."

"Is this a trick?" the woman asked. "We were told we have to stay here."

"No one has the right to tell you what to do," Raena told her. "We'll take you somewhere safe, I promise."

"How did you even get in here?"

"I escaped once," Raena explained. "This is the soonest I was able to come back."

She turned her attention to the door lock. It was coded with a bioscanner. *No way I can bypass that.*

Force was the best option. Raena placed her hand on the glass front of the holding cell and sent a low-intensity telekinetic wave. The glass compound resonated in response.

"Go to the back and turn away," Raena instructed the woman.

As soon as the woman had complied, Raena resumed the telekinetic vibration, this time without holding back. The glass let out a high-pitched trill as it vibrated faster and faster, then shattered in a shower of tiny shards.

Raena closed her eyes and raised a localized shield around herself to guard against the glass fragments.

Jason observed her technique and began a similar process on the cell across the hall.

"Come on," Raena urged the woman. "What's your name?"

"Ruth," the woman replied.

"Ruth, everything is going to be okay. Come with me," Raena said.

While Ruth gingerly stepped over the broken glass in her slippers, Raena moved to the next cell. She and Jason worked their way down the line, freeing seventeen women.

This can't be all of them," Raena thought to herself. She remembered passing at least twice that many on her way in before, and the abduction records pointed to much higher numbers.

"Do you know where they're keeping the others?" Raena asked Ruth.

"One level up," the other woman replied. "I think so, anyway. I only leave the cell when they take me to the labs for testing."

"We're bound to meet with resistance," Jason said telepathically. *"I'm actually surprised no one has stopped us here yet. I'd have thought an alarm would go off when we broke the walls."*

"They must have been successful with taking the surface facility," Raena responded.

"I hope you're right," her brother said. *"Otherwise, we're about to run into big trouble."*

Moving nineteen people through the hallways would be a significant challenge compared to just Raena and Jason. The late-term pregnancies of several of the women would make movement slow, and their lack of training in telekinetic abilities meant they were effectively no more than civilians in their ability levels.

"We're not going to leave anyone behind," Raena told the group. "I'm so sorry you've been held here."

"Why have they been keeping us?" one of the older women asked. "What do they want with our babies?"

"That's… part of a larger conversation," Raena replied. "Suffice to say, they had no right to hold you here like this. I'll make sure you find a safe place to resume your lives. Whatever I can do to help, I will."

"Who are you?" another asked. "No one else has come to help us."

Raena exchanged glances with her brother and he nodded.

"I'm Raena Sietinen, and that's my brother, Jason," she stated. "The Sietinen Dynasty cares very much about people with abilities. We hope that one day everyone can live together as equals."

"But… telekinesis is forbidden," Ruth said.

"It was," Raena replied. "But the Priesthood doesn't call the shots anymore. Things are about to change."

A hopeful spark ignited in Ruth's eyes. "I never thought that things could be any different."

"You've been down here for a while," Raena told her. "But things are definitely changing, and I'll make sure you can make up for as much lost time as possible."

Ruth placed a hand on her stomach. "It's not that simple."

Raena's chest constricted. *What can we do with these children, knowing what they are?* "We'll figure it out."

Jason caught Raena's attention from further down the hall. *"We need to move if we stand a chance to escape."*

"Right." Raena took a calming breath. "All right, everyone, we're getting out of here. Stay between Jason and me—we'll keep you safe. We're going up to the next level to get the others you mentioned, and then we're breaking out of this prison."

"The Priests will come for us," one of the new women, who couldn't have been out of her teens, whispered.

"No, they won't," Raena assured here. "There won't be any Priesthood left by the end of today."

Raena led the group down the hall to the security door. The barrier was solid metal and was outfitted with a bioscanner lock similar to the cells.

Breaking down the door telekinetically rather than trying to override the lock was their best option, even if that meant setting off an alarm. Raena cleared her mind of the fear and doubts swirling in the background and focused solely on the door in front of her. She identified its anchor points and yanked at them with her mind. The door groaned as it rattled in its holdings, and with a fine mist of concrete dust, it came free. She set it along the side wall of the corridor beyond.

Gasps sounded from the women behind her.

She glanced back over her shoulder with a grin. "That's nothing."

Ruth looked like she was about to respond when a pulsing alarm began echoing through the hall.

"Move!" Jason shouted from the end of the line.

Raena ran through the new opening into the hall, searching the walls for signs of a stairwell. Eight meters forward, she saw a sign for one and dashed ahead to open the door.

It, too, was secured by a lock, but Raena smashed in the door in short order and propped it open to make it easier for the group to follow.

She raced up the stairs to the next level, reaching out with her telepathic senses to locate the other women. They were there—somewhere close.

At the top of the first flight of stairs, Raena busted open the next door and waited for the first women to catch up. She wedged the door open and continued ahead once Jason was in sight at the rear of the group in the stairwell.

"They're coming, I can feel it," he said privately in her mind. *"Be ready for a fight."*

A smile touched her lips. *"I can't wait."*

The floor looked identical to the one below, and Raena spotted a security door to the right that corresponded to the location of the holding cells on the lower level. She immediately set to work breaking down the door while Jason took up a defensive position on the other side of the group to the left.

As soon as the door came free, Raena was struck with a wave of telekinetic energy. There were definitely people with abilities inside, and not just the prisoners.

Standing in the center of the hall were two dozen acolytes dressed in light gray and six High Priests robed in black. They stood calmly with their hands at their sides, glowering from beneath their hoods.

Along both walls of the hallway were holding cells like the floor below, except there were two women in every cell—and each held a small child in her arms, ranging from infant to toddler.

"Stars…!" Ruth breathed behind Raena.

The High Priest standing nearest the doorway fixed his gaze on Raena. "Brave, but foolish, for you to come back for them."

"It's over," Raena replied. "The Priesthood has been dissolved."

"No, you can't just vote us out of existence," he sneered. "This isn't about politics or even control. We're here because Tarans need a push forward that they're unwilling to make themselves. We've done what everyone else was too scared to do. You're living proof that our efforts were not in vain—just look at what you can do."

"I'm not some tool you can manipulate," Raena spat back.

The High Priest's thin lips parted in a smile. "We don't need to manipulate you. More powerful forces are at work."

Raena's heart skipped a beat. "You're insane."

"The Aesir aren't the only ones who've read the patterns. We, too, have seen the paths and know what is inevitable. We were ready, and everything is as it should be."

They knew they'd lose here? Then what have they planned? Raena took a slow breath. "Surrender now."

"Oh, you're not the least bit curious?" the High Priest asked.

Now that the baiting was obvious, Raena committed herself to ignoring his statements. *It's probably just lies to distract us. We need to lock them down.*

Raena reached for the pulse gun secured at her waistband—a few well-placed shots would take down every enemy in the hall.

"If you won't ask, I'll just tell you," the High Priest continued. "When the Bakzen became obsessed with the Rift, they needed to be eliminated—they were breaking down the fabric of space. We had hoped to imbue them with ambition to reach beyond our reality here, and they did… just not in the way we'd intended."

"Do we let him continue?" Raena asked her brother.

"For now. I have a suppression net ready to go if they try anything."

The High Priest cocked his head, seeming to pick up on the telepathic exchange. "That, there—the power for remote communication, the ability to travel without physical motion. Those are the abilities we have tried to achieve. The way you can project yourselves is just the beginning. To travel in the dimensional realm beyond our own—that is where we can find true enlightenment."

"That's what you want? Enlightenment?" Raena scoffed. "For that, you're willing to wipe out an entire race, imprison generation after generation, distribute a neurotoxin for mass telepathic control—"

"For one who could so easily read the energy patterns in the fabric, you have failed to see the connections." The High Priest shook his head. "It was you who showed us the way. We had spent a thousand years trying to perfect one physical form, and we're so close, yet you've refused to share in our vision to take the final necessary steps. But when your mind traveled here to Tararia from so great a distance with the Aesir working in unison, we realized we had been focusing on the wrong thing. We had been seeking *one* physical form that could take us to ascension, and so we had missed what was right in front of us—the untapped potential of the collective whole."

Raena drew her pulse gun in one fluid motion and leveled it at the High Priest. Her heart raced, dreading the Priest's next words. "What are you saying?" she demanded.

The High Priest's eyes flashed. "We have already transformed the population to serve us. All those minds, networked as one—that's the only vehicle we need."

"The neurotoxin, it's—" Raena's telepathic warning was cut short by a concussive wave through the air.

She tried to fire her pulse gun but her muscles wouldn't respond. She was frozen in place by a telepathic hold.

"Jason?" she called out through her hazy mind.

"I hear you," he replied. *"We need to break through the hold—the High Priests are going to try to astral project through the spatial tear."*

Around them, all the women were frozen in place, as well. Their eyes were vacant, as though they were unconscious.

"What will happen if they succeed?" Raena asked.

"I don't want to find out. Fight it! They don't have us contained like the others."

The High Priests had closed their eyes and an electric hum in the air was growing more intense every second.

Raena forced back the shackles trying to contain her mind. She was stronger than them—she wouldn't be controlled.

With a cry, Raena broke from the telepathic hold and fired the pulse gun. The beam dissipated around a bubble of telekinetic shielding protecting the High Priests.

Behind her, Jason dashed through the crowd of captive women to stand next to Raena.

They reached out telekinetically toward the shield and tried to force their way through. With each assault, the women in the hall paled and winced.

"They're drawing on their energy," Raena realized.

"Shit!" Jason shook his head. "If we force it, we may break their minds."

"There has to be some way—"

The electric hum in the air rose to a deafening roar, and an aura of white light formed around the High Priests and their acolytes in the hall. The light concentrated into a beam, which shot up through the ceiling.

"They're going for the tear!" Jason shouted.

Raena took her brother's hand and closed her eyes. "Come on, we can't stop it alone."

— — —

An electric hum filled the air, interrupting Wil's thoughts. He was about to question the other Agents when Quadris suddenly stopped in his tracks just shy of the shuttle outside on the hilltop.

"You can't stop us," the High Priest called back to Wil.

Everyone froze.

The fok…? Wil immediately recognized the signs of a telepathic suppression net around himself, stretching as far as he could sense.

Only Quadris was unaffected. The old man stood with his arms at his sides and eyes closed, a white aura forming around him.

Is this what he was waiting for? Wil shrugged off the suppression net and took a step toward Quadris. Mid-stride, a beam of white light burst through the ground in front of him, mingling with the aura around Quadris. The beam shot into the sky, fed by a thin tendril of white light snaking from each individual standing on the hilltop.

Stars! Wil's breath caught in his throat. *What are they doing?*

As Wil watched the energy flow from the individuals into the shared column, the answer became all too clear—the Priests had separated their consciousness from their bodies and were using others to give them the boost they needed to make a run for the spatial tear. It was such an obvious move in hindsight, but he'd been too focused on his immediate surroundings to anticipate the action. Regardless, they couldn't be allowed to reach the tear.

Wil immediately extended his consciousness to assess the column. It was indeed racing toward the location of the Rift, but not as quickly as he could project on his own. However, there was also no way he'd be able to snare it. As strong as he was, the High Priests were a fair match. He'd need help.

"Raena, Jason!" Wil called out. The white column had broken through the shielding that had always shrouded the lower levels of the island, weakening it just enough that he hoped his thoughts could make it through—and that whatever had subdued the other members of the TSS hadn't paralyzed his children, as well.

"Dad!" Raena replied, panic clouding her mind. *"The High Priests, they're—"*

"I know. Up here, too," he told her. *"We need to stop it. Together."*

Jason's presence joined them. *"Are the three of us enough?"*

"We'll have to be." Wil held out his hands toward the blinding column in preparation.

His children gave him a mental nod and he felt them prepare for action.

Simultaneously, they reached out to the column, tracing the individual threads drawing energy from the people on Tararia. It wasn't just those standing on the hilltop and down in the facility, but rather every person on the planet. Additional threads extended toward the column from the moons in orbit and the other worlds beyond. A network was forming, and the more involved it became, the harder it would be to stop.

This needs to end now. Wil began ripping away at the tendrils attempting to merge with the core column, trying to be as careful as he could so as not to harm any bystanders, but speed was imperative.

Raena and Jason backed him up, sheering away the connections. They needed to find the control point for the neurotoxin to keep the tendrils from rejoining.

Wil dove into the column, struggling to keep himself separate from it—to pass through without becoming one.

There it was, deep within the Priesthood's isle. Four High Priests had joined together, merging with a bioelectronic interface not unlike the controls Wil had used in his ships to win the Bakzen War. But this time, the technology was against him. It wouldn't stay that way for long.

Raena and Jason traced their way to the site, as well. Wil could feel their rage over what the Priesthood had done, and he let that fuel them—to fuel him.

A lifetime of manipulation, of disregard for others in the selfish pursuit of 'enlightenment'. It meant nothing. The Priests weren't worthy of using others for their own ends—no one was. Wil had used people himself, and it had almost destroyed him. His only chance at atonement was to make sure that abuse of power could never happen again.

Driven by that imperative, Wil and his children cast a shield around the four central High Priests, choking their access to the Taran citizens they sought to tap as living power sources. Together, they raised the shield, sheering off the tethers.

Soon, the tendrils from the bystanders were all disconnected. Only the link between the members of the Priesthood remained. Their greed would be their undoing.

Wil extended himself to access the energy in the distant Rift—the place where he had always felt most alive. As he did so, he forced Raena and Jason back. This was something he needed to do alone.

He rounded on the High Priests, surrounding them with his mental presence. *"You've lost."*

"We have only just begun," they replied in chorus, fighting back against the shield he held around them.

Wil could feel their confidence—the sense of entitlement that had stripped away their conscience and driven them to commit unthinkable atrocities. Such arrogance… In the end, it held no real strength. Not like the power Wil held, rooted in a desire to help others and unite rather than divide.

The High Priests strained against the shield, but their efforts were in vain. Wil had them cornered.

"You'll never advance without us," they protested. *"We must*

ascend!"

"No. We don't need you—we never needed what you've become." He stabbed telepathic spears into the minds of the High Priests at the center of the network, crippling them. *"You'll never use people for your own ends again!"*

All the bitter anger from the decades of manipulation and sacrifice flowed out of him, entwining with the energy flowing through the High Priests. It seeped into them, poisoning them just like it had poisoned him through years of guilt over what he'd been forced to do.

The Priesthood had stolen his youth, his innocence. They had almost cost him his wife, his children, his parents, his friends—his own life. He thought of the billions who'd died as a result of his actions and the trillions more who were counting on him now to deliver them a better future. His responsibilities to others and the Priesthood's demands had pushed him almost to his breaking point.

But he'd prevailed. He was stronger than them. And they would never hurt anyone else.

Wil drew the sweet power of the distant Rift into himself—more than any other had ever drawn alone. He held it within until he could hold no more. *"You wanted power?"* he said in the broken minds of the High Priests. *"Well, here it is."*

At once, he released the barrage into the network linking the High Priests and their acolytes.

The column of white light exploded into a wave that rippled across the sky of the planet, trembling the ground and sending a shockwave through the air.

The bystanders on the hill collapsed to their knees, and Quadris fell limp to the ground—his mind broken, along with all the others in the network. He would forever be a shell of himself, a fate worse than death, but only fitting after what he'd done in his millennia-long lifetime.

Wil released a shaky breath as his hands dropped to his sides. His eyes stung with tears of relief behind his tinted glasses. Regrets that had weighed on his subconscious for decades were finally gone, his long overdue vengeance served.

For the first time in his life, he was free.

Wil took in the island around him. The energy had shifted—the darkness that had plagued the island was no more, leaving it quiet and peaceful now that the electric hum had faded from the air. *Is it really over?*

"Sir?" one of the Militia guards called to him. "Are you hurt?"

"No," Wil shook his head, gathering himself. *This is the best I've felt in years!* "Secure Quadris. We need to find the others."

Minutes passed as the Militia guards and Agents began working their way through the lineup of Priesthood associates.

Each High Priest and acolyte had the same blank expression. They'd never recover to their former selves, but eventually some of their thoughts would return. For those whose minds had been broken, those thoughts would forever be a reflection on one's past—rehashing wrongdoings that would become a manifest nightmare in their daily life. Some members of the Priesthood would likely never see their actions as wrong, but perhaps, for some, it would be a chance for their own atonement.

If nothing else, Wil had Quadris' confession. Once that was transmitted to the broader population, they could begin to unify.

"Dad!"

Wil heard Raena's voice call to him from behind.

He turned to see her running toward him with Jason, and a group of women were being tended to by the TSS complement.

"Thank the stars you're okay!" he embraced his daughter, and then son.

Raena and Jason beamed at him.

"Psh, it was no trouble," Jason said with the wave of his hand and an even broader grin.

"What you did… that was incredible." Raena shook her head.

"It was a terrible thing to do to anyone," Wil replied. "But they needed to be stopped, and now they can never hurt anyone else."

"Sir!" one of the Agents interrupted. "We're getting reports that all remaining Tararian Guard ships have stood down."

Wil glanced at the High Priests and acolytes from within the underground facility being led into shuttles. "Those on other worlds were part of the network—they'll all be like this, if we ever find them."

Raena nodded. "Imprisonment alone wouldn't have been enough."

"Now they'll be imprisoned in their own minds," Jason agreed.

His daughter crossed her arms, slowly shaking her head. "What about these women and their children?"

Wil drew a slow breath and released it. "The children are clones, but they wouldn't have been imprinted with a new consciousness at such a young age—anyone already in the Priesthood's fold would have been one of the linked acolytes. We'll set their mothers up with a new life as best we can, and either the children will remain with them or they will become Wards."

Raena frowned. "That's no way to begin life."

"We can't help the way we're born," Wil told her. "It's what we choose to do with our lives that matters."

Jason rubbed his sister's back as he glanced at the TSS members going about their work. "I should probably help out."

"Right." Raena pulled herself from her thoughts. "Things are probably a mess at the estate. I should get back."

"I'll arrange transportation," Wil told her.

He looked over both his children. "You were very brave today. You'll make great leaders for our future."

Raena blushed slightly. "I'll try."

Jason shrugged and cracked a smile. "Someone's gotta do it."

That's one torch I'm happy to pass. Wil smiled back. "All in a day's work."

CHAPTER 20

WIL SUPERVISED THE final members of the Priesthood being loaded into transport shuttles bound for a TSS holding facility. All told, only two hundred ninety associates had been inside the Priesthood's compound. *It's remarkable to think so few people were responsible for so much damage. How many died because of their actions?*

There were others, of course, in facilities spread across the Taran worlds, but it all came down to two dozen High Priests who had been running the civilization from their chambers deep within the Priesthood's island compound. That kind of concentrated power introduced too much opportunity for corruption. The dynasties could just as easily fall into those same patterns if things continued along the current path.

Any solution would bring its own set of challenges, but Wil was convinced a fundamental shift was necessary. How, exactly, to get that change implemented would take some maneuvering.

He was pulled from his thoughts by the sound of approaching engines overhead; no additional transports were expected that evening. Looking up, he saw that the approaching vessel was an Aesir shuttle. *What are they doing down here?*

Wil watched the shuttle's landing path and jogged over to meet it.

As the engines powered down, a door in the side of the twenty-meter-long craft slid open, and Dahl emerged.

The Oracle looked even paler under the light of the setting sun, his skin having experienced nothing more than light from the artificial star in more than a millennia. Tentatively, he stepped down the ramp from the shuttle to the ground. His eyes closed as he set foot on the soil.

"Welcome home," Wil said.

Dahl opened his eyes. "This hasn't been home for a very long time, but it feels good to finally return."

"This place belongs to you, if you want it." Wil made a gesture to encompass the island.

"No, we have a place that suits us now. What the Priesthood left behind is yours for the taking."

"On that note, our part is done," Wil stated. "We had an agreement."

"Indeed." Dahl bowed his head. "We shall provide you with the data archive, as we promised. Much of the technology will not be possible for everyone to use, however—it is for a culture where all possess the abilities we take for granted."

"It will be made available to everyone regardless. We'll find common ground to unite us."

Dahl nodded. "That is the future we always hoped to achieve."

"Will you remain out in the galactic core?" Wil asked.

"For now, but perhaps we will one day be among you again."

Wil eyed him. "And what about the Rift?"

"That is an interesting matter," Dahl replied. "Our conditions for helping you were to gain access to the tear and harness its power, but what Jason saw made us realize that doing so would be not unlike the Priesthood's ambition."

"One person's statements have made you change your entire outlook?"

Dahl's thin lips stretched into a smile. "Don't underestimate the power of one person's words. Some people's word should always be heeded."

Wil crossed his arms. "You're talking about what you said earlier, aren't you? That I should fill the role the Priesthood should have been serving."

"Such a role is something to grow into."

"I don't think I'll be hanging around for twelve hundred years," Wil replied.

"You needn't decide that now," Dahl insisted. "We'll provide you with all of our life-extending technology. Once the genetic patch is ready, those tools can become widely available."

And then Saera would be with me… "I'm still not convinced such technology is for the best. Look at what happened to the High Priests when they sought eternal life."

"Their intentions were twisted from the outset. Do not confuse the technology with a person's application of that tool."

Wil nodded. "Fair enough. I'll keep an open mind."

"We shall, as well." Dahl inclined his head. "As much as we like to think of ourselves as ascended, we are still fallible beings. I insisted our intentions with the spatial tear were pure, but when we came face-to-face with its power, I found even myself tempted. We do wish to study it, but we would also ask to have… oversight."

"From the TSS?" Wil asked.

"Specifically, from you."

He laughed. "Yeah, I don't think I'm really the best person for that job."

"You've come closer to that kind of power than anyone and have always come back. I can think of no one better."

I don't have a great counterpoint to that. "Well, I'm not living in the Rift."

"You needn't. Keep watching it from afar, as you have already been doing with Jason."

Wil sighed. "Very well."

Dahl smiled. "In time, you will come to understand you can be more than what the Priesthood forced you to be. That was never your true purpose, Cadicle."

"I'll try to live up to the name."

The Oracle nodded. "I have no doubt you will."

— — —

Waking up the following morning, Cris felt like a new era had begun. For the first time in a millennia, the Priesthood was not the authority over the Taran people. Now, he was one of the select few tasked with ensuring the safety and prosperity of the civilization.

It's not just the Priesthood. We need to make even bigger changes. He took a deep breath and began to get ready for the day, organizing his thoughts for the meeting to come.

Kate looked him over with concern while she finished dressing. "We can't fall into the same trap."

"I know—and Wil knows it. I've already chatted with Ryan and we're in agreement on what we have to do."

"The others might not go for it."

Cris shrugged. "We have to try."

The meeting of the High Dynasties was set for 09:00, a symbolic gesture for the new beginning after what had transpired the day before. Following a quick breakfast, Cris and Kate met the other members of their family in the same conference room. Raena and Ryan had already arrived, and Wil was coming down the hall. Cris waved at him and stepped inside.

"Good morning," Cris greeted his granddaughter and her new husband. "Is it just me, or does yesterday feel like it was all a dream?"

"Hasn't sunken in yet for me, either," Raena replied.

Ryan shook his head. "I don't think any of it will seem real until I've had a couple weeks living the new life."

Wil entered the conference room and closed the door.

"No Jason?" Wil asked, looking around the room.

"I believe his exact words were, 'Politics? No thanks'," Cris replied with a smile.

Wil chuckled. "Sounds about right. I'd be tempted to sit this one out, myself, if it weren't a once-in-a-lifetime historic moment and all that."

"Assuming the resolution goes through," Raena clarified.

"We'll make it," Wil declared.

Kate cast him an evaluating glance. "Even if it doesn't pass, this is still the first meeting under the new structure. It's a historic time any way you look at it."

"Very true. I'll just sit back and observe." Wil took a seat in one of the chairs on the outskirts of the room away from the view of the cameras linked to the holoprojector. "The TSS should be a neutral third-party rather than sitting with one of the High Dynasties."

"All right," Cris agreed. He checked the time, seeing it was 08:58. "We should begin."

He sat at the head of the table with Kate to his right and Ryan to his left, with Raena next to her husband.

The holoprojector created an overlay on the far side of the table, which populated with the Heads from the other High Dynasties.

They exchanged brief pleasantries, and then all eyes turned to Cris.

"So, what's our first order of business?" Kaiden prompted.

"Well, I'm curious about the new laws regarding telekinesis, which were enacted yesterday without going for an official vote," Byron Monsari cut in.

"A necessity to ensure appropriate action could be taken against the Priesthood," Eduard Baellas interjected, much to Cris' surprise.

"Yes, only a majority vote was required," Cris added. "Talsari, Monsari, and Makaris are welcome to submit a vote now for the official record, if you wish."

"I support it," Ellen Talsari said.

"Well, I'm against it." Byron crossed his arms.

Liam Makaris glowered at the Monsari Head. "You really intend to perpetuate that divide between our people? I think Cris has demonstrated that Gifted people aren't dangerous or something to fear. If anything, it'll be better for people to be open with those abilities so they can receive proper training. The greater danger is creating a population of outcasts."

"And let's be honest," Kate jumped in, "I have abilities, and that means Kaiden does, too, but never tapped into them. His children and grandchildren haven't, either, but the first member of a Twelfth Generation is about to be born—we can either keep ignoring those abilities, or we can finally acknowledge what's right there inside us."

Kaiden nodded slowly. "Training as a soldier with the TSS is no longer the only path. We should lead by example and be our full selves rather than hiding behind traditions established to hide the truth about what we lost. The Priesthood told us to hide our abilities because they didn't want us to know what we'd been missing. I, for one, hope future generations will have the opportunity to learn something about themselves I did not."

"We intend to be out in the open," Ryan spoke up for the first time in the meeting. "Dainetris and Sietinen will promote open use of telekinesis in the Third Region. We hope the rest of you will join us in changing the public perception about what it means to have abilities."

"I believe everyone but Monsari is on board with that intention," Ellen said.

Byron's cheeks reddened. "You haven't thought through the implications."

"As things stand now," Cris replied, "the main concern is if the High Dynasties appear divided. If we want a peaceful future, we need to start working together."

The Heads all fixed their gaze on Monsari.

"Fine," Byron yielded. "For the sake of unity, I will support the new regulations on telekinesis, but I must insist we review the wording more closely."

"Agreed," Ryan said. "This wording was meant as a placeholder, anyway. We will find language that's in the best public interest."

Cris nodded. "To that end, we have another matter to consider regarding how to most effectively serve our people. The Priesthood was always meant to be a neutral third-party to keep the High Dynasties' corporate interests from interfering with equitable administration of the Taran worlds. Well, we all know the Priesthood wasn't playing fair. Having lived outside our happy sphere of opulence here on Tararia, I also know from personal experience that things are far from equitable. We need to consider if the way things operate now is really what's best for Taran citizens." He paused, looking around the table. "From my vantage, that is a resounding 'no'.

"The High Dynasties offer the core services required for the operation of this civilization. Without our corporations, things would fall apart. That means we are beyond private interests—we have a responsibility that runs deeper than profit or what's best for our families. We need to think about what will keep the Taran worlds safe and what will allow our people to flourish and have the greatest opportunities for happy lives.

"If things continue along the current path, those with resources will only continue to accumulate more wealth and those at a disadvantage will have very few opportunities to get ahead. Hard work and perseverance can only get a person so far when the entire system is structured to favor those who already have a leg up. If we want to continue to grow and prosper, we must rethink how we serve our people."

"I take it you have something specific in mind?" Kaiden said when Cris paused again.

"I do," Cris replied. "It's going to sound extreme, and it will take time to find an appropriate balance, but I believe that the operation of the High Dynasty's corporations should no longer be private. We provide a public service, and so the public should have a voice in what service they receive."

The other Dynastic Heads' eyes widened with shock.

"That's…" Eduard Baellas began before fading out.

"We need to rethink our pricing and access to products and services in a way that makes it reasonable for any citizen to have a high quality of life," Cris continued. "SiNavTech has already demonstrated that reducing fees on merchants and replacing that lost revenue through cross-promotion and marketing with other corporations has resulted in record profits—even when accounting for inflation. This isn't about making everything free, just redistributing the wealth in a way that everyone benefits."

"And how would you propose 'the public' has a say in these changes?" Ellen Talsari asked.

Cris smiled. "Well, stars, that's easy—almost everyone has a VComm device," Cris said. "Send out a survey and let the people vote."

The Heads did not look convinced.

"What would you have them vote *on*?" Liam pressed.

"Not every individual issue," Cris replied, "but they should certainly have a voice in who represents them. The High

Dynasties have been around for a very long time, and we're still here only because we have made ourselves remain in power—with the exception of Dainetris, of course, but that's another matter entirely. I think we need to hold ourselves accountable. If we're not doing a good job supporting the public interests in our roles as corporate CEOs, the people should have the right to vote us out and get someone who'll think about them, not just personal assets."

Kaiden nodded. "The accountability the Priesthood was supposed to provide, but disaggregated in a way that it would minimize the potential for corruption."

"Precisely." Cris inclined his head. "The question is, are you confident that you're a leader the people will support?"

Eduard chuckled and leaned back in his chair. "It's radical, for sure, but I think it's brilliant. We could all use some accountability."

"All right, I'll support it," Ellen agreed.

"VComm has nothing to hide," Kaiden chimed in. "We do need a change."

The remaining High Dynasties reluctantly cast their vote in support—to oppose would suggest a lack of worth, a social pressure Cris was counting on.

"Then the resolution holds," Cris announced. "Now, we let the people decide if we did the right thing."

— — —

Rolling out the process for universal approval voting was surprisingly straightforward, but waiting for the results of the polls had Raena on edge.

If the results were less than favorable, the other High Dynasties could easily go back on their word and slip into old ways. With any luck, the public would take it as a sign of good faith that the corporations central to their day-to-day lives were now trying to open a productive dialogue—and to support those efforts as a sign of good faith of their own.

"I hate being in limbo like this," Raena grumbled to Cris as she sauntered into his office.

"Well, we'll know in a few minutes," her grandfather replied from behind his desk.

Three days of letting the votes roll in and we have no idea how it's gone. She sighed. "I don't know whether I'll be happy or upset if they give us the boot."

"The thrills of democracy, eh?"

"I wish we could see the results in real-time."

"That would undermine the intent of allowing people an unbiased vote, now wouldn't it?" her grandfather replied.

"Sometimes I dislike the reasonableness of rationality."

He cracked a smile. "Indeed. So, how are the rescued prisoners doing?"

"Well," Raena responded, temporarily setting aside thoughts of the election, "I suppose as well as can be expected."

The fifty-two women rescued from the Priesthood's underground labs were only a fraction of the victims taken over the years, but Raena was thankful they hadn't been too late for everyone. Most of the women had elected to remain with their children, and the others had been placed with foster families. It was unclear what future awaited a clone of one of the High Priests, but Wil had assured Raena that any child exhibiting abilities would be welcomed into the TSS training program when they came of age. For now, she wished them happy childhoods outside the confines of a cell.

Cris gave her a sympathetic nod. "I'm sorry we didn't go after them sooner."

"More may have been hurt if we'd tried," Raena said, knowing it was the hard truth of the matter. "We made the best decision we could under the circumstan—"

"Results are in!" Marina declared, bursting through the doorway. She rushed inside with Ryan and Kate in tow.

As a matter of process, an advisor with each Dynasty had been designated to receive the results rather than the Dynastic Head directly—a step toward the decentralization of power intended for the future. As Cris' longtime associate, Marina was the most logical choice for Sietinen.

Cris rose from his seat. "What's the verdict?"

"I haven't looked at it yet," Marina replied. "I thought we should all review the outcome together."

"I couldn't agree more," Cris said as Kate came around the back of the desk to stand with him.

Ryan took Raena's hand and gave it a squeeze. *"I might go down as having the shortest reign ever,"* he said privately to her.

"I'm pretty sure I read some history article about a guy who only lasted one night. You're already an old-timer."

He smiled over at her and she leaned against him.

"Everyone ready?" Marina asked the room.

"Yes, please!" Cris urged.

Marina placed her handheld on Cris' desktop and selected one of the files to appear on the holoprojector.

The data was organized by corporation, with votes tallied for each of the current Dynastic Heads—who also doubled as CEOs—to remain in their current positions of authority. The intent was for anyone below a fifty percent approval rating to be up for potential replacement, pending a search for candidates and election of a suitable individual.

Raena scanned over the results. "Well, I'll be…"

Every single Head's position had been ratified with at least a sixty percent approval rating. Apparently, getting out the truth regarding the Priesthood had won the favor of most. If everyone did their jobs well in the coming years, they might continue to hold onto those positions.

More impressive, though, were the results for Sietinen and Dainetris. Cris had garnered a ninety-six percent approval score, and Ryan an unprecedented ninety-nine percent—not that there were currently any other employees of DGE.

Cris slumped against his desk. "I'd prepared myself for an outcome where everyone called us scheming liars and demanded our necks."

"I had, too, but I didn't think that would ever happen," Raena admitted. "When it comes down to it, very few people would actually want our jobs. We've demonstrated a desire to change things, and that's more initiative than anyone's ever shown before. Better to stick with what you know than upend everything all at once."

Marina shook her head. "But a rational outcome from the masses…"

"When you break it down to the individual level, people are innately reasonable," Cris pointed out. "Issues have always stemmed from looking only at the big picture. When you treat everyone the same and group people in massive categories, of course you're going to get groupthink going in crazy directions—that's how the Priesthood was able to maintain so much control. But treat people like the individuals they are, you'll get the rational reaction you'd expect from a one-on-one conversation."

"That was our theory from the very outset of this venture," Kate added. "I'm so happy to see it held true." She wrapped her arm around Cris' waist and held him close.

"Now we keep proving ourselves every day," Raena said.

Ryan took a deep breath. "I still have no idea how to go about determining what's best."

"If those answers came easily, other people *would* want our job," Cris said with a smile.

Ryan smiled back. "Fair enough."

"Besides," Raena added, "now we're not in competition with each other. We can work through problems to find mutually beneficial solutions rather than focusing on what will make shareholders the happiest."

Cris admired her from across the desk. "A few public speeches like that and I think Sietinen will have support for many years to come."

Raena gave a bashful shrug. "I really never intended to be a politician."

Kate chuckled. "I think it's a little late for that."

— — —

"Yes, my lord," an attendant said with a bow of his head and withdrew from Ryan's new office.

I'm not sure if I'll ever get used to that. Ryan shook his head and resumed gazing out the window.

While everything was in transition, Cris had arranged for one of the outbuildings on the Sietinen estate to be temporarily repurposed as an administrative center for DGE's resurrection. Even more useful were the staff members who'd been reassigned to assist with the efforts.

Just when Ryan would start to feel like he had a handle on the business scope, he'd inevitably be presented with a new conundrum that made him second-guess his understanding of the entire venture. However, he'd learned long ago that all of life was a learning experience, and he may as well embrace that he'd never know everything. The best he could do was remain malleable and surround himself with smart people who'd help him along the way.

He was pulled from his thoughts by a light knock on the doorframe. He looked up to see Raena grinning at him.

"Hi," he greeted her. "Sorry, I should have noticed you come over."

"You have a few things on your mind, don't worry." She slipped into the room and closed the door. "I hope you don't mind a mid-afternoon visit."

"It's very welcome." He beckoned her over, and she eased onto the edge of the desk next to him.

"How goes it?" she asked.

"Well enough. I think we have a solid transition plan in place."

"About time." Raena sighed. "This has been the longest week ever."

"You're telling me! It still weirds me out every time I turn on a news broadcast and see my face."

"Crazy, isn't it? It's no wonder my dad was so willing to give up his place in the succession line."

"At least you have a mentor on your side of things," Ryan pointed out. "I'm two steps from feeling completely on my own here."

"You're very far from being on your own." His wife placed a hand on his shoulder and looked him in the eye. "Well, at least three steps." She grinned.

"Ha."

Raena leaned in for a kiss, and the good-natured needling

from moments before vanished from memory.

"So," she continued as she pulled away from the kiss, "now that everything is out in the open, we have to think about if we want to introduce any new policies and all that."

"I don't think I have the headspace to think about that quite yet," Ryan replied. "We probably have a solid month of transition activities for DGE to get running on its own power. They want me to go tour all the facilities—it'll be a lot."

"I don't suppose I can go with you?"

The request caught Ryan by surprise. "You have time for that?"

"Well, my grandfather will be helming things at SiNavTech for some time to come. Now that we've weathered the worst of our little revolution, my tasks aren't terribly time-sensitive."

Ryan took her hand. "I'd love to have you along. Truth be told, I was hoping you'd want to come."

"Always." She rubbed the top of his hand with her thumb.

"I'm so glad I don't have to go through this alone."

"Same. It's so much to process…" She eyed him. "How's your mom taking all this?"

Stars, that's right! Ryan closed his eyes. "Fok, I've been meaning to call her. There's been so much on my mind—"

"Oh, so you haven't talked to her since everything went down?"

"No, I have not," Ryan admitted. "Shite, how do I even explain everything?"

"Probably not much to explain at this point. You've sorta been all over the news."

He groaned. *I haven't known what to say so I've put off the conversation, but I can't just leave her hanging.* "You're right, I need to call her."

"I really thought you had last week."

"I'll do it right now." Ryan let out a heavy sigh. "I should probably do that on my own."

"Of course." Raena returned to her feet.

"I don't have much left to get done today. I'll call her and wrap up a few things, then meet you back at the main manor, okay?"

"I hope it goes well." She leaned down and gave him a light kiss.

"Thanks. I'll see you soon."

Once Raena departed, he took a couple minutes to compose his thoughts. After futile attempts at playing out the conversation in his head, he decided to just dive in. He initiated a video call via the viewscreen on the wall.

Nearly thirty seconds passed before Marie accepted the call and her image appeared on the screen.

"Hi, Mom."

Marie's eyes began to glisten as soon as she saw him, on the verge of tears. "Ryan! The news…"

He worked his mouth, trying to find the right words. "I never meant for you to find out this way, but things had to happen quickly, and in private."

She shook her head. "So, you're…?"

"Yes," he confirmed. "You're the descendent of a Dainetris heir. When my father came to you, he knew that. He was friends with Cris Sietinen, and he knew a pairing between those two High Dynasties… Well, let's just say that he found a way to give you the child you wanted while laying the foundation for a much bigger plan."

"Then it's true." Her voice was filled with disbelief. "It really is you on these broadcasts."

"Yes." Ryan took a deep breath. "I've been sworn in as Head of Dainetris. Raena Sietinen and I were married last week."

Marie stared at him in silence for ten seconds. "I don't know what to say."

"There are no words that can set everything right. We had family that the Priesthood hunted down and eliminated like vermin just because they tried to speak the truth. I wanted to tell you as soon as I found out, but we were worried that they might go after you, too, if they suspected you were in on our coup."

His mother shook her head. "I'm glad I didn't know. I don't think I would have had the stomach for it." She scoffed. "It explains so much… why your father insisted on your paternity records being doctored the way they were."

"No more manipulation," Ryan stated. "We've all committed

to a new way forward."

"I'll believe it when I see it."

"Well, I know what my priorities are—and Cris feels the same way. Between Dainetris and Sietinen, we can have a significant impact."

Marie considered the statement. "That's an alliance no one would have expected. I'd always wondered why the Sietinen heiress was never betrothed to another dynastic heir."

"Yeah, that got a little tricky to navigate toward the end. Raena and I have been together for about five years now," Ryan revealed.

"I wish I'd known about the wedding..."

"Her parents weren't there, either," he hastily cut in. "It wasn't a party, trust me."

"Well, I'd love to meet her sometime. She seems like a lovely girl, from what I've seen of her," Marie murmured.

"We do need to get together—and not just a quick visit. Now that people know about me, you don't need to keep living there."

She shrugged. "This is the only home I know."

"I felt the same way when I thought about leaving here, but I'd like us to have a chance to get to know each other."

Marie smiled. "I'd like that, too."

"Well, I'll set up a dinner together for sometime soon and we can take it from there," Ryan told her.

"Where would that be?" she asked tentatively.

"Probably here at the Sietinen estate."

Her face paled. "Me? There?"

"It won't be how you're thinking. Keep in mind that Cris and Kate spent most of their lives in the TSS—they're super casual."

"I still can't believe you're on a first name basis with High Dynasty leaders..."

I am *one of those High Dynasty leaders now.* Ryan gave her a reassuring smile. "It'll just be a nice dinner with my in-laws, don't worry."

She nodded. "All right. I look forward to it."

"I'll be in touch soon." Ryan ended the call and sighed. *It was hard enough for me to adjust to thinking about myself as anything but a Ward, but after half a lifetime, how will it be for her?*

Only time would tell.

Ryan completed his remaining tasks for the day and then locked his desktop and went to meet Raena.

He found her on the couch in their shared quarters.

"How'd she take it?" Raena asked, rising to greet him.

"As well as can be expected. She wants to meet you." He smiled.

"I'd like to meet her, too." Raena placed her hands on his hips. "We can get her out of that quartered housing. For that matter, we'll need to figure out where *we* want to live."

"I was wondering if maybe we should unbury Dain."

Raena thought about it. "Wouldn't that be disruptive to the current population? We'd have to relocate everyone. Maybe it would be better to just complete the repairs and leave it as-is."

"Then where would we go? I mean, I guess we could stay here, but Cris is running SiNavTech for now, so DGE is really where I should focus my attention. We'll need our own offices."

"Well," Raena said slowly, "this might sound strange, but what do you think about the Priesthood's island?"

"You can't be serious."

"It's not like it was when the Priesthood was there. As soon as the final fight was over, it… changed," she explained. "After what happened to us there, I feel almost like it's our duty to make it into something better—to overwrite all the bad that's happened on that island over the years and turn it into a place of joy."

Ryan considered the suggestion. "I guess I'd have to see it for myself."

"Of course."

"It's not something I would have considered, but I can see the rationale."

"After all," Raena continued, "it was set up with administrative facilities and to house full-time residents. There are those smaller structures along the southern coast, and, once you get past its former creepiness, the architecture of the main structure is really quite breathtaking. The center of the island is basically just one giant garden…"

Ryan gazed into her eyes. "That's what you saw in your vision, isn't it? Us there together."

She nodded. "It didn't make sense at the time, but now… it feels right. I think we could make a home there."

"I'm still a little skeptical, but think I can get on board with that plan," Ryan agreed. "I will have to insist on renovations, though."

"I wouldn't have it any other way." Raena smiled. "We could even bring some things from the former Dainetris estate—art, furniture, or whatever catches your eye."

"Perfect." He gave her a light kiss. "I'm excited to be starting this new life with you."

"Me too." She laid her head against his chest, holding him tight. "And this is just the beginning."

CHAPTER 21

CRIS GAZED OUT at Lake Tiadon in the morning sunlight, a warm breeze ruffling his hair. He took a sip of his morning brew, admiring the sight in silence.

Behind him, he sensed Kate approaching.

"Is it still true?" she asked. "Is the Priesthood still really gone?"

Cris smiled back at her. "I'm sure there are some lurkers out there, but as of this morning we're still free."

Kate placed an arm around Cris' waist and leaned against the railing next to him. "We planned this for over fifty years. I can't believe it finally happened."

"And that it worked!" Cris chuckled and shook his head incredulously. "This never would have been possible without you."

His wife squeezed him tighter. "You were the one with the vision."

"I only looked so far ahead, though—you made it happen."

"It was a team effort."

"Indeed it was," he agreed. "We may have set a new direction for Tarans, but there's still a difficult path ahead."

"We'll figure it out." Kate smiled up at him. "We always have."

Cris set down his mug so he could embrace her with both arms. "You have been my constant through it all. I know I can face any challenge as long as I have you by my side."

"Me too." Kate held him in silence for a long while, looking out over the lake together.

"You know," Cris said at last, "I finally feel like I belong here."

"Because we do."

For the first time, he actually believed her. "I do miss the TSS, though," he added.

She let out a wistful sigh. "They'll always be our second family."

"But what we have here and now, with Raena and Ryan—I wouldn't want to be anywhere else."

Kate gave him a knowing smile. "Good, because we have a civilization to run."

"I suppose we do." He took in a breath of the fresh air. "But I have to admit, I'm excited about this future."

— — —

One hundred twenty-seven emails greeted Raena when she checked her handheld in the morning. She took one look at the device and tossed it back onto its charging pad on her nightstand.

"How bad is it?" Ryan asked from in bed next to her.

She rolled back over and nestled into the crook of his arm, placing a hand on his chest. "I'm just going to pretend for a few more minutes that the outside world doesn't exist."

"I'll join you in that."

Raena allowed herself ten minutes of dozing before she dragged herself out of bed.

She showered and dressed. Just as she was entering the common room, there was a light knock on the door—likely a servant with breakfast.

Her suspicion was confirmed when she glanced at the viewscreen next to the door, and she let the servant in to set up the breakfast spread on the round table by the open doorway to the terrace. She thanked the worker and took a seat.

"Smells great!" Ryan emerged from the bedroom with damp hair and sat down adjacent to her.

"I could have these pastries every day for the rest of my life and never get tired of them."

"That's a theory you can test."

Raena took a bite of the flakey deliciousness. "And I suspect I will."

Ryan shook his head and chuckled, but he took two for himself.

"So," Raena said around a mouthful, "what's on the agenda for today?"

"More startup details. Fortunately, I think most of the key staff from the ship manufacturing division of SiNavTech have agreed to move over with the transition to DGE. Selling people on a move to the island has been tricky, though."

Raena nodded. "I don't blame them. I hope the renovation tones down the spookiness factor of the place by… a lot."

"And you're sure that's where you want to settle?" Ryan searched her eyes.

"It'll send the right message," she replied. "We're not them. We can make that place something better."

"All right." He reached over to stroke the side of her face, and she placed her hand over his. "I meant it when I said I'd go anywhere with you."

"Same."

He smiled. "It figures, though, that you'd pick a castle."

"It's not a castle… exactly. More of a converted monastery."

Ryan raised an eyebrow. "Uh huh."

Raena sighed. "Okay, I'll admit it's pretty castle-like. I watched way too many travel shows on Europe while I was a kid, what can I say?"

"We'll have plenty of room to expand operations, I'll give you that."

They finished eating and then went to meet up with Cris in the administrative wing for their morning strategy session. He was waiting for them in his office, looking refreshed and energized.

"Look who's chipper this morning," Raena commented as she sat down in her usual guest chair across the desk.

Ryan took a seat next to her.

"I had a realization this morning," Cris replied.

Raena raised an eyebrow. "Oh?"

"I've actually accomplished something I've been working toward my entire adult life," her grandfather said. "It was always looming out there somewhere in the future, but now it's behind me. I'm free to do… whatever. It's liberating."

"Well, don't get too wild just yet. We still need to make sure this new political structure is stable," Ryan cautioned.

"Don't worry, I'm not going anywhere." Cris folded his arms on his desk. "But on that note, nominations have come in for the Health Council and the Banking Alliance."

"How's it look?" Raena asked.

Cris smiled. "Really good. Lots of smart people with real-world experience."

Raena glanced between him and Ryan. "Hopefully, they can govern."

"We'll have some trial and error," her grandfather said. "I just feel great knowing we have people with their hearts in the right place. I think we're going to be just fine."

"You're right," she agreed. "That freedom you feel for yourself—that's everyone. Rigid status quos of the past have been tossed aside and now everyone has a hand in shaping what we want for our lives, even if it's just in a small way. Slowly, we're giving a voice to those who've been on the outside."

Her grandfather nodded with satisfaction. "We might not get it correct the first time, but a step in that direction sure feels good."

Ryan evaluated him. "I have to ask… You grew up here as a High Dynasty heir just like all the others before you. What made you want to make things different for the common citizen?"

Cris chuckled. "Believe it or not, a couple of drunk guys in a shitey spaceport."

Raena raised an eyebrow. "Seriously? You've never said anything about that before."

"I was just a kid—about a year after I ran away from here." Cris shrugged. "I'd seen what life was like in the Outer Colonies, but it wasn't until I heard someone say that they had no faith in the High Dynasties that I realized they were speaking the truth.

There was absolutely no reason for anyone to trust the High Dynasties, not when the leadership had no idea what was really going on outside the core worlds. And that was never going to change unless someone already on the inside took a stand. I left Tararia to find myself, but what I really found was a purpose. When I met Kate, everything came together. Maybe, just maybe, we could restore trust and find a way for all voices to be heard."

"Here I thought you had a meeting with a wise man while on your internship or something," Raena said.

"Nope, just a couple of drunk guys." Cris grinned.

She laughed. "There's probably something really poetic about that."

"Maybe not the word I'd use, but it's something," her grandfather said with a chuckle.

"In any case," Ryan began, returning their focus to the task at hand, "we should get the new advisory groups in place as soon as possible. If we don't formally fill the administrative gaps left in the Priesthood's wake, others will try to step in and take advantage of the situation."

"Right." Cris' chuckles subsided, but the amusement remained in his eyes. "Let's get to know our new colleagues."

— — —

The mood around TSS Headquarters had changed. Everyone seemed lighter—more carefree.

Jason studied his comrades as he walked down the main administrative hall toward the High Commander's office. *Having the Priesthood's cloud hanging over us must have had a bigger impact than I'd realized.*

Now that public use of telekinesis was permitted, there'd been a surge in applications to the TSS. The Headquarters facility was insufficient for that volume of students, but the interest in training was the perfect opportunity to take the TSS' evolution to the next level. The intent for years had been for the institution to move away from strictly military training and focus on academic pursuits, but that vision had been placed on hold in favor of training teams to assist with the revolution.

The experience had underscored that the TSS needed to maintain a military presence, even if it was at a reduced level, but the individual training team model offered a foundation for other specializations to be cultivated. Under the guidance of experienced Agents, new TSS campuses could be established on other worlds, training those with abilities in the lost arts of healing and craftsmanship using their abilities. The Aesir's former temples throughout the Taran worlds, which the Priesthood had sealed, would make ideal locations to continue those efforts—though he expected that would be a conversation for the future.

It'd take time for those programs to develop, but the building blocks were there. All they had to do was put it into action.

Jason, for one, saw himself remaining in the main Headquarters on the military track. Now that he'd had a taste of high-pressure scenarios on a spaceship, he was hooked.

As far as he knew, Tiff and his closest friends in the Primus Elites intended to make a career on the military side of the TSS, as well, so he'd be among friends. He was certain he'd want something more for himself eventually, but for now, everything felt right.

He reached the door to his father's office and knocked.

Wil beckoned him inside via a flash on the control panel next to the door.

"Hey," Wil greeted when Jason entered. "Have you seen that list of applicants?"

"Crazy, right?" Jason took a seat in his favorite visitor chair on the right.

"Heirs from Vaenetri, Baellas, and Talsari. I never would have believed it."

"No reason to hide anymore."

Wil leaned back in his chair. "No, there isn't. It's a good feeling."

"It really is."

His father studied him. "What about you? Now that you've graduated, you're not stuck here."

Jason shrugged. "I dunno. I was thinking some time as a flight instructor might be fun."

"I am not the least bit surprised by that."

"Does that mean there's an opening?"

Wil smiled. "I think we can make that happen. The position I have in mind would keep you based here in Headquarters most of the time."

"Works for me. I like it here."

"Good." His father studied him. "I was impressed by how you handled that situation out in the Rift. Many people would have backed down."

"I knew what I could do with the ship."

"Still, you have a knack for command, if that interests you."

Jason folded his hands on his lap. "Are you asking if I'd like to be on the advancement track for High Commander?"

"It's crossed my mind," Wil admitted.

"I'm pretty sure there'd be some complaints about nepotism."

"Perhaps, but you have a CR score on record to back it up. After anyone has spent some time with you, I don't think they'd question it."

"I'll consider it," Jason replied. "I'm not ready to make a career commitment quite yet."

"Fair enough. I'm in no rush to go anywhere."

Jason nodded. "Good deal."

"Regardless of what role you want to play, I know the TSS has a bright future. We're finally in a place where this organization can be what I dreamed it could be."

"I'm excited to be a part of that," Jason told him.

"I'm glad." His father paused. "When we chose to raise you on Earth, I was afraid you might reject the life we have here—rebel against us for keeping it from you."

"I almost did. Then I realized I like it too much here to want to leave."

"Good, because I think your mother would be tempted to drop everything and follow you if you wanted to leave. It was hard enough with Raena going to Tararia."

"And she is *not* coming back," Jason shook his head.

"It was surreal seeing her there. She was in her element."

"Totally. In retrospect, I don't know how she made it a year in the TSS."

"Seeing my dad there was strange, too. He was an Agent for my entire life—even after five years, I hardly recognize him when he's not wearing Agent black."

"Still way more recognizable than when I saw you in uniform for the first time," Jason countered.

Wil let out a long sigh. "That day of your Awakening… it was a crazy one."

"I'm sure there'll still be some crazy days yet."

"I have no doubt."

Jason grinned. "But hey, may as well keep things interesting."

— — —

Wil settled onto the couch in the quarters he shared with Saera. It felt even more like home now that he knew his son would be staying close for the foreseeable future. While he missed Raena, at least he knew she was happy with Ryan and near other family. If they couldn't all be together, being in two little groups would have to do.

He'd tried to move on from his final encounter with the Priesthood, but one lingering detail continued to pester the back of his mind. The Aesir insisted that his genetic line held the key to breaking the Generation Cycle, yet the Priesthood professed only direct intervention would produce the necessary results. Every time he'd run a model of the potential outcome, the results had been different—but that lacked the detailed genetic history contained within the Priesthood's data archive. With that information, he could run one definitive analysis.

Saera wasn't due back from her check-in meetings for another half an hour, so Wil decided he may as well answer the question once and for all.

After activating the viewscreen across from the couch, Wil brought up the various records related to the genetic analysis and began constructing the model. He left it to run in the background while he cleared out his email inbox.

Twenty minutes later, he received a notification that the

analysis was complete. *Here we go…*

His heart sank as soon as he saw the results. Without direct intervention, there was no better than a five-thousand-to-one chance of the joined Sietinen and Dainetris line resulting in a viable Generation Thirteen with the necessary sequence to create a genetic patch. Such a patch would be the key to restoring abilities for all Tarans, but without it, the Twelve Generation Cycle would persist and they'd never be able to take full advantage of the Aesir's technology.

Fok! Was the Priesthood right? He didn't want to believe it.

The door clicked open and Saera entered.

Wil quickly minimized the model on the screen.

"Wait, was that a genetic analysis?" his wife asked.

"Yes," he admitted.

Saera frowned. "I thought that was behind us. What were you looking at?"

"Double-checking something. But it doesn't matter."

She tilted her head down and gave him a look that made it clear he'd need to provide a more satisfactory answer.

"It's something Raena had heard years ago, when she was kidnapped," he explained, "that there's no guarantee that our genetic line will produce a cure for the Generation Cycle without further intervention. With the new information we got from the Priesthood's archive, I wanted to confirm those results. So, I ran the analysis myself."

"And?"

"They're right. The only way to be certain the traits will express in the desired way is to cross the lines back: a pairing between Raena and Jason, and then back to me."

Saera's expression passed from initial shock, to horror, back to disgust, and then she burst out laughing.

Wil joined her. After everything they'd been through—all the planning and aspirations to present a solution to their people that would restore lost abilities—they'd still come up short. The Priesthood would have eagerly passed that threshold of decency, but their family was no longer beholden to the perverse whims of their former shadow-masters.

It took well over a minute for them to regain composure.

"So, obviously," Wil said at last, "I just have to say fok the odds—computer probabilities only show so much. Everything will work out, or not, on its own course."

"After all, no one predicted Raena's level of ability."

He nodded. "Very true. And, honestly, I'm sick of plotting the destinies of people before they're even born."

"Amen to that." Saera shook her head.

"You know, fate, or luck, or whatever it is that's had a hand in leading us here—that's only part of it. Our future is what we make it."

His wife took his hand. "I couldn't agree more."

"So, I will choose to focus on the present. We're poised for a new Taran renaissance, the TSS is already transforming into something we'd only dreamed it could be, we're united with friends and family… We may not be able to undo all the harm the Priesthood caused during their reign, but we played our part in trying to set things right."

"You especially," Saera told him. "I officially give you permission to pass off those worries to future generations. You've done your part."

He smiled. "I suppose I have."

She eyed him knowingly. "You're not quite done yet, though—are you?"

Wil shrugged. "Well, there is the matter of Earth."

"Yep, there it is…" Saera chuckled. "You've spent too many years plotting to know how to relax."

"Probably," Wil admitted. "But from here on out, I will be but a humble observer of fate's hand."

Saera smirked. "Until you see it fit to intervene."

"We'll see."

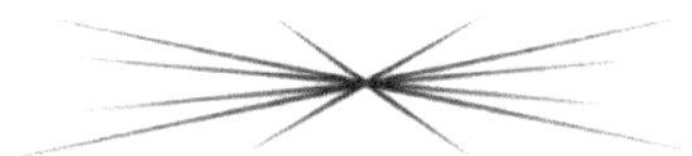

CONTINUE THE STORY...

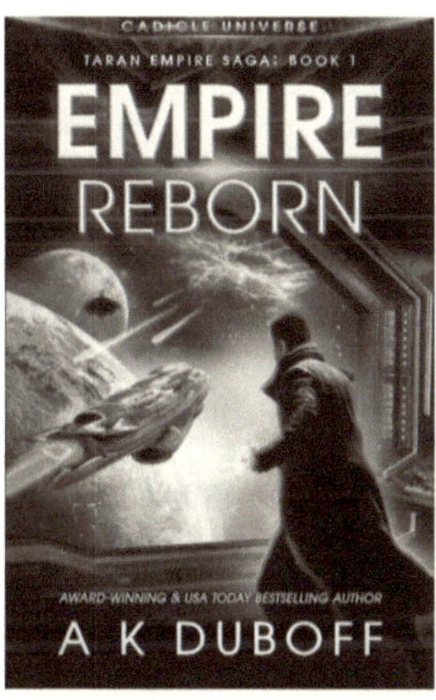

Empire Reborn (Taran Empire Saga Book 1)

A forgotten alien enemy's return reignites an ancient galactic war.

When a civilian starship is inexplicably destroyed, young military officer Jason Sietinen launches an investigation to solve the mystery.

As Jason unravels the clues, he soon learns that powerful, trans-dimensional aliens are behind the attack. A rogue faction within the Empire broke an ancient treaty, and the aliens are back for revenge.

With the future of the Taran Empire hanging in the balance, Jason and his family stand at the intersection of military might and political influence. Facing a brewing galactic civil war, their only hope is to unite the feuding Taran worlds before the aliens launch a civilization-ending invasion.

OTHER CADICLE UNIVERSE BOOKS

CADICLE SERIES
Volume 1: Architects of Destiny (in *Shadows of Empire*)
Volume 2: Veil of Reality (in *Shadows of Empire*)
Volume 3: Bonds of Resolve (in *Shadows of Empire*)
Volume 4: Web of Truth
Volume 5: Crossroads of Fate
Volume 6: Path of Justice
Volume 7: Scions of Change

MINDSPACE
Book 1: Infiltration
Book 2: Conspiracy
Book 3: Offensive
Book 4: Endgame

VERITY CHRONICLES *with T.S. Valmond*
Book 1: Exile
Book 2: Divided Loyalties
Book 3: On the Run

SHADOWED SPACE *with Lucinda Pebre*
Book 1: Shadow Behind the Stars
Book 2: Shadow Rising
Book 3: Shadow Beyond the Reach

IN DARKNESS DWELLS *with James Fox*

TARAN EMPIRE SAGA
Book 1: Empire Reborn
Book 2: Empire Uprising
Book 3: Empire Defied
Book 4: Empire United

ACKNOWLEDGEMENTS

Thank you, the reader! Without you, I doubt this book would ever have been written. When I published *Architects of Destiny*, I was thrilled to sell a few dozen copies. To now have thousands of readers is so surreal and so very super-cool ☺. I am touched by every message I have received from readers saying they have enjoyed this story world that is so near and dear to me. I'm happy I could share it with you!

I began working on this series in the late-1990s as a pet project, never expecting it to see the light of day. At the time, self-publishing was far from an accepted avenue for books, and I never would have considered it. Wow, have things changed! This has been the perfect venue for me, because it's allowed me to tell the story I wanted to tell. The initial books are too short for a traditional publisher to consider, but through the self-publishing platform, I was able to present the story I envisioned.

It's still difficult for me to believe that I've published seven books in just over two years' time. What's even more surreal is that I've been working on a book series for twenty years and I can finally call it "complete". While I wholly intend to write more in this story universe, this main Cadicle story arc is wrapped in the way I originally planned. I hope you enjoyed the ride (and that you will want to come back for more)!

Thank you to my amazing beta readers Eric, Kurt, Liz, Charlie, and Dewald for their helpful suggestions, for their eagle eyes to polish this book, and for their contributions to the rest of this series. Thank you also to Nick and Bryan for their diligent assistance with the final touches.

I owe my mom for her assistance with draft review and editing, and for her continual support. These books would not be what they are without her.

And I must thank my husband, Nick. He's the behind-the-scenes hero of this project. When I met him in 2012, the initial draft of the Cadicle series had been sitting on a digital shelf for years collecting cyber dust. It is his encouragement alone that got me writing again. It's also thanks to him that I was able to leave my day job to pursue writing full-time. That's such a huge compliment to have a spouse believe in me like that—I can't even put it into words. Thank you, Nick, I love you!

Lots more writing is ahead in the coming months and years. Thank you for going on this journey with me!

GLOSSARY

Aesir - A mysterious group of people known to be of Taran descent that live on the outskirts of explored space, engaging in metaphysical pursuits.

Agent - A class of officer within the TSS reserved for those with telekinetic and telepathic gifts. There are three levels of Agent based on level of ability: Primus, Sacon and Trion.

Ateron – An element that oscillates between normal space and subspace, facilitating high levels of telekinetic energy transfer.

Baellas - A corporation run by the Baellas Dynasty, producing housewares, clothing, furniture, and other textiles for use across the Taran civilization. Additional specialty lines managed by other smaller corporations are licensed to Baellas for distribution.

Bakzen - A militaristic race previously living beyond the outer colonies. Originally created through genetic experimentation conducted by the Priesthood, all Bakzen were clones, with individuals differentiated by war scars. Officers were highly intelligent and possess extensive telekinetic abilities. Drones were conditioned to follow orders but still possess moderate telekinetic capabilities. The Bakzen were completely eliminated at the end of the Bakzen War.

Bakzen War - A conflict that lasted approximately five hundred years. The majority of the war was waged in secret within a spatial rift, with the TSS fighting on behalf of the Taran civilization.

Cadicle - The definition of individual perfection in the Priesthood's founding ideology, with emergence of the Cadicle heralding the start to the next stage of evolution for the Taran race.

Course Rank (CR) - The official measurement of an Agent's ability level, taken at the end of their training immediately before graduation from Junior Agent to Agent. The Course Rank Test is a multi-phase examination, including direct focusing of telekinetic energy into a testing sphere. The magnitude of energy focused during the exercise is the primary factor dictating the Agent's CR.

Dainetris Dynasty - Formerly a seventh High Dynasty, the Dainetris Dynasty was responsible for ship manufacturing before its fall from power. Its corporation was Dainetris Galactic Enterprises (DGE).

Earth - A planet occupied by Humans, a divergent race of Tarans. Considered a "lost colony," Earth is not recognized as part of the Taran government.

H2 - The nickname for the TSS headquarters in the rift. The facility was created to serve as a base of operations for the Bakzen War.

High Commander - The officer responsible for the administration of the TSS. Always an Agent from the Primus class.

High Dynasties - Six families on Tararia that control the corporations critical to the functioning of Taran society. The "Big Six" each have a designated Region on Tararia, which is the seat of their power. The Dynasties in aggregate form an oligarchical government for the Taran colonies. In descending order of recognized influence, the Dynasties are: Sietinen, Vaenetri, Makaris, Monsari, Talsari, and Baellas.

Independent Jump Drive - A jump drive that does not rely on the SiNavTech beacon network for navigation, instead using a mathematical formula to calculate jump positions through normal space and the Rift.

Initiate - The second stage of the TSS training program for Agents. A trainee will typically remain at the Initiate stage for two or three years.

Jotun - The codename assigned to the division of the TSS dedicated to the war in the rift, based in H2.

Jump Drive - The engine system for travel through subspace. Conventional jump drives require an interface with the SiNavTech navigation system and subspace navigation beacons.

Junior Agent - The third stage of the TSS training program for Agents. A trainee will typically remain at the Junior Agent stage for three to five years.

Lead Agent - The highest ranking Agent and second in command to the High Commander. The Lead Agent is responsible for overseeing the Agent training program and frequently serves as a liaison for TSS business with Taran colonies.

Leaving (Left) - An act of stepping away from one's life while still in possession of physical and mental capacities. Individuals that exercise this final rite feel that their life is complete and wish to die peacefully in private or with their spouse. Most commonly, an individual will Leave in the night and document instructions for carrying out their final wishes.

Lower Dynasties - There are 247 recognized Lower Dynasties in Taran society. Many of these families have a presence on Tararia, but some are residents of the other inner colonies.

Makaris Corp - A corporation run by the Makaris High Dynasty responsible for the distribution of food, water filters, and other necessary supplies to Taran colonies without diverse natural resources.

Monsari Power Solutions (MPS) - A corporation run by the Monsari Dynasty, responsible for power generation systems for the Taran worlds, including geothermal generators, portable generators, and reactors to power spacecraft.

Rift - A habitable pocket between normal space and subspace.

Sacon - The middle tier of TSS Agents. Typically, Sacon Agents will score a CR between 6 and 7.9.

Simultaneous Observation - The act of separating one's consciousness from the physical self in order to observe multiple spatial planes (i.e., normal space, subspace, and the rift) at the same time.

SiNavTech - A corporation run by the Sietinen High Dynasty, which controls and maintains the subspace navigation network used by Taran civilians and the TSS.

Spatial Dislocation - The act of physically transitioning from normal space to the brink of subspace, either by means of a jump drive or telekinetic abilities.

Starstone – An extremely rare gem. Only ten such gem veins are known anywhere in the galaxy, and each of the six High Dynasties has claim to one. Only enough material for one set of wedding rings is produced by each vein every generation. Starstones emit a luminescent resonance when positioned near other stones cut from the same vein.

TalEx - A corporation run by the Talsari Dynasty, managing mining operations and ore processing across Taran territories.

Tarans - The general term for all individuals with genetic relation to Tararian ancestry. Several divergent races are recognized by their planet or system.

Tararia - The home planet for the Taran race and seat of the central government.

Tararian Selective Service (TSS) - A military organization with two divisions: (1) Agent Class, and (2) Militia Class. Agents possess telekinetic and telepathic abilities; the TSS is the only place where individuals with such gifts can gain official training. The Militia class offers a formal training program for those without telekinetic abilities, providing tactical and administrative support to Agents. The Headquarters is located inside the moon of the planet Earth. Additional Militia training facilities are located throughout the Taran colonies.

Trainee - The generic term for a student of the TSS, and also the term for first year Agent students (when capitalized Trainee). Students are not fully "initiated" into the TSS until their second year.

Trion - The lowest tier of TSS Agents. Typically, Trion Agents will score a CR below 5.9.

Priesthood of the Cadicle - A formerly theological institution responsible for oversight of all governmental affairs and the flow of information throughout the Taran colonies. The Priesthood has jurisdiction over even the High Dynasties and provides a tiebreaking vote on new initiatives proposed by the High Dynasty oligarchy.

Primus - The highest of three Agent classes within the TSS, reserved for those with the strongest telekinetic abilities. Typically, Primus Agents will score a CR above 8.

Primus Elite - A new classification of Agent above Primus signifying an exceptional level of ability.

VComm – A telecommunications corporation owned and operated by the Vaenetri Dynasty.

ABOUT THE AUTHOR

Award-winning author A.K. (Amy) DuBoff has always loved science fiction in all its forms—books, movies, shows, and games. If it involves outer space, even better! She is a Nebula Award finalist and *USA Today* bestselling author most known for her Cadicle Universe, but she's also written a variety of space fantasy and comedic sci-fi. Now a full-time author, Amy can frequently be found traveling the world. When she's not writing, she enjoys wine tasting, binge-watching TV series, and playing epic strategy board games.

www.amyduboff.com

www.ingramcontent.com/pod-product-compliance
Lightning Source LLC
Chambersburg PA
CBHW052019240626
47153CB00006B/1872

9781954344044